This is David Hochman's second novel. The first, *An Apology to Julia,* was published to critical acclaim in the Czech Republic. The son of a prominent political dissident of Prague Spring who risked his life for liberty and truth, and a TV producer mother, he was taught at a young age that some things are worth dying for. He hopes that this novel encompasses the lessons he learned at a young age.

Venesection

David Hochman

Venesection

Vanguard Press

VANGUARD PAPERBACK

© Copyright 2023
David Hochman

The right of David Hochman to be identified as author of
this work has been asserted by him in accordance with the
Copyright, Designs and Patents Act 1988.

All Rights Reserved

No reproduction, copy or transmission of this publication
may be made without written permission.
No paragraph of this publication may be reproduced,
copied or transmitted save with the written permission of the publisher, or in accordance
with the provisions
of the Copyright Act 1956 (as amended).

Any person who commits any unauthorised act in relation to
this publication may be liable to criminal
prosecution and civil claims for damages.

A CIP catalogue record for this title is
available from the British Library.

ISBN 978-1-80016-560-1

This is a work of fiction. Names, characters, businesses, places, events and incidents are
either the products of the author's imagination or used in a fictitious manner. Any
resemblance to actual persons, living or dead, or actual events is purely coincidental.

Vanguard Press is an imprint of
Pegasus Elliot Mackenzie Publishers Ltd.
www.pegasuspublishers.com

First Published in 2023

Vanguard Press
Sheraton House Castle Park
Cambridge England

Printed & Bound in Great Britain

Dedicated to my children, Sebastiaan and Amara, two magical and wondrous souls. I am sorry for what you have had to endure, and may you never forget.

"It is evil to assent actively or passively to evil as its instrument, as its observer, or as its victim…"
— Rudi Vrba.

"Survivors cannot escape their past, or what was done to them, or what they have lost. The physical and mental scars are there for good; one's life expectancy is reduced. But if they are lucky, and strong enough, they can live, and that is a triumph."
— Anton Gill.

"When someone is coming to kill you, kill them first."
— Hebrew saying.

KLARA AND ALBERTO

ALBERTO has killed himself. His sister called from Italy. Said it was Klara's fault — her fault. He left the oven on. Gassed himself, one day after he came back from West Germany. Of course, he did. How else. And now, it was her fault. Forever her fault. What had she done. She wasn't sure she could tell Annie about this. This made her an *accomplice*.

She was such a kind person, Annie, listening to her terrible stories, so patient, but this one, this story, Alberto… no… she could only tell her about the rest. Alberto, *she* was responsible for his death. And Aunt Eva? Was she responsible for her death? She had helped carry her suitcase. She had accompanied her to the transport.

Alberto — if only she had not asked him to go to West Germany. She couldn't tell Annie about Alberto, and his red poppy. *Her* red poppy. He had gotten beaten for plucking the poppy next to the only paved road in the concentration camp. He had been a child then, no more than fifteen. He used to tell her stories, to cheer her up. She hadn't known him long; that's how it was, people came, people disappeared. But he had fallen in love with her. Even though he knew, they all knew, that she was a whore. *His* whore.

She was the one who had told Alberto to go to West Germany. She had called him… from? She couldn't remember. Australia? She had been running since the war, running, always running, to Austria, Israel, England, Germany, South Africa, US, Australia, Canada, back to the US, running, running, hoping to outrun, never succeeding. The past kept running right behind, with, ahead, never letting go. Would *not* let go of any of them. But those that had kept them there, and clubbed and shot and gassed them, for them it *had* stopped running. They had photo albums even. Scribbled on the front of those albums: 'Those Were the Days'. *Schöne Zeiten. Best days of my life.*

What had she been thinking? He had called her from Düsseldorf, Alberto, breathless.

"It's him," he said. "You were right. Living in Düsseldorf."

"He's hiding?"

"No, no, not hiding. Under his own name, just like you said. Made no effort to hide, not at all. But it was the SS-Schutzhaflagerführer. I don't... understand. Klara, it was a big mistake coming here, I had not... I had not... I've been trying to forget, but when I saw him, he opened the door, it was him, of course. He said, '*You*? I remember you. I thought you were dead. How did you survive? I should have shot you myself. What do you want? Why are you here? You're not the first. Stop bothering me,' he said. 'Do yourself a favor, go home, the war's over, forget about it. Move on,' he said. 'You have to learn to move on. It's always about you people, isn't it? You think the world revolves around *you*. What about *me*? Have you thought about that? Me, too, I miss those days,' he said. 'They were the *best days of my life*, but what can we do? You can't travel back in time. I'm back to being a baker,' he said. 'You think I enjoy *that*? Me? A *baker*? Getting up every day at four a.m. It's bloody hard work. *Fürchterlich*. But what would you know about that? You people were always work shy. *Untermenschen*. Subhuman. Patton understood that. He knew you were subhuman. We all did. That's why nobody wanted any of you. They had plenty of opportunities to take you all in, plenty, America, everybody. They all said, no. Now, look at me. *Me*, a baker. After being part of history? *I made history*,' he said. 'What have *you* done with your life?'"

"What did you do?"

"What could... I do... I... I vomited."

Klara listened, receiver in hand. On the line, a long-distance echo, then a click. Maybe the West Germans were listening. Were they any different to the East Germans?

"Disgusting," Alberto continued. "'Now look at what you've done,' he said. '*Untermensch*. You will always all be *Untermenschen*. Leave now, or I will call the police.' I... Klara... he closed the door. He slammed it."

"What did you do?"

"I... I thought he *would* call the police. German police. I had not been in Germany this whole... I swore I'd never go. The faces, everywhere. German spoken... everywhere, it was like I'd never left."

"Police?" Klara said.

"I had images of the SS. I thought he'd call the SS. Oh, I know they don't exist anymore, but are they *really* gone? Dog in left hand, machine gun in the right. Or maybe he would come back and open the door in his white jacket, with his riding crop, or just come out and shoot me or set his dog on me.

"When I saw him, Klara, I instantly reached up and thought, I forgot to take off my cap. *Mutze ab*! That's it. He's going to whip me. Or shoot me. And now... he's a baker. He was always a baker, then... before... a baker," he said. "Klara, I must go, I am at the train station. My train is leaving soon. I think, Klara, it's better if we don't speak to each other again. Yes? I am sorry, Klara, I just... I don't... "

"Yes, Alberto, I am so sorry I asked you to go, I just thought... just a baker, you say?"

"Yes — just a baker... you know, Himmler was a chicken farmer. He wanted to breed only white chickens. Already back then. Can you imagine. If I could laugh, Klara, I'd make up a story, like I used to, remember, to make you smile, about how Himmler would provide chickens and he'd provide the bread... but I can't, Klara, because I see them, all those that died, every night, I'm afraid to go to sleep, they are all there. I am afraid to go to sleep because of that one instant when you wake up, when you think everything is OK, and in that instant, you realize that everyone is dead and the past, all of it, is upon you like a boulder. All dead, my parents, my sister, and my aunt and uncle, my cousins. And all the babies, the children they used to throw into the packed chambers, throw them on top of those standing there, there was no space, twenty-seven degrees Celsius, whenever I see that temperature, I start to shake—"

Yes, Alberto, it's why I live in warm weather, to remind myself of twenty-seven degrees Celsius, here, it's eighty degrees often, and each time I see that temperature... yes, I understand — the babies he used to throw... the baby that I... your baby... *please Alberto, stop...* into the boiling fat — human fat — in the crematoria, I have the blood of hundreds of thousands of innocent people on my hands... *Alberto, please...*"

"Why am I telling you... you know all this... nobody cares... my train is about to leave, goodbye, Klara..."

"Goodbye, Alberto, I am so sorry for asking you..."

No, I never said so, I never apologized, and now he is gone, and it is my fault and... nobody cares... how is it possible. Or maybe it never really mattered. Maybe nobody ever cared. Nobody cared. How is it possible.

ANNIE AND ANTON

"**ANNIE**," Anton started to say.

He looked away, over the canal, at the grey-blue brackish water. It was a late March Florida night, but bright, the moon high above, illuminating, a warm breeze coming from the southeast. They were fishing, as they had done for months on an abandoned wooden pier, under and downstream from the intracoastal bridge, hidden from the footpath along the landmass by foliage and trees from which hung moss known as old man's beard. Old man's beard. *Old Jewish man's beard, maybe,* she heard Klara's voice in her head.

"I see old Jewish men when I look at the old man's beard growing from the trees, hanging from the trees," Klara had said.

"Do you believe in God," the SS-Schutzhaflagerführer would ask.

"Yes," said the old Jewish men with old man's beard.

"Here, hold the bottle," the SS-Schutzhaflagerführer had said. "I will shoot and if I hit the bottle, there is a God, and if I don't, there isn't one."

"Annie, please don't take this the wrong way..."

"Yes, sorry. I was just..."

"I know, I know, thinking about something mom told you."

"Don't take what the wrong way, my love?"

"Annie — please don't misunderstand. I have thought long and hard about this. I am tired, Annie—"

His sorrow tore at her. She held his head between her hands and tears formed in her eyes. "I know, my love."

"I just can't...I don't want to live any more—"

"Please, my love."

"I just can't do it anymore. I can't be without Lucie. I am not that kind of father. I know you will say I am melodramatic, but she is my life, the air I breathe—"

Annie was crying now. Never having had children, she now realized she had been mistaken. She had thought that as long as one person in the world believed in you, loved you, you had hope; if no one believed in or loved you, that hope disappeared. She had mistakenly thought that her love could save Anton. Now she understood that if children were removed from a parent's life, even that one outside love might not be enough.

"Please, my love, don't give up, not now, not when we have found each other, please, I'm begging you. You're the love of my life. I've never felt like this before. We are so close, I promise you. I will make things right, you will see—"

"Annie — how? Don't you see? Everything is against us. This place, this country, fathers count for nothing. They have taken away the only person I have truly and deeply loved—" She looked hurt but understood "—You know what I mean. But it's more than that, she's a part of me, it's as if they've ripped my heart—"

Because she hadn't had kids, she knew it was impossible to understand what he felt. Few things irked her more than presumptuous sympathy from people who somehow thought they could feel a sorrow or a pain they had never experienced. But she knew that without him, she was lost. That her life, too, would once again lose meaning. As Lucie was his hope, he was hers. In that regard, she understood what he felt. If anyone had an inkling of the debilitating pain he felt that life was without hope; that salvation and reprieve lay in the shape of a noose or the sharp edge of a blade; it was she. She had, after all, been there herself. More than once she had woken in a hospital, angry to have been saved. Still, she understood more than others, that hope only existed as long as one lived.

"I need you, Ant, Lucie needs you. We'd be lost without you. Without you, we're nothing."

"Lucie is already lost. They took her away from me."

"You are too important, my love," she was sobbing now. "To me, to her. Anton, please, believe in me."

"I am not that important in the scheme of things, Annie. I am just a miserable human being. I hate the person I've become. I used to be so different. People enjoyed being with me, kids, and friends. Look at me. Now, I rot in my sorrow. I haven't made a joke in months. The world will be a better place without me, believe me."

"You're the most loving man I've ever met."

"In this world, that is a condemnation. It certainly isn't a good thing."

"You have the biggest heart I know."

"A big heart only causes big pain, Annie. I am grateful for you, truly I am. If not for you, for your love…"

"But it is not enough, I know, my love. I can see it in your eyes every second of every day. What has she done to you? What have they allowed her to do to you? By what right? And to Lucie?"

"Don't misunderstand me, Annie."

"Ant — please give me a chance. Some time. Not much. Please, I will right things. You'll see. Please. Just give me some time. Promise that you won't do anything stupid. Because if you do, I'm going right after you, I promise you that. Is that what you want? I won't survive, I know it."

He held her tight until she calmed, and the tears were not so forthcoming. Still here and there she sobbed or took a deep breath.

"I can't promise, Annie, I'm sorry. The pain is too great. It never leaves. Never."

"Then, I'll make you a deal. If I don't make it right, we go together."

"I can't do that to you, Annie."

"You've no choice. I won't live without you, Ant. I won't. And if you won't survive, I'm happy to go with you. I mean it. Deal?"

He wiped Annie's tears. "Let's see, Annie. I do love you, that you must believe."

I know my love. It just isn't enough. She wasn't going to give up, though. Not now. Not when she'd found him, the love of her life. It simply meant she would have to keep an eye on him, somehow, at all times. And that she had less time than she thought she had to correct the wrongs. She'd seen such pain before, and it only ended one way. At most, you could postpone it.

Anton looked to his left, in the distance. "Annie, that bridge—" Annie looked upstream, at a colossal structure under reconstruction, high up over the intracoastal waterway.

"There's a bridge in Cape Town, just ends, high in the air, unfinished. This bridge reminds me of that one for some reason, but, I don't know, this one… when I see it, I always think of the path to the gas chambers that mom told us about — the Road to Heaven as the Germans called it —. I don't know. I see that bridge there, so high, and I think of it as the Bridge to Heaven."

"I think I know what you mean, my love."

"In the rare moments my sadness isn't so great, that bridge makes me homesick. Although I know my cure is Lucie — and you — all of us together somewhere, somewhere safe, far from here. But it's not a place, or a destination. I could be home and inside I would be just as dead. It's always people, isn't it. The ones you love. With them, you can endure anything. Without them, you are nothing."

"Yes, my love."

"Annie, I think, before anything, I want to go home. I want to die there. Not here. You should always die in a place you found happiness."

Annie knew what he meant. He didn't mean that he didn't like the surroundings here, water, beaches, pier. That, she knew, he loved. He didn't mean Klara's house, or her apartment. He also didn't mean the nearby city or state, even. Home meant South Africa. He didn't like this country. It wasn't a dislike, really, Annie thought. It was a disenchantment, a disappointment, at what might have been. But the fact that he wanted to go home also gave her hope. It meant, in all likelihood, that he wouldn't do anything rash here. Not yet anyway.

"Will you help me get home?"

"I will, my love. You'll get home. But with Lucie and me and with your mom. And you will be happy again. And nothing will be missing. That is my promise to you." She touched him, gently, on the back of his neck, then on his ear, taking it tenderly between thumb and index finger. It was a touch of endearment for which he held still and closed his eyes.

Annie looked at the imposing bridge in the distance, the *Bridge to Heaven*, high up as if reaching the sky, then over the flowing water and across the canal, at the thick and impenetrable trees and foliage.

"Sometimes, the only way to get out of a place is to know how you got there first," she said.

"What do you—"

"Sometimes, the hole is so dark, right, and so deep that you can't see a way out. But if you know how you got there, what brought you to such despair, well, then you have some chance to do something about it. See?"

"Not sure I—"

"When was the first time she hit you, Ant?" He looked away. She knew if she asked *whether* she hit him, he'd deny. "You don't have to protect her anymore."

He stayed silent for minutes. Then he said, softly, "I don't remember."

It was a start, Annie thought, finally, an admission. She knew, not only from experience as a police officer, that when victims forgot the first time, the violence had become commonplace, a blur, too numerous to remember specific events. Over time, an accepted part of a codependent relationship. What she didn't say was that her experience with such violence was far more personal. That, she would save for another time. She wanted this to be about his pain, not hers. She knew he was surprised by his admission, but also, quite likely, relieved.

"From the beginning?" she asked.

Annie knew that being on the receiving end of domestic violence was difficult for Anton to admit, as a man even more than a woman, to talk about. But she also knew, better than most, that they had crossed an important boundary.

"I don't remember…"

"OK, my love."

"I don't remember how or when it started. I must have been shocked, I guess. I'd never been exposed to such behavior. With her, it always started with shouting and screaming. There was a look in her eyes she used to get, I guess I must have done something, said something to set it off—" *You did nothing to set it off, my love, any more than I had, as a child and my mother.* "—And this look, I can't explain it, it's like her eyes took on this look—" *Like the insane gleam in my mother's eyes.* "—And then the blows just came, I guess, and I tried to block her fists, she'd hit me anywhere she could, never in my face though—" *Controlled violence, meticulous, measured, no visible proof, I know it, too well.* "—And the rage would last as long as it did, nothing you could do. When Lucie got older, she used to cry, and then Carolien would slap her, too—" *As my mother slapped my brother, Michael, and my father.* "—And I tried to hold Carolien, but it was impossible, and—" *And, and, yes, I know this story, my love, as my father tried to hold my mother, to no avail…*

"You never called the police."

"No."

"Or told anyone."

"No. It never even occurred to me."

"Why?" *Why do I ask such silly questions when I know the answers?*

"I don't know, Annie. I guess, as a man…" *I understand, my love. You were ashamed, embarrassed.* Annie wiped his tears, then her own. "And then, Annie, it just happened. All the time. Twice, three times a week, more, she screamed, too, at both of us, and at Maria, Lucie's African nanny, it just became our life." *It just became our life.* She understood, all too well.

Annie suddenly realized how intricately the stories intertwined — hers, his, Klara's, Lucie's.

"She treated you how she thought you deserved to be treated."

"I never thought of it like that."

"Your mother says, maybe, because you are half black, half Slavic."

"Why marry me, then? Why have a child with me?"

Why do people do anything. "Impossible to say. Your father was famous, wasn't he? A prominent member of the ANC?"

"Don't mention *that* in front of my mother. She likes to think of him as some uneducated African, I don't understand it."

"I've noticed, don't worry. Who knows why anyone does anything. I guess she has her reasons. Still, regarding your ex-wife, in my line of work, there doesn't need to be a 'why'. Innocent people get hurt or killed every day. As your mother would say about the Holocaust, why gypsies, why Jews, why Jehovah's Witnesses, why homosexuals, why children, why old people, why women, why, why, why… it's the why that drives you crazy. When it comes to people, there is no 'why' — in my line of work, we always look for a motive. But, in my experience, motive, often, is just an irrational, sick aberration of human behavior."

"Annie… I—"

"In her eyes, you were simply, all of you, *inferior*." She paused, then added, "How long was it before you got married?"

"She moved in after three weeks and couple of months later fell pregnant and—"

"You married her."

"Yes, of course."

"Did you love her."

"I did, Annie. I loved her throughout our marriage. Despite—"

"You never told anyone about the—"

"No."

"Would you ever have left her?"

He said without hesitation, "No, Annie."

"Say she stabbed you; you wake up in a hospital, would you have left her then?"

"No."

"Do you think she *ever* loved you?"

"I don't know… anything, anymore. In her own way, I guess, or maybe as much as she *can* love… or maybe, not at all, I really don't know, anything…"

"A person like that, in my experience, is incapable of love. And it is that which enrages them. Having to observe something so beautiful all their lives which they are incapable of."

"Maybe, I really don't… it's true, I remember often how I would be playing with Lucie and we'd just be having fun, laughing, messing around, and I would look up and Carolien would be staring at us with such hatred and I just didn't understand it, why she looked at us like that, at me, why not be happy that your husband and father of your child is playing with your child lovingly, I just didn't understand it—"

"Because it was something she could never do herself. You see that, right? I remember, my mother—"

She went abruptly silent.

"What?"

"No, nothing, never mind. One day, I will…" Annie grew angrier. This man in front of her, a gentle man, her man, her love; and his daughter, had been abused and beaten for years. Annie had visions of revenge. Not dissimilar to feelings she was well familiar with. She now thought she was starting to see why Klara had been educating her in the history of the concentration camps, of the darkest side of human nature. Perhaps it wasn't merely confessional. She had an image of Anton now, alone, abandoned, emaciated, in the middle of a concentration camp surrounded by electric wire. All his assets, family, dignity, humanity, dispossessed, as if never having existed or been acquired, a fabrication.

"I'm sorry, my love. I get incensed when I think of her beating you and Lucie."

"Lucie, she only slapped." *Only. If he could hear himself!* "Do you think less of me?"

"Less of you? How can I think less of you, my love? I love you. But I hate her, I am enraged, I want to hurt her!"

She turned her gaze across the canal to the other shore. "I've been thinking, my love," she said. "Those woods, across the way, sometimes… it feels like she's watching us. Do you ever get that feeling?"

She looked at him. "One day, Ant, we'll be free. Of her. Of all this." She waved her hand. "That, I promise you."

"I'm not so sure, Annie. People like that…" He went quiet and his eyes reverted to their usual overwhelming melancholy. They watered and glistened in the moonlit night, and she reached out and touched his cheek. How she wished she could take his pain away. She knew the cure — getting Lucie back into his life, permanently. The injustice of his daughter being with Carolien was too much for her. Not that she hadn't seen such injustice repeatedly. Involuntarily she clenched her jaw with fury.

Anton reeled in the line and pulled out the empty hooks, bait eaten, before placing more squid on the double hooks and throwing the line back in towards the other side of the canal, the weight making a splash upon the water's surface. He remained quiet.

"Somebody called me, Ant. A woman. Someone Carolien knows, I guess."

"Who? When?"

"Last week. I don't know who it was."

"Why didn't you say?"

"The woman said, 'I'm warning you; he's beaten his ex-wife and daughter for years.' She told me to be careful. To stay away."

He looked sadly in the distance.

"What did you say."

"I asked who it was."

"And?"

"They hung up."

He looked at the top of his fishing rod, the pole twitching and he ascertained whether a fish or the current was responsible. But she could see his mind was on her words.

"She's dangerous, and very smart," Annie said.

"Annie don't get all worked up, it's bad enough that she has destroyed me and Lucie. You're not like her, Annie, we're not… and that's part of the problem, isn't it?" *Maybe you are not like her, my love. But there are things about me you don't know.*

She wasn't giving up on him; to give up on him was to give up on herself.

"Ant, listen… one thing you learn in my job — an unemotional liar is more convincing than an emotional truthteller. You see this in court, daily. Which is why I want you to observe some cases in court. See what you're up against." She paused. "Your mom told me a story once about her class of kids watching a documentary about the concentration camps and afterwards the kids said, 'those Jewish children must have done something really terrible to be punished like that.'"

Anton shook his head. "You see, a 'normal' human brain cannot comprehend an atrocity happening to an innocent party without justification — we always need a reason why — and that is to the advantage of the perpetrator. See what I mean?"

"I never… yes, I suppose… I think so… "Anton briefly paused and looked into the distance.

She had seen photos of him before Carolien caused the immense hurt, carefree, smiling, content. Anton was a sliver of the man he had been, she knew. He had been crushed. But Annie thought, not irretrievably, not permanently. There were always ways to save another. Perhaps one could never bring them back to how they once were. But they could always be saved.

"Did the woman say anything else?" Anton said.

"'If you don't stop seeing him,' she said. 'I will go to your boss. You let criminals go free. I can get you fired.' How did she know that?"

"Any idea who it was?"

"Possibly."

"You won't tell me, I guess. Secret police work."

"That's right."

Anton put the rod down on the wooden landing pier, reached out, kissed her, and held her tight.

"What's that for?"

"Thank you, Annie."

"For?"

"For everything."

She looked back at the other side of the canal. He could see her fists clench. "If I knew she was there, Ant, I'd go across… and…" On the other side of the canal, despite the gentle torrent, Annie thought she heard the sound of breaking wood. "Did you hear that?"

"Just a deer. Probably," he said uncertainly, staring into the forest.

"She's like that SS guy your mother told us about, living in Düsseldorf. These people, Ant… they think they've done nothing wrong, it's always the fault of others, and anyway, who will do anything?"

Suddenly Annie's pole nearly slipped in her grip. She reeled in the catch with Anton encouraging. After a minute or so, she pulled out two baby sand sharks, each about a foot long. She was surprised how soft they were. Finally, Anton removed them from the hooks, and they threw them in the water, one each, watching them swim away. She jumped on him with joy and enveloped him in her arms. Across the canal, a piece of wood broke under the weight of a foot.

BELONGING

WHEN she was in high school, Annie had read a short story. It was about a child who didn't belong. She was on a planet and amongst beings that were foreign, and she was foreign to them. She was the unhappiest of children because everyone knew, you had to *belong*. Somewhere. Amongst friends, family, loved ones. You had to be loved and accepted by *somebody*. And this little girl wasn't. But then a miracle happened. There was to be an exchange with a child from another planet, other beings. And once the exchange took place, she (and the other child, too, who also had not belonged on *her* planet, amongst those beings), was suddenly amongst beings very much like herself, who fully accepted her. Who loved her. She was, at long last, home. Home, after all, was not a geographical destination. Home was where you were accepted as you were, where you were loved. It was where you *belonged*.

Often, Annie thought of this story, because she was painfully aware that the little girl in the story was her. Except that there had been no exchange. No place where suddenly she was accepted and loved. Until now. In her own small way, she had found her home and beings who accepted her, seemingly unconditionally. Where she didn't feel different or out of place. Still, she had not been exchanged for anyone. Or maybe she was, in her own way. Maybe she had been exchanged for Carolien. Because now, for the first time, when with Anton and his mother, Klara, and little Lucie, Anton's daughter, and Klara's granddaughter, she *belonged*. She was amongst people who accepted her as she was and enwreathed her with love. Yes, they were broken people. Their overwhelming hurt and sorrow were palpable. And, she had known intimately other broken people. But then, was *she* any less broken? And she could *save* them. She hated all the ridiculous sayings that were ubiquitous these days. *You can't save others; they can only save themselves. Jesus helps those that help themselves*. She remembered a different America as a child, one where people did try to help one another; one where, when one shared pain and sorrow, people tried to help and didn't chase them away with asinine sayings such as, 'too much information'. Really? When did this society become so utterly callous and uncaring? Since when was listening to the pain of another 'too much information'? Since when should another in pain be allowed to languish alone? Since when should you *not* try to save another human being? How were emotional turmoil and pain any different than physical? To Annie, walking away from a person in emotional distress was no different than ignoring a dying man. A human being in trouble was simply that.

And perhaps because this family had accepted her into their hearts so openly, she felt the urge to save them from their hurt and pain. What they didn't realize, and she did, was that they might have come upon a savior. A person for whom no information, no matter how tragic or sad, was not only *not* too much information; it was information to be acted upon. It was information that led to action, not passive acquiescence or the reliance of unjust courts and laws. For Annie knew that situations could be rectified, that people *could* be saved, if one truly cared, if one knew how, and if one had the courage to act. And Annie, she knew, ever since she had set herself free, was that someone.

AMERICAN SCHOOL

PALM City was a small town and, as a police officer, Annie had various duties, from patrolling the streets, to responding to crime, being at the courthouse, guarding the schools; even standing guard over eerie futuristic grocery chains with self-service checkouts and no cashiers (didn't people know that each time they went through a self-service checkout counter, another cashier lost her job?). Every police officer had to do a little of everything. The budget, as it was with all governmental departments these days, was tight and getting tighter. Taxes were being cut increasingly for the wealthy and corporations. Public coffers were siphoned dry. Once empty, the already feeble social services were cut further. It was an unprecedented and at once decisive and simple, ingenious attack on the government and everyone by the wealthy. Unlike years ago, when corporations felt a social responsibility to their employees and communities, today all that mattered were the pocketbooks of investors and shareholders, she believed. Corporations took pride in shipping jobs overseas and paying no taxes. The result was a country that was dilapidated, communities decimated, half to most shops and stores and restaurants closed, homelessness rampant (in her youth, she had encountered the homeless only once, on a visit to New York City. Now, the homeless were omnipresent in every city, town and village, in every community. And the solution? Pretending they didn't exist or moving the homeless out of sight). Drugs and desperation, as one would expect when people had no or several underpaid and insecure jobs, proliferated. And with the social ills and desperation, politicians and the wealthy are of an increasingly dubious and extreme nature.

Annie had been the daughter of a union member, a self-proclaimed socialist; social injustice was deeply instilled in her heart from a young age. She had read voraciously and studied and observed. What was happening seemed self-evident. And yet when she shared her thoughts, everyone acted as if the status quo was entirely normal and unchangeable. Worse, several people had called her 'anti-American'. Since when did questioning the morals of one's country become a question of missing patriotism? Was it not the exact opposite? A quest, a need, to improve one's community and nation. Gone forever, it seemed, were corporate social responsibility and the wealthiest elite paying 90% tax for the betterment of all.

Sometimes she felt that today a police officer's main role was to collect traffic fines, harass the poor and protect the investments of the wealthy. She remembered the police officers of her childhood, affable, friendly, part of the neighborhood and community. Officers who knew to be human. Who joked with children. Who didn't elicit fear. Who understood human failings and frailty and who had compassion when warranted, who gave breaks or second chances. Those times seemed as if from that different planet, different beings. Today's police officers were militarized gung-ho automatons, unforgiving, punishing, arrogant. They would taser and shoot, often without provocation; a body writhing on the ground or lying in a pool of blood was hardly a recipient of second chances or forgiveness or benefit of doubt. And these same unforgiving police officers were unilaterally feared and despised by the public. The policemen and women couldn't even go to public restrooms any more for fear of being attacked or killed; and, she felt, rightfully so. She could not affect the nation's economic policies, but she could, she felt, occasionally and in her own way correct the wrongs of the judges and lawyers and fellow police officers, as much as and whenever she could. Often, when in uniform, she got hateful glances from the populace. If only they knew how different she was.

Annie now stood outside Palm City Elementary School. She always watched the parents drop the children off, mainly by car, some on foot. Still other children walked or biked to school on their own but there were very few of those; when she was a child, she and many other children walked or biked to school alone. Those times, too, were a bygone era; today's parents were either too afraid to let their children go to school alone or too afraid to *be seen* to let their children go to school alone. She was aware that several states were even trying to pass "free-range parenting laws". *How absurd*, she thought. She mouthed the words to herself, free-range chickens; free-range children; free-range parenting laws. What had this country become.

Annie often read newspapers online from other countries. And she felt this country, *her* country, was becoming more alien by the day; or she an alien within. What was commonsense to the rest of the world and had been to previous generations was now considered unacceptable or dangerous (how she hated the overused term 'inappropriate' — when had this ever present, ever imposing, censoring word entered the mainstream and become so controlling, judging and pervasive? Was there a more dangerous and asinine word in today's lexicon? Who decided what was inappropriate and for whom [she envisaged a five-person committee whimsically issuing the next 'inappropriate' saying, term or action])? Few things were more dangerous than censorship, in her mind, which had morphed into something far worse — self-censorship — everyone censoring and controlling everyone else, keeping a beady eye like a sinister concierge or worse, as in some nineteenth century religious community on the lookout for witches to burn (Orwell predicted the ominous *Big Brother* — he could not have foreseen *every* person's ability to become Small Brother through insidious social media platforms — the internet, after all, was originally meant for the few, not the many. Therein lay the contradiction — not more intellectual freedom, but the exact opposite. When *anyone* could be information gatekeeper, without knowledge or discernment, information proliferated, and with it, misinformation; worse, the constant rumbling of judgment and collective and self-censorship. Before the internet, censorship came from the top, from governments, now they came from the bottom, from anyone with access to the internet — who'd have thought. She heard Klara's voice in her head, what about the failings of the electoral college, then? Ah, well, there were anomalies in everything).

She turned her attention to the long line of cars, snaking out of the parking lot onto the street, dropping children off; that was the most common means of bringing kids to school. Elsewhere in the world, children walking to school or playing in a park were the most normal of things. But here, in America, a law had to be passed that allowed children to walk to or from a school or park on their own. Otherwise, the parents could be prosecuted for 'child neglect'. What the heck was wrong with this place? Too many things to count, she thought. And, she was convinced, one of the biggest culprits was the systematic removal of fathers from their children. All hell had certainly unleashed in her life when *her* father had been removed. As more fathers got removed from their children, school shootings were ever more prevalent. To her, that was no coincidence. She knew from official police statistics that there were, on average, two or three mass shootings across the country every day. So many shootings, in fact, that most no longer made headlines. A child whose father was removed from his or her life would sooner or later be consumed with rage. And with parents working longer and longer hours, how would this rage manifest itself? And yet, after every mass killing, everyone turned a blind eye. The official response — more guns and more police officers, even teachers with guns, were needed. Everyone nodded knowingly. No one spoke of the plight of the missing fathers. But then Annie, better than most, had been exposed to such dangers from a young age and could spot the frailties from afar. Other countries had as many guns; the children of other countries played as many video games; other countries' parents were as overworked. But no other country in the world, she was convinced, demonized fathers and removed them from children at the rate of her country.

The fact that her presence, a police presence, was required at a school and that it had become normal — what did that say? (Most parents had welcomed such a presence.

Only once did a man come up to her and say with an accent, "I know it is supposed to reassure me, you being here, but it does the opposite. It makes me realize there is something very wrong with this country. In my country, a police officer in a school would be reason for panic." She was so taken aback by thoughts similar to hers, but before she had a chance to respond, the man had gone.

How and when did things go so horribly wrong? She had theories, of course, about the capitalist system devouring itself starting with Reagan and de-regulation and the continued and insatiable and rapidly growing age of wealthy elite greed, the worst in the history of man, but had learned to keep them to herself. Because when she shared, people looked as if she was indeed from another planet; she didn't need to be reminded. Perhaps there were people like her somewhere. Maybe there *was* a place she belonged. She'd given up hope, until now.

Now, she watched a father she knew say goodbye to his son, tears in his eyes. She knew why. The father would not see his son for another two weeks. And, recently laid off from the nearby car parts factory, closed and moved to Asia, soon he'd not see his son at all, if his ex-wife had her way and the courts condoned her behavior; she had no doubt of either.

The little boy wore the green and yellow uniform of the professional football team in the nearest large city, three hours away to the southeast. He held onto his father and cried, too. It was too much to bear and Annie turned away. What sort of country was this, she thought again. She couldn't stand it. She had spoken several times to this despondent father about his plight. She was determined to do all she could, though at present she wasn't sure what or how. She hoped she'd find a way. Often, she thought there should be an Underground Railroad for children and their fathers to take them to civilized countries like Canada or Mexico, countries that valued fathers (she had thought of this already when her own father was taken away). But there wasn't, of course, and fathers were mistreated more each day and, she felt, it was her role to do all she could, whenever she could, to either save the fathers, or try, in some small way, not to remove them from the children's lives. From a young age, thrust upon her, she felt it was her mission in life.

She turned her attention to the other parents. She took joy in seeing children dropped off by both parents. She also enjoyed seeing fathers drop off children, though she was always aware of the fathers, like this one, who had been removed from children by wives who, she believed, had broken up families for no reason. She had had countless discussions with Carl about this. She knew which parents were which. It wasn't difficult to ascertain. A father and child saying goodbye to each other, knowing they wouldn't see each other for another week or two, presented a whole different picture, one of deep and debilitating sorrow, than ones who felt not the pressure of time. It was a sorrow that she remembered and felt viscerally. Maybe it was true, as Carl implied, maybe she did hate women. She certainly didn't trust them. Any woman today was just as likely to file for divorce and destroy a family as any other, in her eyes, for no reason at all. She had read and was not surprised by the statistics — women initiating divorce by a vast majority (and growing) and college-educated women even more. She and Carl had discussed the phenomenon countless times on the deck at the house in the swamp, beers in hand. She remembered the last time.

They had sat, perched on the deck, backs against the house. Mosquitos swarmed as they often did in the swamp and in the humidity, but she and Carl were well-sprayed and left mostly alone. Three citronella candles surrounded them and provided no lighter than protection, but Annie liked the smell.

"You hate women," Carl had said.

"Not true," Annie said. "I just don't trust them."

"You're a misogynist."

"Stupid word," Annie said. "A convenient, overused insult. What about all the misandrists out there? I see them every day. You never hear anyone being called a misandrist, do you?"

"No, not really. Still — so, do you have *any* female friends?"

"I like — love — Klara, don't I?"

"First time I ever seen you like a woman."

"Plenty of women have only male friends. You hear that all the time. Or you hear plenty of women saying they prefer working with men. For good reason."

"Me — I love women."

"Look where it got you."

"A woman — and kids — it brings out the soft side in a man."

"Sometimes."

"It sure did me. I will say one thing, though," Carl said. "When women get together, there's often the kinds of trouble you don't see with men."

"Such as?" She took a sip of beer. It was warm, but by now she had grown accustomed to it. She even preferred it. She thought that maybe she had some English roots.

"Well, when a woman wants to get divorced, like when Jane started—" even in the poor light she could see the pain in his face "—You know, they tell their friends, they getting a divorce, and the women say, 'Why,' and they say, 'Oh you know, he ain't got a good enough job, or make enough money or he's' — I love this one — 'Emotionally unavailable,' all the women just nod their heads, you know what I'm sayin' — emotionally unavailable my ass, you been married seventeen years, hell, you got responsibilities, it ain't no walk in the park, it ain't no new budding romance, but you make it work, dammit, that's what you do, you don't just walk away, throw in the towel. I mean, imagine a man sayin' that shit to his friends — imagine he said, 'She ain't making enough money or she's *emotionally unavailable*' — I mean, no self-respecting man would ever say that shit, man. If he did, we'd all pack up laughing, think he's some goddam pussy, they'd all say, 'Shut the hell up, go make some damn money yerself or what the hell you talking about, emotionally unavailable, get the hell home and quit with yer nonsense, you got a family, children, responsibilities man…'"

"Now you see why I don't trust them?"

"It ain't right."

"It's bullshit, is what it is," Annie said.

"I was more a mom to those kids than she ever was. Hell, Sara, my little one, sometimes she called me 'mom'. You know what I'm sayin'?"

"My point exactly."

Carl started crying, sobbing softly. She held him in her arms until he went quiet. It was a pain, she knew, that would never go away.

She stopped reminiscing and became alert. In the distance she now spotted a short, frail boy that she recognized, walking down the sidewalk; his name was Toren. His father had committed suicide when his wife had divorced him, and he could no longer see his son. The boy picked up and threw a rock across the street, nearly hitting a little girl on the head, unaware. Annie walked over quickly and grabbed his arm, firmly but not so it would hurt before he had a chance to hurl another stone.

"You're hurting me."

A mother and daughter walked by, looking. Annie took the boy aside, to a small courtyard so that no one could see and closed the gate. In the courtyard was a one-piece gray cement table and two benches. Annie looked at Toren; there was a vicious gleam in the boy's eye. It was a look that she had seen on occasions in the mirror; a look that she easily recognized. Annie suddenly sensed that the thrown rock may have been the least violent of the boy's intentions. It wouldn't be the first time she had thwarted violent plans while saving a child — almost all boys — at the same time.

"Toren — please sit." She pointed at the concrete table and bench. The boy sat but stared defiantly. Annie sat next to him. "I have to look in your backpack."

Toren pulled back involuntarily. His look turned from defiant to nervous. "Just… school stuff."

"Then you won't mind."

Toren glanced around fearfully. Annie felt she could read his thoughts — he was contemplating the route of potential escape. The courtyard was small and there was only one narrow entrance. But he'd have to open the grill metal gate. He must have realized it was hopeless; his shoulders slumped in resignation.

As he handed over his orange bag, his hand trembled. Annie unzipped the bag. Within, next to two books, a notebook and pencils, was a Luger semi-automatic handgun. She rummaged through the bag and under another book found two extra seven-round magazines and a box of 50 .380 bullets. Annie shook the box; it was full. Toren started crying. His whole body shook as he cried but he said nothing. She zipped the backpack and put her arm around him and waited. At first, his body stiffened, then he crumpled into her. By now the last school bell had rung, all the children's voices subsided, and they sat in the quiet morning.

"I knew your father, a little," Annie said. Toren looked at her, surprised, tears continuing to stream down his cheeks. "Sometimes we spoke a bit after he dropped you off." His eyes widened. "He was a good man. I felt that right away. He loved you so much. The way he spoke about you... you meant everything to him. Never doubt that he loved you with all his heart." What she couldn't tell him was that he was one man she could not save. You couldn't save everybody. But now, in this instance, it pained her greatly. Had she done so, she was certain they'd not be having this discussion now.

Toren continued crying. He wiped his right eye with the back of his hand. "My mother says he was a bad man. But he wasn't. At all. He was kind. He never yelled at me." He hesitated. "Like she does."

"You know, Toren, some parents use kids as weapons. And the other parent just wants to move on. That was your dad... he just wanted to move on, rebuild his life, your life, the two of you, but she never let him, always taking him back to court, making his life a misery, it was despicable, until he... died."

Toren started weeping again. "I miss him so much."

"I know you do," Annie said and pulled him closer. She stroked his hair. She continued, indignant, "What happened to your father was unforgivable. I am so sorry. You know, you won't understand this, maybe when you're older. She continued, more to herself, "Bad people exist in the world, I get that. But that a system allows them to get away with it, that's the part that gets me."

They sat in silence for several minutes. A bird landed nearby, brown and black with a white belly.

"Know what that bird is called?" Annie said. Toren shook his head. "A killdeer. Isn't that a funny name." Toren looked at her quizzically, then at the bird, but remained silent. She continued, "So — whose gun is that?"

"My mom's."

"Does she have others?"

"No."

"You sure? I'm going to check anyway, you know."

"I swear," he said. The killdeer flew away and Toren followed its ascent. "Am I going to go to prison?"

"Depends. Why did you bring it to school?" He looked at her, frightened. "I'll tell you why you brought it. You brought it because you wanted to show it to your friends."

"What?" Toren looked at her inquisitively and wiped his left eye. Still, his eyes remained moist, and another tear formed. Annie wiped it with her index finger.

"No. I was going to—" He started sobbing again.

"Right."

"I don't have any friends. Not any more. Everybody makes fun of me, about my dad. Some of the kids, I hate them. Even one teacher… I just want my dad, like the other kids. They all have a dad."

Annie winced. "I understand. Now, listen, do you have anyone you can talk to? Any adults? You know that you can confide in?"

"My uncle, my dad's… but I'm not allowed to see him any more."

"That's going to change if I have any say in this. I'll speak to your mom—"

"But she's the one—"

"Leave it to me. I have my ways. I can be very persuasive. OK?" He nodded. "Now, I'm going to take your backpack and I'm going to get rid of this gun and bullets. You'll say nothing about this to anyone. Not your mother, no one. But you have to promise me that you will never, ever, touch your mother's weapons again. Or any weapons. If you don't promise, I will arrest you. Do you understand?"

There were many other things she was not telling him; things she could never say. Such as that she understood him more than he could ever know. That she, too, had lashed out in her youth. But at the person who had caused her harm, not at innocent bystanders, no matter how mean and brutish they may have been (and she, too, had had her fair share of taunting and bullying). But those days, she knew, were far more forgiving. Today, you only got one chance. If you blew it, it would haunt you forever; what you did at sixteen would follow you at every job interview, every application of any sort, to your grave. Forgiveness, anymore, was a word often heard but seldom used.

"Can you promise me that? Because I am going to keep an eye on you."

"Yes."

"Already then. I want you to go to school now. Take from the backpack what you need. I'll bring it to you later." He reached in and took out the books and a notebook. She gave him a long hug. "Be good now, Toren. Be kind to yourself. I want you to come over to my house one day. Have you ever had self-defense lessons?" He shook his head. "You'd be surprised how quickly bullying stops when you hit one of them hard in the nose. That news spreads fast. I will teach you a little self-defense. Would you like that?" He nodded. "Now, run along." Toren stood and walked towards the gate. Before he opened it, he ran to her and hugged her. He sighed deeply.

"Thank you," he said.

"And you thought nobody cared. They *want* you to think that," she said and smiled. "While I'm around, nothing will happen to you, got that?" She stroked his hair. "Oh, and one more thing, who's been the worst bully?"

Without hesitation, he said, "Jimmy. Jimmy Wilson."

"Jimmy Wilson. Why am I not surprised. He's quite a bit older, and bigger than you, isn't he." Toren nodded. "I may have a little word with Jimmy Wilson, too."

He straightened and with a slightly more confident gait, walked out the gate and to the right towards the school entrance, giving her one final look and the hint of a grateful smile.

THE INTRODUCTION

"**AREN'T** you going to arrest him?" the woman said. She stood in the doorway, pointing at a handsome, light-skinned black man, sitting on a couch, head in hands. "You have to take *one* of us away." *And that is the man. I* know *how things work.* She was tall, taller than Annie, and lean, muscular, had a long face, indifferent blue eyes.

"Who told you I have to take one of you away."

The woman hesitated. "No, I... a friend... I've already reported him to the crisis center. And told the teachers at the school about him." *Paper trail. I* already *created a paper trail. Your role is to arrest him.*

"I see."

Annie looked at the woman closely. She was self-assured and attractive. She had an accent, though Annie wasn't sure which. Annie was certain this woman knew how to use all the tools at her disposal. She had on a very tight-fitting red dress, high heels, make-up perfectly done. She knew this type of woman.

"Are there no male officers available?" *You are not doing this according to plan. A male officer would have already taken my husband away.*

"Would you prefer a male officer?" Unless you're guilty of something, it makes no difference which officer comes to your door, Annie thought.

This is not how this is supposed to work. You take him away, he gets arrested, he gets a record, he gets kicked out, he loses his job, he loses his daughter, he must pay child support, it's all planned out. All you have to do is take him away. (What are you waiting for?).

"I feel threatened. My life is in danger."

"I understand. Mind if I come in?"

"Did you hear me?"

Annie opened the door. On the couch sat the man. He hadn't budged. Annie walked around; she unlocked a door to a bedroom. Inside, an old woman and a little girl sat on a bed. The little girl held onto the old woman, who mumbled something to herself. The scene gave Annie an ominous chill such as she had not felt since the days before she had claimed her independence.

A further oddity was a white rippled candle not long ago lit attached to a small plate on a windowsill, like a lighthouse aimed at faraway ships.

"Are you two OK?" The child had an empty stare and said nothing. "You're OK now. Why are you locked in here?"

"For their safety," said the woman who had let her in, now right behind. "I locked them in."

"Right. And you are?"

"Carolien. C-a-r-o-l-i-e-n. The Dutch way. Not C-a-r-o-l-y-n-e, the American way."

"Right. Caro*lien*, the Dutch way, I am going to take your… husband?"

"Husband, yes, good."

"*And* your daughter? And who is the older lady?"

"My mother-in-law."

"And your mother-in-law."

"What do you mean, take them?" *What are you talking about? He's abusive. I am in danger. Have you not been listening? That's not what you are supposed to do. You're supposed to take him away.* "You're not taking my daughter anywhere."

"I will bring them back." *You are doing this all wrong.* "I assure you they will be safe with me. I am taking them into custody. I am going to take them down to the police station."

"This makes no sense!" The woman raged. "Only *him*! Not my daughter."

"Calm down. Can you step away?" The woman did not budge. "I will bring them back. In the meantime, I need you to calm down. You think you can do that?"

"I am going to call a different police officer." *You will not thwart my plan. You will not.*

The woman was enraged but except for her outbursts, she tried to remain in control.

"All right, you think you can come with me?" Annie helped the old woman up with some difficulty. All three—the father, mother-in-law, and daughter-- seemed to have some sort of trauma. The father now got up, too, with a blank, indifferent expression. Carolien didn't move out of the way;

they had to walk very close to her. It appeared to Annie that they did so with trepidation and fear.

Annie didn't take them to the police station. She took them to a local diner where she knew the manager, a man named Johnny. Johnny made sure they were well taken care of, this sad bundle of humanity that, Annie thought, was immediately evident to anyone with a discerning eye and an ounce of empathy. And Johnny, wrongly convicted for rape at the age of eighteen and only recently released due to a confession of a previously interviewed and released suspect and consequent DNA testing (in no small part thanks to his friend, Annie), had empathy to spare.

They were an interesting hodgepodge, Annie thought. The young girl, Lucie, spoke with what sounded like a half English, half American accent. She was to learn it wasn't English, it was South African. Lucie also referred to her family in terms that they had to explain to Annie were Zulu — *Mama* (mother), *Baba* (father), *Gogo* (grandmother); her father, Anton, spoke with an English-South African accent, having spent time in both England and South Africa (he also had an unnerving way of looking at her, when he finally did so, and she thought once or twice she may have blushed); and the grandmother, Klara, spoke with what Annie presumed was a Russian accent (there were quite a few Russians living in Palm City now), but which they told her was Czech.

In any event, Lucie kept saying how it had been her fault, that she loved her *Mama*, and how her *Mama* was kind and loving, but sometimes she, Lucie, misbehaved and had to be punished. Anton, for his part, took the blame upon himself. When asked, he denied being hit or verbally abused. He said he loved his wife, but he just couldn't make her happy no matter how hard he tried. He said he had moved his family here recently from South Africa so his wife could get a green card and a PhD from an American university — something she always wanted — and so they could be near his mother, the woman seated next to him, from whom he had been separated ('taken', the grandmother interjected) at birth and whom he had only recently gotten to know.

It was a long story and difficult for Annie to follow. For the moment, she was concerned with the goings-on in the house and this evening in particular. The grandmother, Klara, after a few minutes and tea, which she infused with lemon and honey and called *čaj*, composed herself. To the denial and consternation of Anton and Lucie, who were rather upset with her, she said that Carolien had used Anton to get to the US, that Carolien didn't care about her, or them, or anyone but herself, that she, Klara, had survived a concentration camp and had seen plenty of people like that before, and how she just didn't... she wasn't looking for it... how she hadn't initially recognized her for what she was, a sociopath, no different to the ones in the camp, and how she, Klara, had been fooled, again, and how now they were desperate because Carolien was going to divorce Anton and take Lucie, and she had been violent to both, and had even hit her, Klara, and how it seemed like there was nothing they could do, that she felt as helpless as she had when the Germans invaded Czechoslovakia (this whole story was one that Annie at the time knew little about, except some recollections from a class in college, couple of books — she was an avid reader — and movies; but soon, her curiosity and thirst for knowledge and time spent with this family would change that).

Klara rambled somewhat incoherently (later Annie realized that she *listened* incoherently, lacking a frame of reference). Throughout, the daughter kept hugging her father, and he in turn gently touched both daughter and mother. One thing was confirmed to Annie. There was one potentially violent member of the family, and it wasn't any of the three sitting with her now.

Johnny came by to see to them personally and even picked up the check. Not that it was much, the father and daughter had no appetite; Klara ate a sandwich although she ate as slowly as any person Annie had ever seen, chewing each morsel for many minutes. Erroneously, Annie thought it was because of bad teeth or ill-fitting dentures. She would learn later that it was a habit from the camp in a futile effort to keep hunger at bay.

Afterwards, Annie took them home to a Carolien full of what Annie would later describe as a controlled inferno. A raging fire under taut skin and tightly smiling lips. It was a look she remembered all too well; in fact, from her own upbringing she recognized each of the people she had spent time with that night. In Carolien, she saw her mother; in Lucie, a younger version of herself; in Anton, she saw her father; and in Klara an older version of herself. It was that version that scared her the most. It was a version she hoped at any cost to avoid.

As feared, Annie could not stop the motion of events. She reported her suspicions to her supervisor, but upon investigation, they were dismissed. Anton would not press charges and denied any abuse, verbal or physical, as had his daughter. Only the mother-in-law accused the daughter-in-law, but the investigating officer, a male, thought that the wife was very sweet whereas the mother-in-law seemed a little 'erratic' — 'typical mother-in-law'. 'Not quite with it,' he had written in his incident report. 'Rambled about all sorts of things,' he had written, 'the old woman, about war, killings, murders, made no sense.'

Annie was called into the chief's office and reprimanded. A few women had over the years complained that they had found her unfriendly, even biased; this was the latest. Annie didn't deny it.

Ultimately, Carolien had called the police on another occasion. This time it was a male officer who arrived at the scene, and this time he followed her script. The police officer arresting the father in full view of the neighbors. Lucie, held back by her mother, screaming for her father not to be taken away, then running to the back of the house, watching her father through the window. The father seeing her and trying to smile, roughly manhandled by the police officer. Father and daughter crying desperate tears. The grandmother sitting on the couch in the living room as if stupefied, mumbling. The wife telling the daughter, once back inside the house and out of earshot, what a pathetic father she had, but not to worry, lying that he'd be back before the daughter woke up.

And with that began the whole inevitable chain of events that Annie had seen her friend Carl and countless fathers undergo daily in family courts, by the tens and hundreds of thousands, replicated all over America. From that, there was no respite and recourse. It was the removal from the children and the death knell, physical, mental, financial, for the father. In this case, a man who had made a favorable impression on her. Physically, it was true, with his handsome face and build, but also his gentleness. His soft-spoken nature. The immense love that his mother and especially his daughter had displayed for him, her arms constantly around his neck.

FEAR

SUDDENLY, his hand trembled imperceptibly in hers. "Are you scared of her?"

"Of course, I am. We are." *We. All of us. Me, Lucie, Klara.* "I think, Annie, we were scared from the beginning. I think she knew that from the start. And then, she has all the power. Everything has gone her way. I've lost everything. We've lost everything. Everything. Her life hasn't changed at all."

"So, why aren't you angry?"

"We're not all like you, my love. I know you get angry at things, and I love that about you, but we're all different. Where is it going to get me if I get angry? You know where? Arrested, again, and what good will that do? I've had enough, Annie. I'm tired. I just want to crawl into a hole, with you, and never come out. Never have to deal with another person again. I guess I am like mom in that. Look at her — living in solitude — isn't that her little 'hole'?" Anton stared at the trees across the canal from which emanated another sound. "Maybe I've always been scared of her."

"I hate her."

"I hear you. But, please, Annie. Don't do anything we might regret. I need you."

THE VICTIMS' DILEMMAS

THE dilemmas that Klara and Annie pondered often, from same and different angles of experience, were multifold.

The 1st Victim's Dilemma — why did some victims recover from scars ('cracks in their being'), but not others? Why did some victims turn into *Musselmen* (a term of unknown origin given to Holocaust prisoners who had given up), but not others? (Once *Musselmen*, only one fate awaited).

The 2nd Victim's Dilemma — why did the victims often feel a sense of shame, embarrassment and guilt (was this one reason for their frequent, self-imposed silence?), when the perpetrators felt none?

Every victim wanted the same, they agreed — recognition; not revenge necessarily (here, Annie disagreed), but at the minimum, a *recognition* of the pain. Of the injustice. Recognition and revenge, they agreed, were nowhere near the same. At a minimum, the victims wanted the earth to stop, for a minute, an hour, a week, longer, depending on the crime. The way a minute of silence was held in stadiums in recognition of someone's death or a tragic event. That's what they wanted — a moment of silence, the length proportional to the scope of tragedy. Silence spanning across countries and continents. The entire population of the earth, silent.

In Anton's case, had Carolien used him? Of that, there can be no doubt, Annie believes. She is indignant! She wants the neighborhood, everyone, to stop and acknowledge this wrong — she wants Carolien punished, too — but not all victims want punishment, she agrees. Some preach forgiveness, even (this, Annie and Klara agree, is precisely what the abuser or criminal wants and should not be given; still, they know others disagree). In their case, they need acknowledgment *and* indignation and punishment (Annie); or, at the very least, acknowledgement and indignation (Klara). They want everyone to holler and point. There he or she is! Look at them! The former member of the SS — thinking he can just continue as if he has done no wrong! The wife who physically and verbally abused her family, thinking she can continue as if *she* had no wrong! This will not stand! Everybody knows what they have done! Everyone, all the neighbors, people who know them, people who don't, those who can travel, who live nearby, others who travel from afar, equally indignant, are now on the way to his or her house to let them know this will not stand! They are looking at the victim — is he or she the one? Yes, the victim, cries, that is the one. We will not let them get away with what they did to you! Look, everybody! They are dragging them out of their house now, in front of the entire neighborhood, in front of parents, wives, husbands, children, in front of teachers, employers, anyone in any way ever associated, all ashamed, furious, shaking heads, fingers wagging, tsk-tsk, horrified at what the person has done, in unison they put a noose around his or her neck. Tomorrow it will be in the news, forever recorded. Guilt and shame, aptly attributed, in perpetuity.

Should we hang them now? Or should we torture them first and then hang them? So, they can feel at least a little of what the victim had felt? What does the victim say? They should decide. Their pain must be avenged. What did the victim say, let them go? And let them get away with their crimes? Well, so be it, they are magnanimous people, far more magnanimous than us! But the abuser or criminal cannot stay here, not amongst us, they cannot return to their house, they must leave! They cannot live in a community anymore. They must live somewhere alone, atone for their sins, forever immersed in remorse and regret. Best Days of His or Her Life, we will see about that!

Annie wants that for Anton and Lucie, too; Klara wants to see that happen to the SS-Schutzhaflagerführer and Carolien. But it doesn't happen. Their punishment depends on the moral compass of the community. And if their compass remains unmoved, if *they* are not enraged, if they are OK for that person to have gotten away with his or her crimes, if they are OK for that person to live and work amongst them as if they had done nothing wrong, it is hardly the fault of the criminal. Rather, Klara and Annie wonder, it reflects upon their fellow man. Morality and punishment are meted out, if at all, whimsically and individually. Evidently, Düsseldorf and Germany and Europe and the world thought it acceptable to let a murderer of hundreds of thousands return to his previous life; evidently Palm City and Florida and the US believe it's OK for Carolien to abuse her family, for her husband to pay for *her* crimes, and for her to continue her life unabated. But Annie thinks and Klara concurs, it leaves those upon whom the crimes and abuse have been committed forever embalmed in the Victim's Dilemmas, unable to heal, forever asking why, receiving neither acknowledgment nor revenge nor, at a minimum, sixty seconds of silence. They would have thought that the world was capable of at least that.

FAMILY COURT DILEMMA

ANTON walked through the entrance of Palm City Courthouse of the 8th Judicial Circuit. He put his wallet, cell phone, keys and coins in a beige plastic bowl and placed the bowl on a table next to a walk-through metal detector. His only experience with such security until now had been at airports. Courthouse security, he now acknowledged sadly, had replaced airport security as his circumstance.

To the right was the conveyor belt X-ray security scanner, the conveyor belt making a whir. Behind it stood two marshals in green uniforms. The third marshal stood behind the walk-through metal detector. The marshals joked with one another but paid no attention to Anton. Their arrogance and sentiments were palpable. He remembered Annie's words, 'You will feel guilty as soon as you walk through security. Not only because of the marshals' attitude,' she had said. 'But because of the 2nd Victim's Dilemma.' And it was true, he did feel guilty, and embarrassed and cowed and shamed, just as she had predicted.

He replaced his personal items in his pockets and walked past the traffic department on his left. Inside were three people sitting in chairs against the wall waiting to be attended. The door to the court records was on his right. Ahead and to the left were three elevators. He took the middle one to the third floor. There, he walked down the hallway and to the right, following the signs to courtroom 3A. Chairs hugged the walls. On one side sat a woman with two people, a man in a dark suit and a woman in a blue dress suit, pouring over notes. On the other sat a man, alone, staring downwards, his demeanor, expression and posture forlorn, dejected, bent. The man in the dark suit, smiling affably as if it were the most glorious of days, walked over to the man sitting on his own and shook the surprised man's hand and walked back. The dejected man's gaze returned to the floor.

They waited for the hour to turn ten. A few minutes before the hour, both parties walked inside and sat themselves at two adjacent tables. The dejected man now stared down at the table. The woman flanked by people in business suits occasionally glanced at him, her expression haughty and confident.

In the corner, to the left of the judge's bench, stood the bailiff in green with the same expression as his cohorts at security. Behind the bench was the seal of the state and two flags, the state flag and the American flag. None instilled confidence in Anton. Quite the opposite. They made him feel small and oppressed, subjugated. But then again, he thought, perhaps that was the intent, like a medieval cathedral imposing awe and fear from afar.

A cheery older couple walked in and sat near him on the wooden benches in the gallery. The flanked woman turned and exchanged smiles with the couple, the elderly man flashing a thumbs up. The bailiff announced the arrival of the black-clad judge, who walked in with the attitude of the marshals and bailiffs, multiplied exponentially, as the people present, Anton included, stood and sat.

Over the course of several days, at Annie's behest, Anton observed ten such *pro se* proceedings (ones where one party or another could not afford a lawyer and had to represent themselves; in America, divorce proceedings did not provide a court-appointed attorney; by and large, money won — those without legal representation got annihilated — as Annie had explained, 'In America, you have justice and the law — and the two never meet.') Of the ten defendants, nine were male, one female. The plaintiffs, Anton observed, had been alike, unemotional, matter-of-fact, exact, merciless. The defendants, too, had been identical — a blubbering, often incoherent, emotional mess, many breaking into tears; one, unable to pay, asking for immediate incarceration, knowing the circumstances to be futile (the judge replied that incarceration would come soon enough, but first would come 'contempt of court'). The man requesting immediate incarceration left the courtroom sobbing while the ex-wife and her lawyer exchanged smiles and a high-five.

Each case proceeded in a similar fashion. The *pro se* participant was decimated by the party represented by a lawyer or lawyers. In each case, the defendant's ignorance of the law was deemed inexcusable by the judge, he or she expected to be as versed in law as a lawyer with years of law school. Financial limitations were not considered; the defendant determined *pro se* because it was assumed by the court that they saw themselves as proficient in the law, not because they could not afford a lawyer. None of the ten judges, eight male, two female, had pity or patience for the *pro se* defendants. After each session, Anton felt like the party was on the receiving end — utterly despondent and dejected. Each time, Anton wondered what exactly, had been achieved. Each time the judge spewed platitudes about the best interest of the children. Ultimately, in each case, the following was achieved — the defendant could not pay the outlandish amounts awarded; the defendant was either jailed or had licenses and passports revoked; the defendant was left with a prison record and unable to drive or travel, in no hope of finding employment, time with children severely curtailed or removed. The plaintiffs took the defendants to court *knowing* that the defendants didn't have money. This was not about money, Anton realized. And it certainly wasn't about the best interest of the children. (Any more than Holocaust victims had been about relocations; or an *actual* train station or clock [the Germans had faked both, to give semblance of reality and fool the victims]); or the 'ambulance technicians' who delivered the gas pellets or 'showers'. It was about power and control. It was about the destruction of defendants (in that, the similarities were apt). And what was ultimately achieved, Anton wondered? The plaintiffs received no money because there *was* no money. The defendant's life was ruined. And the children, in most instances, lost fathers and in one case a mother. A terrible situation had been taken and made infinitely worse.

After each case, the judge, full of self-importance and grandiosity, the plaintiff and his or her lawyer or lawyers jubilant, walked off, the judge into the judge's chambers, the plaintiff out of the building, 'vindicated'. And the defendant was left behind, broken. *Another parent destroyed,* Anton thought; *more children deprived.* The onerous narrative continued, another deadbeat dad, shirking responsibility. An utter farce and fabrication, Anton remarked.

Later, Annie made her point mathematically. "There are nine court rooms in this courthouse," she said. "On average, each courtroom has three cases per day, twenty-seven total. Of those, twenty are *pro se*. That, in a small town like Palm City. Now, multiply that by the thousands if not tens or hundreds of thousands of courts and courtrooms across the nation," she said. "And you have just had thousands upon thousands of parents, ninety percent dads, robbed of children, employment, money, assets, licenses, passports, lives."

THE VICTIMS' DILEMMA MEETS THE FAMILY COURT DILEMMA

KLARA said, "Now do you see the big picture? Here is what I see — the modern American family law courthouse is the Rothschild Palais in Vienna, circa 1938. You are about to enter the Palais with your children (what time in their presence remains), finances (what's left of them), passport, driver's license, employment, assets, reputation intact. Once the modern equivalent of the *Eichmanns* is through with you, none of those things will remain. You will be no freer to drive or emigrate than could a person of Jewish descent in Vienna (not entirely true, Klara corrected herself, the Jews *were* allowed to leave, especially the wealthy ones, with only their outfits and a suitcase, if a country took them in, until the war broke out). Instead of a concentration camp, you will be sent to prison. Your child will remain alive, but you will hardly see her and have no influence over her life (congratulations, Anton, you have become an anonymous father in the modern version of Lebensborn — Lucie left to be raised by the Aryan Carolien). The inevitable resolution of the Family Law Dilemma."

"The unresolved questions now remained," Annie added. "Regarding the Victim's Dilemma: would Anton recover or become a victim. Would Anton carry shame and guilt while his wife walked around like the SS-Schutzhaflagerführer in Düsseldorf? That remained to be seen." Annie described the realities, she said, while touching Anton's distraught face. The rest was up to Anton.

But, Klara added, "I won't let you become a *Musselman*. Right now, you feel helpless. You feel no different than the wealthy Jewish person facing Eichmann. You feel the force of injustice and history."

Annie continued, "And I won't let you walk around guilty and ashamed. Hold my hand, Anton, don't let go. I will get you through this. Have faith and believe in me. We'll get through this, all of us, together."

THE PHONE CALL

"**GOOD** news, *Gogo*," came Lucie's voice on the other end.

"Does she know you are calling me?" Klara said.

"No, but don't worry, she won't know I called. I am calling from the house phone." *She will find out and punish you, Lucie.*

"What is the good news, my little one?"

"It's not mommy's fault. She had nothing to do with any of this, *Gogo*! It's the judge! She did all this; mommy didn't want it. She wanted all of us to stay together, but the judge made her do it. She told me." *Oh, my little one. Yes, of course, it's the judge. 'It's not me, Your Honor, I was only following orders.' And so it goes, rank by rank, judge by judge, higher and higher, until only one person remains, responsible for all the actions, all the blame. And who is that person, how did he or she get there? In Germany, Hitler was elected. In this country, the judges or the people who appointed them, elected. They and the people who elected them, ultimately, are responsible for one another, one and the same. The elections of those who promise the freedom to act in a certain way.*

"Do you know what a judge is, my darling?"

"No, not really, but she's not nice." *No, no she isn't, my darling Lucie. Very nice. Be aware of those that are not very nice. The trouble is, they are rarely who you think they are.* "Your father, one day, will explain everything to you, my darling."

"Not you, *Gogo*?"

I won't be around any more, Lucie, but "your father will explain. He loves you with all his heart."

"I don't want his heart, *Gogo*."

"What? Why?"

"His heart is broken."

Yes, my darling, how right you are. But a tiny piece of his heart has more feeling than ten thousand of her *hearts. One day you will see. Perhaps you already do.*

"Goodbye, Lucie. Goodbye, my darling."

THE VICTIMS MEET

The Beach

KLARA had been sitting on the beach, off A1A, running sand through her hand. She was nowhere near other people, crowds making her uneasy ever since the concentration camp, the *lager*. Next to her was a small green cooler box, handle torn off one end and in it an empty beer bottle (she had decided long ago that she had chosen the wrong country, one that looked down upon an old woman having a beer on a beach by herself).

Over time she had replaced or changed things less and less; it's what one did, she thought, what was the point of buying or fixing things that would outlast their owner? If one did not have wealth or expensive items to leave to one's progeny, there didn't seem much point buying something short-term that would only clutter and be thrown out upon one's death. It wasn't a sense of sloth or laziness, she thought, or, in her case, a slowing down as much as impending mortality. No point in buying a pet, either that would outlive its owner (although she had always wanted a pet, if for no other reason than because Jews couldn't own pets under the Nazis; but then, she had always moved too much after the war, making it impractical).

And so, she sat on the sand, in old clothes, a cooler box past its prime next to her, staring at the eternal, rejuvenating sea. There was a reassurance in it. Nature and the universe continued unabated, paying no attention to man or his or her insignificance (although, she thought, didn't the Victim's Dilemma, humanity's acceptance, and condoning of evil, prove that it, too, moved alongside, as if part of a cosmic movement?).

Sometimes, the sea brought her a new sense of perspective, the way an astronomer might find looking at infinite stars through a telescope suddenly focusing on a hitherto undiscovered star or constellation. A passerby who didn't know better, she thought, might have mistaken and misunderstood her appearance for lack of pride or dignity or laziness or fatigue or lack of money (not that she was wealthy) instead of a quiet resignation to the movements of the universe.

And so, when nothing else worked, looking at the vast ocean brought a calming, a mysterious easing. Not peace, exactly, or serenity (that, she had given up on long ago); but something akin, a slowness, a determination or at least reprieve to continue, to survive another day (for what purpose, she wasn't sure — she always wondered at those who strove to survive another day at any cost; something she could do as a youngster in the *lager* but found less plausible and certain as the years passed). Sometimes the sea was the only solace she could find.

Reluctantly, Klara stood and wiped sand off her pants. She picked up the cooler box and looked at the ocean one last time. To her right, in the distance, was the fishing pier; on the sea a wind surfer whom for a moment she observed until he was absorbed by a wave. The skies were clear, the sun high above, the heat growing uncomfortable, but she was in no hurry to return. The house would be forlorn, Anton there, almost a *Musselman*, and she at wit's end to find a way to revive him. She had for a long time known that a *Musselman* was only ever brought back to life through having someone to love, romantically or parentally.

Whereas once she would have craved solitude (Anton hardly said a word any more), common for concentration camp survivors, having had her grandchild at her home for nearly a year only to be yanked away had reopened old wounds she thought forever closed and caused pain she hoped no longer possible. That her son fell apart in his daughter's absence only added to Klara's helplessness and despair. If only she had not advised them to move to the US, to be with her.

It was a decision that she felt dramatically shortened her life, all their lives. When she thought herself and others near her to be safe at last from the curse that had afflicted her and seemingly those she loved from youth; the curse reappeared under the guise of a free society, no freer and no more just than she had witnessed under the Nazis. How this was possible she could not understand or comprehend. Society had a habit of allowing injustice to proliferate (the Victim's Dilemma, again) and thrive and run amok, unimpeded and unpunished, she decided. Her daughter-in-law had used her husband, Klara's son; and now Carolien could take their child unimpeded and abandon her son and bankrupt him financially and have him jailed. How this was possible, how it was allowed, in this supposed 'Land of the Free', she could not say (but she had seen many such injustices in her lifetime; and really, had she not learned by now that the countries with the most flags were the *least* free? The incessant national anthem at every paltry event; the pledge of allegiance repeated ad nauseam, hand on heart, by school-age children in preparation for unquestioned and illegal wars in foreign lands. How she despised all forms of insidious and fervent nationalism and patriotism).

Legally, Anton had no recourse. As Caroline had informed him, there was nothing he could do to take her green card away; they had been married at least two years before entering the country. What sort of imbecile, Klara thought, had thought up that rule? Why not two years *after* entering the country? Yes, Caroline had certainly done her research, Klara thought.

Then again, the law, as Klara had forever known, meant nothing; or rather, it was a malleable tool of those with power over those without. After all, no laws had been broken when Jews, political opposition members, homosexuals, gypsies and countless others had all belongings and property stolen and seized, by far most of it never returned, and they themselves deprived of livelihood and lives. No laws are broken. Simply rewritten. How could it be?

For that reason, laws, for Klara, were a means to pursue personal goals; just and often as not, unjust; to be ignored or broken or escaped.

"Lucie."

"*Gogo?*" Lucie whispers.

"Is everything OK, my darling?" *What a silly question, my darling, forgive me. Of course, things are not OK.*

"Sort of."

"Where are you?"

"Chuck's house."

"Does *she* know you are calling?"

"No. I'm using the house phone." *My number will show up, my darling. I don't want you to get in trouble.*

"It's early. What are you doing?"

"I'm making breakfast, and lunch, for school."

"Alone? Where is your mother?"

"She's still sleeping. With Chuck."

"Doesn't she wake up and get you ready for school and walk you there?"

"No, but it's OK, Gogo. I'm a big girl now." *Is that what she tells you? That you're a big girl? You're only eight years old, my child.* "But, Gogo, I'm afraid."

"I know you are, my darling. Is it the new guy? Is it Chuck?" *Because if it isn't, maybe he can stop the violence, at least for a while.*

"No, not really, *Gogo*. He's... OK... sometimes, he touches me, I don't like it. Mommy says he's just being friendly. But it's not him, he's OK—"

"What do you mean, he touches you?"

"No, it's OK — I just don't like it. Mommy makes me hug him, too, but I don't want to. But he's not mean, its mommy, I disappoint her, you know how she is when I don't behave, when I do something wrong." *You do nothing wrong, my darling. It's not you, it's her. How can I explain that to you?* "Like yesterday, I was washing dishes and—"

"What were they doing? While you were washing dishes."

"Watching TV. In their bedroom."

"Does Chuck's son ever do the dishes?" Lucie had told Klara previously that she shared a bedroom every other weekend with a five-year-old boy from Chuck's previous relationship (he also had two adult children, Lucie had said, that she had met once but who were not very friendly, to her or to Carolien).

"He had to wash the dishes once, but it took him an hour, so he doesn't have to do them anymore." Klara seethes. *You are slave-children, my darling. Who makes a five-year-old and an eight-year-old wash dishes while they frolic in the bedroom? Why do people like that have children? But of course, I know why, at least in the case of Carolien — tax breaks, food stamps, sympathy, validation, attention.*

"What else do you do there?"

"What do you mean?"

"Do you have other chores, besides the dishes?"

"Yes. I take out the trash. And I vacuum. Oh, and I clean the bathroom. And last weekend, Chuck paid me nine dollars to mow the lawn." *Those lazy, lazy... you're not the daughter. You are hired to help. You are the maid.* "Oh, and last weekend, mommy had this good idea that I should sell lemonade in front of the house, it was so hot, and I made forty-two dollars, *Gogo*."

"I see."

"Actually, twenty-two dollars. I had to give twenty to mommy. It was her idea." *You have got to be joking.*

"You shouldn't be doing all that, Lucie."

"It's OK, *Gogo*. I don't mind. But yesterday, I broke a glass when I was doing the dishes, and mommy came out and said I was clumsy and slapped me and I started crying and she told me to stop crying, that Chuck would hear it—"

"Does she ever hit you in front of Chuck?"

"No." *Not yet. Still on her best behavior in front of him. But she will. It's a matter of time.* "But, *Gogo*, I'm afraid. The last time she slapped me, it really hurt. And I know I will make a mistake again… I hit my head and had a bump on my head, and she told me to tell Chuck I fell. *Gogo*, please help me."

"I want to, I wish…" Klara says, desperately. *Grandparents have no rights in Florida. This state is medieval. What sort of state allows this to happen?* "I don't know… how."

"I know how. There will come a person, *Gogo*. She can help. You know her. From before. I saw her. I had a dream."

"What do you mean?"

"I saw her, *Gogo*. She's your daughter. But not your daughter. She was young, before, but now she's older. She lives far away, in another country."

No one can possibly do anything for us, my child. "What about her? Is it the policewoman?"

"I don't think so. I don't know. But she will help us. I saw it in my dream. You have to tell her, *Gogo*. Tell her… everything. OK? Promise? Pinkie promise?"

"Pinkie promise." *But, my darling, it is futile. Still, I will do it for you.*

"How is *Baba*?"

"Your daddy… is—"

Lucie says, concerned, "What's wrong, *Gogo*?"

Klara thinks back to the survivors and those that perished. Those that perished thought survival a matter of luck; habits and routines, dignifying existence, were abandoned. Without loved ones or loved ones left behind, their meaning and purpose ceased. The survivors, on the other hand, by and large, thought survival a matter of action, luck negligible. They pretended to wash, even if clean water and soap were unavailable. Her son, now, where does he lie? He hovers between the two. *But these thoughts I cannot share with you, my darling. You have enough to worry about.*

"He's OK, your father. Don't worry, my darling." *Your father has fallen apart without you. As have I. I'm worried. He might become a Musselman, if he isn't one already — remember the word you found funny for your thin father — muscleman, you thought I had said)?*

"Speak to her, *Gogo*, the woman. Your daughter. She will help us."

"I will, my child."

"I must go to school now, OK, *Gogo*?"

"I will hold you, all day, Lucie. I am sending you a kiss on your forehead. I love you, with all my heart. See? I do tell you I love you."

"Me, too, I love you. Bye, *Gogo*."

"Goodbye, my sweet child. Goodbye."

HIMMLER'S LECTURE

HEIL Hitler, class. *Mutzen ab!* Hats off! Welcome to this team building exercise. Remember, you can accomplish anything you set your mind to. Hans — the one there, tenth row, third from the left. A bit slow removing his hat. Not that one, I said, *left*. Please take him into the cafeteria for coffee and soup. What? Please come closer. (Whispering — of course there's no coffee or soup, you idiot. The usual, air pistol, back of the neck — as we did when the transport arrived, and someone asked too many questions or started to raise a fuss. We don't want to excite the masses, not now, not then. Ah, those were the days. Now, get going, I have a lecture to finish). Enjoy the coffee and soup!

Hans — who's the old woman in the back row? She's not Jewish, is she? Doesn't look it. Anti-social, you say? 'Friends' with the SS-Schutzhaflagerführer? Ah, well, looking at her now, that must have been a long time ago. By the way, that was my idea, you know, the brothels in the camps. Well, that's fine then, he's a good man, I should know, I appointed him. Yes — that's OK. Let her stay.

Now, where were we? Today's lecture, class, will cover three things — the Shock Equation; the gullibility of the masses; knowing your audience, knowing your victims. Pay attention. Hans — the lady there, third row, fifth from the right, the one that yawned. Please take her for coffee and soup. *Danke*.

Let's start with the equation, class. *Terror-time=shock*. Rather straightforward, easy to memorize, but write it down, just in case.

What does it mean. Victims blame themselves for going like sheep to their deaths. They are not to be blamed. This is due to German ingenuity, not their cowardice. We, Germans alone, understand the importance of time. Fifteen minutes to create a life, fifteen minutes to take a life. Blitzkrieg. Shock and awe, as the Americans learned from us all too well. Class, the 'normal' human mind needs *time* to absorb terror. Give it enough time, it can get used to anything and fight back. That time must *not* be provided. Is that understood? A person in shock will be docile and be led into the gas chambers or await the bullet in the back of the head. Understood? The time needed to absorb the terror must be eliminated.

Next. Man sees the rest of humanity as a mirror image. If man is good, he or she will see humanity as kind and good, despite evidence to the contrary. That works to our advantage. The person about to be shot, having already witnessed the deaths of others, will await his or her death calmly, not believing in the cruelty of their fellow man. If not, enough time is given for the shock to wear off. Again, time is of the essence.

Hans — that one there — on the phone. Second row from the back. Coffee and soup. *Raus. Raus.*

Three. Know your audience, know your victims. The Eastern Jews were beaten mercilessly and treated worse than vermin upon arrival in the camps. Why? Because they were used to the pogroms in the East. The Western Jews, on the other hand, were treated courteously upon arrival in the camps because that's what *they* were used to. All *Untermenschen*, of course; some more than others. End result, the same. Gas chambers full. Simply a different method. Know your audience, know your victims. Know their mentality. Efficiency and productivity, but also *savoir-faire*, at their very best. That is all, ladies and gentlemen. Class dismissed. Oh, only the old Frau left now. Come with me. *Bitte.* I will take you for some coffee and soup. *Heil Hitler.*

LUCIE (CONT.)

"**Then** what happens, *Gogo*?"

"We go into the hallway. All the other SS cadets are there already, shot, corpses everywhere. One is still writhing. Himmler walks over and casually shoots her in the head with a silent air pistol."

"And then? The two of you?"

"It's almost the same every time. Only once do I shoot him. All the other times I had this dream, he then turns to me, points the gun, but before he can shoot, I smile, say, *Heil Hitler*, and bite on the cyanide pill. Ironic, isn't it? Even when I shoot him, afterwards I still take the cyanide pill. I don't know why. The end is always the same. It's only a question of whether I kill him first. And that, as I said, only happened once. But that one time, I do ask him, 'Why?' And he says, 'Because we could.'"

"What a terribly sad dream, *Gogo*."

If you only knew the rest, my darling girl. Each one sadder than the rest. "Let us not think about that anymore. The woman you told me about, my daughter, I will write her."

"Please hurry. Something bad is going to happen. I can feel it."

"OK, my darling. Do well in school."

"It's hard to focus."

"Do your best, my darling girl. That's all you can do."

Klara turns and wonders about Lucie's whereabouts. Lucie is present but absent. Were they speaking? It seemed as if she could touch her. Or was it the coping mechanism she had learned in the camps? There, she often had conversations with her parents and sister and brother and husband and children (she imagined her babies as children). But the veracity of this she was no longer sure.

Years later, she saw the German certificates giving the approximate dates when all perished of 'heart failure' (the German way to record a gassing — she'd never seen a nation so proficient at lying, something her

Germanic daughter-in-law inherited, in her view, and perfected), her mother and younger sister and father (he would not be separated from them during 'selection' which meant instant gassing — *Sonderbehandlung* — 'special treatment' [who said the Germans had no sense of humor?]), upon arrival at the camp; her brother from typhus two days before liberation by the Russians — *Vernichtung*, 'productive annihilation' — those irascible jokesters; her husband within two months, shot in the head during the insidious *Zählappell*, roll call, because he had not taken off his cap quickly enough — *Mutzen ab!*

Still, it was sometimes difficult to ascertain the reality from the feigned, she reasoned. Just as laws were unreal and whimsical, so could be the good intertwined with the bad. It wasn't always easy to differentiate. One had to be extra vigilant. Klara had read an account after the war how a kommandant at another camp used to bring food to a young teenage goldsmith (she had read and watched anything she could find about the Holocaust; she especially loved the stories of resistance and escapes), whom he had liked and with whom he was friendly (not that the goldsmith was not extremely valuable to the kommandant). The goldsmith years later testified at the trial when at long last society, under world pressure, deemed it could no longer let the kommandant live free. The kommandant couldn't understand, when he had only been kind to him, why the goldsmith testified against him. The goldsmith, too, now a grown man, conceded that the kommandant had been kind to him. And yet, he felt the need to share the horrors he had seen administered to others. The Victim's Dilemma, perhaps, through yet another prism.

Klara had only known Lucie for a little less than a year, but it was an instant connection, an instant love. Lucie cried with a desperation when her father was kicked out of the house, and then when she was forced to leave with Carolien — when Carolien drove them away, Lucie inconsolable, tears pouring from large blue eyes, little fists clenched. It took Klara effort now to return from that dreadful day, a day that brought everything back, her babies being snatched, her husband taken, her mother and sister and father dragged away, into the other line, the line of death, she would only later learn, but she knew, they all knew, the foreboding was real, inescapable (why had she not stayed with them?).

Now, just like then, just when she thought she could and would stop the injustice, her daughter-in-law (again, that dreaded term 'law'!), was dragging her granddaughter away, destroying her son, and there was nothing she could do to stop it. Nothing! She could only stand and cry the same tears her granddaughter cried, clench her fists in the same way, but she could do nothing physically, could call no law enforcement to stop Carolien, could count on no laws or courts. She was just as helpless now as she had been before and during her time in the camps. As equally helpless and without justice in today's America as in fascist Europe. How was that possible? How? She fell to the ground and held her stomach in the same way she had fallen to the ground and held her stomach when her mother and sister and father and Alfons and her babies were taken away. The only difference was that then she had been hit by the butt of a gun. But perhaps that was a good thing. It illuminated the wrongness and injustice and tragedy. Here, now, with her neighbors going about their lives, society once again pretended that the unfolding scene was absolutely acceptable and absolutely normal. She had lain there for hours, cursing her fate and cursing life and cursing a God she was sure was non-existent or malevolent. For how could he allow her family to yet again be taken away?

"*Gogo.*" Klara can hear Lucie crying softly. "Please. Come get me. Don't leave me here alone. I'm not safe. Please."

Klara thinks these thoughts while walking up the wooden ladder and over the wooden pathway leading over the dunes to the parking area next to the road. Unaware, she shakes her head. As she descends the wooden steps on the other side, she walks past the newly built ablution block. She smiles to herself that she still calls the building an ablution block after all these years, from her time in the UK, maybe, or Australia or South Africa, she isn't sure; no one in the US would know what an ablution block is and momentarily she can't recall what the buildings *are* called. She thinks of the German ablution blocks, no hot water, no clean water, no potable water, no toilet paper, no soap.

Nearby, she sees a pelican fly from inland and head over the ocean. She marvels at its grace. She sits in the car and reaches to close the door. A huge, loud crash tears off the door. Shards of glass fly in all directions, one grazing her arm. She looks at the door, dangling from the hinges, mangled. Ahead, she sees a white ambulance with red lettering. It starts to slow. She gets a terrible fright. She believes it might be the 'technicians' arriving with Zyklon B. So, they found her in the end. But she doesn't want to go into the showers. Luckily, the ambulance doesn't stop, it keeps driving. She hears German spoken on the beach; she says, "*Yawohl*," rapidly, apologetically; she doesn't want to be beaten, although sometimes it's better, it keeps you moving; but she definitely doesn't want to be sent to block 11, or the Ka-Be, she just wants to close the car door, make it all go away, but it won't shut. She is parked on the A1A. She came here to look at the sea.

"Lucie — can you keep a secret?"

"Yes."

"I had a baby daughter, once, a long time ago. I never got to know her."

Lucie's eyes widen. "Is that the woman in my dream?"

"No. That's somebody else."

"Who is it then?"

"You had a great aunt. I have no idea how to say that in Zulu, my darling."

"I had an aunt. Where is she?"

"A great aunt. She... died. A long time ago."

"What was her name?"

"I don't know. I don't know her...name." *I never named her. I didn't have time. I didn't have time.*

"You don't know her name?"

"No. I am sorry, my darling."

"What happened to her?"

What happened to her. How did one answer? It was the part she had tried so very hard to forget. But some things were impossible to forget. Some memories *insisted* on not being forgotten. They remained tucked away. *No, time did not heal. Time dulled, but it did not heal.*

"It's OK if you don't want to tell me, *Gogo*," Lucie says, concerned, seeing Klara's sadness. "*Gogo* — why don't you ever tell me you love me. I mean, I know you do, but you never tell me. Mommy tells me all the time."

"Does she? You know I love you; don't you feel it? When I am with you, the way I look at you and treat and hold you and talk to you? *That* is love. Love is how I make you *feel*. People can tell you they love you and be very mean to you. Words don't mean much, my darling. Words mislead. Words change. It's how people treat you that is important."

"But *you* never tell me."

"Because, my darling, the word love mustn't be overused, or it loses its power. These days, everybody is telling each other, 'I love you,' like that mother of yours, she sure has picked up the local habits fast, like it's some normal word, some normal greeting. Like, 'Well, hello there! I love you!' And each overuse makes it less special. But when I tell you, its power has not been lost. Does that make sense?"

"I don't know. I'd like to hear it sometimes, from you, especially now that I am here alone, away from you."

"We have become a parody of ourselves, my darling. This generation has grown up watching and emulating characters on TV. Before, those characters emulated real people. Today, people emulate characters that emulate other TV characters. No one speaks or acts naturally. They act and speak the way they see some phony characters on TV. Writers based on fake characters create fake characters. Goebbels would be proud. And these fake characters run around telling each other how much they love each other. When they love no one at all."

"*Gogo* — I have no idea what you're talking about!"

Klara holds her nearer, but she's not sure she is really holding her and not herself. "Oh, my darling, you are so smart I sometimes forget you are only eight. It's just that I need someone else to talk to. I have been talking poor Annie's ear off"--

"Annie still has ears, Gogo." She giggles. Then she adds, seriously: "I wish Annie could be my *Mama*."

"Oh, my darling girl. Maybe one day she will be. So, you don't think I love you? Let me tell you something. I never thought I'd meet you or get to know any of you. And I only found out you existed last year when your father contacted me. It was the happiest day of my life. Do you know that?"

Lucie embraces her and tucks her head between Klara's head and shoulder. "But *I* do love you, *Gogo*. And I know you love me."

Klara smiles. "In your case, we will make an exception. You can tell me anytime and as much as you like." Suddenly, Klara looks around. Lucie has disappeared. "Lucie? Where are you, my darling?" Klara grows desperate. She starts to weep. She is inconsolable. "Lucie! Lucie! Where are you? Lucie! My darling! Don't go away, I need you." Her cries grow weaker, resigned.

THE CONFESSIONS — KLARA

"KLARA — it's Klara, right? Are you OK? Honey, remember me? I'm Annie, I came to your house, took you and your son and granddaughter for a meal, remember?"

"*Pane bože*," Klara says, clasping her hands. "I wish the ambulance had hit me."

"Are you OK?"

"She took her."

"Who?"

"*Ta kurva*. Carolien."

"You mean, your daughter-in-law took your granddaughter, is that what you're trying to tell me? You mean, now?"

"Not now. Two days after you came, she called the police again, and this time—"

"Klara, listen to me, you have been in an accident. You might be in shock; I may have to call an ambulance—"

"No, please! No ambulance. You see what they are like. It's not a *real* ambulance. In the camps, the ambulance carried Zyklon B, to fool the people. Annie — I am not in shock. I am OK, I just, with the accident, I need to talk. Can I talk to you? Please. I have no one to talk to. I just need Lucie; my son, you remember him, he's not coping—"

"You daughter-in-law managed to—"

"Yes, Annie, she called the police again, he's not going to make it. I am so afraid. I have seen what happens to the *Musselmen*, during the war—"

"Klara, you sure you're OK?"

"Yes, they only hit the door, not the car, I am unharmed. I just need to talk to someone."

"OK, here, take my hand, let's go sit on the beach for a bit, I have to file a report anyway, were there any witnesses?"

"I don't think so, and the car just drove off. The 'technicians'. *Svině*. I am not surprised."

"People do that these days, probably didn't have insurance. You think it was an ambulance? You'd think an ambulance would at least stop — right? Make sure you're all right, even if he was in a hurry to get somewhere. Maybe it was one of the private ones."

"Not a real ambulance."

"You sure you're OK? Here, take my hand, let's walk to the beach, sit down for a bit, we'll wait for your car to be towed, do you know where you want it towed?"

"I have no idea."

"I know a place, they are honest, are you OK with that?"

"OK, yes, fine."

At the beach, they sat next to each other. It was a bit chillier now, the wind had picked up, and Klara pulled her jacket tight.

"Annie. I am tired. I have lived a long time and I am tired. Bad luck follows me, all my life. Whenever I love somebody, something bad happens. They die or get taken away." *Through the chimney*. "*Pane bože*. It's the same, isn't it? In some ways. I don't know what's worse, because if they are taken away, you just wonder, don't you, what happened to them. And now, they came back into my life, and she stole them, Annie… I try so hard no to get close to anyone, to love anyone, but then they came back into my life, my little Anton, well, maybe not so little anymore—"

"Klara—"

"I last saw him when he was a baby, when his father stole him, when they took him away from me, why does that happen to me, all three of my babies taken away when they were born, I thought I had lost him forever, and little Lucie, I didn't even know, you see, I didn't know… that she was alive even… something bad always happens to those I love and the evil ones, they get away with it, always, society does nothing—"

"Are you suicidal? Is Anton?"

"I need to tell you something. I have nobody to talk to. My son, I fear, might have become a *Musselman*—"

"A muscle-*man*?"

"That's what my granddaughter says. In the concentration camp, the *lager*, that's what we called those who gave up living."

"You were in a concentration camp?"

"There is something I must tell you, Annie. I can't carry this grief on my own any more—"

"Have you been to the crisis center?"

"Annie — I don't want a therapist. What is it about this country? 'Too much information', people tell each other. Be positive. What a bunch of nonsense. How can anyone's suffering be too much information? Show me one person whose life is always positive. Up and down, the pendulum of life. Not *enough* information, maybe. So many people go to church in this country on Sunday but won't listen to what ails and troubles their neighbors."

"You might need antidepressants, Klara. I'm not qualified."

"Pills. They think pills solve everything here. If you are a caring human being, you *are* qualified. A heck of a lot more qualified than those *paid* to listen. *They* know nothing about anything and care even less. What I need is a friend, someone to talk to."

"I understand. If I didn't have Carl—"

"Boyfriend?"

Annie laughed. "Oh, no. Just a very special friend. A real partner-in-arms." Annie stood up. "Klara — would you excuse me a minute? I just forgot something in the cruiser, give me a minute, Klara, OK? I'll be right back."

"Of course, dear, I've been talking too much. If you have to go—"

"No, I'm OK, just give me a minute." Annie walked back over the wooden walkway above the dunes and to her cruiser. She radioed the station that she was with a victim of the car accident and that she might be suicidal and would stay as long as necessary. Then she walked back to Klara.

"Everything OK?" Klara said.

"All good." She sat down again next to Klara.

"You know, Annie, thank you for listening to me. You are so kind. I have never talked to anyone about what happened in the *lager* — the camps. Maybe I could tell *you* a thing or two. I tried, I needed to, in the beginning, but people weren't interested, they looked at me like *I* was the crazy one. Isn't that funny? When you recount pain and horror that you have witnessed, firsthand, people shun you. I don't know why that is. You probably have no idea what I mean."

"Actually, I do," Annie said.

Klara looked at her closely. "That pain, Annie it's unbearable—"

"I've known pain like that, Klara, maybe not like yours, but the unbearable kind."

"So, you know. I just want it to stop already. But it never stops, I am afraid of going to sleep. Of waking up. It was like that once, after the war; then it... never really went away, but I guess I could control it... I was much younger... but with age, we get softer, more vulnerable, we cry over nothing, we remember everything, not what we need to buy at the store, that we forget, but all our old memories come flooding back, we get no respite. And into this, they came back into my life, and now they are gone, and I have fallen apart, we both have, Anton and I—"

"Is he in a bad way?"

"Yes. I have seen that kind of grief before, you see, too many times, and mostly people don't recover, and they just... die... and... I can't hang around and wait for that, I can't witness another death, I just can't do it. Oh, Annie, why are there so many bad people in the world, doing evil things to each other. It's something I have never understood. You know, I told people here I have come to know, not friends, mind you, I can't afford to get too close to people, but acquaintances, you know how it is here, old people retiring to Florida, leaving everything they know behind — it's an American thing—" Annie would get quickly used to Klara and Anton's stories suddenly veering elsewhere before returning again and she would always listen patiently, it made her the sort of caring listener so many sought and so few had, one she never had herself until now, and needed just as much. "—elsewhere in the world, Africa, I know from Anton that the Africans, when old, they move back home to the village they come from, to be with loved ones, that makes sense — in America, people move *away* from loved ones to die among strangers — those that can afford it, anyway. Then they must make all new friends, but at our age, making friends is not so easy; and the only friendships worth anything take years and experiences to build; you need depth of feeling that only comes with time and shared difficulties you have together overcome—"

"You mentioned Anton."

"Yes, yes—"

In the meantime, the tow truck came and briefly interrupted their talk. They took Klara's car to a body shop Annie recommended. The driver came to the beach and had Karla sign forms. After he left, Annie let Klara talk. The impact only affected the door, Annie thought, she probably just got a fright and needed to talk. Still, she thought it better to keep an eye on her.

Klara's conversation went beyond the visceral, she spoke of immeasurable grief. And Annie had spoken the truth — it was a grief she knew intimately.

Klara started to recount what she had not told anyone since she was freed from the *lager*. About her family. About other people who refused to part from loved ones and were shot or viciously pounded with rifle butts or gassed. Their bodies lay on the ground or were burned. It was enough to quiet the waiting crowd into submission, those that got shot or killed right away. Always in a hurry, always clubbed. *Raus*! *Raus*! Not that it took much. Already they were all so tired, Klara said, from the cattle cars where they stood for days, hungry, thirsty, dirty, in urine and feces, with dead bodies amongst them, the lucky ones perhaps. Klara said she understood then that it was possible to die if one wished if one was tired enough or without hope. If one had no one to return to if one had nothing to live for. She marveled at those who, having lost everyone, persevered. Who wanted to survive at any cost, desperately, who would do anything to save themselves. To survive for what exactly? The hope of a return to a 'normal' life? How could life, after this surreal horror, ever be 'normal' again? That was the part that horrified her while she was in the camp. That, even if she managed to survive, and that was a big 'if' — how would she ever reintegrate into 'normal' society? How would she pretend as if nothing had happened? As if going about one's day was the most normal of things when one had witnessed such atrocities? And yet, she would one day become one of those. Hope was a dangerous drug reserved for fools, Klara said. Hope could lead you straight into a mass grave or through the chimney, as the Kapos and the SS often warned, bellowing smoke into the air, descending unsuspectingly as ash, or used as fertilizer.

"Now… here is the part I have never told anyone…" Klara started to say. "I could never… never wanted to… tell anyone. Who would I tell? Lately I wanted to tell my son, but I cannot burden him with more trauma, he is barely surviving as it is."

Annie told her she didn't have to tell her anything and Klara said, on the contrary, she said she had to tell someone, or it all died with her. Just the once, was all she needed. She had to get it off her chest, she had carried it too long.

Why Annie was chosen, Annie wasn't sure. Was it a desperation after another close call with death that time was running out? That Klara might take her life? That she might die having told no one. Was it something suprapersonal, larger than them? A connection of sorts that would only become apparent with time, as their lives became intertwined. Annie didn't know. Certainly, Klara said that this was not a desperate moment. That she would not have told just anyone. That she felt an inexplicable connection to Annie, the way one sometimes feels as if they had known a stranger previously.

In any event, later Annie would remember this moment. She would become the holder of Klara's confessions, and Klara of hers.

Klara continued, after momentarily burying her head in her hands. But first she asked Annie her full name. Annie Houbacek.

"Houbáček," Klara repeated. "Married name?"

"No," Annie said, she had kept her maiden name. Annie said she knew that it was of Czech origin, her grandfather having immigrated. Klara gently touched Annie's cheek, and repeated Annie's full name. Perhaps that was why she had been in the accident in the first place, to meet her confessor, Klara said.

"I was separated from my family," Klara continued. "I have never told the next part to anyone.

"Some of the memories had been suppressed so deeply for so long that it now hurt to pry them open," she explained. Some returned from a place she had not known existed and many she had genuinely forgotten. But some haunted her sleep, she said. Recurring images circularly returning. The way her few nightmares had been cyclically omnipresent each night in the camp and ever since.

She told Annie, with great difficulty, that she had been chosen for the brothel. A brothel for the SS. By the second-in-command, the SS-Schutzhaflagerführer. He had spotted her already on the platform. At the time she was still somewhat healthy and beautiful, despite the horrific train ride. She was tall and blue-eyed and as a *mischling* of the second degree (a mongrel with one Jewish grandparent, she explained); then, her records were changed. The SS could be sent to the Russian front for sexual relations with a Jewish person, stripped of rank. But rules only applied if the SS wanted to follow them.

After liberation, she would speak to a woman who worked in a brothel for prisoners — she said those men, many could not perform sex, they were too traumatized, too weak, but they just wanted to hold that woman's hand and tell her stories, about wives and children, gassed, and she said the pain, their pain, was unbearable. Sometimes, she said, she'd have preferred the sex. Most of the men, she said, were gentle and ashamed, but desperate for female companionship. Even those that could get an erection were often premature and, in any event, all were watched by a guard through a peephole in the door as if the pressure were not enough and given exactly fifteen minutes. This woman, Annie said — she could not remember her name, only her nationality — somehow in the midst of the cruelty found time to make a joke. Now we know why the Germans are so many, for them, everything's like a factory, fifteen minutes with a supervisor keeping tabs. Consistently efficient, the Germans — fifteen minutes to create a life; fifteen minutes to gas a life. Unlike the Germans, we are a small nation, we are romantic, this woman said, we take our time lovemaking; those that understand what it takes to create a life, understand they have no right to take a life. Klara didn't laugh at the time, she remembered. The woman touched her cheek and told her to take care of herself. She never saw her again, or any of the other women who worked in the brothel. Klara had never spoken about it to anyone, and she was sure very few of the other women had either.

But Klara was not so lucky, she said, if you want to call it that. Annie held her hand tightly. This was a story from a world of hell. As a child, Annie had experienced her own hell. She at once understood Klara's pain. She could not imagine the specifics, but horror and pain were universal; those, she understood. And she had learned through her police work, although exposed to peoples' pain and suffering, that it was difficult to reconcile personal specifics. It was impossible to know what it felt like to lose a parent, or husband or wife or a child, for example, if you had not done so. But, familiar with pain and suffering, you could empathize and empathize she did.

By the same token, she was always amazed how some of her colleagues, strangers to suffering, could completely tune out to the pain of others, as if they were listening to a program on the radio. How they could remain entirely unfazed and could sleep at night as if they worked in a bank or a store; how they could look at beaten people or dead bodies and feel nothing. There were times she would comment on a dead body they had just investigated and the officer with her would say, what dead body, already thinking of other things. She knew she was different, of course, and now, listening, she felt the chilling effect of Klara's words.

Annie always went beyond the call of duty, and her now sitting here was no exception, no matter if it was at the end of her shift. She was not aware of anyone else at the precinct who took time with victims as she had. She simply could not walk away until she felt certain the victim was moderately stabilized, would not hurl themselves in front of a passing vehicle or take an overdose of pills. Often, the victims called after the incidents and Annie in her spare time would share a coffee. She knew that the victims found solace in speaking to the person who had found the body of a loved one, for example. Sometimes, they called her years afterwards, asking details they didn't have courage to ask at the time; or asking to see police photos they didn't have the strength to look at in the aftermath of the incident.

"The SS-Schutzhaflagerführer," Klara continued. "Was the second-in-command of the camp, junior only to the kommandant." Klara looked into the distance, at a speck, a ship perhaps. "Strange," Klara said, "That I am in the end confiding to a representative of the law. A figure of authority. I feel a connection with you, but why? Is it a personal one, or is it the uniform; or a combination of the two?"

In any event, ever since then, Klara continued, she had hated all figures of authority. No, that wasn't strictly true, she clarified. She had mixed feelings. They were pawns, weren't they, upholding laws which one day made killing a crime; the very next, a sport rewarded. Laws took on comical names, Law for the Restoration of the Professional Civil Service. Or in today's world, right-to-work laws, just the opposite, it's all the same, isn't it, under different guises. Let me continue, so you can better understand, she said.

It would be so easy to say, she added, that she was a victim (not that I wasn't), and that he was a monster (not that he wasn't), but the relationship took on dimensions which she to this day did not understand, she explained, and most likely never would. He could be a bastard and later she would find out that he was a monster, but he also saved her life, whatever it was worth.

The SS-Schutzhaflagerführer had spotted her on the platform and made sure she was taken to the brothel. Normally, Jewish descendants could not work in the brothels, she repeated. But he wasn't interested in technicalities. In the camp, he had godlike powers, of course. He explained, later, that in any event documents could be changed, altered. There were plenty of people in the camp who were adept at such work. She was tall, blonde and blue-eyed, anyway, so it was not far-fetched. Maybe someone had made a mistake. Maybe she wasn't Jewish, he said. He also explained that most central Europeans, Germans, too, had some Jewish blood. He himself had Jewish blood, but it went far enough in generations that under the Nuremberg laws, it did not register (it was in those years, 1933-1935, that Klara realized, she said, that laws had no permanence, were absurd, based on no absolutes).

Klara continued, the building was not uncomfortable, and she had her own bedroom. At first, she didn't know where she was, but soon the other women explained. She was one of the lucky ones, they said, almost enviously. They were in a brothel reserved for the SS. She had been chosen to serve only the SS-Schutzhaflagerführer. There had been one before her, a young Polish woman, similar in looks to Klara, tall, blonde, blue-eyed, but she could not fall pregnant and was moved to a subcamp; later, there were rumors that she had fallen sick and died. Klara didn't feel particularly lucky. To this day, she said, she was not sure if her survival was lucky or not; and of late, she had begun to doubt whether she had ever had any luck at all. Lately she had begun to feel as she had for years, that her bad luck had never truly left. What appeared to be good luck (the unexpected reappearance of her son and the discovery of a granddaughter and daughter-in-law) had turned. And all this, it now dawned on her, with her acquiescence. Her home had, in effect, become the Central Office for Jewish Emigration, the *Zentralstelle*, she explained, in the Rothschild Palais under Eichmann in Vienna in 1938 and she the compliant Jewish Council. Jews wishing to emigrate, she explained to Annie, were fleeced of all they owned, all in a great rush through the building, and left with a passport in hand and hardly anything else. Now she herself had abetted and expedited the very same for her son. He had lost all in the process and been left with a passport in hand, at least for the foreseeable future, and nothing else. All with her unwitting participation.

After the war, Klara continued, she became aware that the description of tragedy was subjective and difficult; that most people didn't want to hear or believe; could not relate; and was sometimes mocked. She understood, as much as it frustrated. When she had at first been liberated from the camps, she had felt the need to tell people she met. It was as if she were bleeding tragedy (the way her son now felt the need to tell people what his wife had done, but nobody was interested, she said), but she found several types of reactions (none what she expected or needed, none the acceptance and understanding she sought and hoped would ease pain, so after a while, she said, she stopped trying), a total and sometimes aggressive shunning or dismissal or disbelief of her story (the listener implying she was lying or making it up); a joy, almost, at her suffering (asking and hungering for ever greater details); feigned sympathy which later turned into derision for victim and empathy for the people who had perpetrated the crimes; listening but uncomprehending; and lastly, people like her with similar experiences, who truly understood, but too full of pain themselves, for whom sharing stories from the camps was akin to comparing war wounds or razor cuts — sooner or later one of them would feel the disinclination to say more.

As a result, she said, this story she was telling Annie, in its entirety, she had never told anyone, and she was not expecting a reprieve, she simply felt the urge to tell someone before leaving this earth. She had long ago understood, she said, that there was to be no reprieve, no cure, for what she and countless others had experienced.

"She couldn't fall pregnant?"

"What?" Klara said.

"You said she couldn't fall pregnant. The previous…" Annie wanted to say 'prostitute', but of course, they had been nothing of the sort. "…woman."

Klara smiled. "I see why you are with the police. Yes, they let her go because she could not fall pregnant. You see… the SS-Schutzhaflagerführer—"

"Did he have a name?"

"I haven't said his name since the war. I can't do it. Giving him a name humanizes him, it gives him dignity. I know it probably doesn't make sense—"

"It does."

"My son now, he cannot say the name of his ex-wife, he just can't — and of course who understands better than me? That's why I call Carolien *blázen* — in Czech, the 'crazy one'. People who haven't experienced what he has, what I have, always tell him he mustn't say anything bad about her. My philosophy has always been, if you haven't experienced that of another, you haven't the right to comment, let alone criticize. Wittgenstein said something similar." Klara blushed. "Does that sound harsh?

"No."

"So, the SS-Schutzhaflagerführer—"

"Yes," Annie said.

"Where to begin. I was his personal… whore. Oh, he always told me I was his mistress and that I wasn't a whore because he didn't pay with money. But he brought presents all the time, taken from murdered prisoners, I was sure, rings, necklaces, fur coats, shoes, watches, even gold jewelry made specifically for me. He said I had to put them on, or he would insist on placing them on, a necklace, as if he had chosen and bought it diligently instead of stealing it from a dead woman, or he would hit me if I refused to put it on, as I had in the beginning, not often, and he would always apologize afterwards, sometimes even cry. He was a short man; I think that was why he loved tall women. A short, rotund middle-aged man, married to a short rotund wife, with five rotund children. But the wife could no longer have children, he had informed me. He was nothing before the war, by the way, a baker's assistant, unemployed even, never the baker or owner of a bakery, took care of the inventory, that sort of thing, whereas I came from a doctor's family, I had been to university, in a normal life our paths would have hardly crossed. I remember his hands, small, and often his nails were dirty. Sometimes I thought I saw blood or human remains on his uniform, I never asked. He would tell me about his days, how hard they were, how demanding, how he was forced to do things he didn't want, to kill prisoners sometimes. He said it had to be done, for the sake of discipline, but also for their own sake, that in some cases they were put out of misery, it was the humane thing to do, he had done a favor. He told me gruesome details. The first time I burst out crying and he hit me, with a fist, cracked my lower lip, then he apologized but I never cried at his stories again.

"Annie, here's the complicated part. Yes, I hated him. But he also saved my life. He could be vicious, a real monster, but in his sick way, I think he also loved me. There were times, Annie, that I actually felt pity for him. Imagine. As he told me atrocious stories and sometimes cried, I actually felt sorry for him. And yet, he never felt sorry for the Jews or children or women; he only ever felt bad when he had to kill a German prisoner; and even then, not if the prisoner was Jewish or homosexual or a political prisoner, not a communist, anyway, sometimes a social democrat, he had it all sorted in his head, what kind of person was subhuman, a vermin, an *Untermensch*, those deaths meant nothing to him, it was like killing flies, he gave it no more thought than that, and yet, they knew, didn't they, that what they were doing was wrong. Why else use misleading terms? Why the 'Final Solution'? Why 'relocation', or 'special treatment'? Or *Stücke* 'pieces' or 'merchandise', or 'load', not 'corpses'. Why not just 'Final Death to Jews Solution'? Why 'heart failure' and not gassing? Why did they want to burn and destroy all remains of their hideous deeds before the Russians or Americans arrived? That's the thing, they could kill without remorse, but they knew that what they were doing was wrong. Otherwise, why not boast about it to the world, if what they did was righteous?

"He did have difficulty, I remember, with killing a WWI Iron Cross German Jewish recipient. 'The man was a hero once,' he said, perhaps it wasn't his fault he was Jewish, but he went no further with his moral predilection. Sometimes killing criminal prisoners, that unsettled him a little, too. Because, when he had been unemployed, he had stolen himself, he admitted; he had to, he said, to feed his family, that was different, and maybe some of these thieves also had done it for the same reason. He felt sorry for the thieves that were killed, imagine that. 'That could have been me,' he said, had the Nazi party not saved him and given him a career and dignity and pride and a sense of purpose. He was respected and yes, feared. 'There was a thrill in that,' he said. 'Being feared. It was a power that one got used to quickly. You could always see fear in peoples' eyes,' he said. 'Always.' And it titillated him.

"Sometimes he put his head in my lap and I actually stroked his hair while he cried about some German thieves that had to be killed — *that* he understood that he could relate to; and isn't that always the case, that you can sympathize only with a condition you know? And I was moved by his sadness. As absurd as it was. Because, when you think about it, in his mind that could have been him, 'there but for the grace of God go I' sort of thing, he was crying for himself; for what he might have been had the hand of providence not played its part. But I was grateful to him, for saving my life. My pity was genuine. Imagine the contradictory emotions swirling inside me; to this day I don't know what to make of them. And, I don't want to say it, but—" Klara started crying and Annie held her; after a while she collected herself and continued "—And this is hard for me to admit, I felt something for him, I hate to call it love, but it was something—"

"The Stockholm Syndrome."

"I don't know, maybe, you have to remember, I had only slept with one man before him, my husband; and so, he was only the second man I had slept with and after a while, I wondered, if I was confusing things in my head, he always complained about his wife and how he had to leave her and, you will laugh, how he would marry me after the war and he had my category changed from Jewish to anti-social so I had a black star, not a yellow one, and so I in the beginning… he said after the Germans won the war we would be together and then when it started to be obvious that they would lose, he said we'd still be together, that he would leave his wife, and he started to be a bit scared, and he kept reminding me how good to me he had been and how he had always treated me well, and we could still get married but wasn't sure we could remain in Germany, we would have to emigrate somewhere, he wasn't sure where, he said he was making enquiries, Argentina or Uruguay maybe, through Italian contacts he had, but he said I could not tell anyone. Like I said, there were days I wasn't fond of him, but there were days I looked forward to seeing him because, you see, the other women, they had to sleep with several men each day or night and here I was, the 'special whore', they used to call me, as if jealous, saying what did I have that they didn't, can you imagine. I could wander around a bit during the day, too, but I saw so many atrocities, killings, beatings. So, there were days when I just remained in my room and had not seen anyone but him. There were days he might not come, called elsewhere, another subcamp, there were many, or Berlin, some conference, and I actually, I don't know, missed him or missed the human company. I know it sounds crazy. I was actually happy to see him sometimes, after an absence. Also, what if something had happened to him, I would become just another… After a while, I felt like a mistress, as crazy as it sounds, and I started to see our life after the war, and I started to be jealous of his wife.

Can you imagine. But I only hated him when I found out, when… so, to come back to your pregnancy question — I have learned since, just been reading about it, really, there are some men, some people, they have certain fetishes, sexual, that appear odd to those that don't share them, comical even. You know, some people, for example, get aroused by feet; or some men like very large women, whatever it is, humanity is awfully strange at the best of times. And so, this man, he also had a fetish. He got aroused by… pregnant women. Imagine." Annie thought back to her own pregnancy, ultimately a stillbirth, when she had felt incredibly sexual, but her husband had found her repulsive — he never said so, but it was obvious, he never touched her, recoiled when approached, didn't make love to her. "You see, when I arrived in the camp, I lost sight of Alfons, my husband, almost immediately. I didn't even have time to say goodbye. I was three months pregnant. Then, *he* came up to me in a white jacket and a riding crop and asked if I was pregnant. I knew instantly, you just know, that life or death depended on it. I just wasn't sure in what way. After the war, I heard that Mengele selected pregnant women for experiments in another camp. In my case, it saved my life. I thought about lying. There was no way to know the right answer. I thought to myself, perhaps I will be seen as useless for labor, and they will kill me *and* the baby. Or, stupid me, even when you are facing certain death, you want to believe in the goodness of people. You want to plead to their 'human' side. You want to believe that a cold-blooded killer is capable of decency and clemency. It's so stupid and yet that is how it is." Annie nodded. She understood the inclination all too well. This inclination but also inability to understand a killer's total lack of empathy. "So, I thought to myself, maybe he will feel sorry for me because I am carrying a child. That's how we think, isn't it, pregnant women, look at us, that the world should show us tenderness, that we are somehow special, propagating the human race. There I was, young, pregnant with my first child, thinking, in this place full of misery and horror, that this man, who personified the cause of the horror, would take pity on me and — what? — say, oh, the maternity ward is over there, they will take care of you until you give birth and then you will have special concentration camp maternity leave, how about that. Decent people are hopeless, they cannot be corrected, they remain optimists until their dying breath. They still hope beyond hope that water will pour from the showers and not Zyklon B. That even with the gas, the doors will open, and it will have been shown a horrible mistake and they will be led out and freed and returned to their lives. Despite all evidence to the contrary, decent people want, need maybe, to believe in the goodness of their fellow man. With blue lips and fingernails in the doors, they die thinking it all some colossal mistake.

"You know how many times one hears, 'what did you do to deserve that?' As if cruelty and horror must be justified, as if there must be a reason for their existence. How utterly foolish. Recently, once again, after I told some random woman what my daughter-in-law had done, the woman said, 'Oh, I bet your son did something terrible to deserve that.' I nearly lost it. So, tell me, I said, the Jews and gypsies and and children and homosexuals and Jehovah's Witnesses plucked from a village somewhere, taken to their deaths during the war, had they done something to deserve *that*? She said, 'Homosexuality is a sin. It's unnatural.' That's all she heard. *Pane Bože*. How ignorant some people can be! Evil exists in its own context, it needs no reason, no origin, no explanation, no justification. It simply exists! Oh, this woman, she shut up and walked away, but later I heard her say terrible things about my son, whom she doesn't know, can you imagine? Why? Why is she doing that? Because she is mean and cruel, yes, but mainly because she is human, with all of humanity's frailties and vulnerabilities and idiocies."

Annie said, "In my line of work, we're always looking for motive, right? But motive needs logic; and murders, killings, heinous crimes, brutality, harm often, are done for the sake of itself, for no reason at all, because someone wants to kill or harm another person. I also get that woman, Klara, who in her head, she *has* to have a motive. That way, she can understand the reason — revenge. The formula, he killed her *because* she had done this or that, people understand that. But when you say, this person was killed for no reason at all, it doesn't compute, right? So, this random woman you spoke about, she almost *had* to make your son the scapegoat, because in her head, it doesn't make sense that someone mistreated him, and he's done nothing to deserve it."

"Yes, of course, you are right, Annie. I have seen so much senseless violence and tragedy, without reason, without motive, as you would say. That I know it exists, it is amongst us every day. One has to be so very vigilant."

"Klara — who was the father."

Klara looked veritably pained. She involuntarily touched her stomach and Annie was sorry she had asked although she felt the need to know.

"Like I said, I was married... my husband, Alfons...I was eighteen — a child — he was twenty-eight, a pediatrician, of all things, we were so happy together, when the Germans... he had a slight limp, Alfons, ever so slight, but noticeable enough for the 'selections'... I... only later found out... I named the baby Alfons, too... oh, my God, Annie... so I told him, this German, that yes, I was pregnant and he was so excited, and, of course, stupid me, I thought, maybe he *is* different, maybe he loves babies, like it was the greatest news in the world and he led me personally across the camp to a building, and left me there with the *aufseherin*, the madame of the place, an older matron, German, a former prostitute herself I would later learn, who took an immediate dislike to me but out of deference to the SS-Schutzhaflagerführer had to be polite if not friendly.

"It became apparent why he had taken a liking to me. Not only was I what he coveted, a tall attractive woman, but I was pregnant. Most men are ambivalent about pregnancies, not he. He was veritably aroused just by the thought of it. And as the belly and breasts grew, as the body changed, the more excited he became. I gave birth twice in those three years. Normally women were sterilized and given abortions. That didn't serve his purpose, of course. Many also didn't menstruate while in the camps, but I was well-fed. I gave birth to a son, Alfons' and my son, five months later. I only saw him briefly, but he was a beautiful baby. A full head of dark hair, like his father's. He was taken away from me. I remember crying like a wounded animal. But the *aufseherin*, I remember she took great joy from this, taking my son away. Although she was trying to justify it, knowing full well what they would do with him. She told me he would be well taken care of, that a brothel was no place for a child. He'd be taken care of by a proper German family. That when the war was over, we'd be reunited. She told me all this with a glee, almost. I was devastated, I remember falling to my knees, clutching my stomach in pain, but I took refuge in thinking that I might see the child after the war. I had my doubts, but there's that hope again, irrational, against all odds or irrefutable evidence.

"After the child was born, the SS-Schutzhaflagerführer lost desire for me. He would still come, and we still had sex, upon his demand, but it was perfunctory, mercifully brief. There were rumors among the other girls that he was looking for my replacement. That he was on the platform, searching, overseeing every arriving transport. I had heard that he had even approached a couple of girls, tall and blonde like me, Polish girls, but was very disappointed when they weren't pregnant. They could have been lying, of course, and going to their deaths, but how could they have known. Imagine, so I was again being saved by this bizarre fetish. The *aufseherin* kept me informed. A bit maliciously, she was taking great joy, I could see. She was certain my time was over, that he'd find someone else, that he'd not want to have sex with me again now that I wasn't pregnant. She hated that I got preferential treatment, they all did. A bit like a man with no water jealous of man with a spoonful of mud. Whether true or not, that he was approaching other women, I didn't know. But the *aufseherin* was not as formal and polite as she had been. She was a big woman, with facial hair above her lip, it was hard to imagine her as a prostitute, and now she was taking liberties, too, with my food, since she knew that the SS-Schutzhaflagerführer had lost interest in me, to a great extent, not completely, mind you. And here, I can tell you, and this is where desperation for survival comes from nowhere, or rather, I was determined to survive for my son and my husband and my parents and brother and sister, in case there was any hope they were still alive, and so I became what I swore I wouldn't be, his whore. That I would seduce him until I became pregnant. It was my only hope for survival. If he was finished with me, there was no guarantee that he'd not have me killed, despite the declarations of love; I was not a thief, I was Jewish, even if he had me reclassified to a black triangle.

"So, on the rare occasions when he did come, to complain about his wife and his life, I still knew the little pleasures he enjoyed, the way he liked to be touched, and when a woman decides to seduce a man, especially a man she knows found her alluring only recently, there is no stopping her. So, I made sure on those rare visits he'd still have sex with me, and I held him tight inside me with my legs around him, making sure he'd climax completely, and I remember how dirty and despicable I felt afterwards, because those times I really did feel like a whore, but I was desperate to survive. I got lucky if you want to call it that. I was young, I was healthy, I was well-fed. I fell pregnant. And quickly, his interest in me returned. It was less than a year before the end of the war then. I was in two minds with this baby. It was a Nazi baby; it was *his baby*. But it also saved my life, for now. I didn't know how I felt about it, not really, not like my son. I didn't know how I would feel about it when it was born. Would he or she forever remind me of *him*? Would I be able to love him or her? And then it was a countdown, wasn't it. Would we be liberated before the baby was born? Because then, maybe, if we weren't killed, we would both be saved. If we were liberated after the baby was born, I had no doubt that the baby would be taken away again. Although, of course, in this case, it was also his baby, and, like I said, you wanted to believe, didn't you, but really, what was I thinking, that we'd live happily ever after somewhere, in hiding? That I would actually love him in the real world? You see, that's how confused your mind becomes, plays tricks, like what is happening with my son now, she has been a monster to him, and yet, he clings on, I think, and believes that somehow, miraculously, she will become a nice person and apologize and come to her senses — you see, we all feel like that, all decent people, we are all the same in that—"

"I understand. All too well."

"—It's human nature, maybe, to cling on to irrational hope, but in my life, evil triumphs over good nine times out of ten.

"So, Annie, I was praying that the Allies would come quickly, and if not, then that the baby would not be premature, or just late enough for us to be free. He still insisted we'd go away together and raise the baby. How absurd. I was still a Jewess to him, an *Untermensch*. I suppose not much different than the American founding fathers and their African slave lovers — and this would become relevant in my life, years later. That's what I was to him — a plaything, nothing more. Not someone to bring to the dinner table, let alone raise a family with. How laughable. I was out of my mind. Maybe I still am. In any event, I wanted the child, sort of, as a mother does, but with ambivalence... I couldn't make up my mind and I was feeling terrible guilt, as one would, you are carrying a baby and that baby has saved your life, for now, and you don't know if you want it and you don't know how you will feel once it is born, will you be a good mother, will you love it? I had visions of being with my two kids, loving my son, not loving my daughter (I had a feeling it was a daughter, or least that's what the *aufseherin* kept saying — I had morning sickness, which I had not had with my son; and I carried high, according to her — in any case, sure signs it was a girl, she said).

"It was just awful, my head and body felt like a constant tug of war, about to explode. In other scenarios, I saw myself with Alfons and the two children. I knew he'd love our son; of course, but how would he feel about the daughter? Other times, absurdly, comically, I saw myself with the SS-Schutzhaflagerführer. In these visions, he wore the same uniform, and the kids and I had to salute him, and of course all three of us would address him as SS-Schutzhaflagerführer — much to his panic, lest people overhear. It was quite absurd, but what does a murderer do after working in a camp? Well, it turns out they go back to their former professions, have no trouble adjusting, unlike the victims and victims' families. They went on to become very successful people in many cases, judges, lawyers, politicians, completely unmarked in modern Germany. Rewarded even. Admired. Nobody cared what they did during the war. Still, at that time, I could hardly imagine him going back to being a baker's assistant, taking orders from a baker, from customers who may have been prisoners in his camp. I spent endless hours thinking about the future. It seemed an unwinnable situation. I didn't think I'd ever be happy again. In no situation did I see myself as part of a happy family, father, mother, kids. Of course, I didn't foresee the most reasonable and realistic situation. One rarely does, perhaps. You remain a dreamer, you hope, don't you, even in the direst situations. At least the food improved, the *aufseherin* realized which way the wind was blowing again now that I was pregnant. Plus, we all knew that the war was coming to an end. We just didn't know if we'd survive, any of us, and what that end would look like, or the future. Suddenly, the guards and the prisoners, including the SS-Schutzhaflagerführer, were equal — well, almost, they could still kill us of course, and we had heard rumors of the guards killing all of us and razing the camp to the ground before the advancing armies arrived. Even the German prisoners were nervous, almost siding with the guards, nationality trumped condition. The mood was shifting because when we were liberated, and now it was only a matter of when, they would be at our mercy, if we were alive. It was hard to imagine, but you started to feel it, the guards were reminding everyone how they had done this or that deed of kindness, as if they really had. And you could see each day they deliberated whether to shoot us. But they were also panicking, trying to find an escape route, a way out. Certainly, away from the Russians of whom they were rightfully terrified after all the atrocities they had committed against them. We knew firsthand how they treated the Russians in the camps, no better than the Jews. The Germans knew what they had done. They knew that retribution was coming.

"So, Annie, here I was, terrified, uncertain how I felt about the baby, but also not wanting it to be taken away. I wanted to decide what happens to *my* baby. I didn't want it taken away. My first concern was that I wanted it to survive the war. Other decisions I'd make afterwards and see with time how much I loved the baby. I know — sounds strange, 'weird', as everyone says these days — but—"

"Klara — please. No need to justify. I can't even begin to imagine—"

"No... of course... I... when you are in a situation, to you it's normal, you only realize how crazy it is when you tell other people, later—" She looked at Annie "—it's different talking to people who have lived something similar or been close to it and maybe because you have been exposed to all kinds of tragedies and you are sensitive, you seem to be... anyway, Annie... so, here I was, nine months pregnant. Artillery fire in the distance. Guards getting nervous. Rumors that they would kills us, destroy the camp. The SS-Schutzhaflagerführer was panicked, too, I could see, but telling me he'd make sure I'd be safe, that the baby would be safe, that both the children would be safe...

"I gave birth two weeks before liberation. Twelve days to be exact. My waters broke. But the baby would not come, I was in labor for sixteen hours, I was in terrible pain, I just wouldn't dilate enough, but then — finally — she was born, a girl, I remember looking at her, holding her briefly, it's true I felt differently about her than my son, whom I had also named Alfons after his father, as is custom for us, but had told no one his name, but she was still *my* baby, I didn't hate her as I worried I might, I still felt this great urge to protect her, I wanted her to remain by my side and I thought this time they would let me, with her being the daughter of the SS-Schutzhaflagerführer. But again, the *aufseherin* — with his blessing! — took her away, I couldn't understand it. They told me again that I was too weak to care for her, and I *was* weak, but I thought, stupidly, with her being half German, and not just any German, but *his* daughter, I remember crying with desperation when they took her, and them telling me that it was for her own good again, that she would be well taken care of, but now a terror gripped me, you see, again I was without my baby… in any event, he could have had me killed at any time. And then, one day, he had come to me and, I hardly recognized him, he was in the uniform of a *Bootsmaat*, a naval petty officer, teary-eyed, said he had to leave. He embraced me as if we really had been lovers and said he'd send for me, once settled. I asked about the babies, the children, and he said they were safe, that they'd be sent for, too, that we'd all be together. You know, in that instant, I think I believed him. Once again. And then he was gone, and the same day all the guards disappeared, and we were left alone and four days later the Russians liberated us… and, Annie, I felt that people, even the other women in the brothel, looked at me differently — as if I had somehow *chosen* my role. As if they were better than me, because I was the SS-Schutzhaflagerführer's whore, maybe it was partially my guilt, I felt as if I was the lowest of the low, but I frantically searched the camp for my children, idiot me, so stupid, so naïve, thinking — what? that there would be a special nursery for my children? With a pink room and a blue room and all the toys they could want. What were these children? Both Jewish, weren't they? Both had a Jewish mother, so they had to be Jewish, no matter who the father was, it could have been Himmler himself, and Annie, I found out from the *aufseherin* — and I swear she told me with a joy, barely disguised, but pretending how tragic it was, she took pleasure in having known the whole time, she told me she wanted to tell me but couldn't because of *him* — that they had both been thrown into the incinerator, alive, upon birth, they had both lived an hour at most, and, Annie, I broke down, and I cried, endless tears, for hours, for all the humiliation, for Alfons, my son, and my daughter, whom I had not named, innocent, and then I found out that everyone had died, my parents, my sister, my brother, my husband, both my children, I was all alone in the world. And, Annie, I don't know how or why I could put myself together, albeit barely. I don't know why I continued to live — there was no point really, and I never saw it more than existence, until Anton was born, and I will tell you about that, but then, you see why all this is like reliving my history, my daughter-in-law has taken away my grandchildren, she has become the SS-Schutzhaflagerführer, as devious and conniving as he, I see no difference, bending and using the laws in her favor, and again, I am helpless, and again I have not been able to stop my flesh and blood being taken away, again I have not been able to save Lucie, or my son. I am as useless as before, and society is allowing it to happen. Nothing has changed Annie.

"So, when the camp was liberated, like so many other prisoners who had lost everything, I was devastated, I was lost, who knows whether I ever recovered, I am certainly not the person I was when they shipped us to the camp, and now, I see myself in Anton — he is a wreck, a shell, I guess that's how I was. Today, they call it PTSD, we had no term for it, but some doctors were studying it after the war and they called it concentration camp syndrome and before that, after the first world war, shell shock, it was the basis for PTSD, it's as if your brain shuts down, you can't cope, focus. You keep moving, just to survive. You think that your pain and tragedy are visible on you, tattooed, like the number on my stomach. Oh, Annie, I was a mess. How many times I have dreamt of my children, my babies, thrown into the flames. Every night. Each time I wake up, drenched in sweat, crying, and each time it's too late, they have been devoured by the flames. My only consolation is that their death was instant, but tell me, what sort of consolation is that? Like now, what consolation is it that Lucie is alive when I can't see her, when I know she is being abused? What is worse. Death, a static event; or your children alive but not with you. Because I could go there and take her by force and kill her mother — is it wrong to kill to save? I have killed before, Annie. I won't tell you that I am proud of it, but I don't regret it, either."

"Was it the SS... I'm sorry, I don't know how to pronounce it."

"No, Annie, he got away..."

"So..."

"Annie — when the Russians liberated the camp. And believe me, the Americans were no different, it's human nature. When they saw all the dead bodies, women, children, emaciated, you should have seen their faces, the rage. And they wanted us to feel the same rage. But most of us, Annie, were tired. And they gave me a gun and told me to shoot the *aufseherin*. She was German, you see, and had a guard's uniform, but she had never really mistreated me, not really, and Annie, as I hesitated, and my hand shook, she said to me, I think she knew they would shoot her no matter what and she wanted one last satisfaction, so she told me, in German, 'I am the one who threw your babies in the incinerator.' Annie, I shot her. And, to this day... did she do it? I don't know."

"Klara, I am so sorry. My God, how have you... lived with all this..."

"I haven't really lived, Annie, not really. I remained alone. I moved from place to place, never got close to people, I was determined not to get close to anyone, not lose anyone. But, in South Africa, I did something stupid, Annie, so selfish. This will sound crazy, but I met a man, a black man, well, I didn't really meet him as such, I saw him, and Annie, do you believe that a woman knows right away the man she will have children with?"

"I see all too often the wrong people having children together, so I'd say no."

"Well, I knew, I knew with Alfons. I knew I wanted him to be the father of my children. And then, in South Africa, I saw this black man, he was just waiting in line to buy something, and this will sound crazy—"

"Not much sounds crazy in my line of work, Klara."

"—I knew he was going to be the father of my child. The child I swore I would never have again. But, and here was my colossal mistake, I was determined to have the child, but without the father, I could not afford to lose another man, not the way I lost Alfons. I just wanted a child to take care of, to protect, since I could not protect my newborns. Of course, it never occurred to me that I might lose that child. It's when we think we're safe that we often find we're not safe after all. I was convinced he would just be happy to give me a child, like a sperm donor. What in the world made me think that? You see, it's that female arrogance again, isn't it, in relation to childbearing and child raising and well, we just assume, as women, we just believe the whole sanctity of motherhood, I was just as guilty as women who automatically assume that the children belong with them in a divorce, I was such an arrogant fool, really. And, let me be honest, Annie, I was racist, too. I assumed that a black man would have even less inclination to be a father than a white man — I know how that makes me sound, so shallow, so stupid — how many of us women see ourselves as doing all the work, being the better parent because we had to carry the child for nine months, thinking ourselves the more emotionally connected than the fathers. God, just when I hear myself talk, I sound like such an idiot." Annie started to cry. It was Klara's turn to hold Annie's hand. "I am so, sorry, child, I am upsetting you. I know my story is disturbing, I had no right, really, to unload it on you. No right. It's probably the uniform again, misleading, isn't it. We think that doctors, police officers, priests, that we can tell them anything, forgetting they are only people, too. All the things you must have seen and heard, too, I am sorry, child—"

Annie liked being called 'child' by Klara. It was sudden, and slightly jarring, but it made her feel… somehow… more intimate, protected, closer, to this old woman who had decided to choose her (if choosing it was), out of all the people she had met in her life, to tell her story that she had kept mostly hidden for half a century. She knew that the car crash provided some answers, Klara was shaken, as people often are when in accidents, as Klara now had been, missing death by a second (had she stepped into the car a second later, she'd have been hit along with the door), all these years later, at a time when death had accompanied her every day. As Annie always said to herself, it took death, or the threat of death, to appreciate life. So now, Klara, this woman with whom she felt an immediate intimacy, made her think of things she herself had tried to forget, things that she knew no one had believed (it was hard to get anyone to believe anything contrary to preconceived ideas; she knew that the crazier and unlikelier the events described by a victim often made the *victim* sound crazy and his or her recounting often unlikely (just as Klara had said). Annie had tried to speak to a couple of people once, a family member (her father's sister), and a figure of authority (a counselor at school), but in both cases she had been made to feel as if she had fabricated events, as if *she* were the 'crazy' one.

Which was why, much to the victims' surprise, she believed the stories (the more improbable, the more she believed, to their utter amazement); and not only listened with empathy, but with a genuine understanding for someone who had not lived through the recounted experience. Because Annie had understood too well, it took someone who had suffered to understand the nature of suffering. And it was acknowledgment, above all else, that a victim required.

"Please continue," Annie said, wiping a tear.

"Are you sure?"

"Yes," Annie said. "I'm sorry. I am crying for me as much as for you."

Klara looked at her closely. "I am so sorry, my child. For whatever it was that you went through."

Annie continued to weep silently. "Please continue," she said.

After a brief, silent moment when Klara looked over the sea, at the distant grey horizon, Klara continued. "So, you will see a double irony here, Annie. I again could not protect Anton, not when he was born, not now. I have been unable to protect anyone I have ever loved. To do so would be to commit a crime. Even though I find the laws unjust, I am not able to do it. Out of fear of punishment more than anything, I suppose. Isn't that the ultimate cowardice? Following laws, you know to be unjust?" Klara sighed. "Annie, he was born in an African village somewhere in South Africa—"

"You don't know where?"

"No. Not really. I had only been in Africa briefly when I fell pregnant and then I was somewhere in the bush. We had to hide a pregnant me with his family. I was hidden in a compartment in the car on the way, and, once there, it was a rural village like any other, to me at least, a European, unaccustomed to the African landscape, plus, they kept me in the dark...

"His father named him Kagiso, I named him Anton, but suffice it to say, I had chosen his father, God, when I look back upon it now, like a piece of meat, how brazen I was, how arrogant, something straight out of the slave trade. You, I had said, you will give me a child. Oh, Annie, the poor man, what must he have thought about this crazy white woman? And yet he went along with my harebrained scheme. And me, what was I thinking? I could not leave their hut. No one knew about me being there, the whole thing was illegal in South Africa, interracial relations, we could have been arrested, but you see, in some ways my madness makes sense, doesn't it? I had in my own way become the SS-Schutzhaflagerführer, hadn't I? I had flouted the law, as he had, to have relations with a black man as he had with a Jewess. Of course, at the time none of that was apparent to me. It only seemed like a noble action, almost, to have a baby with a black man, to break the idiotic laws. It was perhaps my subconscious way to do what I could not do during the war, to carry out an act of rebellion. And yet, with my action, I became no better than a slave master or the SS-Schutzhaflagerführer. I had used him, and then I planned to take the baby away, just as the SS-Schutzhaflagerführer had done. Oh, I'd have taken good care of the baby, of course, I like to think, but who can say for sure what kind of parents we become before we become them, and even then, we all think we're good parents, don't we, even the uncaring or abusive ones. So, in ways, Annie, it was simply history repeating itself again, and my baby boy was taken away, just as I had planned to take him away, and just as my other babies had been taken away. Joseph had given me enough chances for us to be together, in another country, but I wouldn't listen. I had my plan all worked out. Live on my own somewhere with the baby. Had not yet chosen a country but was already thinking back to Europe or the USA; little did I realize I would leave, but alone."

"Why stay there, in the village, I mean, if you knew you wouldn't remain with him, why not leave the country?" Annie said.

"I... don't know. For some reason, I wanted him to be born there, in Africa... have you never done anything you didn't understand?"

Annie stayed quiet for a moment. Then, she said, "Yes, yes, of course, I have. I guess, Klara, we become what we know, don't we? Subconsciously, I mean. If we're abused, we marry an abuser and sometimes we become abusers ourselves."

"Not sure that is an excuse," Klara said. "The lack of introspection and effort to not become like those who have hurt us or those we despise."

THE CONFESSIONS — ANNIE

"KLARA — there's a reason I 'feel' you if you want to call it that. It's not just that I've seen tragedy in my job, though I have. I don't… I shouldn't be telling you this, but I don't always arrest those I should. I try to get to the bottom of things. You know, to find out why somebody did something and then try to solve it or at least help, if I can. Right? Does that make sense?"

"I think so."

"It's gotten me into trouble, at the station, with my boss. He's given me a warning. You know, all the officers these days, they're so gung-ho, so fired up, many of them veterans, or ones who wanted to be soldiers and now have something to prove and see people as the enemy. I've heard the old guys talk about how they used to feel about the community, be a part of it, now it's 'us against them'. But, anyway, I do what I can. And the reason I do, and why I understand you, maybe one reason why you opened up to me, Klara, and one reason why I listened, I don't know, is because *I* was abused… as a child."

"Oh, Annie… your father?"

"No, my dad was amazing, a gentle giant, most tender man you ever knew. It was my mother, Klara, she was vicious, but nobody wanted to believe me, she was charming to others, but she was pure hell to us. Nobody wants to believe a woman can be vicious, and a mother, especially. It doesn't compute. It's always so much easier if it's a man. So, when you tell me about the female guards, I understand. Look at this." Annie rolled up her sleeve. On her arm were old scars, some small and circular, one larger and triangular.

"Burns?"

"Yes," Annie said. "You name it she did it, hit us with anything within reach. Any excuse would do. Or she would punish us in other cruel ways. Her rage was uncontrollable and completely unpredictable. She abused all of us, even my father. He was a big man and yet he cowered in front of her, pleaded. And, he never said a word to anyone. He defended her! Typical abused behavior, I know now. So, do I understand you and Anton and Lucie? Oh, yes. Mother had all of us believing we were at fault. If only *we* 'behaved' better, then none of her abuse would happen. She was the most merciless person I've ever known. So, I know about your daughter-in-law, Klara, she can fool everybody else, but she can't fool me. I know exactly what sort of person she is. You know, when I was called out to your house by your daughter-in-law, accusing your son of abuse, I knew immediately what's what. She hated me, hated that she couldn't fool me the way she could fool everybody else. Your son sat there the way my father used to. It was frightening, Klara. It brought back all the awful memories; I had tried to bury them."

Klara squeezed Annie's hand. "Is your father still alive?"

"It was *she* who left *him*. Imagine. After she had destroyed him. And she took us, me, and my brother with her. We had no choice. To this day, I hate that feeling of helplessness. No, Klara, my father fell apart, the way your son has, he couldn't bear to be away from us, and couldn't bear that he had not protected us. He finally tried telling someone, but nobody believed him. He died a year later after my mother moved out with us, alone."

"It's not so much having someone to take care of you that keeps you alive, as having someone to take care of."

"I agree. He had lost his job, lost us, started drinking heavily — something he'd never done. He got really drunk one night and fell and hit his head and bled to death. They only found him three days later. My mother pretended to cry, acted all devastated when the police came, it was sickening. I was the only one who knew — and my brother, of course, but he was younger, more terrified than me even. But of course, nobody would believe me or us anyway, and besides, we were so scared of her, understandably. Often people commented how quiet and well-behaved I was, but I was just afraid, right, not well-behaved. My brother, he was two years younger…"

"Is he not…"

"He killed himself, four years after dad died. He couldn't take it. Never recovered. He and dad had been so similar in nature, two sensitive souls. Me, I'm tougher. Maybe women are, in general. Maybe we've had to be. Anyway, he pretended to be sick one day, with a temperature, and stayed home from school. I came home to find him. He hanged himself. He'd made a rope out of mother's clothes. How sick is that. Mother acted all devastated again. She should have been an actress. He left a suicide note, apologizing for being such a disappointing son. The police said that it was probably because of my dad's death. And that mom's clothes were symbolic of his closeness to her—" Annie chortled "—I nearly started laughing when they said that, out of pure hysteria, pure fright that I was left alone with her, but I wasn't so little any more, I was sixteen, and I wasn't so helpless any more."

"Is she still alive?"

"She disappeared one day. Nobody knows where. Just went missing. Best day of my life."

Klara looked at her closely. "Never found?"

"Nope. Police suspected she may have just packed up and left to start a new life somewhere, they were surprised that she just left me behind like that, kept reassuring me that she loved me, that I mustn't worry, that one day she would surely come back or at least write or call or send for me—" Annie laughed bitterly. "—that sometimes people just needed to get away from a place where they experienced too much tragedy, having lost her ex-husband, for whom 'she evidently still cared deeply', what a joke, and then her son… how terrible for a mother…" Annie laughed again. "And I had to pretend, Klara, how devastated I was that she went missing and of course, how devastated she'd been, what a farce, when of course she was nothing of the kind, going out drinking regularly at some line dancing dives and bringing home strange men who tried their luck with me when she wasn't watching, not that she cared. God, it sickens me.

"But I tell you, Klara, my ex-husband, he used to beat me, and I let him. A very, very wealthy man. I never told anyone. How sick is that? So, yeah, we have some things in common, Klara. And I am so sorry for all you've been through." Annie looked over the sea and watched a pelican dive into the water, momentarily disappearing before emerging and flying off with a fish tail protruding from its beak. In the distance, low hanging clouds reflected purple and orange from the sun setting behind them. "It'll be getting dark soon. I have to drive you home. Your insurance should cover a rental car while your car is in the body shop, by the way; let me know if I can help with that tomorrow."

"You are kind, Annie."

Annie helped hoist Klara up with her hand. They both wiped sand from the backs of their pants and started walking upwards towards the walkway over the dunes, climbing the wooden steps.

Annie drove Klara home. At the entrance of the town was a large water fountain with a wide moat and a large, lit sign welcoming drivers to Palm City. Several alligators were known to live in or near the moat and were a regular part of the tourist attraction. Annie thought back to how the city had originally started as a retirement community for employees of one of the large telecommunications companies. That was in the early seventies, days when companies saw employees as integral, not a liability. Later, the company disinvested, and the city incorporated and now it was a city like any other with people from all walks of life, a percentage of second homeowners, the 'snowbirds', as they were called, northerners who lived half the year up north (not quite ready to move to Florida permanently) and spent winters in Palm City. By now, Palm City was a town of forty thousand or so inhabitants, subdivided into sections according to the alphabet. Not particularly original, Annie thought, but easy to remember. That way, you lived, for example, in the 'p' section and the like. Klara lived in the 'c' section.

Klara looked over at Annie. "I'm surprised you remember the way," she said.

"Part of the job," Annie replied.

The road was wide and flanked, in keeping with the city's name, with tall palm trees. Once again, Annie thought, not particularly original, but pretty. Klara appeared to be deep in thought herself, reflecting, perhaps, on their confessional discussion, something, it seemed, both thought unlikely they'd share with anyone. But the conversation had also brought back painful memories and Annie wondered if Klara now, too, was immersed in the minutiae of recollections.

Annie thought that Klara appeared so small and frail, swallowed up by the passenger seat. To her surprise, she felt protective of Klara. And not only Klara, but her son, and Lucie, her grandchild. Was it from the first meeting? It had brought back memories, as the ambulance had for Klara. That's how it worked; she had heard someone once say. Memories were drawers that could be pushed and pulled, but never emptied. Annie wished she could minimize their sadness away, sadness that she understood viscerally. But she knew that only one thing could do that. How often had she seen that in her line of work? She was always amazed at how much carnage one person could cause. An abusive husband or wife. A lone shooter in a workplace or school. A serial killer too clever for the police or the court system. A dictator in charge of a nation, an elected leader, even. In Annie's world, it could be anyone, a colleague, a friend, a stranger, a mother. Annie would later recollect Klara's words, 'it took one *Eichmann*, or a *Stangl* or a *Globocnik*; just one was needed to mastermind the wiping out of millions.'

"Klara," Annie spoke at last. She studied Klara's face carefully. "Did you really shoot the — madame, whatever she's called?"

"The *aufseherin*?" Klara stared at Annie who slowed down almost to a halt, then stopped the car by the side of the road and turned on the emergency lights. "I have been a terrible person, Annie. I have been unable to protect anyone I have ever loved. Not my family or Alfons, or my babies in the camp. Not Anton or my granddaughter. No one."

"What happened."

"I couldn't do it, Annie," Klara said. "I lied because I wanted someone to believe that at least once in my life I was capable of killing, of revenge. But the truth is, Annie, when the Russian soldier gave me his gun and told me to shoot, even when the *aufseherin* told me it was her who threw my children into the incinerator, Annie, I… I couldn't do it, that is how pathetic I am, I could not avenge their murder. The Russian soldier took back his gun and shot her. And I wept, for me, for Alfons, for my babies, for all those that had died, not for her, he misunderstood, I could see the look in his eyes, as if there was something wrong with me. I do sometimes think that anyone that can't defend those they love doesn't deserve to live."

"Klara," Annie said.

"It gets worse, Annie. I found out that she *had* thrown my daughter into the incinerator. But my son — *he* had used him as target practice. He threw him in the air and shot him. It took three tries. His own son. Because he had Jewish blood."

"I want you to listen to me, Klara. You're not responsible for that. Right? You were put into an inhumane situation, a situation that no one should ever be in. You couldn't have saved those babies. And your son — you couldn't have interfered with the system. What could you have done? Attack a police officer? You could no more interfere with things now than you could with things then."

"I could have killed him. The SS-Schutzhaflagerführer."

"Right. And then you'd have died, in addition to your children."

"I could have killed her."

"Your daughter-in-law?" Klara nodded. "Yes, but they'd have caught you. Either you can kill someone, or you can't, Klara. And if it's not within you, it's not within you. It's not true that anyone can kill, depending on the situation, as the saying goes. You're witness to that, you're proof. I've seen it. I've seen parents whose children were raped and killed. Who had every reason to kill the murderer. Who had the opportunity. And they couldn't do it."

"How did you know, Annie, that I didn't kill her?" Klara managed to say.

Annie smiled tenderly. "I'm a cop, remember? I can't always tell the guilty ones; but I'm pretty good at telling the innocent ones."

"Annie, tell me something. Your mother—"

"Was one of the nastiest people I've ever met."

"*Was*."

"Was."

"You never tried to find her. She was never found?"

"No. There were rumors, that she had left, run off to start a whole new life somewhere, where nobody knew her. Other people said she ran off with a man she'd met, some even said they'd sailed away together to the Caribbean somewhere. But those people wondered how she could have abandoned her daughter, the dutiful mother most people always thought her to be. Me, I sided with the first version. Still abandoning her daughter, yes, but out of self-preservation because of all the horrible pain she endured." Annie laughed.

Klara and Annie were parked in Annie's police cruiser now outside of Klara's home. Inside, on the right, was a solitary light and suddenly the curtains moved a little to the side. "That's Anton inside. Do you mind saying hello?"

"Of course not."

Klara looked at the window and the curtain pulled slightly aside. "Anton's probably worried about the police car. I am surprised he noticed, the way he is these days."

"We'll go in, don't worry, but first," Annie said, "let me tell you something. After I had lived... my little horror... I had some trouble grappling with a few issues, why people do things to one another, how a parent can hurt a child, some of the things I've witnessed at work, I was really depressed, Klara, and you know, I grew up Catholic—"

"That might explain it."

"I said, Catholic, not Southern Baptist. I'd not been in church for a long time, I was desperate. I went to the one in 'd' section, you probably know it—"

"Yes, a quaint little building, green. Looks more like the SPCA. How I miss European cathedrals."

"That's the one. So, I went in, and I just had to speak to a priest. And Father Muñoz was there. He had emigrated from Portugal with his parents when he was ten. Still had a heavy accent, I remember thinking surprisingly. And, Klara, I told him my whole story, I left nothing out. We sat opposite each other, not in a confessional, and he just listened, dressed in a white and green cassock, he listened intently, I thought, staring at me, but kindly, there was kindness in his eyes, and I cried, I remember, especially when describing the physical abuse and my father's and brother's deaths, and finally I stopped talking but it still took me a while to compose myself. And I remember watching him, waiting, in anticipation, for words that would somehow make sense of it all. And he waited a few minutes, and then he said, 'People… are shit.' That's all he said, right? And somehow it was liberating, Klara. Like, what was I expecting? Seriously? That people are *good*. And I was suddenly almost embarrassed, that poor priest, all the horrible stuff he'd had to listen to over the years and imagine, not only unable to tell the police about it, but having to forgive them!"

Klara sat for a moment, pensive. "People are shit, huh?" she said. "But there are some good ones, not many. And if you meet enough of those, life can be even pleasant at times."

Annie smiled. "Who'd have taken *you* for an optimist. It can be pleasant at times, with the right people, I agree," Annie said. "For example, I'd have not traded our afternoon for anything. Right? I'm sorry you had to be in a car accident for us to meet properly. But… well, do you believe that things happen for a reason?"

"I believe that fortunate things can happen, as well as unfortunate ones. And I believe that having met you, Annie, was most fortunate. Now, should we go inside?"

THE CONFESSIONS — KLARA (CONT.)

"**KLARA**, there's one more thing I need to know."

Klara turned to face her. "Did I ever see him again; did they ever catch him?" Klara said.

"Yes," Annie said.

"By chance. He was living in Düsseldorf, under his own name, completely in the open, as if nothing had ever happened. Imagine. I sent someone to see if it was really him. Someone who had also survived the camps. I didn't want to tell you. I was in Melbourne at the time, I think. And he found him, and... the SS-Schutzhaflagerführer treated him like he had always treated us, like *Untermenschen*. My friend went back to Italy, and... sometime later... his sister called... he had killed himself, left the oven on. I am to blame. Had I not asked him to go..."

"Oh, my God, Klara, I'm so sorry."

"It is my fault my friend died."

"You didn't turn the oven on, Klara. And you didn't send him to a concentration camp, and you didn't do any of the things he had witnessed. Right? No, Klara — it's not your fault."

"I carry the blame."

"Well, please don't. Really. You're not to blame," Annie said. "So, that's it? Did you ever see him?"

"The SS-Schutzhaflagerführer? There was pressure, years later, to finally put him on trial. But he fled to South America, as he had planned. They finally tracked him down; with the help of Nazi hunters, I'd been in contact with over the years in Vienna and become good friends. He'd been living the good life, like many of them. He lived in Montevideo. Had himself a chain of *pâtisseries*, can you believe it. No more a lowly baker, that was a temporary cover in Düsseldorf. Now he could hire himself a *Maître Pâtissier*. It's laughable. With all the valuables he had stolen, he had more than enough money to start his own chain of *pâtisseries*. He finally became what he always wanted, respectable. And it grew to several, nationwide, not that the country is large, mind you. But he didn't need the money. He had stolen enough during the war. You may not know it, but only about ten percent of the camp SS were ever prosecuted. More than ninety percent went on to lead completely normal and respectable and profitable lives with families and children and, like Eichmann, no remorse. We were left to pick up the pieces, to try to live the lives of the dead, and often to die at our own hands. We could not live with all that had happened to us, and *they* thrived. I get so angry when I think about it

"Anyway, I went there. I got his address from the friends in Vienna. They trusted me. I was determined to kill him. This organization helped, they hid me and even gave me a weapon, taught me how to use it. One morning, Annie, I confronted him. He walked to work, unguarded, free, happy, not a worry in the world. When he suddenly saw me. He got a fright. And I saw that he instantly recognized me. I got a fright, too. He had none of the bravado about him, the confidence. Despite his commercial success. He had lost most of his hair, had put on another twenty pounds to his rotund frame, was hunched over, truth be told, he looked a bit… pathetic. It was difficult to reconcile this man with the man I had once known, who elicited such fear.

"We stood there, facing each other, in the bright light. And for a moment, I was convinced I could read his thoughts, that he would try to sweet talk me, as he had done in the camp, but he instantly saw it was hopeless, so he stood there, ready to face death. Annie, I did ask him one question. I said, why? He knew what I meant. Why did you kill our daughter? Was it because she was Jewish? I said. He laughed. He actually laughed. People started to mill about in the distance. A car drove by. I was getting nervous. He took his time answering. Finally, he said, 'I had nothing against the Jews. They were just cargo.' Tears were now pouring down my face. He made a move as if to touch me, I pointed the gun at him. He retreated. Then he said, 'She was evidence. We had to remove all evidence. It was an order. It was nothing… personal…' But I was evidence, why didn't you kill me? And he said, 'You, I loved.'"

Annie stared at Klara. She wanted to say something, but words wouldn't emerge.

"You know, I think that in his own demented way, he meant it," Klara continued. "And, I tried, I really tried pulling the trigger but I couldn't, my hand started to shake and the bastard started to smile — *ta svině* — and I was so determined to kill him, so I did the only thing I could, I shot the gun, over his head, but it was enough, I thought, that he would know he'd never be safe, he'd been found out, and he fell to the ground, in a little heap, covering his head, and I ran and along the way I threw the gun into a storm drain, I remember it was early, but more people were out now, and I heard the gun fall to the bottom, hitting water, and I just kept running, and the people who had tracked him down for me, they picked me up and I was in hiding for a few weeks before they flew me out of the country. I felt like such a failure again. I held a gun pointed at his head and couldn't shoot. I was at most three feet away. But they got him, in the end, and he went on trial and spent the rest of his years behind bars. I didn't testify against him, though, I just... couldn't. I never saw him again."

"I'm sorry, Klara, I shouldn't have asked. It doesn't matter. I knew the answer. I'm sorry. You did nothing wrong." Annie exited the car and walked over to the passenger side. They were parked in the driveway. A solitary streetlight from in front of the neighbor's house illuminated them slightly. A palm tree swayed with a light breeze. A flock of wild turkeys could be seen in the distance, by the fir trees across the street. Annie looked up higher at the large moon rising in the sky. Inside the house, the curtain had closed, but no one came to greet them. Klara took Annie's arm, Annie helping Klara out of the car, and together they walked slowly towards the house, the sound of frogs in the canal behind the house a reassuring evening concerto.

KLARA'S HOME

INSIDE, the house was humble, as Annie remembered. But now, after their conversation, she saw the contents in a different light. Inanimate objects were given no preference; it wasn't so much, Annie thought, that someone old lived here as someone from a different world, a different culture who, despite years of living in the US, still did not, by choice, fully belong or integrate. Who could, if she wanted, leave at a moment's notice. Or who, at least, prized people over possessions, even if for the sake of self-preservation, she had chosen to keep a distance. As if waiting, unwittingly perhaps, for loved ones to at any moment reappear.

Annie looked around. On the windowsill, again, the burning white rippled candle, this time burnt halfway. Underneath, the kitchen table and chairs were plastic. Elsewhere were dilapidated faux wood furniture and an old TV. A few paintings and a couple of photos hung on the walls. Two paintings stuck out, one, an elongated drawing of an old city, in panels of three: the other an oil painting. When Annie looked closer at the drawing, she saw 'Praha' sprawled in black chalk above the drawn city. Next to it hung the oil painting of a woman, attractive, blue eyes, curly blonde hair, dignified face, gentle looking. Annie looked closely at the painting. But what grabbed her attention were three black and white framed photographs. The one on the left was of about twenty women, all nude, at the bottom of a ravine, standing in a line, a man with an armband in front, looking down. All faced forward except the third woman from the front, who faced the photographer. At the end of the line of women, as if catching up, was a pregnant woman holding a baby. Annie squinted. She was fairly certain that the woman facing the camera was the same as the one in the oil painting. Klara noticed her taking a closer look and said, "My aunt Klara. 1941. All those women and children, minutes before their deaths. Those photos were taken by a member of the SS so he could show them off to his girlfriend, friends, and family. He sent the film home to Germany to be developed by a local chemist. The SS man got in trouble — not for killing people — for developing the film and showing people."

The photo in the middle was of a crowd of people sitting down on the ground perhaps. In front was a young mother holding a small child. Next to them, looking directly at the camera, was another child, older, in a furry black hat. And to the right, a photo of a pile of corpses, all female, a hundred perhaps, and two men pointing machine guns at a body.

The image of Klara's aunt was disturbing, but no less than the naked pregnant woman with baby or the young mother with her sleeping son. Annie wondered what any of them could have possibly thought at the time of imminent death for them and their children.

"They were taken, nine at a time, to the edge of the ravine, with nine more behind them who had to watch the execution," Klara said. "Below them in the ravine were the dead bodies of friends, family, people they knew; behind them were more loved ones, neighbors about to watch them die and take their turn. And the SS would write home how hard it was on *them*."

Annie said nothing. She was overwhelmed, had no idea what to say. She walked onwards. There were hundreds of books on bookshelves that strained and bent under the weight.

Annie returned to the small kitchen scattered with worn appliances, an old microwave, an old-fashioned juicer. Klara opened the fridge door. On it were several photos of her granddaughter. Some in magnet hearts that read, 'who am I missing today', below the photos.

Annie sat on one of the plastic chairs and waited for Klara to find Anton. Klara came back, saying Anton would join them in a while.

"My boy is broken," she said, apologetically. "Please excuse him."

Klara offered Annie a beer. Off-duty now, Annie accepted. It was one that Annie was unfamiliar with, Pilsner Urquell. Klara had placed it in the fridge for a moment, saying beer should not be served cold. It was bitter but rich and Annie liked the full taste. As they resumed their tour of the home, Annie studied more drawings and notes, declarations of love, that Klara's granddaughter had left for her. There were reminders of her everywhere and it was evident that nothing had been touched since her granddaughter and daughter-in-law had left.

Annie studied every detail of Klara's home. Annie walked up to photos on a bookshelf of Klara and her granddaughter. Some with Anton, too. One of the frames had been taken apart and the daughter-in-law had evidently been cut out. The remaining photo was an awkward size. Of the daughter-in-law, only a partial leg and high-heeled shoe remained. She looked at Klara, who shrugged.

"It's childish, I know, I cut her out, I liked the photo, and I couldn't stand looking at her," Klara said. Annie nodded. She'd have done the same, she thought. At the very least. She tried to imagine the scene of departure and aftermath; the silence of a house used to a child but suddenly deprived.

Klara took her by the hand and led her through the living room, to the back of the house, then through the sliding door, onto the enclosed porch. Outside, Klara turned on the overhead fan, and lit two candles, one shaped like a heart. The frogs sang nearer now.

"Klara — those candles. On the windowsill."

"Yes, Anton remembered." Klara sounded sorrowful. "Sweet of him. On hot days, when it's over eighty degrees, twenty-seven degrees Celsius, to be precise, I always light a candle." She wouldn't elaborate and Annie thought it better not to pry.

They sat next to each other, the chairs nearly touching, looking into the night. The moon hung in the sky. A wisp of a cloud moved slowly across its shadows.

"When they left, Annie, I can't tell you how bad it was. Lucie…" She paused. "One of the greatest regrets of my life is when the first wave of Jews had to leave their homes. My Aunt Klara, whom I loved, the one in the photo and painting, after whom I am named, was in that wave. She was the sweetest woman. Unmarried, bad luck with men, she poured all her heart and attention to us, her nieces, and nephews. Always had something, small presents, something baked, a book, a toy, a knitted sweater. And we had to help her pack her suitcase, having no idea where she was going. Relocation to the East, they said. I helped her pack for her death, Annie." Klara cupped her face with her hands.

"You couldn't have known."

"That's the thing. For a split moment, I was grateful it was her, and not us. To this day, I have carried the shame of that selfish thought."

"You were young. And scared."

"People are always so relieved when someone else is singled out. People so rarely go to the defense of others, Annie, not realizing that often they are next. Needless to say, we never saw her again. I came across that photo by accident in a book about the war."

"You can't blame yourself."

"When my daughter-in-law decided she was moving out and taking Lucie — my granddaughter was crying, saying she didn't want to go with her, and pleading for Anton to help her, to interfere, to stop her mother from taking her, and she was pleading for me, *pane bože*, Annie—"

"You've said that a few times now. What does that mean?"

"What? Oh, *pane bože?* Sorry, it means, I guess you would say, 'Dear God'."

"Oh."

"I was crushed, it reminded me, later, of my Aunt Klara, we were powerless, again, here, today, in this society, can you imagine, there was nothing we could legally do, she had every legal right to go, and there was nothing Anton could do, I had already been at the lawyer's office, I had a foreboding, I took Anton, he didn't want to go, there was only one way to stop her, Anton would have had to file for divorce, and even then, the lawyer said it was temporary; and of course, Anton kept saying he didn't want a divorce, *pane bože*, Annie, I feel sick again, and I had to help Lucie pack her suitcase, as I had helped Klara, I threw up, I was sick to my stomach, *how could history be repeating itself*, I kept thinking, and there she stood, I am sorry, like the Germans used to, telling us to hurry, *raus, raus*, like we were nothing, *Untermenschen* again, and Lucie crying the whole time—"

"Sounds like she took Lucie out of spite," Annie said angrily.

"Yes, I think so, too, why else does a person like that—"

"A chess piece," Annie continued. "Out of usefulness — nice tax break, sympathy from strangers, looks nice on your arm, trophy child."

"You seem to understand, Annie. The neighbors said, 'Well, of course she took her, she's the mother.' And one person at the pool said, 'Why would she have wanted children if she was mean.' I started to laugh, hysterically."

"I have yet to meet anyone who sees themselves as mean or unkind," Annie said.

"I remember the guards at the camps, they laughed amongst themselves, joked, they could be kind to each other or to their dogs, while beating or shooting a prisoner, quite often at the same time. We often heard them celebrating late into the night, eating, drinking, singing, dancing. They celebrated Christmas as eagerly as anyone."

"I know when I tried to speak about my mom, everybody shut down," Annie said. "Nobody wanted to believe me."

"I think people are uncomfortable, Annie, for the same reasons all of us are uncomfortable. You're wondering, can it happen to us? We are living proof that it can. You're also wondering, how would any of us — how would you — act in a similar situation, if made guards over life and death? Maybe that is the part that scares people the most. People are always uncomfortable with something they don't understand. I lived it and I don't understand it. I am as uncomfortable as anyone, believe me. More. I am consumed by it, I think about it, all the time, I read everything, watch everything. I have nightmares, daily."

"Not possible to move on, is it?"

"Move on," Klara repeated softly, sadly. "Forget about it, forgive. Such silly terms. I often wondered, lying in my room in the camp, what did they talk to their loved ones about? What did the SS-Schutzhaflagerführer tell his wife and kids at the end of the day? Did he — did they — tell their families how many people they killed that day? Somehow, I doubt it. And yet, between breakfast and lunch he had killed five thousand people. They had 'normal' conversations, didn't they? About how the war was going, and about shopping, and books and the theater, maybe, and what the children learned at school, and all the time, meanwhile, at 'work', every day... you see why I am obsessed, maybe, why I can't get it out of my head... it's the how... how did they do it, how did they live with it, all of them, how did they completely forget about it, how come they had no regrets, no remorse? I simply can't understand it and yes, it's driving me crazy, I admit. And yet, surely their partners knew precisely what sort of 'work' they had to 'perform' just the incessant sweet sickly stench of burning corpses and the constant pestilential cloud and ash from the crematoria even on sunny days — how do you live with and love a killer? I understand that they didn't think of us in those terms, as humans, that they believed their spouses had to do a 'hard job' to save the 'Reich' from undesirables, to propagate the 'master race', but still... we have a hard enough time comprehending serial killers that kill a few people, how do you live with someone that has killed thousands, tens of thousands, hundreds of thousands, millions of people?

Knowing, deep down, surely, that those victims are innocent children, women? How? Some of the SS were even doctors — doctors! performing medical experiments on people, killing people, thinking surely, they were doing it for the betterment of mankind — but they didn't really, did they, else why try to destroy all evidence — including the children — you see, that conundrum, they all knew their actions were 'wrong' and yet they performed them without hesitation — how? They could go home, all these people, and be loving to their wives or husbands or parents or children or friends or pets. Or is that what scares us, that there were so many willing killers and sadists? I know one thing — there is no truth in the saying that anyone is capable of evil deeds, that evil resides in all of us, I have seen too many people unable to perform evil, even if it meant losing their own lives. That is a simple excuse for all those who *have* committed evil — that anyone in their shoes would have done the same. So often you hear perpetrators say, you'd do the same, anyone is capable, and I knew that was entirely untrue. I have seen proof, people shot, killed, unable to commit evil deeds."

"I understand none of it myself."

"You do try to put things out of your head, you temporarily forget, you have to, don't you, to go about your daily life, else you'd go crazy, or crazier, thinking of all this. But there are reminders. It might be a Christmas carol, seeing a German appliance like Krupp or a Volkswagen or BMW, overhearing someone speaking German, a person who reminds you of someone you lost. It may be a smell, a sound, a sight. And then, you are back there again, as if you never left. With all the sights, sounds, smells, all the fear you experienced. I read about a woman who would wake up not knowing if she was back in the camps and her husband had to walk her about their New York apartment and show her the sights. And that is what I have been reliving with this experience of my daughter-in-law. It has reminded me of my family, the loss of lives, children taken, innocent people destroyed. She brought me right back to that world, Annie, which I have tried to keep at bay, albeit not successfully, but enough to survive, and now here it is again, and this time, Annie, I am older, weaker, and I am not sure I can keep it at bay enough anymore to survive."

"You will survive this, Klara. For your son, for your granddaughter."

"I am so tired, Annie, so, so tired. You know, the day that Carolien was moving out with Lucie, and Lucie wouldn't go, she was holding my leg. And Carolien, she slapped her and I was frozen with terror, I could do nothing, again, all over again, and it was like I was back there during the war, all the same emotions of helplessness and horror and Lucie crying, letting go my hand finally and walking away, holding a stuffed animal I had given her, and I kept saying, don't worry Lucie, we will do what we can, but I didn't know what that could possibly be, with these stupid, useless laws; and our worlds, mine, his, Lucie's evaporated, like gas. And Carolien walked away, arrogant, haughty, smiling, at our impotence, her power and control, giving her unlimited pleasure, *pane bože*, how many times I'd seen that same look of contempt and arrogance in the camp, the very same look, expression, and again I was transported back there, all the same feelings… oh, Annie…"

"Klara — I may need you to visit someone. Get some counseling, maybe go on antidepressants. Would you do that for me? How about your son? Sounds like you two are in the same boat."

"I was afraid you would react like that. That's the solution in this country, Annie. Pills—"

"No, Klara. Only until you feel better."

"I know what would make me feel better, Annie. My granddaughter under my roof again, that would make me feel better, it would make Anton feel better. This entire country is on antidepressants. All the kids are on Ritalin."

"It'd only be temporary."

"I have tried those things before, Annie, they didn't help. Antidepressants only made me feel numb — I didn't like the feeling — and a therapist who doesn't know me, doesn't care about me, no, Annie — no more… like I said, I am tired… maybe you and I could just talk, meet up for coffee sometimes…"

"I am concerned, Klara."

It was then that Anton opened the glass sliding door and walked onto the porch.

"I was worried earlier, Mom, you weren't answering your phone."

"Your mother was in a car accident. Nothing to worry about, she's fine. We just spent all day talking."

Anton was as she remembered, a tall, lean, attractive light-skinned black man with very short hair. He looked a little disheveled again, Annie thought; and probably looked different until not long ago. And now, it was Annie's turn to be transported back in time. In Anton, she saw her father, broken, devastated. She felt the overwhelming sadness and despair and helplessness she had felt in her youth, at the mercy of her mother. And she vaguely entertained the thought that she might try to help them, and Lucie, that she would try not to allow what had happened to her father and brother. She knew that it was the same feeling of helplessness, but also determination. Because unlike him or Klara, Annie didn't feel as helpless. After all, her mother had mysteriously disappeared.

Anton sat next to her; she was between him and his mother.

"How are you, Anton?"

"Would you like the American answer or the South African one?"

"Let's start with the American one."

Anton smiled wistfully. "Living the dream."

"And the South African one?"

"Up to shit," he said.

"I'm sorry," Annie said. "You have every right to be angry."

Anton looked at Annie attentively and his expression softened. "But not at you, I'm sorry. I think the uniform… threw me off… coppers—" He pronounced 'coppers' the English way "—Haven't been too good to us lately."

"So, I've heard. I'm not like other police officers."

"Annie understands, Anton," Klara said.

"Does she?" he said, and attempted a half-hearted smile which he couldn't quite manage. "Thank goodness somebody does."

He put his hand on Annie's arm. The touch took her by surprise. She looked away. "Thank you for taking care of my mom today," he said.

"It felt like we were taking care of each other," Annie said. "It turns out we have some things in common."

Annie observed Anton and Klara interact. There was an affection, an attentiveness but also an aloofness. She couldn't imagine what their relationship was like. For him to have been taken away at birth (as had been Klara's other babies); for him to believe all the years that he had been abandoned; for them to be reunited and for him to move his family to the US to be near her; for his wife, Klara's daughter-in-law to have used them for her own gain, break the family apart and abandon them, taking the daughter against her will (and continuing the cycle of forced abandonment). There would probably be resentment on his side (being brainwashed, perhaps, to some degree by his father and his family), but also excitement at the reunion; a natural distance between two people who had not grown up or spent much time together; and then the sudden joy of getting to know each other only to have the person most precious to them torn away, united now in a broken grief. In addition, for Klara, the reliving of so many sentiments she had previously felt in the camps, thinking her children were forever gone and suddenly one returning. Annie could little imagine how the two felt.

"I asked your mother, Anton, to consider counseling and antidepressants," Annie said at last. "First thing she said to me as I found her sitting there, door knocked off, shaken, was, 'I wish the car had hit me.'"

Anton looked ahead with great melancholy. "It has been hard, without Lucie—"

"You know, Annie, we're not Americans," Klara said. "Yes, I have lived here a long time, but I continue to think like a European. We don't believe that popping pills is a solution. It only masks the problem. We also don't believe that wanting to die is a sign of depression necessarily."

"As long as you're alive, there's hope," Annie said. "That things will improve. If you die, what then? What about your granddaughter? Your daughter, Anton? She needs you, both of you. You can't give up. What will happen to her? If anything happens to the two of you — think about it, Klara — she'd be all alone, like you'd been after the war, all these years. Surely you don't agree with your mother, Anton."

"I am not optimistic, Annie," Anton said. His calmness was unnerving to Annie. She now thought she understood the meaning of '*Musselman*'. The way he spoke. Monotone. Like an acolyte, like he knew something no one else did, like he had clarity of vision and thought. Like there remained only one thing to do. She'd seen suicidal people before. Anger she could handle that was still a sign of life. Frustration, too. Any emotion, really, was a sign of a person not giving up. But utter calmness unnerved her.

"I see Lucie under supervision once a month for an hour." He turned to Annie and smiled, a smile that rattled her. "My life has been ruined."

"It hasn't been ruined. It has changed. The question is, what do you do about it," Annie said.

"We're not depressed, Annie," Anton said. "Or at least not in a conventional sense, where people are depressed, and they don't know why. We know why, and we know that we could be instantly cured, if Lucie is returned to us, especially if we could live back home, overseas, but that's not going to happen, is it? The courts won't allow it. And now, they will place greater and greater restrictions on me, squeezing child support I can't afford, more each month, financial suicide, take away my driver's license, my passport, how will I find work then? And for what? An hour a month under supervision?"

"That little girl needs you. I saw how much she loves you. Maybe things will change. You never know."

"Unkind people live forever, Annie," Klara said. "So many survivors took their own lives after the war or died young — you know what stress does. All sorts of health issues. They never had peace of mind. They had to relive and redream all they had endured, all those they had lost. No, Annie, look at Carolien, happy as can be. And look at us. It's the same thing all over again. Nothing seems to change. No matter which society you live in.ND Dictatorship, 'democracy' — makes no difference. I never thought it possible. I never thought that here, in America, in a *democracy*, in a *free* society, I'd be reliving the same nightmare, but I am. We are. It has taught me this — there is no such thing as a free and just society."

"I know it's been hard on you two, but don't give up. Not now." She reached out and held their hands. The hands held little strength, but they weren't lifeless, and, most importantly, they didn't let go. That gave Annie hope. She had seen marasmus, from lack of human touch. Maybe that's what Klara meant by *Musselmen*.

"I said I wished that the car had hit me—"

"You did."

"Because it was an ambulance, Anton. Like in the *lager*. I told you about that. In the gas chambers, Annie, they used to deliver the gas pellets in an ambulance, to reassure people. I had a feeling they would come for me, one day." Klara paused. "Have you ever heard of the Masada?"

"No."

"The Masada, dear, was a fortress where Jews killed themselves rather than be conquered by the Romans. The men killed their wives and children and then themselves. Like people jumping from buildings on 9/11 — are not life *and* death better on one's terms?"

"Klara, if I think you're suicidal, I have to take you to a hospital, have you both committed, or at least get you professional help. You understand that."

"Please, Annie, no hospitals," Klara said. "Can you help us?"

"How can she possibly help?" Anton said.

Annie looked at them carefully, understanding Klara's query. The women exchanged glances, but Annie quickly looked away for fear her meeting Klara's eyes would somehow mean acquiescence. The evening after Annie had taken them to the restaurant, she had cried herself to sleep, memories returned as if they had happened the day before. And they had remained, both her memories and this family's grief. She wasn't all that surprised to meet Klara again, only regarding the circumstances, as if a premonition. Common grief had perhaps intervened.

"Before I go, I have to ask. Is there any danger you two will do anything that might harm yourselves or others?"

"No," they both said, not altogether convincingly, but reassuringly enough for Annie. She'd have to take the risk. She didn't think the hospital was an option. Not for Klara. What a mess, she thought. And poor Lucie. She pictured the girl she had met at the restaurant, defending her mother, eight years old, wise in many ways, but also stilted, wise and stilted and abused. And then, she wasn't sure, was she picturing herself at the age of eight. Whether she was or wasn't, she knew exactly what Lucie was going through, now stuck only with her mother, at her mercy — like her father and grandmother, brain numb, protecting itself, wondering when the next pain would come, from one of two people who should have loved her the most.

Annie looked at her watch. She had been sitting with them for nearly six hours. She committed just enough to Klara to make sure, inasmuch as she could, that they would hold on and give her the benefit of doubt, both in terms of possibilities, and a future visit. Then she said goodbye, and hugged Klara. Anton walked her to the cruiser. There, he gave her a hug, too, and Annie felt the same sensation that she felt when he had touched her arm. She thought she may have blushed and was glad it was dark. As she drove away on the circular route in the 'p' section, she watched him, standing forlorn, looking at her drive away until she rounded the curve.

POSTCARD

IT was an off chance, really. A distant and unlikely plan B. A whim of an old woman. Sending a postcard to Germany. Who did such things anymore. She did so on a pretext, in a way. To a person she planned to kill but learned to love. Nothing in life ever went according to plan, she thought. Man thinks, God laughs, as the saying went.

Dear Katrin, she had written. It was cursive, of course, as she had been taught in Czech schools. Cursive and pretty (not as steady perhaps as it once was), each letter distinctive and definitive. She thought of her first-grade teacher, deported and gassed, who had taught her how to write and whom she had loved and who had loved her, with great affection and gratitude. *I had breakfast with your grandfather. He sends regards. The day has come. I need you. Please think carefully before coming to see me. If you come. I will not blame you if you don't. I love you from the bottom of my heart. I always will. Klara.* Below the signature, in small but equally precise letters, was Annie's phone number.

Of course, there had been no breakfast with a grandfather. He had died long ago, a crushed cyanide pill on his tongue. It was an agreed homage to the veiled letters forced by *lager* inmates under gunpoint to fool those still to be shipped. Still, the grandfather was real. And he was, indeed, Katrin's grandfather, that much was true.

Klara had sent the postcard and almost forgotten about it. Maybe she had even wished that it would never arrive. For she understood the monumental significance, if not specific consequences for those involved. She also knew that for Katrin it would be incredibly difficult to refuse. It was a call for help that would be a success or a failure. It would either cleanse Katrin and set her free; or it would taint her forever, more than she was. It would set Annie free, too, to be sure; and give her and Anton an unmarked beginning.

She hesitated only a moment. From her car, she threw the postcard into a blue mailbox outside the Palm City Post Office. In the distance, the top of a palm tree blew lightly in the wind. The sky above, a light blue.

She sent it and forgot about it.

KENTUCKY

"Annie."

"What?" She looked at him and smiled, the way she always did.

They sat next to each other as she drove the rental car, a black Ford Escape. As a passenger, she suffered from car sickness, but she enjoyed driving and he didn't mind. It gave him the opportunity to relax and look at her. Which he did, regularly, putting his hand on her elbow. Her spirit was vivacious, childlike, he thought, and her pink sweater and pink sneakers reflected it. Anyone would be hard pressed to guess that she was a police officer.

In the 12-volt charger she had put an essential oil diffuser that she had brought with her for the occasion. He loved such things about her, the quirks, the foibles, that made him love her more. That was the thing about love, only the lucky few found the right ones. And that's how he knew, the things that used to drive his ex-crazy. Annie either didn't notice or loved about him. And he knew it was the same for her.

"Does this or that bother you?" She would say.

"I haven't even noticed," he'd say.

And she would say, "Because that used to drive my ex crazy."

He stared at her as they drove. He didn't understand what she saw in him. Why she loved him. He didn't think he was worthy of her love. Sometimes he just wanted to end it all, to disappear so she could move on with her life, find a man that was worthy.

Bit late for that, he thought.

It was a big weekend. She was taking him to visit her aunt and uncle, her father's brother, outside of Lexington. They had flown into Cincinnati and now drove an hour south, the only family she had stayed in touch with since.

He stroked her cheek. "Why do you love me," he said.

"Who says I love you? Aw, honey, just kidding, don't be like that. Why does anyone love anyone?"

"I'm serious. I'm not worth it. You can do much better."

"Better? How? Some guy with a lot of money?"

"Yes. And no baggage. Look at me."

"I've had that, remember, a man with money. Thought he owned me. I didn't love him. Often, I felt like a high-class hooker, don't smirk, I did. Nothing worse than that feeling that you sold your soul for money and comfort. Lying in bed, letting a man touch you that you don't love, it's a death. I remember thinking late at night, while he snored in bed next to me, his paw on me, or when he would roll over and poke my back — that was his way of telling me it was time for sex — that I was no better than a high-class hooker. In fact, worse, at least the high-class hooker is honest with herself. The husband pays for everything; we pay with our souls. All in the name of marriage, being a wife, being a mother; but deep down, we know better. Right? Just selling our bodies and beauty to the highest bidder. When I see wives of rich men, I feel sorry for them. I *know* the lives they lead. Often thrown away for a younger model. By then, you're usually middle-aged with fewer prospects. And here comes the hot new wife, selling her soul, moving into your house. *Their* lives continue as before; and you get visited less and less by old friends or kids, because you are the cranky old bitch who can't get her life together."

"You're hardly a cranky old bitch."

Annie smiled. "I would be, if it wasn't for you," she said. "I married him when I was twenty-one. I thought, he's so glamorous, a rich family. I thought, with my past, that I was lucky anyone would have me. Then the abuse started. Then *he* left. I became a police officer because I had to do something, right, and money was running low and because I thought I'd be good at it. But mainly, because I thought, maybe I can prevent others from being hurt. It's not prestigious, it's dangerous, and I know that my ex and his new wife and friends must have had a good laugh about it. I enjoy my job, but, sometimes seeing them around town, me in my uniform, it was humiliating. I didn't fight for money, Anton, I thought I did the noble thing, I just walked away, proud. Stupid and proud. But then, when you really are at your lowest, along comes a man with no money—"

"Thanks."

"—But a kind heart, and he puts you back together, and you put him back together, and you know that you'll both be OK — right? And you're grateful that you can start again. When I am with you, Ant, I feel alive. Sounds silly, I know. I am hopeful. You make me feel like I'm a teenager. The way you look at me, the way you touch me. Life's full of possibility, when before it was a slow road to death — sounds melodramatic, I know, but what else do you call not living and one day dying at the end of a monotonous life. I know I want to spend the rest of my days with you, Ant.

"And none of what you've been through is your fault, by the way. You blame yourself too much. You married a psycho. So what. So, did I. We're not the first. You could be on one of those real-life crime shows, you know. All that says to me is that you're a kind and loving man. People like that see you coming a long way off. In my line of work, I see it every day. You have 'sucker' written all over you. Aw, honey, don't be like that. It's a good thing, believe me. It's only a bad thing if you end up with a psycho. But what if you end up with a decent person?"

"Are you saying you're a decent person," Anton said.

"Funny man. *My* man."

"I am."

"Want to know why I love you?" Annie said. "Because you love me for me, you don't try to change me, you don't belittle me, you treat me as your equal. Because you pay attention to all my needs and you know exactly what I need, sometimes before I do. Because you are kind and gentle to me, always. Oh, and because you are the best dad I've ever seen. *Baba*, right?"

"Well done."

"*And* you're hot, even though you don't realize it, which makes you hotter and you're great in bed. There. Does that answer your question?"

Anton's eyes were moist. "I don't think so. I may need to hear it again."

He never thought he'd be with anyone who cared for him again in his current state.

But sometimes, help arrived late. He felt that he was back now at a crossroads; whereas before he had been down one of the paths, now, maybe, he wasn't ready to give up. There wasn't always time to resist; giving up was inevitable.

"Ant," Annie said. She touched his arm. "I have to tell you something."

"Yes?"

"You saved me."

"What?" He was shocked to hear it because that's how he felt — she had saved *him*.

"I mean it," Annie continued, "I've told this to no one else. I thought about taking my life. I just felt... I couldn't... Carl talked me out of it, but it was touch-and-go. I just felt... a constant emptiness... I don't know how else to describe it." He started laughing, a good-natured laugh. "You laughing at me? I shouldn't have told you." He put his hand over her eyes while she drove and continued to laugh. He felt ecstatic. "I can't see. You stinker," she said. She pulled by the side of the road.

"I tell you I thought of killing myself and you *laugh*?"

"You've saved *me*, Annie."

"I've had no such thoughts — since we've met." She paused. "Have you?"

"Yes — I don't want to be a burden to you. I thought maybe your life might be easier without me. You could go back to being 'normal'."

She scoffed. "Normal? I go home, sit on my own. I've no one. Nothing. Carl — on the odd day." Suddenly she smiled. "Sometimes I feel that I may not be... enough for you?" She grew serious. "Promise me you'll never do anything stupid, Ant — I need you. I wouldn't survive that. I mean it. You must believe in me. Things will turn out fine, you'll see."

"Will they?" Anton said. "Annie, I need to go home."

"Alone?"

"Don't be silly," he said.

"I know, my love. I've known it since we met." Anton held her. She felt his chin quiver. He always held her tight when he wept, so she couldn't see. She wouldn't have minded; she wouldn't have thought less. After all, she had been with a mother and an ex-husband who didn't cry or when they did, only for themselves; her pain had been an irritant, a weakness.

They pulled up to a building and exited the car.

"Annie — why are we here?"

"As in, the meaning of life?"

"Yes," he went along. "As in the meaning of life."

"I can't tell you that. Although, I think *you* might be the meaning of my life." She thought he blushed. "Have you ever been here, to Keeneland?"

"Keen-land? No."

"Keeneland Racetrack — that's where we are." Then she added, "You know, I keep thinking about your mother."

"My mother? As far as I know she's not a punter."

"A what?"

"Someone who bets on horses. What does my mother have to do with horse racing?"

"I, er, no, never mind. So — Keeneland. A racetrack. I want to show it to you."

"You want to bet on horses."

"Don't be silly. There are no horse races this time of the year. But I want to show it to you," she said, as they approached a set of stone buildings. They walked through the main building to the track. Along the way, Anton was amazed that it was open — back home it'd be fenced and locked. Even the restrooms were open and clean, to his use and relief. In the courtyard and behind where the horses were shown before the race stood a green Rolex clock and behind it a magnificent sycamore tree (he couldn't help wondering if the clock was real). It was an overcast day, but the sun was bright behind the clouds, and he had to squint. They took time and held hands as they walked underneath the building to the racetrack, along the way hearing the loud calls of predator birds. Annie explained it was only a recording to keep vermin and pigeons away and pointed at a small speaker above. The loud menacing shrieks emanated from a red, round speaker.

They looked at the track and walked backwards and still Anton wondered why Annie had brought him.

"This place—" She made a sweeping gesture. "—This part of Kentucky is important to me. It's my home. The way South Africa is important to you. Integral to who you are."

Anton looked closely at her. She beamed, the way he beamed, she said, whenever he spoke of South Africa. He kissed her, held her close.

"What?" she said, smiling.

"Nothing. I love you."

He walked over and touched the wall. "Limestone?" he said.

"Well done, my love. Limestone, but importantly no iron. Only three places in the world you have that — Scotland, Ireland and here. That will bring us to the third destination of the day. But for now, why did I bring you here — not quite as random as you might think, my love. I used to come here with my dad, when I was little, seven, eight, Lucie's age. It was the only place I remember feeling happy, safe. Mom wouldn't come here, right? Thought it was beneath her. Gambling on horses. The only place my dad was himself, among friends, free, not looking over his shoulder to see whether she *approved*.

"He was so proud of me. Loved to introduce me, show me off. Held my hand as we walked around. I was as proud of him as he was of me. He let me read up on the horses, we'd study them in the courtyard, he'd let me choose the ones we'd bet on. We never bet much, never more than ten, twenty dollars. It wasn't about that. This was our sanctuary. She couldn't hurt us here. He'd tell me about the history of the track and how it was the last in the country not to have a public announcer, that it was for the purists. You had to watch the races with binoculars. Dad got me my own pair, I was so proud — I remember when I got them for my birthday, mom was of course angry about it — out of jealousy, envy, it was a joy, a pleasure she couldn't understand — but you know what, fuck her! I even took them to school! You'd think the teacher would disapprove, but it's Kentucky, she had her own pair of binoculars! The best present I ever got, because it was from my dad, because it was only between us and, most importantly, because *she* couldn't interfere. It was our little secret place, free from her madness. It was amazing here, and we were free, happy here. I'll never forget it. Well, and then it all came crashing down."

"She put a stop to it."

"If only. No, it was my own stupidity. My own weakness, my sensitivity. We watched a race on TV. It wasn't even here. Somewhere in New York. And there was a horse that everybody was all excited about, won several races, and I decided that was my favorite horse. You know, the whims of a little girl. And so, we watched this race, my dad and I, and I remember there were only two horses racing, this horse, Ruffian, and another. Ruffian was leading, not by much, but pulling away when suddenly its leg looked like it was made of rubber — you know how sometimes you see athletes break a leg on TV and how horrible it looks and it was just like that, it flailed, and yet it still tried to run and of course, that damaged the leg even more. I was traumatized and my dad tried to explain that this was really rare, such a bad injury, although horses did get injured sometimes, and they operated on this horse for hours, it was all over the news, but then it went wild when it came to, and was destroying itself so they had to put it down. Anton, I was quiet for days, I couldn't talk about it, you know, I was a little girl, don't forget, traumatized by *her* violence, well, and then I saw this, and I just couldn't ——"

"Oh, Annie."

"—I couldn't, Ant, I just couldn't get myself to come here again, or to any race, and with that went the only sanctuary we had, and I never remember being happy like that again, not until I met you, no — Ant — I mean it, it's true — my father was devastated, just devastated, as if it had been his fault for introducing me to horse racing, but he loved me so much and he never pushed me, never tried to force me to come to another race again, he respected me, you know, but that was it, the last of our happiness, and then a couple of years later he got a job in Florida and we moved there, but we were never happy again.

"She was happy, though, ecstatic, gloating, and in spite of that, I couldn't get myself to go to another horse race, I was so terrified of seeing another horse… I so desperately wanted to go, but just couldn't. I knew that dad was devastated by it, but also feeling guilty that he introduced me to horse racing in the first place, but I think it also pleased him that I was sensitive, as if he didn't know that already, although at the same time, I bet it terrified him no end that I would end up with someone as he had and sure enough I did, because that's all you know, right? You always marry what you know, don't you, unless you can one day break away."

"I am sorry, Annie."

"We've all lived our inferno, Ant, you, your mom, me, my dad, my brother. And the bad ones, your mom's tormentors, my mom, your ex, my ex, they walk away, don't they, like it was nothing, like we were nothing, any of us, nothing at all—"

"Well, you said your mom—"

"Like it was nothing, Ant, like we were playthings for them to torture, which is why, here, I was thinking of your mom. The happy places she told me about, the happy times, before the war…"

"Annie—"

"What."

"What's the story with your mom?"

"That's the second part of our trip. Ready?"

"Is she buried here? In Lexington?"

"In a way. Come. Afterwards we'll reward ourselves with a bourbon tour—"

"I know nothing about bourbon."

"That will all change today."

"We won't be drinking much bourbon in South Africa."

"Red wine, I know, can't wait. And Amarula. That stuff is *addictive*. But this is not about bourbon. This trip is to introduce you to my parents."

"*Parents*? I thought they both passed?"

"Sort of."

"Sort of?"

"My father *did* pass away. So, the racetrack, the bourbon, are my way of introducing you to him." She looked away. "I had — almost — forgotten how happy we were on those days at the track, just the two of us. We never had such alone time again. And, you know, by moving there, to Florida, he was even more at her mercy. There was no escape. The house here in Kentucky was his, she had moved in after three weeks and fell pregnant with me two months later, he had no idea what hit him, he told me." She started crying. "Shit. Shit. Shit." He held her. "But he always said that I was the best thing that ever happened to him. How much he loved me."

"Annie — your brother."

"What about him."

"You never talk about him."

"He bet on the wrong horse," she said. "How appropriate is that?"

"What do you mean?"

"The more my mother beat him, the more he loved her. I couldn't stand it. He followed her, like a dog. Never complained, always defended her. He never went with my dad and me to the track, anywhere. Ever. We invited him, then we stopped inviting him. He always stayed behind, waiting to be beaten—"

"You never — your father never — reported her to the police?"

"Of course not. You know all about that, Ant. Have you reported Carolien? It becomes commonplace, the violence, I have no idea how, but it does, they have a power over us, and we defend them." She paused. "So, at those times, when my brother stayed with her, she'd smile at us, when he refused to go, like she got one over on us, like, look at me, he prefers me to the two of you. I hated that smile." She gritted her teeth, then said, "I hate her. I will always hate her. I will never forgive her for killing him, for taking him away from me, my dad. I can't stand people who tell you that you have to forgive, I agree with your mom." She stayed quiet a moment, angry. They still stood by the racetrack, no one around; Anton wondered what the track looked like when Annie was little, when she had come here with her dad. What people had dressed like. What the two of them had looked like. He wondered if she had any photos, and hoped he wouldn't forget to ask. Suddenly he thought of Lucie.

"What're you thinking about? Ant? What's wrong?"

"Annie — Lucie — she's in trouble."

"Calm down, my love, we'll get through this. You're not alone anymore, OK? You have me."

"She's not safe, Annie."

It was Annie's turn to hold him. "Shh," she said. "We'll get through this, together, OK? Shh, my love. Please. I've thought about everything, there is only one solution, I'll take care of things, you'll see. We'll be in South Africa, all of us, safe. We'll be drinking wine together in the sun on a beach somewhere, some of the places you've told me about. You'll see."

"Annie — I'm afraid."

"Don't be, my love. Please. Nothing to be afraid of. Look how far we've come, all of us, we've survived this far, haven't we? Not much longer now, my love, you will see. OK? Please believe me. Please believe in me. Please believe in us. I need you, Ant, OK? I need you like I've never needed anyone. I want to share a life with you. A home with you. I want to hear you puttering in our home, I just want to know you're near me, to know I can walk over and hold you, kiss you, to know everything will be all right. Know what I mean? I can't live without you. And don't laugh, I want to marry you one day. I've already been thinking about it. On a beach, there, just a few of us, Lucie, your mom, Maria, a friend or two, and us, laughing, I can see it, and we're free, you know, and all this is behind us, in the past." Anton held her, put his face next to hers. "I need you to believe in me, OK?" she said. He didn't respond but looked at her imploringly. "At least don't think about all that for now, OK? Please, my love, stay in the moment. Believe in me. Sooner or later, you have to believe in somebody." He nodded, not exactly convincingly. "So, listen to my story. Maybe it will take your mind off things."

"Annie, I need to hear Lucie's voice." He felt a desperation that he often felt, unable to be with his daughter. "I have to know she's all right."

"You know that *she* won't let you speak to her." The 'she' sounded precisely as the 'she' used for her own mother. Anton had bought a cell phone for Lucie, but it kept being turned off, or the volume turned down, or simply hidden from Lucie. He was cut off from her for continuous days and it felt like he was going crazy. But, at this precise moment, not being able to get a hold of Lucie — he pulled out his phone and tried anyway, against Annie's pleading, only to go straight to Lucie's voicemail.

Annie persevered. "So, my dad sold *his* house to move us down to Florida — that's where *she* was from. He didn't want to go, only did it for her, she of course just wanted to cut us off from all we loved, I didn't want to go, change schools, leave all my friends, leave dad's family, but she kept saying how she hated Kentucky, how she had only moved here for him — they had met in Florida when he was on vacation — how backwards it was — can you imagine — we're talking Florida here, not France. Seriously. Kentucky has this backward reputation but look at this place. It's horse country. You saw how pretty it is here. The wealthiest people in the world have horses here. Arab sheiks, you name it. The queen comes to watch horse races. You've seen the properties and mansions. Heck, just the barns look like mansions. What has Florida got compared to this? Nothing. Miami. Garish, false Miami. A lot of glitter, no gold. Plastic surgery heaven. He didn't want to go, but he did it for her. My poor dad. Thinking, somehow, he was going to save the marriage, make her happy, like she would be a different person."

Anton realized that was precisely what he had done, moving Carolien and Lucie to the US, hoping for a miracle, that Carolien would somehow become a kind person.

"It was a disaster, of course. She was even worse in Florida. Much worse. Now we were *completely* at her mercy. No outlets, nowhere to go. No support. Alone with her all the time, which was precisely what she wanted. God, I remember how devastated he was, so much more even than he had been Kentucky. And now he had nothing, he had given her control of his money, he never saw another penny. I remember I once asked him, dad, why didn't you kick her out of your house in Kentucky, and he said she was my mother, that decent people didn't do that sort of thing. And I said, had you kicked her out then, she would not have kicked you out in Florida. And he said he had no idea she would do that. And I said, but dad, crazy people do crazy things. The look on his face, you should have seen it, Ant, the coin just dropped, you know, child's logic, but of course it was too late, for me, for him, for my brother. He often quoted me, 'crazy people do crazy things'. I'm not sure what he could have done then, you know."

They sat down on green benches pulled under the roof and bunched up, away from the track. The day remained misty, overcast, but bright. On a timer, they were interrupted by the piercing sound of the birds of prey recording, ominous, lurking in the background, meant to keep vermin away.

"The next part of the trip, before we reward ourselves with bourbon." She looked at Anton, who looked in the distance. "Are you listening to me? Where are you?"

"Yes, of course, I heard every word you said," he said. "It's just that, I remain worried about Lucie, I can't help it, I think there's something wrong, I can feel it. Something bad is going to happen." Annie flinched involuntarily. He continued: "You know, she was the sweetest child, from the very beginning. Just the sweetest. She used to feel everything, see everything, every little thing, it was amazing. I remember, she always had to touch me, as a baby. One day, I tested it, I thought it was coincidence. I'd move her away on the bed and she'd roll right back to be next to me, no more than two, three months old. To this day, she's always touching me, has a hand on me, a foot on me."

"I've noticed that. It's adorable."

"She was always very perceptive, very tactile, I'd fill a tiny little crack in the wooden floor, for example, and she would see it right away and feel it and let me know, this was when she still crawled, before she could talk. She'd touch it and look at me to let me know she noticed. Or, when I held her, the smile she had for me. I still remember her first smile, toothless, in the bedroom, it was the most amazing thing. Or she would pat me on the back, and I knew exactly why she was doing it but one day I asked anyway, when she could talk, and she said, as if it was so obvious, 'Because I love you, because I am so happy with you.' God, Annie. It took my breath away. They are so pure, kids, aren't they. And then we fuck them up. I always say, kids aren't the problem. It's the parents that are the problem."

"I know, Ant. I've seen what you two have. You're the best dad I've ever seen. *Baba*. What happened to you is tragic. We'll set things right." He shared none of her optimism; he could in no way see how they would 'set things right', not when the justice system protected the strong and failed the meek.

"The rage that Carolien has, Ant, I've seen it before." She didn't elaborate. She continued, "It wouldn't have made any difference anyway, you tried calling 911, told them your wife was beating you, and what happened?" He had, a few days earlier, just to find out. The operator on the line was unconcerned, she kept repeating, is your life in danger? And he had said, "Well, I don't think so."

And she casually said, "Well then, nothing we can do."

A man being beaten was acceptable; a woman being beaten was a crime. The message was unequivocal.

"Anton? What am I going to do with you today. Is it Lucie? Are you worried about Lucie still?" She didn't wait for a response. "Ant — the next part of the trip — it's important, are you ready?"

"I think so."

"You'll have to do something for me."

"What."

"Come," she said and took him by the hand. They walked through the underpass. To the left were windows where the punters placed bets. Across from the windows were computers to the same effect. He hated the propensity to replace all employees with robots or machines, just to make more profit, livelihoods forsaken — he thought of the eerie feeling he had had of walking into a grocery store in Florida at night to find no employees, only self-checkout tills, a policeman making sure no pilfering took place. Or having to place orders in restaurants or convenience stores on computer screens, the employees, if any, hidden behind. What were companies afraid of, human interaction? Perhaps they were, that's how unions start. He smiled. The ANC ran through his blood, it always would. His father had made sure of that.

Annie was right, he *was* all over the place today. And here he thought she was. No — it looked like she had the day meticulously planned. He felt that none of today was without representation. And, some semblance of a plan, her plan, a vision, started to emerge, though he could not pinpoint it.

She led him to the empty parking lot; their rental car the only one. They started to drive through the countryside. She told him that Ruffian had been foaled on a farm not far away. She explained about how the blue grass buds seen in the springtime made it seem as if the fields were almost blue. She said that the grass grown in the limestone soil made the horses stronger (evidently, not her poor Ruffian; anomalies were nature's way). And how the same immigrants who made the first bourbon also built stacked rock fences with no mortar dating back hundreds of years that looked like something straight out of those two countries, and how she said the older locals sometimes still called them 'slave fences'. She explained that in all likelihood, Irish or Scottish foremen had built with slave labor, although the locals now disputed that, understandably. As he listened, he watched her beam, animated, he'd not seen her like this in Florida. He realized that in Florida they were both unhappy, not just he, and that he had erroneously assumed it was her home. He realized suddenly that in Florida, they were both without a home, away from their homes. And he looked at her lovingly as she spoke. What he didn't know yet was why she had remained in Florida; why she had not moved back to Kentucky. He began to understand, he thought, that this trip had an altogether different purpose than he had been led to believe, that there would be no visit with an aunt and uncle; that it was a way of introducing him to her home; clearly, it was a place as important to her as South Africa to him, but in ways entirely different. But, somehow, it felt to him suddenly as much an introduction to her home, as much as a goodbye, a final goodbye, to her home; and that not every home was a home, not in that sense. This was a sentiment he could not shake or understand.

THE THREAT

THEY finally arrived at a new looking neighborhood. The houses were brick, mainly, some wood. They were medium-sized; the neighborhood looked clean and well kept. Nobody was in the streets, as if aliens had sucked all human inhabitants into a saucer and flown away. That was the thing about the neighborhoods, Anton remarked, the one thing that really had shocked him when they had arrived in the US, no one socialized with anyone like people did back home, they hardly spoke to one another, hardly anyone knew their neighbors. Carolien, for whom relationships were of no relevance except usefulness, didn't mind, of course, quite the contrary; but he felt the solitude acutely. And so did Lucie. They felt terribly isolated. Every evening they would walk around the neighborhood but would see no one. From the street, the eerie glow of television sets could be seen in practically every home. Often, too, the garages had been turned into a living space of sorts, sparsely furnished but always with an oversized TV hanging from a wall, and several large cars parked in the driveway. A few of those garages had the door raised and inside sat invariably a man, mostly alone, watching a sporting event, a can of beer in hand. Even in the homes, it seemed, the family was sequestered, disjointed, each family member behind his or her TV or tablet or phone. *Familial apartheid*, he thought. He imagined a nation where no one spoke to one another and when they did, it could only be about things they'd seen on TV or a screen. The solitude was crippling. He had never seen Carolien happier, though. She treated them as unkindly as ever — worse, perhaps — but on the outside, she seemed much happier, as if now in a place she belonged. Perhaps it gave her pleasure that now he, too, was without friends.

After he had moved out, he had met Annie; at least their love had provided some hope, if not liberation. Still, the situation with Lucie terrified him, and he had no idea how it could be resolved.

"What are you thinking about?"

He hesitated. "You don't want to know."

"About how much you love me?"

"Something like that," he said, and as he looked at her, he did feel a pang of love, joyous as much as hurtful, as if it could not end well. It was the first time he had felt that with her; and it unnerved him.

"You OK?" she said, concerned.

"I think so."

"Not much longer to go now." To what, a physical destination? Or a mythical place in the future he couldn't see? He hated the mood he was in suddenly. Annie slowed and stopped by the curb. She had a look of fierceness on her face that was completely unlike her. Fierceness and, perhaps, rage.

"Annie? You OK? You upset with me?"

"Of course not, my love. How could I be upset with you? But am I OK? No, not really. Ant, listen, this is important to me, what we, what you are about to do. After this, you mustn't think less of me or love me less."

"Yes, OK, of course," he said.

"Ant, see that house?" She pointed at a ranch-style brick house.

"With the green Subaru?"

"Yeah. I want you to ring the bell—"

"And run away?"

"Please be serious. I need you to do this for me, trust me on this, OK?"

"I don't understand."

"A woman will come to the door. I don't want to see her. If I do, I might do… something… Look, I'm going to back up and wait over there—" She pointed her thumb; he took it that she would be waiting out of sight, down the street.

Annie continued. "This is what I want you to tell her." Anton listened intently, puzzled; but thinking, too, that he perhaps understood. He felt his complexion change, lighten. As he listened, up the road he saw a girl on a bicycle riding away. It gave the neighborhood a strange feeling, suddenly, the appearance of the only human being, and a child at that. It seemed to Anton an uncanny time for a person to appear.

"I don't know if I can say those things, Annie."

"She made my life hell, Ant. She is—"

"I know, Annie." Anton held her for a moment and kissed her on the forehead. He stepped out, walked up the driveway and past the Subaru. Inside, the car was spotless. The lawn was tidy, but there were no flowers or bushes. No personal touch. He waited in front of the door, mulling over what Annie had told him to say. He turned to see if she was within sight; she wasn't. He rang the bell. After a few minutes, he heard shuffling inside. A woman opened the door, seemingly leaning to one side, holding a walking stick. He even held out his hand, which she shook, and he was immediately sorry he had done so, the very hand that had beaten his Annie. The trouble was, despite everything, he had expected to find signs of a monster, something, anything that would give her away. He could kick himself, he thought, for falling into the same mistake that angered him when people met Carolien for the first time. Instead of telltale signs, the woman was diminutive, frail, ordinary looking. Her voice was squeaky. He couldn't envision her swatting a moth, let alone a small and defenseless daughter. For a moment, they looked at each other as if for recognition. He could see some resemblance. More the father, to be sure, from the photos he had seen. Still, the forehead, and maybe the mouth and chin. The color of Annie's eyes, the nose, her small ears, those were her father's. The red scar that ran from this woman's cheek to her neck was hers alone. When he told her who had sent him, she stiffened. For a moment he almost felt sorry for her. He told her she must immediately end whatever relationship she was presently in, that if she didn't, Annie would come back and finish what she had started. He could see that she was visibly shaken, fingers trembling. She wanted to know how Annie had found out. He said he didn't know. She asked if Annie was with him, and he said no. She started to whimper that she was just a frail old woman, in bad health, walked with difficulty and that she had been punished more than enough and that at her age it was inadvisable to be alone. Again, he almost felt pity. Until, that is, she started to blame Annie, that Annie was the violent one, look at the scar, look at what she had done, I can barely walk, and with that verbal attack, he saw her precisely for who and what she was, and his face hardened. She noticed immediately, too. She was good, he thought, she had surely fooled many others in the past and evidently even now, but she wouldn't fool him, not today, maybe he had learned something, maybe he was not as pathetic as he thought he was. Now he surprised himself, he almost snarled that if she said one more word about Annie, he would come back himself. His own anger surprised him. He was inches from her face, hands in fists and now afraid he might do something. For Annie, for his mother, for Lucie, for himself.

She cowered. She had seen the look before. She didn't dare say she'd call the police. She knew better. She also knew that Annie meant what she said, and that she was lucky to escape with her life. He repeated Annie's demands and was certain she'd follow them. He turned around and walked into the deserted street. He turned to see the woman's hunched figure still in the doorway. He didn't turn again.

He walked to the end of the block and saw Annie parked in the street several houses across the way. She wasn't taking chances. When she saw him, she started the car and slowly pulled up. He jumped in.

"How did it go?"

"She invited us for Thanksgiving." She wasn't in the mood for a joke. "I think I scared the hell out of her."

"Unlikely," Annie said. "*Was* she scared?"

"Yes. Annie — the scar — what… happened." She remained quiet. As they drove away, he looked at the north-central Kentucky countryside, large farms with mostly black, four-board wooden fencing without corners. She, too, looked at it, he remarked, almost reverentially.

"What did she look like."

"Old. I almost felt sorry for her." She shot him a disapproving look. "Don't worry — you know what these people are like. First, she was trying to make me feel sorry for her, then she said how it was all your fault—" He noticed Annie smile bitterly. "—That's when I lost it. You would have been proud."

"What happened?"

"I was stern, that's all. Told her what you said." He paused. "Annie — what was that about, exactly?"

"Let me see. Where do I start. Remember what I said. Don't judge me."

"I won't," he said. "Tell me — that scar… and I don't know, all of it, I thought she hated Kentucky, she's from Florida, so how did she end up here?"

"Some things, Ant, it's better if you don't ask, but it's good you know. I guess. I don't want you to be afraid. I am not like her. If you beat up a bully... or take revenge, is that wrong?"

"It's a fine line, Annie."

"Is it? Really? What's the alternative? What would have happened to you, to me, to your mom if certain people who hurt us had been stopped first. I don't see how you can compare—"

"I don't mean like that."

"Sure, in a perfect world—"

"I'm sorry, Annie."

"*I'm* sorry. I just get all worked up. You know, your mom — she understands — laws don't work, Ant. They are porous, pliable. You've seen that with your own divorce. Sometimes you have to take justice into your own hands."

"I thought that's why you became a cop, to uphold laws."

She gave him a quizzical look. "Once, after mom beat me so badly, I couldn't go to school for days, something snapped inside, Ant. She drank at night, wine mostly, I mixed sleeping pills into the food one night, she didn't notice. I tied her up. For a week. That scar you saw is one of several."

"Jesus, Annie."

"Your mother told me, had there been more people like you on the transports there'd have been no concentration camps."

"My mother knows?"

"Not in any great detail."

"And she approves?"

"When she said that, I took it as one amazing compliment, coming from her. She said if people stood up to each bully, imagine that world. Instead, she said, we put up with all sorts of abuse for God knows what reasons. Anyway, the thing with my mom was pretty easy. She had no friends, I called her work, said she was sick, wasn't difficult. Summer vacation for me. Best one I ever had. *Best time of my life*." She looked to see if he got the reference. He hadn't. "She got off easy, Ant. I made her a deal. She knew she more than met her match. She knew that next time, I'd kill her. And yes, I would have. I think she even took some perverse joy in thinking she had created a bigger monster than she was. But it wasn't true. I haven't hurt anybody who hasn't hurt someone first.

"Once I started, once I had her all tied up on a chair in the kitchen, it was all fairly liberating. I gagged her so she couldn't scream. She passed out a few times. I could have killed her but didn't. I wanted her to suffer, the way I had suffered, the way my father had suffered and my brother, for the rest of her life. I didn't feed her or give her water for days. Kind of symbolic, right? I didn't let her go to the bathroom and I didn't wash her. It was, needless to say, quite a mess. When I finally let her go, she hobbled around cleaning up, terrified. I enjoyed it, Ant. Sounds horrible to you, probably, I know. I told her she'd move back to Kentucky, the place she hated, with her scars and her limp, and she would never get into a relationship ever again — she'd remain alone — not get another opportunity to hurt anyone. Well, I found out last week on the internet that she broke that deal, got involved with some man — amazing how many lonely chumps are out there, to take her in the condition she's in. Still, I didn't want her dead, I just wanted her as she is, suffering, she's old now anyway, but I couldn't let her hurt anybody else." Anton looked at her for a long time. Annie's information was a lot to absorb.

Without him noticing, she had parked on a narrow side road; ahead, behind a wooden fence, were three horses, two brown and one white. He stared at them. They were majestic.

"Ant?"

"Annie — I… am not judging you. I'm not. It's one aspect of our love that is precious to me, that we don't judge each other, we accept each other. I think I understand why you did what you did. But Annie — I don't want you to live the life of a vigilante, now that we are together, I don't. I don't know why. Well, I do know why. Something doesn't sit right with me; something is bothering me. I think I might be an idiot, that it's irrational, but it's a fine line, Annie, do you know what I mean? Where does it start, where does it end? Who decides who deserves to die? You know the old saying, terrorist to some, freedom fighter to others. I'm not saying it's the same, not at all. I'm not even saying it makes any sense, because I'm not sure it does. It just scares me, I guess, that's what it is. Do you know what I mean?"

"Sort of. I debated for a long time whether to bring you here — I thought of coming alone — but then, I thought, I need you to see my home, but also, I needed you to know. Even though I was taking a big risk. I was terrified it would change things between us and I can see that it's still mulling around in your head. I'll give you time to think things through, OK? I have no regrets that I brought you here. I didn't want there to be a secret between us."

He held her tight and realized that whereas he had seen her as a fellow victim, even though she was a police officer, she had long ago shed that past and left victimhood behind; and that in his own way he'd have to do the same one day. He just wasn't sure how. Was it perhaps her strength that now made him weak? His limitations, his failure to protect Lucie, his mom and himself? Was that what was bothering him? That she had done what *he* should have done? What perhaps all victims should have done? She had punished the perpetrator in perpetuity but did not kill her (as she could have); and she made sure the perpetrator would never cause harm again. She took power and control from the perpetrator into her own hands and liberated herself. Perhaps part of the purpose of today was to show him that there was hope, that he *could* be strong; or maybe that were he not strong, she'd be strong enough for him, for them; or maybe there was no message, just a day spent together, doing things that had to be done. But he knew one thing — he loved her, still. He was frightened, yes, of what exactly he couldn't say, but then, maybe he always had been. But he loved her, more than ever, and he took her hand and she smiled. A wide smile that said many things, but one of them was the most important, relief. Relief that he had not stopped loving her. That today had changed nothing between them, that he had not judged her, that they had only been brought closer together and that their love was stronger than before. She had been worried, he could see, that he would judge her, that his heart would change. But he hadn't. He understood. He had understood that there comes a time, unless one is lucky, when someone will want to cause harm and no one will come to your aid, not the police, not the courts, not friends, neighbors, no one. And that at those times, you perhaps did have only two choices — fight and preserve something of yourself; or give in and slowly wither, like the *Musselmen* had proved.

"God, I sure could use a bourbon," Annie said.

THE DISTILLERY

It was one of Kentucky's oldest bourbon distillers, started by Irish immigrants. Annie's father had taken her there when she was young, before they had moved to Florida. As a child, she had been amazed most by the huge cypress wood fermenters, the sour mash bubbling on the surface. Her father had always said that one day, when she was old enough, they would go together and enjoy the tasting, which she was too young to attend. Of course, the day never came. But this was her way, again, as it had been at the racetrack earlier, to say hello and a final goodbye to her father for she was certain she'd not return to the US or Kentucky once she left.

They were with a group of tourists; she stood with Anton overlooking the sour mash bubble. She told him he'd have to waft it with his hand to appreciate, which he did, choking and smiling in the process at the strong alcohol smell. Then they tasted it on a small wooden stick dipped into the mash in a plastic cup.

"Crikey," he said. "It tastes like *umqombothi*." He laughed. He explained that *umqombothi* was traditional African beer back home, rumored to be made with battery acid. "Lights you up, so to speak."

"I'll remember that during the next power outage." She had no idea if he was joking, but she loved it when he used terms from home. He'd always cheer up when he said them, unknowingly, and it only made her love him more. And again, they exchanged glances. The shared fates, how seemingly they continued to be intertwined. Strange that here, in bourbon country, he was reminded of beer back home, she thought. She took him by the hand, and they followed the tour. They went by the huge copper pot stills; below, one of the workers labeled the sides of the barrels. They went onto the barrelhouses, the barrels stacked in rows to the top, near the ceiling, arranged by dates. The guide explained each bourbon batch was deemed ready only when the official tasters agreed it was, not a day before, not a day later.

Outside, Anton again remarked on the limestone architecture, much of it over a hundred years old. Finally came the tasting. They went into the tasting room and sat on bar stools behind the center of a u-shaped wooden table. In front was a gas fireplace. Annie's eyes grew moist, and she made a toast to her father. They drank the bourbon in the glass on the left in three sips, as instructed, the first to acclimatize the palate. A non-bourbon drinker, he admitted there was much more to bourbon than he had imagined. The difference between the first and second sips was dramatic, and he decided he'd sip everything like that from then on. They studied the tasting wheel, deciding on vanilla, butterscotch, honeysuckle (Annie), almond and cloves (Anton). The guide said there were well over thirty potential flavors that the professional tasters detected, many undiscernible to the untrained drinker. They ate bourbon chocolate balls between sips and then tasted the glass on the right, the double-barreled bourbon, much smoother, and a bit sweeter, but both decided they preferred the one on the left, which tasted stronger, more potent, but also where the kaleidoscope of tastes seemed farther ranging. After the day they had had, they felt giddy. Annie felt that they had passed a momentous test. As if the last obstacle had been overcome. That was how it felt. She was sure of this as they walked outside and found the skies still overcast but not so bright. They still felt exhilarated now from the tasting, even if Annie was also emotional about her dad. Anton put his arm around her, hand on shoulder. But there was no question they were happy when Annie's phone rang. They were on the way to the parking lot, still rather full of cars when it rang. They were a bit taken aback because it wasn't as if either one was called much by anyone, except by Klara, and she wasn't much of a caller. The number had their Florida area code. When Annie answered, it was a hysterical Lucie, sobbing uncontrollably. She was difficult to understand. What Annie could make out almost made her buckle. Anton took the phone out of her hand. He tried to calm Lucie, but tears started to roll uncontrollably down his cheeks. From what Annie could hear, Lucie had been home with Carolien when the police came to the house. Lucie had overheard them tell her mother — since they couldn't find Anton — that Klara had been found dead, an apparent suicide, had jumped from the intracoastal bridge, the one under repairs. The conversation was still going on and as he tried to placate Lucie, Annie placed her ear near the phone and heard Carolien in the background wailing, saying how much she had loved her mother-in-law and how she would tell him, Anton, soon as she could, although, sadly, they had recently divorced, something she had never wanted. Annie saw something change in Anton's countenance as he listened. But the transformation was brief, unlike hers, and then it went back just as quickly. She knew there could be a side to him, not unlike hers, but that he kept it under control, unlike her. All this went through her mind in a split second.

He hung up with Lucie, desperate. She didn't know what was worse, losing a parent you loved all your life or one you only met as an adult and grew to love.

He kept repeating, "Mother, please don't go," arms outstretched. He swayed back and forth. She held onto him. She knew he was in shock. She knew there was nothing she could do but hold him.

They sat in the car and Anton wept and moved back and forth as if autistic and the tears continued to roll and Annie too felt the shock, but in her own way. She thought of all the times she and Klara had spent together, the conversations, intimacy.

His eyes met hers briefly with such despair that she said nothing, just continued to hold him. He turned the key in the ignition and found a song he wanted to play, a version of *Mack the Knife* by a country musician from Texas they had come across recently in a French movie. It was a haunting rendition that Klara had loved, and they listened to it now:

'Oh, the shark has pretty teeth, dear

And it shows them pearly white

Just a jackknife has MacHeath, dear

And he keeps it out of sight

when that shark bites through his victim,

Scarlet spreads amongst the pain

But white gloves wears our MacHeath, babe

And the blood is never seen.'

He put it on repeat and the rendition played over and over; she didn't mind if he played the same song for a hundred years, until the pain became more manageable. She knew that grief was a unique and individual process.

She was lost in her own grief, remembering something Klara had told, "Where the Germans failed, Anton's Germanic wife will succeed." Annie had known precisely what Klara was talking about; she now blamed herself.

Annie wiped her tears and wiped Anton's as the singer sang:
'Now on the sidewalk, Sunday morning,
Lies a body just oozin' life,
And someone's sneakin' 'round the corner
Could that someone be Mack the Knife?'

She started the car and pulled out of the parking lot. The clouds burst open, and it rained so hard she could hardly see. She flipped the windshield wipers to the highest setting.

The song continued to play. As they drove, in the distance lightning lacerated the darkness with menace. She slowed further and put on emergency lights. There was no question of flying to Florida tonight. She was grateful that Anton had not suggested it. She was just as terrified for Lucie as he; but she knew there was nothing to do just yet.

"Annie, it's my fault," Anton said.

"Let's get back tomorrow and find out what happened. It's going to be one horrible, sleepless night. Your mother… I loved her, Ant. You know that. She was the closest to a mother I've had. There's only one thing to do."

She wasn't sure he was listening. He stared listlessly. The singer sang the last stanza before the moritat started again.

KATRIN

Soon as Katrin saw the postcard, she recognized the beautiful old-fashioned handwriting. Her hand shook and she started crying. She innately knew she'd never again see the woman who had been like a mother to her. She had not even read the contents, but she knew.

She stood in the kitchen of the two-bedroom apartment in the neighborhood of Prenzlauer Berg near the Kollwitzplatz. It was chilly and she buttoned her jacket. Outside, rain and wind lashed the large, double-pane windows. She had not seen Klara for many years and now knew she never would again. She understood why they could not have seen each other. Katrin had reminded her of loss, through no fault of her own. But Katrin would never forget her. Klara had been the only true parent Katrin had ever had. When old enough, because of what Klara had taught her about the Holocaust and Katrin's parents' roles and support and acquiescence, Katrin would renounce her immediate family and leave and never see or speak to them again.

After a few minutes, Katrin managed to pour herself a glass of Riesling. She walked over and sat on a beige leather sofa in the living room. Although a beautiful, intelligent woman, she'd never married. A long line of suitors politely but firmly rebuffed, she took no chances, intent never to hurt anyone. Still, she had not entirely given up on one day having a partner, but at her age, she had a specific picture of the type of man it'd have to be and the kind of place they'd live. It would be a truly special man in a special place. Someone who kissed her forehead and someone who loved pets (she still grieved for her recently deceased basset hound). Someone who truly needed her, she'd have to feel useful. And, it wouldn't be in Germany, of that she was certain, and he wouldn't be German. It would have to be in a warm and humid location. She was tired of dark skies and unpredictable weather (yesterday's hot day being an anomaly). But she wasn't counting on anyone and if she ended up alone, that was fine, too.

Katrin had had herself sterilized. She'd never have children of her own. She would not risk giving birth to a monster. Not with her genes. Her life had been solitary and lonely. But it was not purposeless. She had studied diligently her family's past. She had given talks at schools. She had given interviews and published articles. She was determined that her family's history is not overlooked or forgotten or forgiven. Even if it meant that she herself was punished for things she'd never done and for which she bore no responsibility.

She was certain her life had two purposes. To exonerate lives taken by her ancestor, and to save a life. She had assumed that life would have been Klara's. Now, whose life it would be, she wasn't sure. But she had known somehow, innately, that the day would arrive, and such a card would be found in her mailbox. When she had found it, she'd dropped all other mail to the floor and leaned against the wall and cried, childlike, until a concerned neighbor had escorted her to her second-floor apartment.

She now sipped the wine and continued to weep. Somehow, when the time came, she assumed that she'd see Klara again, before doing whatever needed to be done. She had not envisioned a life without Klara out there, somewhere. The world had become depopulated. And she worried about herself, just a bit. She now had only one purpose left. She didn't know specifics, but she knew that once transpired, there'd be nothing left to do. Perhaps, goal attained, she'd go the same way as her great-uncle, cyanide pill on tongue, he very much guilty, she, until now, guilty by association. Providence would judge, she decided once her purpose had been fulfilled.

Outside, the rain grew lighter. She took the final sip of the sweetish wine, glanced at the remains of a burnt candle on the windowsill from the day before, and thought back to time with Klara. Was she her granddaughter, some people would ask Klara on their walks, both blue-eyed, one blonde, one with gray hair but still blonde enough.

There was something about the nanny that from the first moment attracted Katrin. Klara had tried to be stern initially, but unlike Katrin's cold and aloof parents who were rarely home, Katrin had felt instantly at ease with her, at ease and, ironically, safe. When they had met, Katrin was seven years old. She was eleven when Klara left, both with broken hearts. They had grown inseparable. During that time, Klara had taught Katrin much about the Holocaust. Ultimately, it was to be her only revenge if truth and knowledge count. It was a secret that Katrin never shared with her parents (not that she would have anyway; as if from birth there had been a separation).

Only once in those four years had Katrin walked in on Klara while she changed (normally Klara was extra careful and locked her door). Katrin saw a number tattooed on Klara's stomach. A large, ugly number. It was shortly before Klara had left. And later Katrin wondered if Klara had left because she had seen the tattoo.

Ultimately, Klara had to leave. Her purpose for coming had changed from the first time that Katrin smiled at her and thrown her arms around neck. Many years and much research later, it would become apparent to Katrin why Klara had become her nanny. She would specifically remember a moment, in the beginning, when Klara had held her head under water while washing her hair for a moment too long. When Katrin emerged and gasped for air and cried and there was a momentary look in Klara's eyes that only later made sense, but it passed just as quickly, and despite that Katrin inexplicably hugged her and cried. It was later evident to Katrin why Klara had become her nanny; instead, Klara had fallen in love with her. And because Katrin had fallen in love with Klara, too, and because she was the only mother Katrin felt she ever had; and because she ultimately found out who her grandfather had been; she knew that one day she would perform an act to avenge her grandfather's deeds. At the time and even now, she didn't know precisely what that act would entail.

One thing was certain, she didn't trust her countrymen. She couldn't stand their excuses, their complicity, their covering up of the past. She found them disingenuous, trying to trick the world into believing there existed two entities, the Nazis and the Germans, that the two were separate. It was ingenious, she thought. How easy to say, not us, it was the Nazis. As if the Nazis and Germans weren't one and the same. As if they hadn't acquiesced and partaken and profited. As if they hadn't all stolen or worn property, businesses, money, gold, diamonds, jewelry, watches, clothes, hair, shoes, glasses, baby carriages, food.

The lies and deceit never stopped, nor the details to which they extended. The fake train stations with a fake clock; the soap handed out; the Star of David on every tile within the gas chambers to make them look like a Jewish bathhouse; the ambulance with its red cross and Zyklon B. Endless.

If a nation didn't confront its past, could there be redemption and forgiveness? She couldn't stomach her compatriots, any of them, and during her lectures openly told them so. She didn't listen to German or Austrian music, didn't read German or Austrian writers except those that had escaped the Third Reich: Remarque, Feuchtwanger, Mann, Zweig; otherwise, she shunned as much of her culture as she could. Now, typically, Offenbach played in the background.

She always assumed that the act which she would be asked to perform, if it arrived, would entail taking one of her countrymen's lives. She didn't know whose.

At the bottom of the postcard was Klara's beautiful signature. And underneath that, in small but neat handwriting, a US phone number, with the leg of the number seven neatly lined through. She threw the empty bottle into the recycling bin. She took out of her coat a photograph which she always carried and stared at the body of her grandfather shortly after being hanged for his crimes, lying in a grey striped jacket. She placed the postcard next to it and inserted both back into the coat pocket.

She could never bring back any relatives of Klara's that had died in the camps, or indeed any of the victims. But this wouldn't be only about them. In some small way, she, a German, would avenge a crime. But equally importantly for herself, she would sever, she believed, the ties that had connected her to her great-uncle, of whom her parents always spoke in reverential tones, much to her later disgust — the notorious originator and overseer of the extermination camps, Odilo Globocnik. Perhaps, she would forever purge the shadow and presence he had held over her life.

LEAVING KENTUCKY

AT the airport, Annie and Anton stood at the gate, devastated, like two trees clinging in a hurricane. Travelers lingered in seats, some stood fidgeting and a few college students played a board game on the floor. Nearby were the ubiquitous airport shops full of souvenirs and fast food. But what got Anton's attention were four children, the eldest ten at most, with parents. They had light blue plastic holders on red ropes around their necks, inside of which were boarding passes. The parents and children looked forlorn and dejected and, to him, represented symbols of societal failure. He knew suddenly who they were and why such a despondent and desolate picture they made. But it was a father and son that specifically caught his eye, holding each other, knowing they would disappear in an instant from each other's lives until the next time and that they would never have the luxury of parents and children who had the freedom of seemingly endless time, who didn't have the incessant and odious presence of a ticking clock. Both were on the verge of tears, the father even more than the son, and he could hear the son whisper to his father, as he held him tenderly in both hands.

"Please don't cry, Daddy, please don't cry. It's only four months, Daddy, and I will see you again." And the father's chin started to quiver and then the tears poured for both, and they tenderly embraced. Anton was aware that he was witnessing the best his future might one day bring and knew it was not an image survivable, not for him, not for Lucie.

Since they had received the news of his mother's death, Anton had felt an overwhelming urge to speak to Lucie. Against Annie's advice, he had tried to call Carolien's cell number several times. But the cell phone and number he dialed (the same cell phone and cell number he had acquired for her), conjured the usual and unavoidable array of remembrances and images. All the things which had been crucial to her stay or which she had coveted, and which she acquired through him, remained in her life — the green card, the social security number, the PhD, all his money, the bank account, the cell phone and phone number, his daughter; only he had been cast aside, once his usefulness had been fully depleted. It momentarily struck him as odd that he had been at once so useful for so many things and, once acquired, so utterly expendable.

When he had forgotten about making the call and perfunctorily held the phone against his ear, lost in thought, Carolien's curt voice suddenly said into the phone, "The parental agreement forbids you to call me."

For an inexplicable reason, he had the vision of a figure, rigid, military, decreasing by one a number in chalk on the side of a railroad cattle car.

"My mother died."

Carolien said nothing. He had the feeling that the silence had turned to noise. Peering at him through round rimless glasses was Carolien's cheery face.

The adjoining gate announced an impending departure and a line of passengers shuffled to the front.

"Where are you?"

"At the airport," he said.

He remembered their wedding day. First the city hall of a small town; then the lavish garden of a local restaurant. He had always remembered it as a jubilant event, they, and the wedding party exuberant. Now, he was not sure what he remembered. It all seemed long ago.

"Good," she said. "Are you going back to South Africa? I think that's the best thing for you. You have nothing here anymore."

He had nothing here anymore; he had nothing there anymore. She had taken everything.

"I want — I need — to speak to Lucie."

"Lucie isn't here." He heard Lucie pleading in the background and then the sound of flesh against flesh and then sniffling and finally silence. He shook his head. He never learned. Why had he not listened to Annie who now looked at him disapprovingly. "Don't call here again, Anton. I am going to tell my lawyer that you broke the parental agreement by calling me. Are you still *pro se*? So sorry."

The phone went dead and for a moment he held it against his ear. They had to board the plane and he and Annie walked by the little boy who a minute ago had tried to assuage his father. At the entrance to the gate, the little boy suddenly turned and ran back to his father, crying how he didn't want to go and the father crying now, too, and trying to reassure his boy, and one or two onlookers looked on with genuine concern. Anton, though, couldn't look and his eyes watered, already emotional from the death and all that had transpired since their arrival in the US, and Annie took him by the hand and led him into the plane where the stewardess greeted them with a ubiquitous smile, quick and fleeting, and they sat in the middle of the plane, near the wing, and Anton took out his passport and fingered the pages until he came across an entry stamp to the US.

He showed it to Annie and said, "The stamp of unhappiness."

"I know, my love," Annie said, and wiped a tear that rolled to his upper lip. She fell asleep well before takeoff, only to be awakened as the plane's wheels touched the ground in the state aptly named, 'God's Waiting Room', now with one person less.

BACK IN FLORIDA

BACK in Florida, Annie had to take over. Anton had no one there, his father's family was back in South Africa; having come to be with his mother, newly discovered. Annie could not imagine what it felt like for him, losing his mother a second time. He was gutted, almost useless. He was in shock. He had lost everything that he had loved, his daughter, his home, his country, his friends and family there, and now his mother, too. He had nothing left. She was terrified. She hated to leave him alone, but she had to go to work. Their life had to continue until she could put a plan together.

In the meantime, he remained alone in Klara's house. Annie knew it was a terrible ordeal. She had a hard enough time getting him to go there. First, they drove very slowly from the airport, as slowly as she could, making multiple stops. Once in town, he wanted to go to the sea, just sit there, as Klara and he and Annie used to do, and so they sat there, he crying, she holding him, looking out at the grey ocean, the occasional seagull or pelican flying by, a turtle egg area demarcated with yellow tape on sticks nearby. He was afraid of going to the house — she understood that she'd seen it before — ghosts of those one loved, it took time getting used to seeing a house without a loved one that had occupied it. Once there, Anton saw his mother everywhere, Annie knew. She did, too, to a lesser extent. He saw his mother, in all her familiar places, in her bedroom, which he reluctantly entered except to smell her clothes (which made him cry), in the kitchen, her study, on the porch. He saw her by the canal in the back where she would sit in the afternoons. He perused her numerous books, many on the history of the Reich. He looked at the photos she had framed on the bookshelves. When they had first returned to the empty house, they had found all the picture frames turned upside down — something which puzzled them — but they also found, importantly, a chicken in the slow cooker, which evidently Klara had planned to eat the night she died. Also of great importance to Annie was the absence of a suicide note. Also absent was a will. She took charge of all administrative things, informing banks, governmental departments of his mother's death. She also helped with collecting the death certificate. She was adamant that cause of death not be listed. Of course, that was a simple matter of pride, since suicide was ruled. There was no changing that. Carolien, of course, had an alibi, a Filipino woman who lived in town, volunteered at the crisis center, and who had been advising her on American divorce procedures. There was Carolien's boyfriend, too, an extremely wealthy 'snowbird', a retiree who lived in the north of the country in the summer and at his Florida house in the winter — but Carolien was with him only briefly, she had told the officer who had delivered the news.

There had been no foul play suspected, in any event. The officer had confirmed how distraught Carolien had been at the news, how close she and her mother-in-law had been, and how this was not unusual for a Holocaust survivor. Not being an expert on Holocaust survivors and never having known one himself, the officer nevertheless readily accepted Carolien's opinion, which, after all, made sense to him. And Carolien was European. And attractive. Annie pictured the scene.

Annie's goal now was to make sure that Anton didn't do anything rash, stupid. She knew that his love for her and Lucie were the only things keeping him alive and she hoped they were enough. They saw Lucie as allowed, but Anton was distraught, even more than before (she had a feeling during the Kentucky visit that he was coming into his own, becoming himself again, as Lucie told her he used to be, he had even said so himself). But her visits were presently not as much help as before. She had the feeling they hurt as much as they helped.

Annie also couldn't tell him of her plan, only that things 'would be all right' which hardly sounded reassuring to a man who saw himself as doomed and condemned. She needed time. Her plan was not one that she could fulfill in a day; it needed a few months for nothing in any way to arouse suspicion. But she knew what solution was needed; that much, to her, was clear. Annie had come across enough divorced men through her work to know that only two types ever recovered — those that miraculously got their children back; or those that started new families and could somehow leave the old family (children), behind — these, she understood far less than the former. In any event, she was convinced that Anton belonged in the former and, either way, her plan was to get Lucie back *and* give him a new family. To do that, there was only one solution. And Annie was anything if not determined. She was also, through her work, incredibly well-schooled in crime. The saying that there was no such thing as a perfect murder was not entirely true. There were enough unsolved murders. Whether this was because of police incompetence, she wasn't sure. But it did mean that there *were* 'perfect' murders — or at least perfect in the sense that the perpetrator was never caught. In that way, each of those murders was planned and committed differently. And it wasn't like anyone was going to come forward and tell Annie how to commit the perfect murder. But the advantage that Annie did have was that she knew the downfall of every single murder she had ever solved. She precisely knew the mistake or mistakes that the perpetrator had made which inevitably gave him or her away. And that, already, was a huge advantage. She had come across hundreds of pitfalls, mistakes, some silly, some small, some large, that those perpetrators had made, and which got them caught. So, she had a 'how not to' guide, and that was certainly a great start. In addition, she had come across criminals that *had* been caught. Granted, the smartest got away. Still, she had had at least some insight into the criminal mind; and, although perhaps no expert, she'd been able to study criminals in detail and up close, starting with her mother. And what better school than that? Who'd have thought that growing up with a mother like hers would one day come in handy. Maybe all the suffering had not been in vain. Her endless talks with Klara further gave her insight into that type of mind, from an individual as well as collective perspective; and Klara and Anton's description of Carolien provided more insight still. Lastly, she was not afraid to stand up, for herself or others, when justice was nowhere to be found. That, she had already proven, and perhaps that was the most important lesson of all. She knew that she would not allow more harm to come to those she loved.

  The death of Klara had surprised and shocked her. That, she had not anticipated. That, she regretted, terribly. She remembered Lucie's wise words to Anton: 'crazy people do crazy things.' Of course, you never knew precisely what such people planned, but they always exceeded your expectations, that she had learned. She also had no doubt, from her talks with Klara, had more individuals, more communities, more nations stood up to the Nazis, to use one historical example, then the Holocaust would have had little chance of success. It was the collective compliance and acquiescence that allowed it to happen. All the time, the Nazis were terrified that the victims would rise, or that help would come the victims' way, on the transports, in the camps, in the communities, cities, countries. All the time, the Nazis resorted to lies and deception so this wouldn't happen. All in all, she reckoned now, she probably could not have been better prepared for the task that lay ahead. She knew which pitfalls to avoid; she understood what made such people tick, inasmuch as a person like her could; and she knew she had the courage to take justice into her own hands, when required, knowing well that laws were arbitrary and whimsical and too often unjust; that waiting for karma to arrive or a hand of justice to correct a wrong was as good as waiting for a miracle. How many in the camps had learned that lesson Klara had taught her, and how many more learned that lesson every day. Klara — her presence was ubiquitous. Annie understood only now much of what Klara had been trying to say, to teach, to instruct, to prepare her for what needed to be done. And Klara's death now, in light of that, seemed the logical conclusion. {stopped reading here}

Still, Annie was a rational person, and she knew planning took time. It would be too suspicious if anything happened to Carolien now. Anton would be the immediate suspect and knowing how the justice system worked, she could not put it beyond some random court and random judge and a hodgepodge investigation that he'd be placed behind bars. After all, he already had a reputation; as far as the system was concerned, he had been an abusive husband; he could already only visit Lucie under supervision; and he had a motive — to get Lucie back. There could be no perfect murder while Anton was living in town. He would have to have a foolproof alibi. She would take care of that; in any event, she wanted to involve Anton as little as possible. Just enough to get the job done. She still worried that he would be too decent to go along with her plan, if verbalized. But, perhaps now, with the death of his mother, perhaps that look in his eyes she had seen if for an instant, perhaps that symbolized that he understood what had to be done.

In the meantime, Klara had been cremated as per her wishes. Even so, Annie and Anton had long deliberated, as must Klara have. How ironic that Klara would ultimately be killed at the hands of a German-born granddaughter of a Waffen-SS volunteer, and that she would depart this earth 'through the chimney', as the Germans had so often threatened. Annie had never spoken to Klara about this last wish of hers, but Annie was certain Klara must have deliberated long and hard and still Klara had decided to let bygones be bygones and had decided she had no time for symbolism; or perhaps it had been just the opposite, perhaps she *had* wanted to depart in the very same as the rest of her family and so many compatriots and millions of other innocent human beings. Either way, Annie and Anton had followed her wishes.

She and Anton picked up her ashes from a portly man in a crumpled suit at the nearest funeral home. He was polite but formal, any attempt at small talk would in any event have made them feel worse. Even so, the few words spoken had a rehearsed quality; they'd have preferred had he said nothing at all. Still, Annie admitted that at such times no words could bring much solace to anyone unless the deceased was truly old and truly ill and in pain, and even then; or the deceased was truly hated by the party picking up the ashes. Neither was the case. The man handed them the remains in two wooden urns, one large, one small. The large one had a cover on top and within were the remains in a clear plastic bag. The small urn was a box that had a candle at top and a tiny drawer. Inside that, too, was a sample of the ashes, for those that wanted to keep it for good or perhaps travel to other destinations to deposit. In their case, that was the intent. As per Klara's wishes, they would take the small box, depositing half of it in a body of water near where they would ultimately make their home, and the other half depositing in the Vltava River running through Prague. They planned both for a move and a trip another time.

In the meantime, one sunny day they took the ashes in the large urn on a boat up the intracoastal waterway. It was just the two of them. They arrived at an area where the waterway branched off towards the sea if one went far enough. Across the way was a wooden deck on which stood fishermen (Annie had been there with Anton multiple times); next to it was a concrete launching ramp. In the distance, not far, was the intracoastal bridge, ominous, high above.

They threw the anchor into the water and the boat pulled against the tide, the rope taut. They were overcome with grief. Anton wept as he held the large wooden urn. Annie put her hand on his leg. It felt incongruous to scatter ashes, not only for the act itself, but because life went on for others while they paid tribute to a death. For some reason, Annie remembered stories that Klara had heard of the *sonderkommandos*, the prisoners who had been forced to help empty the gas chambers of thousands of dead bodies and move them over to the crematoria to be burned, three per oven, into the same ashes that Anton held now. She remembered Klara telling her how the builder who had built the crematoria had continued his profitable and successful career after the war. She was thinking she would do her best so that the person responsible for at least for these ashes would not be able to get away with it.

Annie took the bag out of the urn. It was heavier than she anticipated, although she was surprised how little remained of the human body. It was nearly impossible to fathom that this dust of different sizes and shade was only a few days ago Klara. Anton took the bag and put it into the bottom of the boat to collect himself, then glanced at Annie and finally at the other side. Annie followed his gaze. She wasn't sure whether her eyes were deceiving her, but she thought she saw Carolien helping a middle-aged man launch a speedboat, a cigarette dangling from his mouth. Lucie stood nearby but separate. Carolien wore a bikini and a pair of sunglasses; and, reflected in the sun, a gold ankle bracelet. She laughed flirtatiously at the man, sipped on a bottle of beer and, in her left hand, held a cigarette.

"Ant let's move up the stream, up that way," Annie said. "Please."

In the meantime, Carolien and the man, unaware, had lowered the speedboat and all three were about to go past Anton and Annie, Carolien sunning herself in the front, the man at the helm, and Lucie in the back. It was only then that Carolien spotted them and waved and smiled with what, if Annie didn't know better, could be construed as genuine affection, as if she were seeing long-lost friends. At a slow pace, they rode by (one could not ride quickly here).

Suddenly, Lucie started crying and screaming for Anton and reaching out her hand. "Baba! Baba!" she yelled over and over.

Carolien moved towards Lucie and put her hand over her mouth; the man pretended as if he saw nothing. Anton, too, yelled for Lucie and held out his hand. Carolien with her free hand continued to smile and wave. One or two people at the ramp looked at the puzzling scene, then turned back to their boat. Soon the speedboat disappeared behind the bend, but not before Carolien gave one last wave, Lucie sitting limply beside her.

Slowly, the speedboat picked up speed, and in a moment, they could only hear it, and then, they neither heard nor saw it anymore. Annie had been watching Anton carefully and she was happy to see that, initially, to Carolien, he had made no motion to wave back, if for no other reason than reflex or habit.

"Annie... Lucie—"

"I know, my love. It tore at my heart. It will be taken care of—"

"God, Annie, did you see her…"

"It broke my heart," she repeated. "There is nothing we can do. Be strong, just a little bit longer, OK? In the meantime, we are saying goodbye to your mother and putting her in her resting place, as she wanted."

He stared dejectedly at the bend where the speedboat disappeared.

"Did I ever tell you about the time I overheard her telling some coffin salesman on the phone how she didn't want a pine coffin because the smell of burning pine was unbearable?"

In spite of himself, Anton smiled. "She could have a wicked sense of humor," he said.

"Helped in the camps", she said. "You know, I think she'd have a good chuckle about all this, the absurdity."

"Maybe, Annie—" His eyes started to moisten again, and Annie leaned over and hugged him, the boat rocking from side to side.

"Will you help me with the ashes?" he said.

They picked the bag up together. Annie said, "Klara, you are the only mother I've ever had. Wherever you are, I hope you can see us. I want to thank you for everything, I mean that, for everything you taught me, for treating me as your daughter, for the love and kindness you always shared. And I want to make you a promise. I will protect your son and granddaughter and make sure they are taken care of and safe. That, I promise you. Take care, Klara, and God bless you."

She looked at Anton. "Mom, I don't even know where to start. For so long I — I wouldn't say I hated you, but I cursed you, I did, you know that — I thought you had abandoned me, but then I found you and you explained how it all really was, that I had been taken from you, and Mom, I am just so grateful that I had a mother, at least for a brief while, for the past year, and I know it hasn't been easy and that I brought her into your house, I am the cause of all this, I am the guilty one—"

"Anton, please."

"If it weren't for me… and, when you asked that day on the beach, I never said I forgave you. Of course, I forgave you, Mom. Please forgive *me* for not telling you…" He choked up and couldn't speak.

"Anton, your mother told me that in spite of everything, the past year was the happiest year of her life because she had her little boy next to her and that that was a joy she thought she'd never experience, and that it was far more amazing than she could ever have imagined and she said she knew you felt guilty and she did, too, for telling you to come, but that she was so grateful for you, Lucie, me, so please, my love, just say goodbye, that's what she would have wanted."

Together they lifted the bag and slowly poured the contents into the sea. The wind blew it a little upwards before depositing it back on the surface for it to finally start to sink. It took a while to pour, heavier than she had expected and yet such a little pile was left of the human being they grew to love. Annie marveled how you could have people in your life since birth whom you did not love at all; and others whom you knew briefly and yet to whom you'd given gratefully and completely your heart. She was grateful now for the love she had experienced with Klara and the love she had experienced with Anton and Lucie and that she still would. The bag was finally empty, and they sat back down in the boat, holding hands, wordlessly, lost in thought, looking at the clouds on the horizon, above the bridge, reflecting orange and purple and pink. She wondered, without sharing, if it was a sign of any sort and hoping it was. Or that, at least, Klara was at peace, knowing that they were together and that her son was not alone, and that Annie would take care of him and make sure he and Lucie would be all right.

They pulled up anchor and Anton still ran his hand in the water, in the place where they had strewn the ashes, a final goodbye to the mother he and they had come to know late in life. Finally, they started the motor and just as slowly went back to the marina from where they had rented the boat. As they touched against the wooden posts with used tires buffering the landing, Annie jumped up and handed the rope to an employee of the marina. He tied it to a round wooden post. Anton looked around and asked about the plastic bag and Annie replied, "It must have blown into the sea."

SCHOOL LUNCH

ANTON sat with Lucie at a thick, prefabricated cement table. Already it was cold to the touch; but colder still, sitting in the shade. In front were the courtyard, grass, and trees, and next to it the school canteen reserved for visiting parents who wanted to have lunch with their children. Anton never missed a day. Few other parents came, mostly the same ones.

Lucie sat on his lap wrapped in his bearhug, something they both loved. Partially, he knew, she sat on him to avoid the cold cement; but it was something she did anyway at home sometimes; and, he hoped, she would for as long as possible. The pleasure of having his child in his lap, or walking hand in hand, was one that he knew was on a time limit; the day would come when she would simply no longer hold his hand, or sit in his lap; like so many aspects of parenthood, he hoped always for each to last as long as possible and always remembered when they ended — when Lucie stopped crawling, when she stopped needing her favorite stuffed toy to sleep with, when she stopped saying 'huptup' instead of ketchup.

Minutes later, two mothers he didn't recognize, one blonde, the other Asian, sat at tables on each side.

Lucie ate what he had brought — a submarine sandwich with her favorite toppings, mayonnaise, olives, tomatoes, ham. As she did, they stared at the courtyard full of trees, branches stripped, ready for a mild winter. Lines of children walked by with teachers headed for the canteen next door. The children held one finger to their mouths in silent obedience and another in the air, as instructed, without reason. The children were small and guileless and waved to Lucie, sometimes mouthing 'hello'. Lucie generally didn't respond.

At the table to his right sat the Asian mother with her son, Toren — Lucie whispered the boy's name, cupping Anton's ear with her hand; and a little girl, whose hair was twirled into cat ears, that Toren had chosen to have lunch with (the children could always choose one friend to sit outside with when a parent visited).

"Are you catgirl?" Anton asked.

The girl turned a hue of pink, looked askance, and said, "It's batgirl, not catgirl."

"Hello, I'm Suzette, Toren's mother," said the Asian woman.

"She's from the Philippines," Lucie whispered in his ear. Then she added conspiratorially, "She's friendly with *mom*." He understood. *Watch what you say.*

"Hello. And you must be Toren." Toren didn't respond. "Does your father also come for lunch?"

"I don't like to talk about him. My father was a very bad man," Toren said.

"I am sorry to hear that. Bad man, eh?" said Anton. Toren moved closer to his mother. "Is he with the Mafia?"

"It's not a joking matter," Suzette said. "He was a bad husband and father."

According to whom Anton wanted to ask. But, of course, he didn't. Lucie looked at him and smiled. It was a smile he had come to love, full of implicit complicity and understanding. He was sure in the world few parents were as attached to the soul of their children as he, and the children to their parents. He kept quiet and held Lucie closer.

Soon, the half hour was up. Lucie collected and crumpled the wrappers, told him to finish the rest of her sandwich and chocolate milk, and gave him a big hug. He watched her saunter off to the cafeteria, join her class and then, in a line, walk to her classroom across the courtyard. Every few steps she'd turn and wave until she waved one last time and disappeared through the door. Anton always remained a few minutes longer, it was his way of remaining close to Lucie. Suzette, too, waited until her children were finished and said goodbye.

When they were alone, Suzette said, "So, you're the dad."

"Yes. I'm sorry, by the way, about his dad — I had no—"

"Don't worry about that. By the way, I'm so sorry about what's happened. We all are."

"*We?*"

"Carolien's distraught, she's just devastated."

"Oh, I see. Is she? Distraught, I mean?"

"*Of course,* she is, what a silly thing to say. She has cried to me many times, how she wanted your marriage to work—"

"You seem to know a lot about us."

"Carolien has said... things."

Anton wondered what she had said to Suzette and why. But suddenly, unconsciously, he did know. "How long have you known each other?" he said.

"A month. Or so. We're very close."

"In South Africa, in all the years we were together, she made no attempt to make any friends. I guess she would have told you that I don't want any of this... this... divorce. I don't understand, really, what's going on."

"We hang out. She has told me how hard she has tried, how hard you have both tried, how much she still loves you, but sometimes there are just... it doesn't matter how much a couple loves each other... there are just... I don't know..."

"Irreconcilable differences?"

"Precisely."

"I learned that term recently. I have learned quite a few, actually. All rather sad. Like 'no-fault state'. Had no idea there even was such a thing. Wasn't quite sure what it meant — any of it — not sure I still do. These... irreconcilable differences seem to have sprung up once we arrived in the US."

"Well, I don't know about—"

"We only came to the US because I got citizenship through my mother. My wife... found out that my mother, who I thought abandoned me at birth, lived in the US. Naturally, I was grateful to her. We visited mom several times and I thought we all just fell in love with each other. I was devastated at the time we had missed out on, and all the time Lucie and she had missed out on, and I was kind of determined to make up for that. Incidentally, Carolien had always wanted a green card and a PhD from an American university." Suzette looked visibly uncomfortable. "She kept saying, 'How perfect, we could move there and spend time with your mother and, well, she said she might as well also get her PhD, as an afterthought almost, but certainly something she wanted since we met, so, I thought, why not? Sounded reasonable. We didn't have to go forever, I thought, let's see how it goes once she finishes her PhD." Suzette fidgeted. "So, I packed us up, sold all my premarital assets, paid for everything, thinking we are a family, together, that's what families do, but you see, she had other plans, unknown to me—"

"I am not—"

"I thought that's what you do in a marriage, you're a team—"

"You know, you sound… bitter. I think you need to… get over this, move on—"

"That's what Carolien says. Anyway, she got her green card upon arrival — we had filled out all paperwork before we left South Africa at the American consulate — and then when we arrived, I got her social security and set up her banking and gave her half the proceeds from the sale of my premarital assets, and then, soon as the PhD program accepted her, she announced she was leaving me and taking Lucie with her. Needless to say, my world fell apart."

Suzette looked discomfited still, but her voice hardened. "I've been praying for you," she said. "All of you."

"That's helpful."

"You *are* a bitter man. Maybe if you hadn't been a violent and abusive piece of… none of this would've happened."

Anton was dumbfounded, speechless. For a moment, he didn't know what to say. So, Carolien was accusing him of the very things *she* had done. Yet, he still didn't have the courage to say that it was *she* who had been abusive to *him*, to Lucie. He still, inexplicably, found the need to keep quiet. As if telling would somehow betray her.

"She reported you at the crisis center," Suzette said.

"Did she," he said with sadness.

"I knew you must have done something terrible for her to be so angry."

Anton was silent. It felt like his brain became slow, obtuse. As if the scene was outside his realm, independent, a barely discernible TV show crackling in the distance.

He said, "Suzette, forgive me, my mother survived the Second World War, I have learned a lot about it from her since we arrived here. One of the things I learned was a story she told me. Maybe this will make sense to you, I don't know. She showed her class—she had been a teacher once--a documentary about Jewish children being gassed in the concentration camps. You know how her class responded? They said, 'Those Jewish children must have been really bad to be punished like that.'"

"Precisely. When she told me you beat her, it all made sense."

He shook his head and looked at the courtyard with great melancholy. His heart, his entire being slumped. "I think you may have missed the point of the story," he said. Then, after a moment, "Did *you* advise her to go to the crisis center?"

"Yeah, of course, she asked me if she should. I volunteer there. She deliberated for so long. She has such a kind heart. It was such a hard decision for her. She didn't want to go, to get you in trouble." She scoffed. "She so wanted to protect you, lie for you. That's what people do in abusive relationships. I know all about it. I told her she must go, that it went on long enough, that she had to, for her, for Lucie, that she also deserved to be happy, that you had destroyed her life long enough. I went with her; she didn't have the courage to go alone. She is so terrified of you."

"Is she," he said softly.

Suddenly Anton felt the full ramification. He realized that Carolien was tightening the noose, that the walls were closing in, that she was waging a war against him and, still loving her, that he was essentially defenseless. Now if he reported the abuse, it would look like he was only reporting it to deflect attention from *his* abuse. She could even say it wasn't her idea, she didn't want to report it, but Suzette had insisted. It was smart, he had to admit. Carolien was that.

"Don't you think it strange that I wasn't violent and abusive in South Africa, but suddenly became violent and abusive after we arrived here?"

"She says you've always been abusive."

"Why not divorce me in South Africa then? Why drag me across the world, take everything from me, and then once she's taken everything, divorce me only then? Strange, don't you think?"

"Listen, I don't really want to get involved—"

"You don't want to get *involved*? You *are* involved. Are you kidding me? She's playing you; you are helping her—"

"All I know is, she always says that she wishes you two could just get along, you know, for Lucie's sake?"

"Right."

Suzette grew quiet. Then she said, "I also married my husband for a green card. There's nothing wrong with that. It's not like it's against the law or anything."

"Maybe it should be, don't you think?"

"Well, it isn't."

"No."

"Anyway. He was in the military. I left him, too, after we arrived, people do that all the time, Anton, it's no big deal—"

"No big deal. I see. I bet he never saw it coming."

"That's not my fault."

"Of course."

"The thing is, he was only a soldier, I wanted a better life—"

"I see."

"My second husband was a professor here at the university. We had a good life — until—"

"Until?"

"He left *me*. For some graduate student. You probably think it's karma or something. Like I deserved it."

"You will be surprised to hear it, but I actually take no pleasure in bad things happening to others."

"Carolien can do better. You're like my first husband — a deadbeat dad."

"I am sorry you think that."

"You shouldn't have been violent and abusive."

"Suzette. Do I look violent to you? Have you considered asking Lucie?"

"The courts won't let a girl that young testify."

"You didn't answer my question."

"I gave Carolien the name of an excellent lawyer."

Anton felt terribly exhausted. "OK," he said.

"You're bitter and negative. You have to be positive. You should just learn to move on. You don't know how things work."

"How is that."

"She will take Lucie and you will see her every other weekend and pay child support. That's how it works in America."

"I don't get to see her much and *I* pay child support."

"That's how it works. The courts will decide how much there are guidelines. If you don't have a job, it's the median income. It's all very fair—"

"Is it? Paying child support when you have no income? Tell me, how is that fair?"

"Children belong with the mother."

"And the father?"

"A father can never be a better parent; a child needs a mother—"

"And doesn't need her father?"

"No. Not like a mother. Besides, you are abusive. We won't let you get you away with it."

"*We*? Did Carolien send you today, I haven't seen you here before."

"I knew you'd be here."

"I see."

"I told Carolien what to do in case you don't listen to reason."

"And what might that be?"

"You'll find out. But I suggest you do what she wants. Be reasonable. It's better you go along. It's in the best interest of the child."

"You seem an expert in such things."

"Carolien is terribly worried about you. She's afraid you might be imprisoned, lose visitation rights, lose your driver's license, your passport, you won't be able to find a job and if you do, your wages will be garnished. She doesn't want that. She wants all this to be amicable. For Lucie. For all of you."

"What happened to your husband?"

"He never lost his passport."

"You said he wasn't abusive."

"He wasn — I know how it is overseas, in Asia, I can only assume Africa is the same. The man has the power—"

"In the indigenous communities in Africa, Suzette, the families try to talk sense to the couple. They view divorce as something *bad, especially* if they have children. There is no such thing as a no-fault divorce over there, you can't just wake up one day and decide marriage doesn't suit you, to hell with your partner, to hell with the kids. You know what I think? I think that the parent with the child should pay the other parent child support, for the privilege of having that child, now that would change everything, don't you think? Suddenly we'd see the more committed parent, right?"

"That's not the way it works here. The child belongs with the mother."

"You said. Thanks for letting me know that the cards are stacked against me. Please thank Carolien for her concern. And send her my love. I haven't stopped loving her."

"You've got issues, obviously. Caroline is reasonable, she's a *mother*, she loves you, she loves Lucie, she loves your mother, she's devastated by all this, wishes there was something she could do, it's just so hard—"

"There, you are right."

"You're not reasonable, Anton. You're angry. You have to be positive. Move on. Act with dignity," she repeated.

"Right," he said sadly. "Do I look angry to you, Suzette? Sad, devastated, yes, angry, hardly." He stood up. Suzette slid slightly away. He smiled wryly. "I forgot my brass knuckles today."

"You should just go back to Africa and leave them alone."

"Back to Africa, black man. Where would you like me to go precisely, Liberia?"

"I didn't mean it like that, I am not a racist—"

"It's been a real pleasure talking to you."

Anton walked left, down the cement pathway, past the auditorium on the right and the library on the left. He had been tried and judged. It seemed that in this country, every man was a whisker away from being accused of being a violent, abusive, *deadbeat* dad and shipped off to private prisons. Not likely that he was going to convince anyone otherwise. And, suddenly, it seemed like one big racket, like everything else in this god-forsaken country, all set up to take everything away from you and leave you in ruins. One colossal American *nightmare*.

He walked up the stairs into the main brick building and turned on the linoleum floor. The hallway wound to the left. He entered the office. Mrs. Matthew, the senior clerical assistant, sat in front of her computer screen, eating an apple, without looking at him. He unpeeled from his shirt a black and white sticker and handed it back to her. She said not a word, took it and registered its return in the computer before throwing it away. Behind her sat Marta Porter. And to her left, leaning against the bookshelf was the ubiquitous presence in American schools, the police officer. It was a man he'd not seen before, with shorn neat hair and a goatee, standing erect, glowering, thumbs on belt. Only Marta smiled at Anton and wished him a nice day. He smiled back unconvincingly. She was the only friendly one at the school who, seemingly, was willing to give him benefit of doubt. He walked out, forlorn, emotionally drained, shaking his head involuntarily not only at the conversation he'd just had, but at the need for an ever-present police officer in modern-day American schools. Something was very wrong here, he thought to himself.

THE ELEPHANTS OF PILANESBERG

THEY sat on the beach off the A1A, where Klara had first sat with Annie. This time, it was the three of them, Anton, Annie, and Klara.

A couple in their thirties played with two small children nearby and intermittently Anton gazed at them. In between, he recounted a story of the young elephants of the Pilanesberg National Park, northwest of Johannesburg. Klara and Annie were not aware of the story and listened, sharing a bottle of chardonnay while Anton sipped a beer.

Anton explained how the Kruger National Park found itself with too many elephants to sustain its ecosystem. Some were culled; most transported elsewhere; but no adult male elephants could be moved at the time with the harnesses available. Pilanesberg National Park, several hours to the west, was one of the recipient parks. It found itself with female elephants and young male elephants, but no adult males.

Sometime later, the rangers were confronted by a series of mysterious rhino mutilations and killings. Poachers were ruled out since horns hadn't been taken. The mystery continued; hidden cameras were installed in the bush. To the rangers' amazement, the young male elephants were found to be the culprits. Some were put down. Then some of the parks' personnel decided to try a novel idea, introduce adult male elephants as role models into the Pilanesberg herds. By now, the harnesses had been improved for such a move. With the introduction of a father figure, the killings ceased immediately.

They remained quiet for a moment. Anton continued to look at the young couple and their children, then out to sea. Annie held his hand.

Klara broke the silence. "The Germans had a program called Lebensborn to procreate the Aryan race, thought up by Himmler. Aryan fathers mated with Aryan mothers who gave birth to children raised in state homes according to Third Reich ideals. The fathers remained anonymous. The children grew up fatherless."

"Seems a common theme," Annie said.

"The things people do," Klara said.

"What's the solution?" Annie said.

"Good question. Hitler was a vegetarian, moved by animal suffering — look where that got us."

"Without a father, young girls drop out of school and fall pregnant at far higher rates," Annie said.

"And boys grow up aggressive and shoot up schools," Anton added. "And yet this country removes fathers from their children."

"You can't hate an entire nation, Anton."

"This country has killed more people than any other since the Second World War. Vietnam, Afghanistan, Iraq, Libya, Syria. Not to mention deaths by drones. Boys sitting behind computer screens killing like it's a game. This country vanquished a legitimate enemy and became one. It's arrogant and bloodthirsty with power; it believes power gives it moral legitimacy."

"When a nation's military is too strong, it is too easy to go from Goethe and Beethoven to Hitler; from Lincoln to Bush," Klara said.

"This country was once a beacon of hope; not anymore," Anton said.

"It was no more innocent then than today," said Klara.

"Do you hate this place, Anton, because of what it's done to you," Annie said. "You can't hate an entire nation."

"Mom does."

Klara sat quietly for a moment. "It is illogical, I know. I can't help myself. I hate the Germans. I always will. Not the young ones as much, perhaps, but I trust none of them. A nation that is capable of doing that once is capable of doing it again. That is what I believe."

"You like Katrin," Anton said.

"Yes, I do like Katrin," Klara said, pensively. "Levi said that the Germans committed those crimes precisely because they were German. But I have come to believe, in my more rational moments, that evil resides within humanity, but not within humans. I think that when you are born into a nation that has committed such crimes, you have to make extra effort to make sure such crimes are not repeated. And, I believe, Katrin has done exactly that."

"That's one German you like."

"And *you* love Annie," Klara said. Annie smiled, as did Anton, eventually. Klara continued, "That is one, too. So, I guess, neither one of us hates an *entire* nation."

"Surely not everything is great about South Africa?" Annie said. "Right?"

"It is imperfect, of course, but Annie, it tries. It is not obscenely wealthy like this country. Yet, it has built millions of low-cost housing for the poor since the ANC came to power. What has this country done for its poor? It treats its most vulnerable like noncitizens, like they have no value, no rights. This is the *richest country in the world*. Its currency has the audacity to proclaim, 'In God We Trust', and the poor haven't access to health care or decent education or a proper meal; schools in poor neighborhoods haven't the resources of those in wealthier neighborhoods. From day one, the odds are stacked against them. Yet, everybody goes to church. And on the way from church, this *Christian* nation walks over the homeless and destitute. Every day I see so many homeless, people living in cars, one in five children goes hungry in this country every night; a third of the nation or more is unemployed or underemployed, working two or three lousy jobs; or so many hours a week that no time is left to spend with one's children. But nobody talks about it. At least, in South Africa, we don't pretend that poverty doesn't exist or isn't a problem. This country is no less corrupt than South Africa and far less caring. That's what I can't stand."

"Anger is not always rational, but it is not always unproductive, either," Klara said. "I saw many survive on anger alone."

Suddenly, Anton said, "Mom — why did you not look for me? When I was born?"

It was Klara's turn to look pained. And it took several minutes to answer. "My dear boy. I looked for you, as long as I could. But I could not go to the authorities. Having you was an illegal act. And the Africans would not help, they are incredibly loyal to each other, to their detriment at times. Your dad was an important figure in the ANC — our meeting wasn't quite as random as I made it out to be. I was politically active, I had joined the Czechoslovak Communist Party, of course, as so many had done after the war, so it made sense. I went to a couple of conferences, we met… and… after you were born, I stayed as long as I could. You said yourself how much you traveled with him within Southern Africa, Lusaka, elsewhere, even went to England later, but I had no way to track you down. In those days. But know this, I thought about you every day of my life. Never a day went by that I did not think of you. Not a one."

"*Baba* always said you didn't want to stay with us. Is that true?"

Klara looked away. "In a way—"

"He said he asked you many times."

"I wanted to take you with me to the US."

"Take me from *Baba* and raise me alone?"

Klara started to weep. "Yes. I know, now, how terribly… what a terrible person I sound like…"

"You thought a son didn't need a father."

"I don't know what… yes, I suppose that's what I thought."

"Didn't you love him?"

"I loved him, Anton. Which is why I thought I had to go."

"That makes no sense."

"I know to you, today, it makes no sense. But back then—"

"Because he was black?"

"Yes, no, I don't know, Anton. I think I was just afraid to lose him, to lose you."

"You lost us both."

"Yes." Klara wiped a tear with the inside of her sleeve. "I lost you both." She paused, then looked into his eyes. "Can you ever forgive me?"

Anton didn't respond. They kept quiet for several minutes and sipped the drinks.

"Let's go home, my elephant," Annie said.

"Am I? Like the elephants?"

"A troubled one. But incapable of too much mischief and harm, my love."

"Your father did a good job," Klara said. "Perhaps I was unneeded. You grew up just fine without me."

"No, mom. I missed not having a mom, every day. I asked about you all the time. You know, he only spoke nicely about you. Who knows how I'd have grown up with two loving parents, two loving examples. But I did say to one or two women, I wish you could be my mother."

"Like Lucie."

"Yes."

They finished their beverages. The sun had set; the young family had packed the plastic beach toys and towels and left across the dunes. Anton helped both women by their hands, then he hugged his mother for several minutes. Finally, they, too, drove along the coast, the sea to their right, eventually turning towards Palm City from the east.

SIGNS

THERE are signs, always. People ask, were there signs? Did you not see it coming? Anton thought about this a lot lately. Of course, there were signs. There always are. But he ignored them. *That* was the difference. Something he tried to figure out about himself in the aftermath. Why had he not walked away when signs appeared? Was that the difference between those embraced and those exploited? Those that found good relationships and those that found failed ones. When others would have walked away, he remained. Where others wouldn't let themselves be screamed at or hit, he forgave. He excused it in all sorts of ways. *He* was the one at fault, if only *he* had acted differently. *He* was not doing enough in the relationship. He, he, he. Never she, she, she. Never even we, we, we.

He had learned a lot from his mother. It was a lack of self-preservation, she had said. He'd have not lasted long in the camps, in her opinion (he wasn't sure how he felt about that, but he didn't think it was a *compliment*). Still, he had to wonder, did the Germans not kill the gentlest and the softest? The tough ones, with luck, survived. Maybe all of life was such. The toughest ones climbed the corporate ladder, ending as CEOs; the gentle ones worked in social care or shelved books at the local library.

He had stayed with Carolien, as long as he had, because he had lacked a strong sense of self-preservation, his mother had repeated. Some in the camps, she explained, did anything to survive, *anything*; others, the *Musselmen*, gave in. But she told him, don't despair. It's not necessarily a bad thing.

Just when he thought she meant he'd be shelving books at the local library (still much better than stocking shelves at the local Publix), she mercifully continued, "It also means you are more willing to upend convention, to not follow banal rules and laws, to try new things; you do not have an inflated sense of self-importance or self-worth; for what you believe, you are willing to sacrifice. Pros and cons. Had more prisoners fought back before the transports, during the transports or even in the camps, far fewer people would have died," she had said.

The Germans did anything to avoid resistance. They lied, deceived, manipulated the victims to avoid revolt (she had told him this several times, on purpose, he assumed).

That was the first reason so many died in the camps, according to her, lack of self-preservation. The second reason, she said, was 'godforsaken hope', the downfall but also survival of humanity. Two similar inclinations, she had said. She reminded him — again — of the visit of Himmler. The Himmler Effect. Imagine experiencing the hell of the *lager — pane bože —* and knowing that Himmler is ultimately responsible, but still, despite all evidence, thinking, Himmler is here, he will see what is going on, he will set things right. Imagine. So, that is you, Anton, you are that mix of lack of self-preservation and eternal hope. Hope that suddenly Carolien will come one day and say, 'I am so sorry Anton, for everything I have done, I don't know what came over me, I love you, I will be different.'

'You are waiting, hoping. At which point do you discard hope? In your case, never. Of course, *she* is incapable of acting with decency and love. Any more than Himmler would have bellowed, what in God's name is going on here, start treating these prisoners with some respect! They are human beings, for God's sake! When I come back, I want them treated well, dressed well, fed well, housed well. This is an abomination.'

"But of course, he doesn't. He smiles. He looks benevolent, almost. He can be charming if he wants. He is thinking the exact opposite behind those round rimless glasses. He is thinking, *they still have it too good, the vermin, the Untermenschen, there are still too many, we are still too good to them. We are still too civilized, we Germans, it's in our psyche, it cannot be helped.*"

Anton listened to his mother, whom he had missed. He thought, *yes, she is right. She knows. It is who she is; it is who he is*. He doesn't think the lack of self-preservation can be changed. As far as the eternal, senseless hope, that might be something that perhaps can be. If it's not too late. Whether it should be changed, he cannot say.

THE FIRST SIGN

THEY had been together three weeks, if that, he and Carolien. She was living with roommates in Pretoria at the time, he alone in his house in Johannesburg. It was only natural that they spent time at his place. They explored the neighborhoods near Louis Botha Avenue, the decades-old Portuguese pubs, the Italian bakeries and restaurants, all the antiquated places he had come to love. And she professed to love them, too, all the things he had come to love, all the people he had come to love. Of course, before and after him, it would become apparent to him, in the company of others, she would profess to love none of what she had loved with him and only the things the new man loved. And he would wonder if he had ever known her at all. Later still, he wondered of this chameleon-like transformation; opinions altering to fit objectives.

Three weeks they had spent together. He sharing the life he had built, happy and willing to share it with her. Now, he supposed that she had studied every aspect of the way a farmer inspects a cow or a horse, weighing, sizing, inspecting the teeth. She professed to love each nuance, habit, interest ('we have so much in common'). In the end, wasn't this the beginning of perceived love, the supposed sharing, the commonality? he wondered. What was it about commonality that those in love found as if magic symbols within the whims? 'You like that band? Amazing, I love that band. You love this cuisine? I love this cuisine.' As if, somehow, sharing the same tastes or experiences could in any way explain the notion of love.

And then another thought, couldn't someone who loved nothing pretend to love anything? It wouldn't take much to say, 'I also love walks on the beach.' Or 'What a coincidence, I love that author.' Or 'I like that beer,' or, 'I am also a Catholic.' When none might be true. But of course, Anton thought, to one with no defined personality, how difficult was it to pretend a like or a love or even a dislike or a hate for something or someone as long as it suited? To ingratiate oneself to those with eternal hope would be easiest of all.

In the third week, the veneer cracked. Suddenly not everything was liked, loved or shared. Inexplicably, she had flown into a rage. What struck him was the omission of a reason — she was a student, they were under no pressure or duress of any kind, it was simply a matter of enjoying each moment — whatever the trigger, it could have been of no consequence because later she could not remember what had made her so irate — as it would be throughout their relationship. It was a frightening transformation — he remembered the expression in her eyes, the redness of her neck and face — at the time he thought the rage had been the anomaly, now he understood that the rage burned always within, like a large engine always stoked, a diabolical, eternal flame, and it was calm that was the anomaly.

'Good and evil,' Klara had said. 'Yin and yang. Call it what you will. The person that is capable of one small act of evil is capable of a million; the person that is incapable of one small act of evil, is incapable of multifold. Walk away, soon as you see one small act of evil, whether pointed at you or another. Put a stop to it or walk away.' Easier said than done, of course, he thought, when your self-preservation mechanism, for whatever reason, doesn't kick in.

He remembered watching Carolien, like a wild beast, uncomprehending. He told her calmly to pack her things, that he would drive her back to Pretoria. That he was unfamiliar with such behavior. His parents and his family had been good-natured; there had been disagreements, of course, but he had never seen rage or yelling such as she had just exhibited.

She packed up the few things that she had at his house. They drove along the N1 through Midrand northwards towards Pretoria. She cried the entire way, pleaded, begged, that she had no idea what came over her, that it had never happened before, that it would never happen again. As he listened, his heart was moved. He suspected that this was by no means the first time; he also supposed that were he to turn and drive back, she'd do this over and over (though he didn't know at the time that it would lead to violence).

This was the point where he diverged with people who ended up in successful relationships and marriages, he later concluded. Whereas others would have driven her to Pretoria, he hadn't. He asked her perfunctorily never to act like that again, she promised. He had ignored the warning sign, utterly aware; he had ignored self-preservation, utterly unaware. He'd entered a personal hell, to find out that a personal hell was rarely personal; that it often pulled in those one loved the most.

THE SECOND SIGN(S)

ANTON wanted to propose the old-fashioned way, so he and Carolien traveled to Holland to meet her parents. They stayed at their three-story home in the small, quaint town of Vianen, of which the parents were very proud. No particular effort had been made for their arrival, however. Their allotted bed was a lumpy, uncomfortable one, split down the middle, although the guest bedroom had a perfectly comfortable bed next door. The parents were formal but friendly enough. There were a few strange things that occurred that later lurked in Anton's mind, once he had been cast aside.

When the family ate, they never invited him to the table, and he had to get his own plate and cutlery and ask if he could join. The mother did the laundry, including Carolien's, but didn't do his — that, he had to do on his own (Anton didn't mind doing it, he was simply surprised that as a guest he was singled out to do his own, when she had done all the others' — her excuse had been that all men in Holland did their own washing). Anton went along with the story although Carolien's father did absolutely no housework at all, let alone the washing (a portly man with a thick grey beard and hair, he mostly sat in front of the TV all day, complaining how hard work was — he was in charge of a German industrial lubricant subsidiary, but what he actually did, Anton couldn't say). When Anton hung his clothes on the balcony rack, the young wife living next door couldn't stop laughing, saying she had never seen a man in Holland hanging clothes and that she hoped he would be a good influence on all the men in the neighborhood (Carolien's mother acted as if she heard none of this, although he could see her in the courtyard below).

Years later, when he had been used and abandoned (Annie: 'say it as it is, Anton, she didn't *leave* you, she *used and abandoned* you'), by Carolien; when she had taken Lucie and moved away, he went into a terrible depression. For the first time in his life, he couldn't sleep. He would wake up every two hours, sometimes on the hour. And all the signs would keep recurring, repeatedly, over and over (Klara, clasping her hands, finding him awake in the kitchen in the middle of the night, 'now we both have nightmares, *pane bože*'). All the signs he had seen and ignored. Like the time they visited Holland with Lucie as a five-year-old and Carolien's mother commented on how dark Lucie was, how she had hoped for lighter features. All signs that at the time he laughed off; but they hung on to him; and he wondered, late at night, would it have made any difference had he said or done anything. Was he not just like the prisoners who accepted beatings or went obediently and quietly to their deaths?

Carolien's parents and brothers used to visit twice a year, take advantage of his hospitality, but soon as he and Carolien arrived in the US, they ceased all contact with him. Had they known about her plan? Were they in on it? What other explanation could there be when they had visited them in South Africa just a month before their departure for the US and had acted ever so friendly, ever so pleased that they were moving to the US so Carolien could at long last get her green card and PhD?

But the sign that he remembered most vividly, late at night, had been their first dinner together at their house in Holland. He came downstairs to find them already eating. It was an uncomfortable moment since no place had been set for him. He had to apologetically ask if he could join. No effort was made. He rummaged, blindly, looking into cupboards, trying to find a plate and cutlery. They continued eating as if he wasn't there. Barely anything was left of the food, but he served himself and joined at the table. He felt ill at ease, they acted as if it was the most normal thing in the world, to let a guest, the man who came across the world to ask their daughter for her hand, dish himself slim leftovers.

During dinner he was suddenly exposed to the rage he had witnessed when he had driven Carolien to Pretoria. He sat across from her mother, Carolien across from her father. Out of the blue, Carolien and her father started to scream at each other, that same look in their eyes he had seen in hers, both red in the face, veins popping out on their necks. They continued to scream, in Dutch, lost in a blind fury, for more than fifteen minutes. He remembered looking at the mother, hoping she would interfere, but she ate as if she hadn't a care in the world. He had no idea how to react, a most bizarre of moments. Later, he asked Carolien what the argument had been about (his perfunctory Afrikaans had been only a little helpful), and she had for a moment acted as if she didn't know what argument he was speaking of, and then said, 'Nothing, nothing of relevance.' But the thing he would remember later, staring into the darkness of his bedroom, alone, unable to sleep, was the distinct impression of looking at her father and thinking that one day he would replace him, and it would be at him she would rage.

He remembered thinking those thoughts and yet... and yet, the next day he asked her parents for her hand. It was not met with the grandest of enthusiasm. The father said it should be OK. The mother said she only had one demand, he had to take care of Carolien. He said of course he would, he loved her. And she had replied curtly that she meant financially. He had to take care of her *financially*. 'And,' added the father. 'Don't expect us to contribute to the wedding, or anything else for that matter, we Dutch *don't* do that.'

Their approach to finances was made even clearer when the four went to dinner the next night and after dinner the father, who made several times more than Anton, said he would put in a third of the bill and Anton could pay the rest. Later, a friend would remark, 'just remember, the Scots were thrown out of Holland for being too generous.'

Now, as Anton lay awake, he couldn't help thinking, there were signs throughout, in this and many relationships, from day one, glaring red flags so big he was practically enwrapped; and yet, he marched along like an obedient, quiet boy.

THE THIRD SIGN (Out of an Endless Array of Signs)

IT was the third sign that would haunt him the most. The one where he truly didn't understand why he had not left Carolien when he could. When Lucie would later reprimand him for not doing so (crazy people do crazy things, reverberated in his mind). Although he still suspected that, besides the lack of self-preservation, besides the eternal hope, lurked something else — incomprehension. The absolute incomprehension for the unempathetic mind. It was inconceivable to him that a mother could hurt her own child. That she hurt him, Anton, somehow, that gradually became understandable. And after some time, it became acceptable. How, he didn't know, but it had. But Lucie — how she could allow Lucie to be hurt; that, he didn't understand. But, of course, that was before she, Carolien, did the hurting herself, when he would restrain her and she would mostly beat him instead, Lucie crying helplessly at the sight of her father being beaten by her mother.

At that time, Carolien had decided to fire the nanny, Maria, an old, wonderful and kind lady that Anton had employed and housed for years. As far as he was concerned, she was part of the family. Carolien hated her; Anton had no idea why, when she was kindness personified (perhaps that *was* why), and Lucie adored her. Carolien fired Maria and hired a different nanny, one of her own choosing, without consulting Anton. Within a month, Lucie, who until then spoke beautifully (she was three years old at the time), started stuttering and peeing and pooing everywhere, something she had never done. Anton, who was often away on business, didn't know what was going on. He kept asking Lucie why she was stuttering, she couldn't reply. Only when he asked, when did you start stuttering, did she say, when the new nanny hit me on the head. He was horrified. He approached Maria, their former nanny (who still lived on the premises behind the main house). She told him that she was not allowed in the house anymore but that she often heard Lucie screaming inside and that she had told Carolien about it and had assumed Carolien had told him. Carolien hadn't. He was furious.

He confronted Carolien, who had the most frightening look on her face that he had seen and would see until his mother passed away — a look of complete nonrecognition. Not a look of someone who knows they had done wrong and now feel caught in the act. It was the look of someone who indeed knew what was happening to her own daughter but was entirely indifferent to it. She couldn't care one way or another whether Lucie had been beaten. It had meant nothing to her. And now, or so he excused himself, he was stuck more than ever (he went to the authorities about the nanny — who in any case disappeared once fired — but it never occurred to him to go to the authorities about Carolien's abuse). In fact, when he had recounted the story of the nanny to Carolien's visiting parents, they acted as if they had heard nothing out of the ordinary, as if the story of their granddaughter's beatings was entirely commonplace. They had had the very same indifferent expressions. Then they had asked what he had planned for dinner.

SCHOOL

ANTON parked in front of the brick building and walked across the street. In front of the building was parked the ubiquitous police car. He walked up the stairs and into the school. Anton was nervous. He wasn't allowed to see Lucie except for the once a month supervised visit. But Marta Porter, the executive assistant, had called him saying she could not get a hold of Carolien (who was away at a conference); so, he rushed over.

Inside, he walked to the right and down the hallway and entered the office, also on the right. Marta flagged him down and motioned to come over. Mrs. Matthew, the senior clerical assistant, looked on disapprovingly. The police officer leaning against the wall observed, too, in her case with feigned indifference. As Marta took him into the adjoining room where Lucie sat across Mrs. Valdez, the school vice principal, he thought he could hear Mrs. Matthew going, "Tsk, tsk."

The vice principal was middle-aged, blonde and attractive, but presently stern. She was no happier to see Anton than she was to have Lucie in her office. What she was thinking, Anton wasn't sure, but if he had to hazard a guess, he'd say she thought about an apple not rolling far from a tree. If so, she got the analogy right; she had, however, mistaken the trees, one for the other; a common enough mistake.

"Lucie, would you like to tell your father why I had to call him?" said Mrs. Valdez; the way she pronounced 'father', Anton believed, was less than flattering. The rest of the sentence was said calmly, but with an underlying menace. *Why don't you, Lucie, criminal in the making, tell your criminal father what you've done.* Mrs. Valdez, it was apparent, would much rather have had the mother there, who in her opinion would know how to feel, what to do, how to react. How could this father possibly be of any use? But here they were, they had to call a parent and he was the only one available.

Anton looked at Lucie staring at her shoes. He had full confidence in her; he wanted to sweep her in his arms, protect and escape with her, from Mrs. Valdez, from Carolien, from the courts, the school, city, country. Once again, he became aware that he was in his very own prison, surrounded by barbed wire, an electric fence, guards, dogs, machine guns, towers. (What, then, was the role of Mrs. Valdez in this personal scenario?). He wanted to envelop Lucie in love and protection — no less than had any parent upon entering the camp gates, the gas vans, the gas chambers — and, it seemed, no more effectively.

He looked at the clock; had very little time now and hoped he wouldn't get in trouble with the law for coming here, knowing Carolien would report him to her lawyer and her lawyer to the judge.

Lucie kept looking at her shoes.

Mrs. Valdez turned to Anton. "We had a situation where Lucie wasn't being respectful, isn't that right, Lucie? Lucie? And instead of being respectful and using words, she used her hands. She will lose her recess privilege and sit in the room while the other children play. She will also have to apologize to the little boy. And there will be expectations going forward to use words, not her hands."

Mrs. Valdez spoke as if to Lucie, but over and beyond as if Lucie had no comprehension.

Once the vice principal stated her case, there was some discussion about whether Anton would be allowed to take Lucie to her mother's house. In the end, with the mother and her new boyfriend unreachable, they didn't feel they had much choice. Mrs. Valdez expressed conviction that Lucie be firmly and properly reprimanded at home and her behavior not repeated. Anton pleaded obsequiously and, he felt, shamefully, to the hands of authority on behalf of his daughter.

They exited the office to the stern looks of Mrs. Matthew and the police officer and walked out the school and down the brick stairs.

Anton and Lucie drove to Chuck's house, the last place either wanted to go. Lucie pleaded with him to drive her to Klara's house, his house; he knew if he did, he'd be in even bigger trouble. In what sort of country did a loving father have to drive his daughter to the house of a psychopathic mother's boyfriend, he wondered? In this one. Love and care and paternity be damned. Anton was sickened, but more than that, he was tired, browbeaten. He was afraid to go to Chuck's house, afraid he might say or do something untoward, should either he or Carolien in the meantime return. He had a feeling he should call Annie, but he didn't want to bother her at work; besides, he had a feeling she'd be panicked by the situation. Or that she herself might do something rash. He was starting to feel she was a person of action far more than he could ever be.

As he pulled up to the house, he had the distinct feeling he was delivering Lucie to *her* very own little prison, the way his mother had helped deliver her namesake.

"What happened at school? Do you feel like talking about it? It's OK if you don't." Lucie looked at him with imploring hazel-green eyes. "You know I believe in you. I am sure you had good reason."

Through tears she explained that she had been quietly playing a game with her friend, Jaden, when another boy came over and called Jaden fat. Jaden was hurt, she said. But Jaden was really nice, too, like you, *Baba*, so she had to defend him, she said. She tried to sort it with words, as they had been taught. She told the teacher, but the teacher told her to sit down and did nothing and the boy said, 'See, I can do anything I want.' And he called her friend fat again, so Lucie hit him.

"I tried to use words, *Baba*, I did," she said. "But when I was told to sit down, I didn't know what else to do when the teacher wouldn't help, so I hit him. You told me, *Baba*, if I ever see anyone hurting anybody, I had to protect them. I tried with words, *Baba*, but when that didn't work, ooh, *Baba*, I am like her, aren't I?" She started crying and Anton held her tight.

"You mean like Carolien," he said, and she nodded. And he said, "No, you are nothing like her, I am so proud of you for standing up for your friend."

What he didn't say was how unlike him and his mother she was, too, and how like a certain person he loved he thought she might be and how that really wasn't such a bad thing. On the contrary, he was incredibly proud; and he was incredibly relieved.

Finally, he watched Lucie walk away, up the pathway to the large house, the backpack heavy on her frail frame. At the door she turned and waved for him to go, chin quivering, tears streaming down their faces. He'd rarely experienced the pain he now felt of having to watch his daughter walk away, into an uncertain and dangerous environment, and he was unable to stop it. If only he were more like her, he thought.

LUCIE

ANTON and Klara weren't the only ones suffering from sleeplessness. Lucie lay in bed, staring into darkness, tears pouring down her cheeks. She could not understand, why her, what had happened to her, what had she done? She didn't realize that in this, too, she was well within the full circle of family history.

All she knew was that two years ago, she was happy in South Africa. She had *Baba* and she had Maria, who loved her — until Mama replaced Maria with someone who beat her. She couldn't explain to *Baba* at the time what was wrong, and Mama didn't seem to care. She had just learned to talk, and when that person hit her, she started stuttering, the words wouldn't come. But, finally, she made herself understood to *Baba* and he had put a stop to it. She was frightened of Mama, too, though not like the other woman, that was different; but she didn't fear *Baba*, who often tried to protect her from Mama, but she loved her mother all the same. And she believed that if she were only a better child, kinder, well behaved, that her Mama wouldn't hit her anymore, that it was her fault, just like Mama said. But try as she might, it just seemed like she could never be good enough. Sometimes she was hit so hard that her head snapped all the way back and her neck hurt. If she could be a good girl, then none of this would have happened, she was sure of that.

Her mother also beat her father, her *Baba,* but never in front of other people, never when they were out, only at home. Aside from that, she loved South Africa. It was sunny every day, she remembered, and the food was delicious, all the fruits and vegetables the vendors sold on the street corners, and all the beautiful artwork the street vendors used to make (she used to watch them with *Baba*, fascinated), and her *Baba*, he was happy there. Except when he was hit, too. Lucie remembered crying when that happened, and the first time she started crying she got smacked so hard that from then she went to her room and closed her door, but she could still hear the sound and him trying to calm *Mama* and it was terrible and she would cup her ears, but it only helped a little.

At least in South Africa, her grandfather, *Umkhulu*, was there, too, and he was very nice, he always brought presents and she loved him so much and they had a big family, aunts and uncles and cousins, she used to visit them in the countryside, it was lovely, and of course there was Maria who took care of her until her *Mama* — she wasn't supposed to use the Zulu words any more, they were in America now, and when she did, her mother got angry and slapped her. But *Baba* didn't mind Zulu words, and neither did her grandmother, her *Gogo*, she was really nice. When mommy made Maria leave, there was the other woman... but she didn't like to think about her, the other woman, she had also found her a bad girl and also had to hit her like her mommy until her *Baba* sent her away. If only she could be a good girl, then none of this would have happened, but she began to understand some words, like mommy going crazy, being *the blázen*, so angry with them, and how, really, she always would. And she didn't understand why she had to lose everything, why they had moved here. She didn't like this place. Her *Baba* also didn't. Only her mommy loved it here. Meanwhile, she had lost everything, why did they have to come here? When they first came it was OK, it was hard, she missed everything and everyone so much, but at least she met her *Gogo*, and that was wonderful, she didn't know she had that *Gogo*, even *Baba* didn't know he had a *Mama*, it was amazing, and they started visiting her and it was OK here, they used to go to the beach and everything seemed nice and mommy acted nice around *Gogo*, she never hit her in front of *Gogo*, she was calmer, but of course all that changed when they moved here. But back then it was nice, she loved being with *Gogo*, *Gogo* was so nice and she listened and told her stories and they loved being together, they'd go for walks and to the beach and to the parks, too, there were a lot of parks here, not with any African animals, though, not like on a safari, and the library, that was nicer than back home, the children's section, but that was about it, everything else was nicer back home, here it rained a lot and everything.

She really should be going to sleep, it was late, but she could hear mommy and Chuck, he was kind of old, they went on his boat and everything and they went to church here now, too, which was boring, but, he was not so nice sometimes, the way he looked at her or touched her, she didn't like it, mommy always said she had to hug him, but she really didn't like him hugging her. But mommy liked him, she didn't know why, she left *Baba* to be with him and they moved in with him, to this new town with a university because mommy said she had to study here.

She really should be sleeping now, it was late and there was school tomorrow, but she didn't like school so much anymore. She used to like school a lot, back home in South Africa, all the kids were really nice, and the teacher, but then here, at *Gogo's*, she also kind of liked that school, but then mommy brought them here and she said they didn't need *Baba* anymore and when she cried, she sometimes hit her because she cried, and she tried not to cry. And when mommy went to university and she came home from school the man was here, Chuck, and he always wanted to watch TV and put his arm around her and she really didn't like it, but mommy said it was OK, so she just sat there. Mommy said he was a really nice man, that he let them stay with him for free in his big house and let mommy drive his car.

She could hear them sometimes making noises in his bedroom like the sounds she sometimes heard mommy making with *Baba* before, but back then, it didn't bother her, she didn't know why, but these sounds, they just made her sad. So she was all alone now, she had lost everyone, her family back in South Africa and Maria and then her *Baba* here and her *Gogo*, and now it was just her and her mom and Chuck and she was sad all the time, and she cried all the time, but she didn't show it to mommy or else she would slap her, but sometimes she cried at school, too, and the teacher just said she was homesick, that it was normal and that it would be OK, but she didn't think so, she didn't think it would be OK, because now she saw her *Baba* once a month and there was always some person there, they were never alone.

But she liked Annie, she came with *Baba* sometimes, she was a police officer but not like the bad ones who took *Baba* away. Annie took her out to eat and also *Gogo* and *Baba*, and now she came with *Baba* to visit. And she thought that Annie liked *Baba* and *Baba* liked her and Annie was always really nice to her and really nice to him and Annie said she really liked *Gogo*. But she still sometimes wanted her mommy and *Baba* to be together even if mommy hit him and her, but it was confusing sometimes,

Annie was so nice. She also told *Gogo* when she came to visit *Baba* once that she wished Annie could be her *Mama*, too. She was not scared of Annie.

It was hard. She wanted her parents together, and *Gogo*, but then mommy put her in a car one day and said they were leaving *Baba* and *Gogo* and she wouldn't even let her take her toys, the toys that *Baba* and *Gogo* got her, or her stuffed animals, only this one, this little dog that mommy bought her later, but she liked the little dog and she held him when she cried at night, he kept her company when she was sad, and mommy said they couldn't get a real dog because Chuck didn't like pets and it was his house and they were lucky to be living there, mommy said. But it wasn't mommy's fault, mommy said, that they were not together and that they had to leave, it was someone called Judge Pullard, what a funny name for someone so mean—what sort of name was Judge, anyway?--she did this, Lucie didn't know why, but she wasn't very nice, breaking up families.

And now, she was just so tired, but she couldn't sleep again and she was crying again like she always did now, and tomorrow she had school, but she didn't want to go, she didn't like anybody there and her grades were bad now, she didn't study anymore and mommy didn't help her with homework the way *Baba* used to, *Mama* had no time because she had to study all the time, *Mama's* stuff was really important she said, not like hers, and *Baba* wasn't allowed to come to school to have lunch with her anymore, so nobody came, and Chuck said she shouldn't bother mommy when she was studying, but he also wouldn't help with her homework because he was always watching TV, football and golf and stuff, always sports and stuff.

The kids didn't like her at this school, they said she was a crybaby, and she was stupid, which was probably true now, she never used to be, but now her grades were bad, she couldn't remember anything, and nothing made sense when the teacher talked, she didn't understand it.

How she missed her *Umkhulu*, and Maria and her cousins, especially Hlengiwe, she was always so much fun, and she missed her *Baba* and *Gogo*. They were not far away, but she wasn't allowed to see them anymore, not since that night when the policeman came and mommy said *Baba* had been hitting her, which wasn't true, mommy had been hitting him, but she, Lucie, was too scared to say anything, and *Gogo* was crying and she thought *Gogo* was too scared to say anything too, and they took him away, and *Baba* was crying, looking at her and she was crying, and finally she whimpered,

"Please, he didn't do anything, please don't take him." But then she saw how mommy was looking at her and she got scared, so she just cried and said nothing. And since then, she hardly ever saw him and mommy said it was because he didn't care about her very much, but she didn't think it was true, and *Baba* gave her a cell phone, but it got lost, she left it on her bed when she went to school but when she came back it was gone, so he couldn't call her and she couldn't call him, mommy said she couldn't use her phone, so she was all alone now, all the time, with no one, just mommy and Chuck.

Sometimes, they went on his boat, that was nice, but mommy and he drank a lot of beer and smoked, for her it wasn't so much fun, she was by herself, mostly, and mommy forgot to put suntan lotion on her, and she got really burned and it hurt, and once, she saw *Baba* and Annie on a boat and they looked so sad, they were throwing something in the water, she didn't know what. And they just looked at her and she started crying and calling for *Baba*, she just wanted to be with him and with Annie, but mommy came over and grabbed her mouth really hard and she couldn't yell anymore, and mommy got really mad again and later, when Chuck was sleeping, she hit her.

She really did have to be a good girl and maybe all these bad things wouldn't happen anymore and maybe she could see *Baba* more and Annie, she didn't know. But she missed *Gogo* so much, she had been so kind to her, she never yelled, was never angry, was always so patient and kind.

Sometimes Chuck teased mommy that she had married a black man, but she, Lucie, was also black, so… and he thought that was really funny, he laughed about it and mommy laughed, too, but she just looked at them, now she was the only black person, and she just wanted her *Baba*, and she was sad because she had no one, just this little stuffed dog she called Hlengiwe after her cousin, mommy wasn't happy about that, she wanted her to forget about South Africa, she didn't know why. Mommy said they were really happy here, but she wasn't really happy here. And she really had to sleep now, because it was really late and tomorrow she would be really tired in school again and she might fall asleep, and the other kids would laugh at her and make jokes.

She really didn't like it here, she just wanted to go home. She just wanted to go home. She just wished… *Baba* was here now… she wished he was holding her like he used to when she went to sleep and read her a story and make her warm milk with honey, he always made her warm milk with honey, she wished he was here… she wished she could go home… and she was feeling a little tired now…a little tired… and she had to go go…sleep… or mommy would would would… really angry again… her fault, she was bad…bad…goodnight, Hlengiwe… she was the only only one she had now… aanobody else… bad… goodnight… goodn…

KLARA

NOT far from a sleepless Lucie was a sleepless Klara. She turned and thrashed and thought of Anton and Carolien and Lucie and all that had transpired since they had moved to the US and she had to admit, she no more understood it than she had her experiences in the *lager*. In fact, it was the first time since that she had given the *lager* as much thought. She had been plagued with several recurring nightmares since the war, but she had learned, more or less, to keep them in check. When the sleeplessness got worse, she would resort to sleeping pills. She didn't like to, but sometimes there was no other way. She knew how debilitating lack of sleep could be. In the *lager*, she knew from women performing hard labor that they were so exhausted that falling asleep normally wasn't a problem. She knew that for them, the nightmares started upon liberation. But, of course, for her, sleeplessness had already been a problem in the brothel. At first, the SS-Schutzhaflagerführer was rather perfunctory with her. She was surprised that he, too, with his power, was smitten by her youth and beauty. She was old enough to know what sort of power she held over men just by walking down the street. Men of all ages had gazed at her with lust in the streets of Prague. Even her father's friends, many married and honorable, would make passes or whisper suggestions when they thought her father was not listening. Many of them at first, even ones much older, were intimidated by her beauty, which she found charming, even exhilarating at times; that something she had been born with and had no control over could make men do practically anything, shower her with expensive presents, offer to take her on exotic holidays, give her anything she wanted, many offering to abandon wives and children if only she would acquiesce to their overtures. Many were even unconcerned about unrequited love; it was enough that they loved or thought they loved or lusted after her; many said she shouldn't worry, that love would come with time.

Then, in the camp, a young Italian boy would come — he had to be careful — outside her window, Alberto, and he used to bring her news from the front, good and bad, but also, he used to make up stories, just to see her smile, so she wouldn't be so sad, and once he brought her a flower, a red poppy, she learned later that he traded his bread for it, poor boy, went hungry to give it to her — who knew where he got it — and got a beating for it; she remembered it was springtime, and that flower meant more than all the gold and diamonds *he* could ever bring — and she used to give Alberto a bit of salami, he was so thin, from *him*, until one day Alberto was caught and she didn't know if he was killed or transferred, only to find after the war that he had survived and had moved back to Turin. *He* had flown into a rage that she had given Alberto food, the food that he had brought her. But he didn't strike her this time like she thought he would. When he calmed, he simply said, 'I am sorry. You disappointed me.' Afterwards, he still brought delicacies, but not as often, and portions not as plentiful.

The SS-Schutzhaflagerführer in his white jacket and always with his riding crop, emulating his kommandant, which scared her at first, hadn't been very different from other men. Despite his power of life and death, he was intimidated by her beauty. In the beginning, he used to come into the room and sit quietly without saying much, looking at her shyly, while she read or ate, aware of his glances. He would ask if there was anything she needed and what he could do to make her more comfortable. He always brought a present, diamond jewelry, some truly magnificent, and always a delicacy, bottle of wine, Champagne, caviar even, salami, cheese, the best foods and drink, and left it for her. Only much later did she find from whence all came — the arriving transports; and only then did she realize that the goods depended on the nationality of transports. If he said that next week he'd have salami, a transport of Hungarians was expected, and so forth. She had assumed that a man of his position could purchase whatever he wanted, but of course there was no need, not when treasures were brought on transports every day for free.

Once she found out, she forbids him to bring any more prisoner goods and he had hit her (regarding jewelry, though, he obeyed; the delicacies continued, however, first plentiful and then, after her *betrayal*, fewer and in smaller quantities). He had found this naïve and foolish but charming and berated her, saying if she didn't take it, then someone else would steal it, the bastard Jewish prisoners (he often spoke as if she wasn't Jewish), the thieving Kapos, even members of the SS. He spoke disdainfully of all, all thieving, all untrustworthy. He explained that what he brought her was her safeguard in case anything happened to him (he made it seem like his position was as dangerous as any on the eastern front). That once the war was over, she would be a very wealthy woman and that, ultimately, he would leave his wife for her.

Still, he had been relieved when she had asked about the gassings. Because by then their relationship had taken a strange turn. Besides sex, she had become his confidante. He often complained how he had no one to speak to, how, when he had at last told his wife about the gassings, their intimate life took a turn for the worse, how they often now slept in separate beds. He complained miserably how little his wife understood him, how he only did everything for the Fatherland, and yes, for his wife, for his family, how else did his wife think she got to live in luxury. He called his wife a hypocrite. But Klara — it was strange — despite the circumstances, he felt she understood, the stress he was under, the difficulty of his work. He felt that she understood him as no woman ever had (not that he had been with very many — in fact, only four, excluding his wife and two of the *real* prostitutes). That, according to him, Klara didn't seem to judge, but accepted him as he was, with all his goodness (Klara kept a straight face), but also flaws. With her, he didn't have to pretend. And often he used to joke with her, make fun of his rotund wife, of his children (though not the middle son, his favorite). Here, with her, in her room, was the only place, he told her, where he could be himself.

And so, he used to come and tell her of his days, and she listened, as indifferently as possible, trying to show no affectation, but after he had left, often she had to clutch her stomach and vomit; but mentally she was determined to commit everything to memory so if and when the day came and he was tried, she would be the most useful witness and send him to the gallows. She also knew, of course, the danger she was in. She was the one witness he could not afford free if he had even the smallest doubt he'd ever be caught or that she would use the knowledge against him.

In the end, before the camp was liberated, he had come to say goodbye. He was tearful and made no effort to hurt or kill her. He was entirely convinced of his plan to escape, said he had been planning and putting it in place since Stalingrad, but that he would send for her one day, when it was safe to do so. He was completely unafraid, she noticed, that she would ever tell anyone of the atrocities he had partaken in and told her about. Either that was because he had deluded himself that she cared for him; or he was certain that his escape was foolproof; or he believed that what he had committed were not atrocities.

She knew in any event that he was a multi-millionaire many times from the pilfered prisoner wealth. At his goodbye, she had managed to squeeze a tear, sufficient enough for him of her feelings, and then to throw up once he departed at the years of humiliation and abuse and duplicity.

For months on an almost daily basis, he had been coming to her room, even on days when nothing sexual had occurred (his sexual prowess, he admitted, was not what it had once been), right after his work ended and told her, as any husband to any wife, of his day, often in great detail and gruesomeness, sometimes laughing, often complaining about the complexities of the job, never, however, remorseful. The only empathy he ever showed was for fellow members of the SS, some of whom, at least initially, had trouble killing women and children. He was nearly distraught when describing the nervous breakdown of an SS subordinate who had to be sent home, he had become useless, because some random little girl had reminded him of his daughter.

Now, the night was quiet except for the rustling of the breeze through the trees outside. The house was empty, which she found disturbing. Anton was here, but he had become a *Musselman*. He couldn't eat, he couldn't sleep. He had the vacant expression she was all too familiar with, not of those of indifference and cruelty; but of those who had given up on life. By moving here, to her, he had lost everything — his country, his home, his house, his friends, his family (he still didn't realize he had not had a family — not with a wife like that), and of course the person most precious to him — Lucie. Klara's only hope of late was the lovely police officer, Annie, who had, miraculously, she thought, in his current condition, started coming over more frequently and who also took a genuine liking to her, Klara, and with whom they now spent more and more time, individually and together.

She had seen a flicker of hope in Anton's eyes. She knew there was only one thing that could save a *Musselman* — she had seen it in the *lager*. She also knew that she herself could not save him. But Annie — well, that was a different story. Annie could. Her love could. And in turn his love for her, was it developing or were it to develop. Annie had also gotten to know Lucie a little and they took a real liking to each other. It was Annie's gentleness and calmness and kindness that naturally attracted people to her, especially an abused child like Lucie.

Klara also alone understood and felt ashamed about something else — why Anton had never left Carolien, no matter how abominable she had been. Having lost Klara, his mother, as a baby, he was determined that Lucie would not lose Carolien, even if it meant his demise. Klara was certain that he did not understand this himself. That he was playing out the scenario unawares, that he couldn't understand why he had not left Carolien before, when it was safe to do so without losing Lucie, back in South Africa, before they had moved here and his and Lucie's lives came apart (and of course hers).

Klara wondered why suddenly she had opened up to Annie so completely, and then to Anton, to a lesser extent. Something had triggered the avalanche — Annie said it was the accident, but Klara thought it was everything combined, that the accident may have been the detonator, but that the explosion of emotions had been building a long time, and that recent events had only reminded her of her past. It was as if now that the dam had finally broken, every word had to emerge until no words remained.

Klara was determined that she would not die with any recollections unshared. She also felt that it was unfair of her to do so, but they assured her that they didn't mind (what else could they say) and besides, she couldn't help herself. For hours, she would sit with Annie or Anton and go on and on, much of it she thought had been forgotten, suddenly coming to the surface as if it had happened yesterday.

Often her stories brought herself to tears, stories that she thought she viewed with a blunted indifference. She even told some stories to Lucie, guiltily, but she wanted Lucie to at least have some understanding of what had happened to her, one of the last remaining witnesses, before she passed away.

Klara felt reasonably healthy, considering, and had every inclination to live for another several years, but at her age, you never knew, all too often old folks she'd run into at the store or in the neighborhood or at the pool would suddenly disappear and she'd never see them again, but she could be pretty sure their end had come. And perhaps that too was a reminder of the *lager*, the disappearance of people from one day to next. But more than anything, she knew that the trigger had been the similarities of fate that she felt she shared with Anton and his family — Carolien's indifferent coldness and cruelty reminded her of the SS and Kapo guards; Carolien's lies and disingenuousness, reminiscent of Nazi behavior; Anton falling apart and in front of her eyes becoming a lifeless *Musselman*; the violence that Carolien exhibited once she was sure of all her powers and plan; Lucie losing her father as she, Klara, had lost her family; Anton losing Lucie as she, Klara, had lost her babies in the camp; Anton losing everything of importance to him and finding himself alone and helpless as Klara had once lost everything of importance to her and found herself alone and helpless; the police and the courts as callous as any fascist police and courts she had witnessed; the injustice of laws; Annie and her father's abuse at the hands of her mother. The similarities were endless. And it may have been the confluence, some aspects perhaps unconscious, that broke the dam and made her talk as she never had; a necessity she awoke and fell sleep with.

So now she lay in bed, thinking, pondering. She listened to see if Anton, who slept in the bedroom across the house, made any noise; he didn't. She was certain that he was not sleeping any more than she and was ruing with urgency and desperation the day he had set foot on this continent. The entire world dreamed of coming here; but how many found purgatory instead of nirvana at the end of the trip? The irony hadn't escaped her.

Since she couldn't sleep, she decided to get up and warm a glass of milk in the microwave. She tried to be as quiet as possible, walking through the living room into the small kitchen to the right. She heated the milk and sat down at the kitchen table in the dark. She wondered about empathy, something that had troubled her since the war — why some people had it, but not others. And was a person capable of feeling something they had not experienced? Was there any way to understand what it felt like to be abandoned by a lover or be diagnosed with cancer unless one experienced the exact condition and emotion? It was one reason why she until recently had not been able to speak to anyone about her experiences during the war. She felt that trying to explain them to another was like sharing pain with a stone. And yet, because of their own experiences, Anton and Annie and even Lucie understood and empathized. But could they feel what she felt?

Could she feel what they felt? Perhaps empathy had limitations. Still, she thought, because a person could not feel another's feelings, did people not assume that everyone's feelings were the same?

Anton turned on the lights and pulled up a chair. She hadn't heard him approach and got startled. For a moment, he reminded her of Alberto. He looked haggard, dark marks under his eyes. She knew he had not slept well for months. Still, his expression was not as dead as before, she remarked. Annie was doing her magic and inwardly Klara smiled and felt immense gratitude. Not that Annie spent any time with them out of anything but love. Still, Annie coming into their lives was a miracle if there was such a thing.

"Mom — what are you doing in the dark."

"Did I wake you?"

"No — I couldn't sleep."

"Want a sleeping pill?"

"No, Mom, I don't want to become addicted to those things."

"Think of it as temporary. Don't let yourself become too run down. Body needs sleep."

"Annie invited me to Kentucky for a weekend. To meet her aunt and uncle."

Klara couldn't help grinning. Anton smiled in return. She realized he had not smiled for a long time.

"So, she wants to show you her home," Klara said. "Sounds serious." They both continued to grin. "Can I give you some advice?"

"What?"

"Sometimes the quickest way over a woman is to get under another one."

"Mom, seriously?"

"Just trying to be helpful."

"What the heck were you doing in the dark anyway?"

"Thinking."

"About?"

"*Really* want to know?"

"Is this going to be a long story?"

"It might be."

"In that case let me grab a beer. Want one?"

"Sure, it'll go well with my milk."

He got up and took a beer from the fridge. He twisted off the bottle cap and sat down.

"I was thinking that we assume that everybody feels things the same way, hate, love, pain, rage, but how do we know that it feels the same to all people? What if *that* is the problem? We think that someone lacks empathy, but what if their version of empathy is simply inferior to another's?"

"That's what you were thinking about in the dark."

"I warned you."

He took a long swig of the beer and swirled it around his mouth before swallowing. "I needed that," he said. So, all right, that doesn't sound entirely implausible. But, it is possible, even probable, that some people experience no empathy at all."

"Of course, but look at the SS, the Kapos — they had empathy when it came to themselves, their own families, their own children."

"Goebbels killed his own children, all six of them," Anton said. "You told me so."

"Actually, it was his wife, the mother, Magda, she killed them. They say the eldest child was found with bruises on her face. They suspect that Magda had to force the cyanide in her mouth."

"Jesus."

They went quiet for a moment and Klara wondered whether she should have mentioned that it had been a Magda. Her words now hung in the air like a foul stench. Wordlessly, she worried about Lucie, even more than before. She felt that if Lucie were to remain with Carolien long-term, something horrible was going to happen.

"Carolien's mother's name is Magda," Anton said.

Klara remained quiet for a moment. Then she said, "I remember." She paused. "Anton—"

"Yes?"

"I want you to promise me something." Anton waited. "If anything should happen to me—"

"Mom — stop — what should happen to you."

"Listen. If anything should happen to me. I want you to know it was not by my own hands, do you understand? I wouldn't do that. I fear that where the Germans failed, your Germanic wife will succeed."

"Mom, stop." They drank their respective drinks in silence.

"Should I rather continue with my philosophical ruminations?"

"If it's cheerier than your last comment."

"Fine. So — I always wondered why some people returned from the camps or the war scarred forever, and others seemed to fall back into their previous lives, as if nothing happened."

"What if everybody was affected terribly."

"I don't know. Today we call it PTSD, 'shell shock' in the First World War. When psychiatrists started to see symptoms after the Second World War, they called it 'concentration camp syndrome'. The precursor to PTSD—"

"Annie sees a lot of PTSD at work."

"—She told me. You could tell, some people had it really badly, almost incapacitated, could never hold down a proper job again, and others thrived. Here's the thing, we regret that we cannot *read* the minds of others. But wouldn't the world be a better place if we could feel what others feel?"

"That's what you were thinking at four a.m. And here I was thinking, why do I wake up every day at exactly four a.m. What the heck is that about?"

"Imagine if we could feel what others feel. No more pain, no more hurt, no more wars, no more killings. All gone. Just like that. And only things left, compassion and understanding."

"Nirvana, mother," Anton said. "Unless people took pleasure in the pain of others."

"I hadn't thought about that. You know — that man…"

"Who?"

"The SS-Schutzhaflagerführer. He used to tell me everything. Every day, like I was his… like I was his wife, like it would have no effect on me. All the 'problems' he had been facing, he said it was so stressful, they couldn't figure out how to dispose of the prisoners quickly enough. He wanted to impress Himmler; they all did. So he told me how one of his subordinates had tried Zyklon B on a bunch of Russian prisoners of war and how effective it was, and how before that they had to use car exhaust and how slow and impractical that was and how shooting the women and children only demoralized his troops… and he told me, *svině*, that the corpses looked peaceful, how very humane it all was—" She turned red in the face "—Why didn't I kill him, Anton—"

"Mom."

"—That… *kurva*. You know what else he used to do? On purpose, he would let a prisoner join the *Sonderkommando* — you know, the Jewish prisoners made to strip and rob and carry out corpses from the chambers and burn them — and make sure that his wife or children would be gassed, and the prisoner would find them among the bodies and the SS-Schutzhaflagerführer used to watch them. Anton — he used to study their reactions... tell me like it was some sort of an experiment involving mice..." She started to sob, and Anton held her. After a while she collected herself. "You know what terrifies me, Anton. I thought, I really believed, that I'd be able to recognize one of these people, capable of such things, if I saw one again, but I didn't, did I? Once again, I was completely fooled. She fooled me, Anton. Me. Who had seen countless such people... like her... She fooled me, completely, that wife of yours. Even when I saw her smack Lucie once or twice, she apologized, saying she didn't know what came over her, I was shocked, I was frozen, again, I did nothing, it was Lucie, later, who told me it happened regularly, but Lucie — *pane bože* — she was defending her mom, too, telling me that it was her fault, it broke my heart and the way she treated you, in my house! And still, I didn't think right away that she was like... him... like them... you see, again, I so badly wanted to believe, I didn't want to think that here was one again, in my house, in our house—"

"It's my fault, mother, I let her into your house. She had already been violent for years. In South Africa. I had... I had done nothing... it became 'normal' — part of life..."

"I am one of the few to understand that Anton. You... are like everybody else. Nobody wants to believe the worst. Even if they are savagely beaten. Until the last moment, everybody thinks, surely these really are showers, surely they would not kill women and children, surely... you know, sometimes I think of those Pearl Harbor photographs, you see the civilians looking at the planes bombing the ships and flying at them with machine guns. And the people just stand there. The Shock Equation — just like the lecture I see in my dream. Terror takes time to seep in, difficult to comprehend to those who don't think like that, impossible maybe. And those without empathy, it is said, are one percent of the population. That's seventy-five million people in the world. *Seventy-five million.* Ironically, a little less than the population of today's Germany. An entire country. And here I am, me, trying to excuse such people, saying surely they feel *something*, surely, just not what we feel. You see, even me. After everything I've been through. They feel nothing. Nothing. And that gives them great power over the rest of us. The rest of us see terror and we freeze, our minds go numb, we don't comprehend. And only later, sometimes much later, do we understand what happened, but we don't really, we keep asking ourselves 'why' for the rest of our lives. We can't sleep, we drink milk and beer at four a.m."

"Five, now."

"Five a.m. And they sleep comfortably in their beds, as if nothing happened at all. And to them, nothing has. I know that after the war, they moved up in German society, the highest ranks even, as if nothing happened. The best days of their lives, that's what they were to them. The best days of their lives. How? How is that possible? How come so few were ever punished? I will never understand it, Anton. Never. Any more than I understand Carolien."

"Mom. Listen, I am sorry I brought her into your house. That's my fault. I'm sorry for everything. But I'm not sorry we got to spend this time together and I'm not sorry Lucie got to know you."

"Had you never moved here—"

"But we did. So, I — we — have to live with the consequences. Now, should we go to sleep?"

"At five a.m. Shouldn't we rather wait for the sunrise?"

"Let's go on the porch then."

They picked up their drinks and went outside through the glass sliding door. They sat on the canvas fold-out chairs, putting their drinks in the cup holders. The air was crisp but not chilly. A wild turkey mother and her three young ones paraded nearby on the way to the canal. Klara and Anton turned to the east and waited for the sun to rise. When it did, both were asleep.

KLARA AND ALBERTO

THEY sat at a café on the Via Antonio Bertola in Turin, Alberto's hometown. Alberto had suggested the café two blocks from his apartment. Sitting at a table by the windows, it didn't have much of a view, but Klara thought maybe that's why he chose it. In front were tram tracks, and across the street a five-story building. In fact, she thought that she could be in any number of Czech towns. On the triangular building across the street and to the right was a sign that read, 'Via Antonio Bertola, Ingegnere Militare', and to the right of that was what looked like a women's clothing boutique. To the left of the café when they had entered was a store that advertised lotions, perfumes and creams.

She looked at Alberto closely, touched his hand on the table, and smiled. Although he didn't take his hand away, he didn't smile in return. It was the first time she had seen him since his disappearance in the camp. At liberation, she had searched for him, had found out he had survived, miraculously, but he had disappeared before she could find him.

Now, six years later, he was twenty-one, three years her junior, but looked no less than forty, she thought, eyes burrowed deep in dark sockets, hair speckled with gray, skin prematurely aged. The light-blue eyes that she had loved in the camp, that she had thought had reflected a blue she'd only seen in southern hemisphere skies, appeared to her now a grey blue, the color of the cold Atlantic sea. She wondered how she appeared to him and preferred not to know.

Klara had found him, as if, somehow, finding him would bring her, bring them, solace.

"You should not have looked for me," he said.

Klara didn't answer for a moment. She wondered why she *had* searched for him. But it was natural, she thought. Neither had hardly any family left. Neither had anything familiar to return to. It was true, she had run and been running, moving from place to place, whereas he had returned to his hometown. Still, she, like he, she assumed, searched for familiarity and the only familiarity that existed could be a face from the camp, a face that understood all that they had endured. But, looking at him now, she wasn't sure she understood the face in front of her as much as he understood the face in front of him. For he had now informed her a few minutes before that he had been condemned to work in the *Sonderkommando* for having befriended her, ushering fellow prisoners to their deaths, collecting their valuables, cremating their remains, a fate, perhaps, worse than death and, despite shared fates, entirely unfamiliar, she now realized, to her worst imagination. And she now realized, too, or thought she realized with what he had been forced to live with — the constant acquiescence of death.

"Nobody can blame you for that," she said.

"Nobody needs to blame me for that. I blame myself. Every second of every day."

"You had no choice, Alberto, they would have killed you otherwise."

"I should have killed myself." Tears streamed from his eyes. Klara wiped his cheeks. A young couple seated nearby looked at them, then averted their eyes, as if observing a lovers' quarrel.

"What would that have accomplished?"

"It would have freed me… from me." She tightened the grip on his hand. He turned to look out the window, tears freely streaming down his face. "There's something else. I… Klara… I had to leave, forgive me for not waiting for you when we were liberated. I couldn't face you. I didn't want you to find me, afterwards… but I have to—"

"I was so relieved to find out you had survived. I thought you were dead."

"I am dead, Klara. On the inside, I am dead. I live with my sister. She takes care of me. I am dead." He paused. "I have something for you…" He reached into his jacket pocket and pulled out its contents, hidden in a fist. When he opened his hand, a necklace with dark red garnet stones fell into Klara's hand.

Klara started to weep. "It's my mother's. I bought it for her. Where did you get it?"

"Klara… she gave it to me… for you… in the gas chambers… crematorium two…"

"How?"

"I recognized her, from the photo of your family you showed me. She took the necklace off and handed it to me, crying, but so dignified, Klara, so calm, she stroked my cheek, I started to cry, too, I was determined to get gassed along with them that day, but then she hugged me, told me I had to survive, to tell the world, and she walked off into the crowd and I only saw her… afterwards…"

Klara held the necklace tightly to her chest. Tears continued to roll down her cheek; they were now in a place, far away, the hell they never left, years back, not free in a café in Turin anymore; they were utterly unaware of the shy and concerned glances they occasionally received from fellow customers seated nearby or entering and departing.

"There's something else, Klara, I have been holding inside, but I must tell you, Klara, I can't hold it in anymore." Klara wasn't sure she could hear more now, but she knew she had little choice. "Your baby… Klara… his baby… it was me…"

"What was you?"

"I am the one who threw it into the incinerator."

Klara sat, stupefied. She pulled her hand away, unfairly she knew, inadvertently, involuntarily. After several minutes she said, "Why?"

Alberto's face remained unmoved. Only the tears betrayed his emotions. The now grey-blue eyes looked into hers. The look was one of immense pain, but also a final resignation.

"He… he said he'd shoot us both if I didn't." As he said it, Alberto crumpled his face into his hands. Klara at once wanted to touch him, to hold him, but found herself unable. She knew her actions were irrational, unfair, but she couldn't get herself to embrace him. The one thing he now needed, the semblance of forgiveness, she was unable to give. Completely unjustly, she knew, she felt in his presence the deaths of millions and his complicity in it. She didn't say it, but she knew he felt it, too. He had been condemned by sadistic murderers and killers to their guilt while they roamed the earth free of remorse.

They finished their coffees and paid and departed. Originally, she had planned to stay for several days, or much longer perhaps, envisioning a possibility of a life with the boy who had brought her a red poppy and got a beating for it, but they both knew this was now not possible. They stood on the sidewalk in front of the cafe separated by no more than an arm's length, but they came no closer and could not be farther apart. The long ominous arm of Nazi brutality remained with them, between them, even here, on a sunny day in Turin, peace long ago returned, like an icy wind.

She told him that she would remain in contact but wasn't sure she would. Unbeknownst to her at the time, they would speak twice more by telephone.

Alberto replied, "You are the only love of my life."

He made as if to hug her, but she stood still, and he stopped the forward motion and said goodbye and slowly turned and started walking back, down the street, towards his sister's apartment, away from her. She watched as he disappeared around the corner, a young man already old, crumpled, hunched, a life never returned.

KLARA MEETS KLARA

KLARA sees a young girl in a summer dress. She's forgotten the dress, her favorite that glorious spring, light, quality cotton, beige with black and yellow flowers, tainted only by the venomous threats from the North of a fist-waving demagogue.

The girl sits with a group of friends. Klara knows them all, intimately. They smile, they laugh. Not a care in the world. Time seems infinite. The future can only be glorious, they believe. But, of the six girls, only two will survive. The girl in the summer dress. And her friend, Emilia, with fashionable glasses, drinking, ironically, Viennese coffee. The rest will disappear in mass graves as if they never existed. Only the old Klara knows this, nobody else. As the young girl in the summer dress walks by, the old Klara beckons her to sit, briefly. The young girl does, reluctantly. She is trusting, and in any event, the woman is old.

"Please, sit, for a moment. I have dreamt of this, of our meeting, for a long time."

The young girl looks at her friends who share harmless banter and jokes and do not see her. She sits, fidgeting, playing with the hem of her dress. But her demeanor remains friendly and open.

"Dreamt? I don't... understand. Do we know each other?" She is polite, of course, to a stranger, someone older. She uses the formal '*vy*', not the informal '*ty*'. She says, "*Známe se?*" And not, "*Znám tě?*" She has beautiful white teeth and lustrous hair and radiates unadulterated joy and optimism in her eyes. She is unaware that soon her teeth and hair and eyes will never exhibit the same radiance. "Are you a friend of my parents?"

"In a way," Klara says.

"I haven't much time, I am sorry, my friends are waiting for me."

"I understand. Your name is Klara."

"How did you--"

"I overheard one of the girls and besides, we've met each other before."

"Oh? At one of my parents' soirées?"

"There, too. Klara, listen to me. I need you to talk your father into emigrating."

Klara laughs. "You know he won't go anywhere. No one is more Czech than he." She looks around. "Besides, I'd never live anywhere but Prague — no city is as magical. Last year, we went to—"

"Paris."

"How did you… my parents told you, I guess? Yes, Paris, and Paris is special, but it's nothing like Prague. Nowhere is like Prague, not staid Vienna, rigid Berlin, antiquated Budapest. I will never live elsewhere. I might travel, a lot I hope, but this will be my home." *Oh, my darling girl, there is so much I want to tell you, to warn you about. You must talk your dad, our dad, into emigrating. Quickly. There is no time to lose.*

"You must get out, all of you, before it's too late."

"Why? We're Czechs. Where would we go? We belong here."

"There'll be war."

"What, you mean that buffoon? Hitler? You can't take him seriously. No one does. Besides, we have a treaty, with England, France, he wouldn't dare, daddy says." *This is no time for reason, my child. The English and the French will be as reliable as the weather in the English Channel. They will sell you to the Germans and declare world peace.*

"Please speak to him. Please, before it's too late."

"I must go. What is your name, I will tell my parents I saw you."

"Klara."

"Ah, another Klara. What a coincidence. I am sorry, I have to go. It was a pleasure."

Then, suddenly Klara sees him. In the distance, coming through the entrance, limping imperceptibly. Dressed impeccably, in a grey fedora. His eyes darted the room, looking for her. She runs towards him, not as quickly as she'd like, forgetting her aching joints, but she runs, full of love and longing.

Still, he doesn't seem to see her as she gets closer, but it doesn't stop her from throwing her arms around him, and saying, over and over, "Alfons, oh Alfons."

He hasn't put his arms around her, which surprises her, perhaps she's done something to annoy or upset him, but she can't think what. She finally releases him only to find him looking at her with utter puzzlement. She looks around; several tables are looking at them, and the young Klara approaches now, too, wondering, of course, what the old woman has in common with Alfons. Clearly, the relationship is intimate, familial perhaps, but she's never met her and has heard no reference or at least seen no photos. The old Klara slowly releases her embrace and steps back.

"I am so sorry," she says, crying.

"Madame, do we…"

"Please forgive an old woman. I can imagine what this looks like."

"But you knew my name."

"I remember you, from long ago."

"Oh, I see, when I was a boy perhaps."

"Yes, yes, when you were… still young."

"You know my parents?"

"Yes. They were always very kind to me."

"She seems to know both our parents," the young Klara says, holding Alfons' hand now.

"And you are?" says Alfons.

"Klara," says the old Klara.

"My favorite name," he beams, and kisses the young Klara on the cheek.

"I suppose I'd better be going," the old Klara says. "But, Klara, please promise me that you will speak to your parents, and to Alfons, and to his parents, about what we spoke."

"What was that," said Alfons.

"Klara says we should emigrate. Leave Prague. Before the Germans invade."

"That's nonsense. With all due respect. The Germans got what they wanted — Austria. They won't attack us. Our army is strong; besides, they tangle with us, they tangle with the French and the English. And *they* won't allow it."

"That's what I said," said the young Klara.

"This is our home," said Alfons. "We are to get married—"

"I know," said the old Klara.

"—and a couple years down the line, start a family. Besides, Klara grew up in the Sudetenland, she speaks German like a German."

The old Klara stands still and continues to weep at the thought of their dead son, and touches Alfons on the cheek. "You must leave. Or you will all die. Except for you, Klara. *You* will remain, alone."

Now, they look at her as if they hear the ramblings of an unstable old woman. Alfons pulls the young Klara closer by the hand and starts to walk towards the table with their friends. He tips his hat.

"We must go."

Then the old Klara looks after them mournfully and when the young Klara turns, their eyes meet one last time. For a moment, the old Klara thinks she sees a glimmer of recognition in the young Klara's eyes. Then the young Klara turns and almost skips with happiness, the groom-to-be by her side. The old Klara wipes a tear. She glimpses through the window the 'twenty-two' tram approaching in the direction of the castle, the metal emanating sparks on the wire above. Across the street lies the national theater, soon to be national no more. At the table, the young Klara waves to the old Klara and speaks to her friends, who look over at the old Klara. Young Klara continues to say something out of earshot and her friends, whom the old Klara remembers intimately, turn away. Soon, they rejoice in their company, in youth, in life. Within three years, only two will be alive. Neither will ever look as healthy or joyful as they look now.

Old Klara knows there is nothing to be done. Always, she imagined being able to warn her family, warn herself. Little did she realize that she would only end up absurd and comical, warning deaf ears. History indeed repeats itself, she thinks, even if one has lived and studied and forewarned those who had not. No one listens to anyone. Or rather, people listen, but only to those *with authority*, even an authority usurped and illegitimate. People follow a leader. It can be a leader of a nation or a family or someone one looks up to and respects. More often than not, if diabolical or malevolent, the leaders are blindly followed to atrocities or graves. Few resist or follow an independent path. It takes courage to say, Mr Himmler, go to hell. But, if action is taken, perhaps fate does not need to be an unavoidable, preordained destiny. But Klara thinks, man has to *act*.

Lastly, two things surprise her — if one couldn't warn oneself, whom could one warn? And, she had warned Alfons and feared for his life far more than her owns. Perhaps from her Anton inherited his whimsical sense of self-preservation.

AN OUTING

"ANNIE?"

"Yeah, Mom?" One day Annie had called Klara 'Mom', and it was the most natural of things. "We need eggs."

"Right." They were in the Publix grocery store on Palm City Avenue across from the new library. Annie now helped around the house and spent more and more time with Klara and Anton.

"Is that what you wanted to tell me?"

"No. You know I have been imprisoned by the Germans and the Soviets."

"Mom, seriously? We're shopping..."

"Time is running out, my child."

"What do you mean?"

"Please, Annie, humor me. You know what the difference was between the Germans and the Russians?" Annie waited. "The Russians never beat us."

They were walking through aisle nine and Annie picked up and tossed four two-liter soda waters in the cart for Klara. She smiled good-naturedly. "Mom — you sure this can't wait?"

"This country tortures prisoners now," Klara said.

"All right, Mom, I give up," Annie said. "Is that what you wanted to tell me?"

"No — here's what I wanted to tell you. The Germans are accomplished liars. I have never seen better liars. We all knew in the camps, never trust a German. Well, there was one that I told you about. And there is another — I trust her implicitly. Besides those two, they lied about everything, we were so desperate to believe. You know about the gassings and showers, but it was also the pervasive, everyday lying. They would lie to our families back home, for example, tell them we'd be released and then say it was cancelled because we misbehaved. Of course, no date had been set and no misbehavior had taken place. It was all to alienate the prisoners from their families and vice versa. Or they forbid you from having any photographs, for the same reasons. Of course, I managed to keep one."

"I think I know why you're telling me this."

"Carolien is a natural liar. She is just like the SS — there's something about Germanic people, they can't help themselves. Never believe anything she tells you."

"Is there anything specific—"

"Lucie called me at home one day — Carolien had gone somewhere with Chuck — I think he is too friendly with Lucie, by the way, it is just a gut feeling, maybe I just do not trust anyone anymore — so Lucie called me. I am sure she got in trouble for it, Carolien checks the phone logs. And you know what Lucie said? You remember me telling you about the Himmler visit, and stupid me, thinking, now things will improve, he has seen the conditions we live in."

"Yes."

"Lucie said, '*Gogo* — you know how she calls me that — I have good news, Mommy doesn't hate Maria.'"

"The African nanny?"

"That's right. The one that Carolien detested, the one that Lucie loved. The one that Carolien treated abysmally — I heard all the stories from Anton. So, I said to Lucie," Klara continued. "Really? What makes you say that? And she said, 'Because we mailed Maria a letter together and Mommy wrote how much she loves Maria.' So, now, I said nothing to Lucie, I said something like, well, isn't that interesting, but there is poor Lucie, she has lost everyone she loves, she gets slapped all the time, maybe not in front of the new guy, not yet, but she will, she knows all this, and yet, and I know that is how children are, she wants, she needs to believe that her mother is not unkind, that she is loving. You see?"

"It breaks my heart, Klara."

"But this is the important thing. Now, imagine the mind of someone like Carolien. And you know what, I have to say, hats off, I do, in her duplicity. She is there, thinking all the time, wondering what she can do next, heaven knows where she finds the time with her PhD studies. She is thinking, how can I make Lucie think I am a nice person. Why that is important to her is anyone's guess. But it is to those people, isn't it? Surely Lucie remembers how Carolien had been to Maria, and to her. So, Carolien devises this plan, she says, 'Why don't we send a card to Maria?' Lucie can't believe her ears, of course, she would love to do that, and they go pick out a card together, they write it together, Carolien writing how much she loves Maria and how much she misses her, and they go to the post office together and they mail it together!"

"Let me guess, it never arrives."

"Of course not. Anton called Maria. She laughed for such a long time, I spoke to her, too, she sounds so wonderful and all that Anton told me about her — but, imagine that Carolien would go through all that trouble, go buy a card, write it, go to the post office with Lucie, throw it together into the mailbox and send it, to a totally made-up address, one humongous lie so that Lucie might think, *wow, maybe mommy is not so unkind, maybe she is a loving person.*"

"That's diabolical."

"The night that Carolien had Anton thrown out of the house and arrested, a month or two later — children are funny how they think, it takes time for them to process things — Lucie said to Anton, '*Baba*, why didn't you come back?' And he said, 'What do you mean, when?' And she said, 'That time you left the house.' And he said, 'But you know that mommy kicked me out and I couldn't come back anymore.' And she said, 'But mommy said you would be back soon and, *Baba*, I watched you leave through the window, and I was crying and waiting for you to come back, and then when you weren't there in the morning.' And Carolien told her, 'What a bad daddy you have, he didn't even come home to see you.' Or another time, Annie—" Klara spoke rapidly as if she didn't want anything left out, as if afraid to forget something, as if time seemed ever so fleeting. "—Lucie called again — for these stories she's allowed to call me, of course — all happy and said, '*Gogo*, good news, it wasn't mommy who wanted the divorce. Oh, I said? It was the judge!' Lucie said. 'Mommy told me, she had nothing to do with it!' *Pane bože* — you couldn't make this up if you tried. How do you explain to a child what a judge is, that he or she does nothing without instructions…"

Annie was quiet. "Mom — no more stories for now, please. I know why you're telling me; I do. It breaks my heart to hear all this. Don't worry, I understand all too well what sort of person we're dealing with. You forget I was trained by one of the best, my own mother."

"I know. It's just… I guess I am making sure you have as much information as possible. Knowledge is power, as they say. You can't have enough. Have you heard of Pastor Niemöller, by any chance? No? He was a German, but anti-Nazi, sent to a concentration camp, but when the war broke out, he wanted to be released and be a U-boat commander as he had been in World War One. Patriotism won over morality. Hitler, though, turned him down. He survived the war, lived to an old age. Anyway, he said, '...The Nazis first came for the communists, and I did not speak up because I was not a communist. Then they came for the Jews, and I did not speak up because I was not a Jew. Then they came for the trade unionists, and I did not speak up because I was not a trade unionist. Then they came for the Catholics, and I did not speak up because I was a protestant. Then they came for me, and by that time, there was no one left to speak up for me.'"

"A wise quote."

"Reminds me of our current president, attacking the Mexicans, and no one is speaking up for them. The Jews should be the first ones to speak up, to defend them, you'd have thought they'd have learned their lesson. But do people learn? Which reminds me of Santayana, who said, 'Those who cannot remember the past are condemned to repeat it.'" She paused. "He could have remained a Harvard professor but in his forties decided to move to Europe. He never came back to the US." Annie studied her closely. "Yes, I am trying to make a point, you are right, of course. Once you leave, Annie, once you all leave, promise you will never come back. This place is unsafe now. I fear the rise of fascism. And remember — I saw the rise of fascism in Europe. For what is fascism? As Mussolini said, *El Estado corporativo* — the corporate state. And what has this country become, if not that? I should have left a long time ago. Didn't know where to go. Europe... for me, was unthinkable. I didn't want to be too close to the Germans, I just do not trust them, never will."

"You're coming with us."

"Oh, Annie... oh, oh, grab the pasta there, will you, the macaroni, thank you... you know I love you with all my heart, but no, you will go alone, and Annie, I can't tell you how grateful I am for you."

"I love them, Klara."

"I know you do, and that, to an old woman, is the greatest gift of all. To know that my little boy will be taken care of. You know what I mean — he is too kind, too gentle, people like that aren't meant for this world. No good can come of it. In this world, you have to be a fighter, sometimes even fighting dirty, and he has none of that in him, we've spoken about it, you and I, no self-preservation, he just doesn't have it. He'd have died within days or weeks in the camps, if he lasted that long. Look at me — I know history and I let it repeat itself. I hadn't learned a darn thing. So, you see, maybe it makes no difference if you know your history, humanity is simply doomed to repeat all its folly all the time, one big circle. It's because Anton and I are alike. We are soft, we are weak. We had no idea what to do, how to stop her, and she knew, took full advantage of it. You know, Höss, the kommandant of Auschwitz said his favorite prisoners were the gypsies because they were like children, always laughing and playing and singing, even when they went to their deaths. Not a one, he said, ever looked at him with hatred. So, who knows, maybe Anton and I have some gypsy blood, it wouldn't surprise me. We're not like you, Annie, you are strong. I knew that the first time I saw you. Had I not been chosen by the SS-Schutzhaflagerführer — there is no way I would have survived either. Oh — grab the OJ, will you?" They both smiled. "Yoghurt, grab a few, dear, thank you. Fruit on the bottom. Strawberry. Christ, my back is killing me. Give me a minute, dear." Klara held onto the cart, pushing it along, as much as a crutch, while Annie walked next to her, grabbing, and putting the items in the cart. They walked by an older man stocking the shelves who said hello to Klara.

After they were past, she whispered to Annie, "I think he likes me." Her eyes twinkled and Annie thought how sad it was that she had not had the opportunity to have a family, husband, raise children, that there was probably nothing that Klara had wanted more.

"Mustard?" Annie said.

Klara pointed to mustard in a glass mug with a handle. "The German one, she said." Then she smiled sheepishly. "What can I do. It's the closest one to Czech mustard." Then, "Am I boring you with all this?" Annie was familiar with victims of crimes. Several of her colleagues, too, were veterans, and victims of PTSD. She understood the dire need for some of them to remain silent; and others to talk until little more could be said. She also knew enough old people in the neighborhood, it being Florida; and she knew that many in old age suddenly felt the need to unload burdens, of whatever nature. And that often they took on forms of a confession, of crimes or injustices to them, or, less frequently, crimes they had committed, sometimes decades ago. The time of reckoning had come, for many, and they didn't wish to die with hidden secrets. Sometimes what triggered the confession was a tragic event, perhaps a death of a loved one, or a terminal disease, and they felt an urgency.

Such was the case with Klara, Annie felt. The shock of Carolien's behavior and subsequent abandonment, made Klara almost always talk now about the war, or at least her experiences in relation to what had transpired with Carolien. Annie had to admit something else, too. She welcomed the stories. Never a fan of history in school, this felt different. To hear the recollections from someone who had lived them made all the difference; she also understood that when this generation died, the stories died with them. Plus, the more she heard and learned, the more interested in the topic she became. She had even checked out a few books from the local library that Klara had recommended. And the more she learned and read, the more she *wanted* to learn and read, and the more she peppered Klara with questions. Knowledge was like travel — once begun, there could never be enough.

"I look forward to our time together," Annie now said, "I love our talks. I feel privileged that you chose me. Truly, I mean that."

"Tell me if I become a bore, dear."

"Don't count on it."

Suddenly, urgently, "Annie — listen, this is important."

"What — the mustard?"

"Yes, the mustard. Humorous. Now, this is not the right place, but then, what place would be, the beach? In the camps, you learn that you can share the most intimate knowledge with someone on a latrine next to you. If you share at all."

"Let me guess. We need toilet paper."

"Comedian, you."

"But you did say, eggs, right, because they're right here?"

"Yes, jumbo, please check them." Annie picked up the carton and started feeling every egg to see if it stuck to the bottom. "You know, we are one of the few countries that washes eggs. So, they have to be refrigerated. We sterilize everything."

"What?"

"Never mind, just moaning as usual. One of the advantages of old age. People expect you to be cranky. Now, Annie, you and I, we understand each other."

"We do."

"This whole big mess. There is only one solution."

"I've been thinking about it."

"So — you have come to the same conclusion. I knew you would. Anton, God love him, is paralyzed. He is soft and weak, like me. I've already said so. Had it not been for you, he'd have turned into a *Musselman*. He has no idea what hit him, no idea how to get out of the mess. I have been lying awake every night, just thinking.

"Now, Annie, I think you are far smarter than me. Hear me out, you are. You are also professionally trained. That is going to count infinitely, it is a huge advantage. You will have to be extra careful, and you will have to be extra meticulous and plan, but also take your time. I don't think I am telling you anything you don't know — far more than me, like I said. The only thing I can say is that — and I know you know this already, too, but I just have to say it. The person we're talking about is extremely dangerous. I truly believe that, because of what I have seen, in my life, but also since they moved here. They lived under my roof, remember, while it suited her. I had ample time to observe her behavior. She brought back so many memories. I saw so many similarities. These people, they are what they are. By nature. They can't help themselves. I don't know if I am making sense. But — you have been reading some of the books I recommended, *Levi*, for one—"

"Yes."

"Remember what he says. The part where the Russians are getting closer. Everyone in the camp can hear the artillery. It's getting louder. The end is near. But the Germans continue to destroy and organize and command and fight and kill. Why, Levi asks? Because they are Germans. Do you understand?"

"Yes, Mom. Don't worry. I'll be extra careful. I've already been thinking, all the time."

"Good girl. I've had thoughts. Annie — I have seen love do amazing things. It is enigmatic. No two people give the same definition. No one can really explain why they fall in love with this person and not another. I do know one thing, though, people are willing to die for it. Now, in your case, I want you to live as long as possible, do you hear me?"

"Yes, Mom."

"Don't tell Anton, anything about this. Ever. He needs to remain in the dark. Always. This will have to be our secret. You will have saved him, and he won't realize it. That is just how it has to be." Klara stopped and took Annie by the hand. "That accident with the car was the greatest thing that ever happened to me."

"You sure went to great lengths for us to meet."

"And when you are sitting there, on the tip of Africa, and having a glass of wine, I want you to think of me, occasionally, and make a little toast. That's all. And, Annie, on hot days, when it's over eighty degrees, would you please light a candle?"

"I've been meaning to ask, Mom — what's that all about?"

Klara's expression grew mournful. "One day, I will tell you, my dear. Just think of me occasionally, OK? And please do that for me."

"You will be right there with us."

"No, my dear, my time has come."

"You're a spring chicken," Annie said.

"A winter chicken, more like," said Klara. "Grab some ice cream, would you? Oh, and some chocolates."

"Mom — you're not supposed to have sugar."

"You know what, let's live a little, what do you say?"

"Sure?"

"Absolutely."

Annie grabbed a tub of ice cream — Klara told her to choose whatever she wanted (Klara remarked that she had chosen Anton's favorite) — and a couple bars of high-cocoa dark chocolate, ones they both liked.

"You know, there was one good German that I heard about in the camps. The SS-Schutzhaflagerführer told me about him. Later, I even read about him."

"Oh, yes?"

"The SS sometimes acted friendly to the prisoners, especially the leaders, the politicals, and they tried to talk them into escaping, making them feel like they could help, and then betray them, that was one of their favorite tricks. But this young member of the SS, he talked one of the prisoners into dressing up as an SS officer and escaping together."

"Did they get away?"

"They did, incredibly. I remember the SS-Schutzhaflagerführer was livid. But the story doesn't end there."

"What happened?"

"The SS man actually did it to see if his plan worked. Because, you see, he had fallen in love with a Jewish prisoner from France. He came back for her, sneaked back into the camp, and tried to get her out, but this time, they were caught…" For a moment, they were both silent. "That man didn't have the hard heart of a German; he had a Slavic heart."

"How terribly sad."

"Hitler said that one German equaled ten Slavs — Stalin corrected his faulty arithmetic. I say, one Slavic heart equals ten thousand Germanic ones, and that might be a vast understatement. And you, my darling girl, have one huge Slavic heart."

Annie blushed and squeezed Klara's arm.

Suddenly, Annie became alert and stopped. She stared ahead and Klara followed her gaze. "What's the matter, dear."

Annie waited until the person walked by, then said, "Did you see that woman?"

"The Asian lady?"

"Filipino. She's a friend of Carolien's. Her name's Suzette. Ant had a run-in with her at the school."

"If I had known he'd be called 'Ant' one day, I'd have named him, '*Mravenec*'."

"'Ant' in Czech? That's funny, Mom."

"Anyway, a run-in you say. That's interesting. How long had she been standing there?"

"Not long."

"Think she heard anything?"

"I don't think so."

"Good. I think it's OK."

"I'm not a big believer in coincidences."

"I've seen a few in my lifetime. This isn't a big town. Either way, I wouldn't worry. Grab those mushrooms, would you, dear, I am going to make *kulajda* for you, would you like that?"

"The mushroom soup? Oh, yeah."

"Good. Now let's get out of here. And not through the self-checkout line, dear, you know me, I am not going to be responsible for another cashier losing her job so the capitalists can make more money. Once a red, always a red. You know, I do believe that was the thing that upset me most in the camps, the fact that I had to wear a yellow star and then a black star but never a red star — *ty svině*. You know, it's always so much more fulfilling to swear in your mother tongue."

As they walked out into the sun, Klara squeezed Annie's hand. She didn't think it necessary to tell Annie about the threatening text messages she had been receiving from an unknown number. She didn't think there was a need. It was a bit of superfluous information she didn't want to muddle the plan. If anything, it was a handy bit of news. In some ways, she knew that the next part she was to play was important to the overall plan. It would lend an extra bit of motivation and credibility. In one small way, she would outsmart Carolien. It was simply a shame that she wouldn't be able to enjoy that glass of wine with them. But she had lived long enough, she was tired, she didn't want to be a burden, least of all to them. She just wanted them to find a slice of contentment and to heal each other, and mainly Lucie, and she knew they would. She had written her last will and testament, leaving them what little she had, and she was satisfied. Anton was in the best hands. That was more than she could ever have hoped.

PREPARATION

ANNIE sat at a restaurant alone, having lunch, or at least pretending to have lunch. On her phone, she kept a sharp eye on the time. A little over twenty minutes to go. Meanwhile, she inspected the salad in front of her, probing it with her fork. The tomatoes were large, with no flavor (she had to admit), the chicken pieces were big and white and, she learned recently, bleached (and, not surprisingly, also with no flavor). The salad dressing was rich and greasy and who knew what ingredients it contained. All GMO *rubbish*, she concluded. She sat in a box cutter, ubiquitous American restaurant that she used to like; with the atmosphere, she had been informed, of a church bingo parlor. Sterile like the eggs, Klara might have said. Jesus, listen to herself, Annie thought, she sounded just like Anton and Klara. Down to the 'rubbish'. They had worked her over.

Since they met, she had lost ten pounds — she knew it wasn't just their dislike of local cuisine.

She ate a mushroom and pushed the rest away. She smiled. Soon she would find out whether what Anton had told her about South Africa was really true. Whether or not, she knew she'd follow him anywhere. Or rather, was it not she that was to lead *him* back home, if things turned out all right (and why shouldn't they, she tried to reassure herself, not entirely successfully)?

There weren't family restaurants in Palm City, anyway, she thought in her defense; had there ever been. If so, they long ago closed and been replaced by identical chains that crisscrossed the country (Klara's words). Each chain opening eliciting great excitement from the locals until the next chain opened with great fanfare and lines out the door, taking the clientele from the previous restaurant (she had made the mistake once before, telling Klara, "You won't believe it, Outback is opening up next month, we have to go!" And Klara rolling her eyes and saying, "My dear, I don't eat at chains").

Annie thought now in mitigation that the mushroom, at which she picked with her knife (since she met them, she started to use a knife, too, or at least tried), she was fairly certain, tasted like a mushroom, but she admitted that she had been brainwashed, and how was she to know what a mushroom tasted overseas versus this one. How would she know whether the food here tasted like it was meant to taste? Their opinion (they really were two peas in a pod in some regards), was that the US was the only first-world country that did not have to declare which foods were GMO, and that, in fact, they were all GMO here, that in fact Americans were the only nation in the first world where people were dying younger, and that the food had no flavor (Anton once complained in the store how the tomatoes were too large and without flavor; the chicken meat too large and with a strange hue and without flavor, and everything had corn syrup, and all was either processed with no flavor or fried with no flavor and all of it a bunch of rubbish, and she started laughing at his diatribe and then he did too and she had never thought about any of these things, and well, she had to concede, that had put a damper on her proclivity for the usual junk that she had previously enjoyed). As bad as the food was, Anton had said the Dutch cuisine was worse, that those people would eat a used tire if they could fry it — not that that made her feel much better.

Now, she had to admit, when at the store she checked all the ingredients and yes, all the bread had sugar (how was she to know that bread wasn't to have sugar), and everything did indeed have corn syrup, and all of it probably *was* GMO (Klara and Anton had informed her; and the internet concurred, 'we're living in Sinclair's *The Jungle* all over again,' Klara had said, which made Annie run to the library at the first opportunity — she liked old-fashioned books, not electronic ones), and found that the vegetables and fruits *were* too big and without flavor and rotted from the inside. Anton said that Americans were unhealthy, overweight, and overworked. Once or twice, he had approached strangers in the town (this wasn't Miami exactly, but they still had their share of tourists), and asked if they were European (now that was embarrassing), and sure enough they had been, and he came back gloating, saying he knew because they looked so healthy and because their kids were well-behaved. "Are you trying to tell me I look unhealthy? Or that you won't have kids with me?" she had said then, suddenly self-conscious.

"*You* are the exception," he had said, charmingly.

But it was the mention of the children that put a wide smile on his face and, in turn, hers. He didn't have to explain why he was smiling, but she knew, and in turn he knew. And it was an important moment because they had not spoken about having children (more, in his case, for the first time, in hers), but suddenly it became clear what the future held and she felt that things would be fine, just as she had promised. That the things stolen from him she would provide; and the things stolen from her, he would provide.

It had been a special moment — at a coffee shop by the beach (the coffee was OK to drink in the US, he had assured her, not without mirth, it was all *imported*—only source of anti-oxidants Americans get, he had said) — and after they had knowingly smiled at each other in complicity that only love can provide, he walked over and hugged her and she could have sworn that his eyes were moist, and she knew how important and symbolic the moment had been.

Now she smiled, lost in thought, playing with the salad but not eating; and, she thought, one thing she did have was her love of sports (in college she had played volleyball), and she still swam and cycled and worked out at the gym and here and there went to yoga. So, she made up through exercise what she lost through the food supply. If Anton had been telling the truth (not that she didn't trust him, but she wondered whether he may not have exaggerated all the flavors and tastes back home and denigrated all that he found here because his life had disintegrated since his arrival), she couldn't wait to be with him in South Africa. She couldn't wait to be with him there in any event for other reasons. He only truly lit up (not that he didn't light up when he saw her or when they were together), but he lit up doubly when he was with her and he reminisced about his life there (and how much she loved him at those times, his voice animated, the sparkle in his eyes well and truly back), and she would smile and he would say, 'What?' And he'd kiss her.

And of course, another reason was because they would be safe, away from here. They'd be free. She could picture it so easily and had to admit (though she had not told him), that when she pictured it, it was a wedding, on a beach, and it was just them, Anton, Lucie, Klara, Maria, and she was pregnant, not showing yet, early, and the sun was shining of course, the sea majestic and the food glorious and the wine, and all of it, magic, they lost in the moment. And she thought (stupidly, in her opinion), how she couldn't wait to take care of him, in their own home, in their own kitchen, and she would cook for him; and she would do all the things that she swore she'd never do for any man again, even his laundry (what the heck was wrong with her, she thought), but she did, she just wanted to take care of him, and see him happy, and give him, give *them*, a child and have a family and be content, because she believed that she had a truly tender man, and they would be kind and loving to each other, of that she was certain, and their children would be kind and loving and Lucie would be healed, over time, with great love and tenderness and gentleness, they would envelop her and she would never be threatened again, and Maria would be with them, treated kindly. She couldn't wait.

Then she looked at the time on her phone and she had four minutes to go and suddenly grew nervous. She could feel herself sweating despite the relentless air-conditioning (Klara's term or maybe Anton's, she was sure). God, how she loved him and how she loved them, and how grand—his word--things were suddenly, when she had purpose, whereas before she had no life, she felt, she had no purpose (well, it could not be said she did no good for the community, though she could not declare so openly, of course), she would only work and go home and too often drink herself to sleep, always alone. It was true that aside from her exercise three or four times a week, she had no social life. She had become a recluse and then she met them, and suddenly, she felt alive, Anton made her feel alive, and she knew she wanted to share her life with him and with them and not be alone anymore. She knew she had a purpose again, not only of correcting wrongs, but of loving and being loved. She was so grateful to him, to them; and she knew, too, that she had brought him back to life, as it were, and that gave her immense pleasure. If only they could already be there, on that beach, in the sun.

Then he came, on cue, a non-descript man (possibly light-skinned black man, according to witnesses later, medium height, a little on the heavy side, but overly so; possibly Hispanic, it was hard to tell, one witness said he had a tattoo on his neck of a heart and next to it a four, but that it all happened too fast, another witness said the tattoo was a star and crescent but it was on his arm, and another said he had no tattoo at all; they all agreed that he spoke unintelligibly, mumbled, probably not a native English speaker, one of those immigrants more than likely that the new president was always talking about, probably a *Muslim*) with a pantyhose over his head, blue rubber gloves like the ones found in hospitals, making a racket, slamming the door, yelling at the manager in some strange Hispanic/Cajun/Arabic accent — it wasn't entirely easy to discern what he was saying, the only words that were clear were 'floor', 'kids' and 'money' — making it clear enough that everybody got on the floor, which they all did with the exception of a heavily-tattooed young white man with a beard and an NRA baseball cap — there's always one in every crowd, Annie thought — reaching for a gun, ready to blast the criminal, and potentially half the restaurant so he could be the hero and make the news. That's what Annie had been keeping an eye on. When the young man reached for the gun, she walked over and kicked it away, kicking his hand in the process.

"What the—" he started to say, grabbing his hand in pain. Around were mostly elderly people, some hiding under tables, and some just looking on, as if numb (the shock equation). She had pulled out her own gun and showed it to the man with the beard.

She mouthed silently, "Police."

She walked over and picked up his gun and put it in her pocket just in case he had ideas.

The robber stood with his back towards her. He held a gun and pointed threateningly at the manager, once again barking unintelligible orders but clearly pronouncing 'money'. The manager had in the meantime opened the till, shaking, and whimpering,

"Please don't shoot, mister, please, you can have it all." The manager took out the money, not that there was much, hands shaking uncontrollably, and handed it to the robber. He watched Annie sneak quietly on the robber from behind, trying not to look directly at her. Annie put the gun against the robber's head and told him to give her the gun.

"Gonna something something something, bitch," the man said.

"Just give me the gun, and nobody gets hurt."

After hesitating, he handed it to her. She took it and said, "Jesus, it's plastic."

"Something something you something something my money?"

"*Your* money?" she said. "Why are you doing this?"

The man started to plead, almost crying, saying, "Something something something food something kids."

"Get out of here," she said.

The robber shrugged and hauled and raised the crumpled small wad of money in his fist for the restaurant to see. The gesture was noncommittal, not exactly celebratory, nor a resignation. It was a sad gesture of involuntary motion, almost like an apology.

Then the robber turned and ran out the double door, not quite like a deer, Annie thought, or, if like one, then an older, arthritic one. He weaved with difficulty between several parked cars. He continued towards a forest not far away, across the parking lot, nearly colliding with an old Chrysler parked across two spaces. He froze, stared at the light-skinned black driver, as if recognizing him, then started running again. As he reached the forest, he turned around. He held the money in the air, this time like a victory salute. Then he disappeared into the cascading foliage.

The man in the red baseball cap now got up and started running, intent on going after the robber. Annie pointed the gun at him.

"Sit down," she said. The man stopped by the door, uncertain.

"Give me my gun back. Are you going to let him get away with that? What kind of police officer are you?"

"The kind who doesn't want to see innocent people get hurt, and that includes you."

"I can take care of myself," the man said.

She waited still for a few minutes until she knew the robber was safely away before handing back the gun. "You should be careful with that thing," she said. "People might get hurt." He snarled an expletive, not quite at her, he knew better, and ran out into the forest. By then, Annie knew the robber was long gone.

"That was a very brave thing you did, Miss," an old woman said. She had been at the nearest booth, hiding under the table. She got up with great difficulty and now straightened her skirt.

"Not so brave," Annie said. "It's only plastic, the gun. Want to feel it?"

"Oh, no," said the woman. "Still, you didn't know that did you? Very brave. Are you a police officer?"

"Off-duty."

"You let him steal the money," the manager said. "I am going to report you. I know the chief; I know his whole family. They go to my church."

Annie pretended to read the manager's nametag. "Johnny — do you have kids?"

"How much was it, dear," the old woman said to Johnny. "I'd be happy to pay. The man said something about food and kids, I could hardly tell what he was saying, could you? I almost felt sorry for him, truth be told. I'll pay whatever he took."

"No," the manager said. "*She* must be held accountable, it's not right."

"Oh, dear, come now. Just tell me how much he took, I'll write you a check, we can forget about the whole thing. This police officer did a very brave thing indeed, and well, so he took a bit of money. No harm done."

"No, Miss, it wouldn't be right—"

"All right, you listen to me, I am going to write you a check for a thousand dollars. If that's not enough, you will have my address and phone number, so call me, I can write you another one for more, Got it?"

"I am going to report her."

"Sometimes rules are meant to be broken a little, young man. Live a little, for chrissake." She walked over and took out a checkbook from her purse. She wrote out a check and handed it to the manager. "Here you go. Knock yourself out."

Quite the character, Annie thought and smiled, too bad she could never get to know her better and introduce her to Klara.

"You be good now, dear, you hear?" the woman said, grabbing Annie's sleeve and walking out. An elderly couple in the back of the restaurant stood up and clapped. Meanwhile the young man came back, sweaty from the Florida humidity. He was out of breath. He held his sides and leaned over, then straightened up.

"I ran as far as—" He struggled for air. "—I could. Until the swamp. He—" Gasped. "—Disappeared. I hope the gators get him. You let him get away."

"He needed money for his kids."

"Are you kidding me? Are you an actual police officer?"

"I am."

"I also need money for *my* kids. It doesn't mean I can hold up a restaurant, does it? Besides, he was a foreigner, you heard the way he talked, he could barely talk English. Those people are coming here taking our jobs."

"Good day, Sir," Annie said.

"That's it? Good day?"

"Don't worry, I am going to report her," the manager said.

"Good, you do that, this is ridiculous."

Annie walked out. The humidity hit her immediately. She realized now that parts of her body were completely drenched with sweat, even with the air conditioning. Meanwhile, the light-skinned black man whom she knew intimately had driven off. She had not been happy to see him. But at least he didn't get involved. He merely watched. She knew why he'd been there. He'd have been worried, concerned for her. He'll have to learn, she thought, that some things he'll have to leave up to her. That he's not up to those tasks anyway, whereas she was the only one in this family that was.

As she drove away, she thought that the plan went well. The only unforeseen scenarios were the young man (that was not entirely unforeseen), and the old woman (that was). She didn't think it was overly concerning, though. The young man would tell a few friends in a bar, she thought, but he'd let the manager report the crime. The old woman would wonder why her check was never cashed, but not for too long and not overly so. She would simply assume that the restaurant couldn't accept her money, no matter how well meaning. She would hope, Annie was sure, that Annie wouldn't get in trouble and that the robber would get away. But not enough to go speak to the police just in case the whole thing had not been reported. Sweet old lady, thought Annie.

Annie got in her car, realized she was famished, that she hadn't touched any of the salad except for the lone mushroom and decided to drive to the nearest burger joint, GMO food, sugar, corn syrup be damned. Anton didn't need to know everything.

THE ROAD TO HEAVEN

KLARA was at home alone. Outside was dark and gloomy, almost hurricane weather, she could hear the wind howling and the rain battered the windows. She had not seen Annie all day and Anton had borrowed her car and went out. She hoped they were inside somewhere, dry. Since she had no transport, she decided to watch a documentary on TV.

It was about a German-made passenger ship which had been headed for Stockholm on the Baltic Sea and had capsized from a flooded cargo bay, the large hydraulic door faulty. Hundreds of mostly Baltic and Scandinavian passengers had been trapped below deck in the middle of the night.

Now Klara received a text message and paused the film with the remote control. She checked the phone to make sure it was not from Annie or Anton or (miraculously), Lucie. It was from an unknown number again, and the messages were getting more frequent and uglier now, graphic, threatening. This time it alluded to an imminent arrival, wrapped again in explicit threats. Well, if it was time, so be it. She felt reasonably calm, she thought. She wasn't overly fearful, and she wasn't panicked. It was the panic that worried her more.

She still hadn't told anyone about the texts. She put the phone down and pressed the play button on the remote control. The movie restarted.

A reconstruction showed water flooding the vessel now at tons per second. People scaled and climbed the toppled, jutting internal structure. For some, the survival instinct took over. They'd do anything to live. They trampled children and the old. They ripped life vests from each other. Some even turned to thievery, ripping jewelry off the necks of fellow passengers.

To Klara, none of the behavior was surprising. She had seen thievery on a grand scale, much of it by people who could not hope to survive. She had seen, too, the desperation to survive. What she didn't see on this ship were the few courageous souls like Father Kolbe who volunteered to take the place of a fellow Pole in a concentration camp, a randomly chosen married man with two children, to be punished for another's escape. Kolbe died from a phenol shot to the heart. The man he replaced survived. The documentary didn't mention acts of similar bravery.

Klara didn't feel that in the camps she had been brave or had done anything courageous. She had never volunteered to die in anyone's place. And there were ample opportunities. Ample. She had been young, of course, but she didn't think that was an excuse. She had seen young people be courageous and die. It just hadn't been her. And, of course, Kolbe, too, had only been in his forties, a young man still, plenty of life ahead. And yet he took the man's place.

So, what she was going to do now really held no merit, as far as she was concerned. In fact, no merit, no courage at all. Kolbe took the place of a person completely unrelated to him. Now, *that* was courage. Klara was old, and volunteering for her son.

The movie now showed other people dazed, confused, stricken, paralyzed with terror. They could not walk. Their minds and bodies shut down. The survivors recounted how they could not think, could not hear, moved erratically if at all. Their brains stopped functioning, they said. One young man related how he started to climb stairs, surrounded by pushing, panicking crowds, thinking his parents and girlfriend were right behind. When he turned, he saw them far below, frozen with terror, unable to move, standing still, all three, staring vacuously at him like wax statues. People pushed him upwards, farther away. And here, the worst of possibilities merged. The mother, otherwise immobilized, suddenly gestured for him to continue; and he did, leaving his loved ones behind, seeing them for the last time. His survival instinct kicked in; theirs turned to stupefied terror. How often had she seen that in the camps, too. A paralysis that led to certain death. A command given by a Kapo, by the SS, the man or woman or child stricken with fear, a paralysis mistaken for disobedience, and a clubbing to death or a bullet to the head or neck. Or those lined up to be shot, with those next to them already killed and the executioner moving closer, not running but standing, awaiting fate, staring emptily. Or the ten thousand or so passengers arriving on cattle trains not storming the few guards with guns. Or why, forewarned, were people meekly led into gas chambers. Or why during Pearl Harbor some bystanders remained motionless, observing enemy planes spraying them with bullets. Or why, in a recent terrorist attack, with a man aiming an AK-47 at their heads, people sat or lay still, motionless, or cowered and waited their turn and did not run. Klara knew, or thought she knew, that for the vast majority, the paralysis, the stupor rested in the unfathomable nature of terror. That the mind could not compute what it could not understand. Like thunder blaring only after lightning had struck. The human mind could not simultaneously process the action and the terror quickly enough. In the face of horror, for the vast majority, the mind shuts down. Klara hoped this wouldn't be her.

Klara remembered how she had read somewhere that the horrors people experienced were passed to the children, genetically, how scientists had done studies, and how the effects of the children showed up in MRI images of the brain; and that the children continued to bear the wounds their parents had endured. And she wondered, then, whether the terrors she had experienced and suffered she had not passed onto Anton and now he onto Lucie? Was that perhaps why he had been incapacitated by Carolien because he already carried Klara's terror and it had simply been too much?

There was a knock at the front door. The wind and rain continued unabated. It was dusk now, almost dark, and she wondered if Anton was somewhere with Annie. She hoped that he was. It gave her immense pleasure and relief to watch those two together. Few things were as joyful to observe as watching two people falling in love, especially two people you loved yourself. And she really hoped that they were somewhere dry and safe, Annie's place maybe. Young lovers needed privacy after all, they couldn't always be with her.

She was sorry now that she would see neither one again and she tried to remember the last time she had seen Anton and Annie and Lucie. She remembered each instance and she was sorry she had not told each one how much they meant to her and how much she loved them (Lucie's conversation coming back to her), but she showed them often enough, and who knew, perhaps it was better this way. Then she wondered whether she had told Anton and Annie about Father Kolbe. She wasn't sure she had. And then she realized she had never answered Annie's question about the candles being lit on hot days. She hoped that Anton would tell her.

There was so much she had not told them yet, even if they were so patient to listen to all her stories, so many sad and tragic and unpleasant. And they really did take such an interest in them, for her sake perhaps, but still. And they both, Annie especially, had started to do their own research, it was very sweet, they really took an interest, and read books from the library, some that Klara had not heard of, and they had even taught Klara a thing or two. She was pretty sure that Annie would come across Father Kolbe in those books somewhere, or at least she hoped she would, and tell Anton about it, and maybe Lucie when she was older; or find out about the courageous parachutists who had killed Heydrich, had she told them about that? She couldn't remember, but she didn't think so. Oh, she thought, I really hope they learn about all these people because there were some truly courageous ones, it wasn't just a matter of people voluntarily going to their deaths, although there was much of that of course, too.

The doorbell rang again, and she thought the person was really impatient. With the weather, it wasn't surprising, but she took pleasure in knowing they were outside in the pouring rain. Lightning struck a tree nearby and she shivered.

She thought of writing a note, but of course knew that wasn't possible. If she could though, she'd write how grateful she was to all of them, how they had brightened the end of her life, at a time when she thought only solitude was omnipresent. She'd write how much pleasure they had given her, and that she was sorry that she brought Anton and Lucie pain by encouraging them to move to this country and to her house, and that maybe this would make up for it a little. She would write, she thought, that she was sorry she wouldn't see them in South Africa, but she had some unpleasant memories of the place and although she knew it to be different now, for the better, memories had a habit of creeping up and she had enough fodder for nightmares, hadn't she?

And she saw that she had not frozen and that the spirit of Father Kolbe and all the courageous ones like him would now channel through her and help her be strong. She went through the sliding door in the back, through the porch. She opened a large blue striped umbrella and went into the backyard to the canal, her bare feet sloshing in the St. Augustine grass. From the muddy bank, where on occasion she had seen alligators swimming or even sunning themselves in her yard; she threw her cell phone into the murky waters, avoiding poison ivy, not that it mattered now. She looked at the ominous clouds, another lightning not far illuminating the night, and she was surprised at the vehemence of memories of her parents and brother and sister, but it wasn't from the camp. It was from before the war, her mother cooking, her father reading the newspaper, jazz playing on the radio, Benny Goodman, and she dancing with her brother while her sister looked on, laughing. She was happy now that this would be her last memory of them.

She returned through the porch, wiping her feet on a towel hanging there so she wouldn't bring mud inside and through the house and opened the door to the find the person she had been expecting. The person drove an unfamiliar car with no license plates, Klara remarked, and was dressed in a baseball cap, quite low, covering her face, and men's sunglasses, even in the dark, not the usual large and feminine ones, and rather manly clothes, Klara thought, jeans and a men's shirt, the jeans soaked at the bottom, and wet tennis shoes, not the short skirt and tight top and high heels and heavy make-up and bright red lipstick she was used to seeing on this person. This person told her they were going for a drive to the intracoastal bridge. Klara said she had been waiting for a few days, since the first text messages started arriving, and with dignity and grace she went with this person to the car, getting soaked, not that it mattered, and they drove slowly together, the streets wet and nearly deserted, and she thought of Father Kolbe and the phenol heart injection and hoped his death was quick and that he hadn't suffered much.

UNDERSTANDING

"Mom?" Klara loved it when Annie called her mom. It was a pleasure she thought she would never get to experience and now, in old age, in her remaining days, she had two people calling her mom and one calling her *Gogo*. "Do you remember the first time I called you 'Mom'?"

"Of course. In the kitchen. You weren't feeling well, so I told you to go lie down and I tucked you in and made you good Czech lemon and honey tea. And later, *kulajda*."

"You tucked me in and put the blanket all around and under my feet so my feet would be warm, you know how they're always cold, even here in Florida, in our mild winter, on rainy days." Annie teared up and walked over to Klara and gave her a big hug. "And you made me *čaj*. You know I can't say tea anymore, right? And then, when I felt a bit better, you made that delicious mushroom soup. And I just felt so... loved and appreciated, as I have never been loved or appreciated, of course, by my own mom. In that moment, I had a mom; I never thought I'd have one. And then, you had introduced me to your son, and I saw how much like you he was, and well, it was inevitable, wasn't it. When I saw how much pain he was in, other women would probably have run — heck, other men would have run from my baggage, too — but I know all about that, and I just wanted... I needed to help him; I couldn't help it."

"I know, dear. You have no idea how grateful I am."

"As grateful as I am for you," Annie said. "I guess I just needed you to know. It's all the little things you do, that every mother should but many don't, that Anton does with Lucie — heck, he's like a mom — he told me when Lucie was little, she would sometimes call him 'Mom'. I get that—"

"You know what Lucie told me the other day?"

"What?"

"She said, 'I wish Annie could be my mom.' Actually, she said, '*Mama*'." Annie's eyes welled and she started crying and held Klara a bit tighter. "I wish that, too. Maybe one day," Klara added.

"Oh, Mom—" Annie started to say. It took her a while to compose herself.

"I'm sorry — I thought you should know. So — you were telling me…"

"Oh, that Anton understood why she had called him 'Mom', he told me, and he saw it as a badge of honor, as well as he should have, I told him! But it's the little things, you know, that you notice, that I like, or things you do that you don't have to, he does, too, remembering what flavor ice cream I like or what type of chocolate, or how I like my coffee, or which type of wine I like, and you always have it here, or when we went to Kentucky, you got up extra early and made us schnitzel sandwiches for the road, those were *so* good, and you packed it for us and of course, I found later in my little bag my favorite chocolate, and we ate it on the plane, Anton and I, Mom and oh, it was good, and you should have seen everybody looking, it smelled so good, too, and the lady next to us said, 'Wow, that looks good,' And I said, yeah, my mom made it for us this morning, she got up real early, I looked at Anton and said, *our* mom, and he smiled at me, our mom got up extra early and made this for us for the road. And the lady said, 'That's mothers for you, I wish I still had my mom, and I said, not all moms are like that,' And she kind of thought about it and said, 'I guess *we* are the lucky ones.' To which I smiled, you know, but felt wistful.

"Anyway, Mom, the way you take care of me, you always hug me when I arrive and you always walk me out and hug me and wave to me when I leave, and you always ask if everything is OK. I never had that before, but always dreamed of it, and, Mom, sometimes I drive away and I cry, I try not to show you, but, you know, good tears, but I also cry for everything I have missed out on, and that you were deprived of, and now Anton and Lucie, and I swear to God, Mom, I will make things better. You told me how history repeats itself; well, you have to *do* something, don't you, if you don't want it to repeat itself."

They sat on the porch as they often did. They watched the rain through the screen. It was raining so hard that the water streamed over the gutter. "I will have to ask Anton to clean the gutters again. It's those darn pine trees. They sure make a mess," Klara said.

"He's at the store, right?"

"He is. You need anything?"

"No, Mom, just checking. I wanted to come over when he's out. So, we could talk, alone. There's something important I want to talk to you about."

It had been a busy day and Annie had gone home from work first to take off her uniform; now relaxed, she was glad she had. She sat in her gym clothes — she planned to take Anton for a workout afterwards and before having dinner, the three together. But as she took another sip of wine, she thought that the gym idea was quickly dissipating. Not that Anton would mind, particularly. Gym wasn't his favorite, but he went for her.

Klara ate half a piece of chocolate she wasn't supposed to have, and offered one to Annie who turned it down.

"Mom, I don't want you to think less of me" -- she started.

"For bringing me chocolate? Hardly."

"Funny, Mom. No — for what I'm about to tell you."

"I assure you, that's not going to happen."

"You might not remember, but when we talked once before, I told you that the only thing I like about Florida is the swamp. Oh, I also like gators."

"I remember, about the swamp — not the alligators."

"Well, one in particular. You should see this monster, Mom, fifteen-footer, no lie. I've named him Odilo."

"After Globocnik? You have a good memory. That poor gator, though."

Outside, it had stopped raining and the sky had cleared. The moon, almost full, now lit up the surrounds. A deer walked by on the way to the canal.

"So, the swamp," Annie continued. "You might not know it, but I have a little cabin in the swamp, on stilts. It's not easy to get to. In fact, the only way is by boat, which I keep hidden. No one really knows about it, well, except for Carl who lives there."

"I remember you telling me about him when we first met. I was relieved when you told me he was not your boyfriend."

"Wow, Mom, you really were planning ahead."

"You never know."

Annie smiled at how things turned out. "So anyway, Carl takes care of it for me. Doesn't really leave. Here and there, at night, not much. Well, he did leave once recently but he doesn't like people, you see, not any more.

Until I saw Anton, Carl was the most amazing father I'd ever seen. Four girls. They adored him. You should have seen them. They did everything together, everything. They used to go trick-or-treating in the neighborhood, it was the sweetest thing you ever saw. He always drove them around everywhere, to all their activities. The mother was kind of just... absent... present, but absent..."

"I see."

"This mother—"

"Is Carl a black fellow? Medium height?"

"Light-skinned, yes. Why?"

"Just wondering."

Annie smiled. "Yes, he his. Light-skinned black man, medium height, as you put it. Until I met all of you, the closest human being to me. Not what you think, never a boyfriend, he was broken, and I was broken — we still are — and we had no time for any nonsense — you know all about that, we were just friends, but incredibly close, and he could trust me, and I could trust him—"

"That's an extremely rare thing in this world."

"Right. So, now, his wife, Jane, they both liked to eat. He was — is — an amazing cook. Loves to hunt and fish, too, so that family ate well. They weren't fat in those days, mind you, but they were both pudgy, kids were nice and round, too, to put it nicely. They were just happy, you know. You know how food can do that. Carl's lost a lot of weight since then. Anyway, his wife, who I knew well too, she decided one day to go on a diet. It was sort of strange to see. I mean, she loved to eat, and he loved to cook for her, for them. God, his ribs were to die for, they still are. Anyway, here's where it gets a little tricky. When one person in a couple starts to lose weight, a lot of weight, I get suspicious."

"Another man."

"Right. That's what I thought. Now, I can't tell you if she met this man first and started to lose weight or if she lost the weight first and then she met him. I don't think it matters either way. I think you know where I'm heading with this. It was an older white guy; I have no idea how they met. He had moved here from Jersey with his wife, oh, yes, that was it, and she had passed away, and now Jane is a nurse, used to make house calls. Now she works at the school for the deaf in Daytona. Anyway, one thing led to another and there you have it. People like that, it's not enough that they cause all the damage. They accuse the other person of the same things they are doing. The lies that woman spread, but she was convincing, I'll give her that. And Carl — he was broken. Just broken. Devastated. He used to cry, out of the blue, couldn't stop.. Had no idea what happened. One of those situations where he had done everything for the family, lived for that family. A real family man. He used to come over to my house and cry. I was the only one to believe him. Because of my mom, I'm sure. I just knew he was telling the truth. All the other people in the neighborhood, all the women especially, they all sided with Jane. Just because she's a woman. No idea why people do that, it's appalling. I mean, get a brain. And all the men, their husbands, they didn't want any trouble at home with the wives, so they started to keep their distance from Carl. Mom, it was just heartbreaking. And that Halloween, she told him she would take the girls trick-or-treating — this was the first time she'd ever done something like that, he did all that stuff until then — suddenly she's supermom in public, putting on a show — and all the women were saying what a nice family they made, the three of them and the old white guy, and there was Carl, for the first time not trick-or-treating with his girls, crying in my living room, watching through the window his family walking with the new boyfriend around the neighborhood. He stayed there, Mom, even after they had gone back home, and he just cried for hours. It broke my heart. And of course, after that, yes, you guessed it, she accused him of abuse, and she just destroyed him. Needless to say, he lost everything. Everything. It was the usual story. The courts slapped him with crazy child support that he couldn't pay in a million years. And she knew that, and the courts knew that. I see it at the courts all the time. And I wondered, what was this judge thinking? Judge Pullard was her name, complete idiot, but, really, they are all the same. The man has no money, the woman seeking child support knows that, the court knows that. They order him to pay unaffordable amounts. He is in contempt of court, he gets arrested. He can't find a job afterwards with a prison record, he's lost his driver's license. It's abysmal. All they have accomplished is to destroy another man's life and remove him from his children and then they call him deadbeat dad — go figure. Well, a lot of good that does. And that's the warpath Jane was on. So, I'm supposed to arrest him. And I'm driving him to the station and he's crying, and we both know his life's finished. So, I turn, I turn around, and I drive, and park and we take the boat to the cabin, he knew nothing about it before, nobody did, and later I said he had overpowered me and ran off. He's been hiding and living at the cabin now for over twelve years. But you know, Mom, it was the first time as a police officer that I had acted against the *in*justice system, that's what I call it now. It was *empowering*. And I decided that I wouldn't, if I could, follow the laws and punish the innocent and let the guilty free — not every time anyway. That, when I could, I would actually *do* something. Now, I've been smart, Mom, I've never been caught, but the chief has been suspicious for some time. One more thing like that, letting a criminal go, whatever, I'm out of a job, I know that.

"Now, don't get me wrong, he's not the man he once was, Carl. He's not completely broken, but he's broken. Still, he's free, or at least not in prison. I bring him food, and books or whatever he wants, which isn't much, and he hunts, and fishes and I think, considering, it's the best the situation can be. And of course, Jane completely brainwashed those girls, and they don't even want to speak to him to this day. I sometimes see them and ask them about him, and they always complain about him and just say nasty things, ran off, deadbeat dad, all the crap she has fed them. I never told him that, it'd hurt him more. It's just awful.

"So, now mom, this is the part where the story gets a little complicated."

"I had a feeling."

Annie played with a curl of hair. "There was a pedophile, Mom, I saw him sometimes driving by the middle school, a very wealthy man in a fancy car. I always thought he looked kind of weird. Unmarried, no kids, always near that school. Only later did it click, at the time I hadn't thought much of it, but by then he had molested a couple of girls before they caught him. He was wily and smart as hell, in his own way. They finally caught him, but you can imagine, he had the best lawyers and got off. Two of the girls refused to testify, who can blame them. The last girl he molested was from a poor family, her father used to work at the thrift store, her mother too, as a cashier, they had several kids, it was just awful. I remember that the girl never recovered. Not long afterwards, she became promiscuous, until then a good student, and got pregnant in high school and dropped out. She moved away to South Dakota. Last I heard she was some exotic dancer up there, you know, for the men working in the oil fields or whatever.

"Mom, I saw this man a couple years later by that middle school again. And, I don't know, something just snapped, and you know, it was history repeating itself, nothing changes, the injustice system is crap, it's corrupt, it's anything but just and I was so sick and tired of it, I had become a police officer precisely because I thought I could do some good, prevent those things, after what happened to me, and my dad and my brother, and everything just turned out the opposite and I was seeing innocent men destroyed and guilty men walk free and I had enough. Something just snapped, you know. I just couldn't take it anymore. I was off duty, but I followed this guy home. Then, one night when he was out, I waited until it was dark. I was very careful. All the things I had learned, all the ways they could trace me, I took care of all that. I entered his house through the back door and waited for him and when he came back I tasered him and then drugged him and I took him to my cabin. Now, of course, being a police officer helps. Nobody's going to automatically suspect you, are they? I was in no way involved with the case before, either. Anyway, when I got there, Carl was apprehensive at first, but, he understood, pretty fast, being a father to girls and all, and let's just say that this guy never left the swamp. Carl helped me and has ever since. He's been a real godsend, and sometimes I go there, and we just talk late into the night, and, until I met you three, I had no one else. And I do worry if Carl will be OK. I've told him that I might have to leave soon, leave the country, but I don't think he was that surprised, he understood, I guess I knew he would. He told me he's going to be all right and not to worry about him and he's just so happy for me." Annie wiped a tear. "I told him, of course, about you three, and he was so happy. Really. I think he would have loved to meet you and I've thought about taking at least you out there, to meet him, but you know, I wasn't sure…"

"I'd have liked to meet him."

"Do you mind me telling you?"

"That would be rich, wouldn't it?" Klara said. "Coming from me?"

"I had to tell you, Mom. Just like, I like to think, you had to tell me all you've told me. You know what I mean?"

"I do."

"So, afterwards, after the first time, I felt guilty. I did. Which is funny because I never felt guilty about Mom. Then again, she's still alive, so… and I thought, am I like… her? Am I worse?"

"My dear, hardly. Is the person who injects the murderer on death row the guilty one? If you are anything, you are a vigilante, aren't you. You take justice into your own hands. Your motives are different. Don't for a second believe that murder is murder. You are trying to prevent another person being killed or hurt or damaged. You are like the person who kills a serial killer after he has killed two people who otherwise, if left alone, would have killed twenty. You made sure that there wasn't another girl molested again. There are reports that the American GIs who liberated Buchenwald went crazy and slaughtered all the remaining SS guards. Does that make them equally guilty? In what sort of moral universe could it? Sure, the Nazis would like us to think that they are the same. How in the world anyone can compare the two is beyond me."

"You don't think less of me."

"If only I had your courage and moral conviction, perhaps I could have saved my Aunt Klara, or who knows, my parents and brother and sister or maybe just some random people in the camp. But I didn't, Annie. I was too scared. I was too entrenched, too taught to follow the laws, to obey figures of authority and look where it got me. Look where it gets anyone. Think about it this way, you know the Wannsee Conference."

"Where they formalized the Final Solution?"

"Yes. There were fifteen people there, all high-ranking Nazis. They spoke about in the most matter of fact, bureaucratic manner. Not one questioned why it had to be done, they only questioned how it ought to be done. Amazing, don't you think? Educated people, some with PhDs—"

"Carolien's getting a PhD."

"Case in point. . So, there they are, in a magnificent villa on the western shore of the Wannsee lakes, southwest of Berlin, fifteen of them, all senior people from the ministries, agencies and the SS. Heydrich — I told you about the parachutists — announced plans to scour Europe, including nations not yet occupied, and transport eleven million Jews to the East for extermination. Now, I always wondered, if he had said, we're going to collect eleven million potatoes or squirrels or whatever and transport them to the East and destroy them, you would think that at least one of these people would pipe up and say, 'Uh...why?' In this case, with innocent human beings at stake, no one said a word. No objections whatever.

"I like to imagine someone barging in, and saying, 'Gentlemen, sorry to intrude, is this the conference on the Final Solution?' 'Why yes, it is. In that case, please follow me, I have someone I'd like to introduce you to.' 'Oh?' 'Yes, his name is Odilo.' 'Globocnik, is he here?' 'I'm afraid not, this is a different Odilo. Please follow me.' And they do, and they meet your Odilo and... no Final Solution. That person would be a hero, wouldn't you say?"

Annie looked at Klara lovingly. "Thank you."

"We spoke of it before, not as directly perhaps, but we spoke of it."

"We have," said Annie.

"Sometimes, there is no other way. Annie, you are like my own daughter, my own daughter-in-law. You are the only hope I have, that we all have, Anton, Lucie."

They heard a car arrive in the front. Anton had returned. He took a moment to unload the groceries in the kitchen, they could hear the rustling of plastic bags and the opening and closing of the pantry and the refrigerator. Finally, he came onto the porch, sliding the glass door open.

"There you are," he said and hugged his mom and kissed Annie. He pulled up a chair. "The store was packed. What is it about old people having nothing to do. I'd swear they go to the store ten times a day."

"Seneca said, 'Never have I been busier than when I had nothing to do,'" Klara said.

Anton took a sip from Annie's glass. "What have you two been talking about?"

"Women's things, make-up, knitting and such."

"Make-up, knitting and such," Anton repeated, smiling. "Right."

"Girls must have secrets. Now be a dear and bring us some more wine."

Anton went to get the bottle while Klara squeezed Annie's hand.

While they waited, Klara looked at the silhouettes of three trees that she had planted about a decade ago, when she had been a little younger and quite a bit stronger. They were a lemon, grapefruit and orange tree and their yield had been plentiful. She had taken good care of them, diligently covering them on cold nights in case of frost. Still, there had been four. There used to be two orange trees. But in the last winter, no matter how carefully she tried, the fourth tree had died. In the end, she had to cut it at the root. It had made her terribly sad. Of late, she liked to think of the remaining trees as one being for Anton, one for Annie and one for Lucie, as if she had divined their arrival in advance. And she wondered what would happen to the trees without her, but it wasn't a major concern. She thought she had a legacy in the three people whom she loved, and that her lineage would after all not die out, and that Lucie, although scarred at present, would be brought back to life by Anton and Annie, especially when they were back in South Africa.

Klara felt more hopeful than she had in a very long time. She continued to hold Annie's hand. She believed that Annie knew where the conversation had been heading; after all, they shared an uncanny connection in so many ways; *and* she wanted to let Annie know that she would make absolutely no judgment; in fact, just the opposite, that she held her in the highest regard, and was counting on her, precisely because of what Annie had told her. She reached out and placed a curl of hair behind Annie's ear and felt that Annie understood.

CAROLIEN AND SUZETTE

CAROLIEN stood inside Suzette's kitchen, sobbing. It was the middle of the day, and the children were at school. Carolien had come unexpectedly. They had met once or twice at school, the way parents do, first at a PTA meeting, exchanging pleasantries and backgrounds, and Carolien had suggested that they should get together for a coffee one day and the children could have a play day. Although Suzette did have some reservations, seeing as Lucie was black, light-skinned but black, not that she had anything against blacks, mind you, but still...

Still, she was surprised to see Carolien at the door when she had answered. Immediately upon entering, Carolien had broken into terrible sobs and started telling Suzette the most heartbreaking story about her husband abusing her and Lucie.

"You mean... he hits you?"

Carolien again started sobbing. It didn't surprise Suzette very much, admittedly. She had found the couple a bit incongruous. She had wondered why such a pretty woman like Carolien, always in very sexy, tight-fitting clothes, make-up always nice, high heels, nails done, why she was with... a black man. Again, it wasn't that Suzette was racist, she knew she wasn't, but still, she had to admit that there was *something* about black culture, the inner cities, the music, the drugs, the unwanted pregnancies, the violence. She herself, Suzette, had married a *white* American soldier based in the Philippines. She was of Chinese origin, too, which made her higher in social status than the indigenous Filipinos. In fact, she didn't really like to be called Filipino. She preferred to be referred to as a Chinese who had emigrated to the Philippines. It just... sounded better.

"You must go to the crisis center, Carolien," Suzette now said. "You can't let this go on. Next time he hits you, you have to call the police. Promise me. I'll go with you if you want." Carolien sobbed in her arms, each breath stilted, anguished.

Finally, Carolien said quietly, "Yes, please, Suzette, do you mind? I don't think I'm strong enough to go alone, I don't want to hurt him."

Suzette felt Carolien's chest heave uncontrollably in sharp outbursts. Suzette hugged her new friend. So, they were friends, Suzette thought. Of all the people Carolien could have gone to, she had chosen Suzette. And Suzette liked that Carolien was Dutch, European, who had also lived in Africa, to her it seemed very *worldly* — that was something they had in common, Suzette thought, she had been Chinese living in the Philippines, Carolien had been Dutch living in South Africa; and both had married American men, at least by nationality and emigrated to the US.

Now she held her new friend, Carolien's warm tears falling on her shoulder.

"It's my fault, Suzette."

"What is?"

"That he beats me. Look at me, the way I dress. He says it's provocative, that I flirt with other men. But, you know, I don't. He's the only man I ever loved. He can be so incredibly kind, it's just when he drinks, sometimes, you know how some men get. But he's not really like that."

"How long has this been going on?"

"It started about six months into our marriage, I was pregnant the first time he hit me. In the stomach. He said he didn't want the baby, that I trapped him, but it was him, he told me to go off the pill, I just wanted to make him happy. I always have."

"Listen to me. This is typical. You're in an abusive relationship. People like that, they manipulate, they brainwash you, to make you think it's your fault. They always say those things, they wouldn't hit you, but you did this or that... I know, I volunteer at the crisis center."

"Really."

"Yeah, so you see, I see abused women all the time. I know all about it, everything you're telling me, it's typical. Have you ever told anyone?"

"No, never."

"You've been defending him, lying for him."

"He's a good, kind, loving man. He is. And he's a good father, it's just that... when he drinks, then... or when I don't listen to him, or misbehave, or look at another man, I don't even realize I'm doing it, but I'm sure he's right, why would he say that--it, and, we are living at his mother's, she's been so incredibly kind to me, like my own mother, I really love her, if anything ever happened to her, she's old, I would be devastated, she's been so kind to all of us, I am afraid for her, too, because when he drinks, he goes into a rage…"

"Listen to me, Carolien, listen. I'm going to tell you something now, OK?" Carolien looked up, eyes red, mascara smeared. She looked at Suzette imploringly, then averted her eyes. "I have to confess something to you. I married my husband to come here, for a green card. My husband was a good man, he never beat me, I just… I don't know. But I said he did. I have never told this to anyone. I'm just telling you, well, because, I don't know, you might understand. I had had enough, know what I mean? We were struggling, financially. I was tired. I wanted something new, something different, exciting, I wanted someone that could give me *more*, I guess. It sounds so shallow, mean, doesn't it? I just wanted him out of my life, out of *our* lives. Is that… terrible? Sometimes, when I watched him play with Toren, I was just… I don't know… enraged… does that make sense?" Carolien stared at Suzette and for a moment Suzette thought she might have made a mistake opening up to her new friend. She grew apprehensive. "Carolien?"

"I know *exactly* what you mean."

Suzette smiled, she thought she had been right about Carolien from the start, when they had met at the school, at the PTA meeting. She had noticed Carolien immediately, tall, light hair, blue eyes, pretty, lovely smooth skin, very feminine, short skirt, all the men noticed, too, a demeanor at once friendly, but melancholic. There was something very sad about her. Suzette, on the other hand, was short and dark, plump, not very attractive, she felt. In Carolien, she saw the person she wanted to be. Or at least to be *with*, to be *seen* with. A person she'd be proud to call a friend, to hang out with, to introduce to others.

That evening, at the school, Carolien's husband had been there, too. A light-skinned black man, bit darker than Lucie. Handsome — for a black man. Suzette smirked as she reminisced. But nowhere near handsome enough for Carolien. And, well, thinking back now, you couldn't account for taste, could you, there was something not right about him, aggressive even, Suzette thought. They had made an unlikely couple. Like one of those couples, you see on TV — Seal and Heidi Klum. She used to like Heidi Klum, but then she married *him*. Something didn't feel right. Maybe

Carolien's husband had been wealthy, who knew. These days, you couldn't be open about such things, black people were almost...popular, what with all the famous athletes and all the hip-hop stars, but Suzette had old-fashioned views, not that uncommon in the South, that black people weren't at the same level. It was not popular to say so before, with the black President; still, now, you could be more... *open*... there were plenty here in the south, she knew, who thought just like her.

"Carolien — your husband — he's South African... he's black..."

"*Colored*, actually," Carolien said. "His mother is white, Slovak; his father was a black South African." Carolien wiped a tear and smiled.

"We used to call it colored here, too, it changes all the time, they don't know what to call themselves anymore, do they?" She scoffed. "They've been colored, negroes, black, now they're *African American*. Who can keep up? Black, to me. Same thing, isn't it?"

"Not in South Africa. There — colored is... métis, mixed blood — it's a matter of pride almost — you're colored, not white or black — they speak differently, Afrikaans, not one of the African languages normally, different culture. He's more African, though, because of his father..."

Suzette frowned. "Well, here, he's just black. One drop rule." She stood on her tiptoes to appear taller. Every few minutes, she looked at herself in the mirror behind Carolien. Next to her, she felt ugly. *She* had to try so hard. Baggy clothes to hide flab and extra pounds. Extensions to make her hair fuller. Breast implants. And here stood Carolien, tall, lean, good skin, all real — nothing fake. A true, natural beauty.

Carolien almost whispered, appearing distraught, "This is a stereotype, but they, the coloreds, drink a lot, and beat their wives—" Carolien started to weep again. "—I didn't know it at the time, of course... I just fell in love with him... I still love him... he's the only man I've ever loved..."

"So often women find out too late. I see it at the crisis center all the time. That's how men operate. They hook you, and then, when they have you, that's when the manipulation, the threats, the violence begins. It's terribly difficult to get out of."

"I don't want to leave him, he's a good man," Carolien said. "I don't want to deprive Lucie of her dad. I don't want to get him in trouble, Suzette."

"Does he ever hit Lucie?"

Carolien started crying again. "Not really, not hard, not when she doesn't deserve it, she's not an easy child—"

"OK, that's it, I will help you through this. I know how difficult it is, Carolien."

"Tell me, Suzette," Carolien said. "What happened, with your husband?"

"I'm not proud of it, Carolien, but I felt, at the time, I didn't have money for a lawyer, and I didn't want to lose Toren, I didn't want to give up any time with him, didn't want to share him, I know that sounds a little cruel—"

"I don't think so. Me, I *am* afraid of Anton, even though I love him. I'm afraid for Lucie, even though *she* loves him. Kids belong with mothers, anyway."

"I totally agree. So, anyway, I hit myself with an empty plastic bottle till I got bruises on my arms. Then I called the police. When they came, I was very convincing, I cried, told them that he was abusive, had been beating me, that I felt threatened. I remember they asked if I felt that my life was in danger, and I said yes, like you, I said, I love him, but yes, my life is in danger. He had been taking a nap, I remember, they woke him, took him away, he had no idea what hit him."

"I *do* feel threatened."

"You see? In your case, you don't even have to lie."

"Is that it?"

"Yeah. Let's go to the crisis center tomorrow anyway, so there's a trail, a record of the abuse. And start telling people, don't lie for him anymore. Tell people at the school, the teachers, other mothers. Anyone you can. The more people that know, the better. That will help. And then, I'm not sure, you really don't want to wait until he hits you again, you should do what I did, call the police, it'd be better if you have a couple of bruises, tell them your life is threatened, they will take care of the rest. This is America. Not the Philippines. I am sure South Africa is the same. Third world. Men have all the power. Here, we do. You're so lucky you're living here now. The police — they have to take somebody away, like I said, when they come to the house. And guess who that's going to be? This country is just wonderful like that. A mother's paradise.

"Don't worry, Carolien, you're not alone anymore, we'll sort it out. You've suffered long enough. You and Lucie. He won't get away with this," Suzette said. Then she decided to change the topic. Carolien had endured enough, the poor woman. "How do you like Palm City? The US?"

"What's not to like?" Carolien said. "It's just like in the movies." Suzette was pleased. She had heard Anton say at the PTA meeting how he preferred South Africa. Americans hated that. Even Americans who'd emigrated here, like her.

"We're so lucky, aren't we."

"Suzette, what happens after he gets arrested?"

"He gets what he deserves. He goes to jail, he gets a record, can't find a job, can't see Lucie except under supervision, basically, you get rid of him for good."

"I'm not sure I can do that……"

"You're too kind. Forget about it for now, Carolien, I'm just so grateful you came to me. Tomorrow we'll go to the crisis center. He beats you and Lucie. He deserves everything he gets…"

"Lucie's crazy about him. If you ever ask her if he beats her, I am sure she will lie for him."

"Kids do that. But you are the adult here, Carolien. You have to do this, for you, for Lucie, for the both of you. Give you both a new start."

"I don't want to be… alone."

So… even a woman like Carolien was afraid of being alone. Who'd have thought. Such a beautiful woman and she had the same fears and insecurities.

"You will be alone for exactly five minutes. A woman as beautiful as you? Are you kidding me?"

Carolien blushed. "You really think so?"

"You kidding? Heck, yes. And, you will be with someone that is… better suited for you." She thought about saying 'white' but then she added, "Wealthy. Someone you deserve. Know what I mean?"

"I… I think so…" She burst out crying again. "Oh, I don't know, Suzette. Do you know any men like that?"

"Seriously? I know plenty of men like that. There are so many single men here, widowers, divorced men. In fact, there's one I am thinking about right now, Chuck, incredibly wealthy, lives in a huge house near the marina, a retired executive, widowed, he's got everything, a yacht, speedboat, several houses, even a plane, he'd be perfect for you. I can introduce you."

Carolien smiled sadly. "You're such a good person, Suzette. I am so lucky." She gave Suzette a long hug. "Tell me something. Is your husband in Palm City?"

"My first husband? No," Suzette said and hesitated. "He died."

"Really? How?"

"He... well, he had Toren one night, and... well, he, you know, he had kind of fallen apart after all that, he wasn't a very strong person to begin with, he was weak, I always thought that fatherhood made him soft, he was different when I met him, you know, in uniform, a soldier—"

"What happened?"

"Uh, he... when he had Toren one night, he... already wasn't too well, mentally I mean, couldn't find a job, couldn't drive, lost his driver's license... also, we had agreed that he would see Toren a lot less, that it was better for Toren, well, I suggested it and he had to agree, he had no choice, and, well, at that time he was only seeing Toren under supervision, but I had a date with the professor and I couldn't find a babysitter and Toren had been whining that he wanted to be with his dad, so that night... uh, he killed himself."

"How? You mean, with Toren there?"

"Yes, he waited until Toren fell asleep and then he... slit his wrists... and held Toren until..."

"Toren found him?"

"It, uh, Torren woke up, the bed was of course, all wet, sticky he didn't know what from, when he turned on the light, there was blood all over the bed, Toren couldn't wake him, he was terrified, he called me, I called 911, rushed over there, it was awful... he was dead by the time the ambulance arrived... what kind of person does something like that? So irresponsible."

"Did... anyone blame you?"

"Me? No, why would they blame *me*? No — they all agreed, my friends and stuff, people at the school, teachers, the other mothers at the school, I mean, they knew about his... behavior, I had told them, and they all agreed it was utterly irresponsible of him to do that."

"And how does Toren feel about that?"

"He was traumatized, of course. It's taken him this long to get over that, I mean, can you imagine finding your father like that?"

"How does he feel about his father?"

"He can't stand him. Hates it when he's just mentioned, you know. I mean, after what he'd done, who can blame him."

"Sometimes, these things... are just for the better..."

"That's what I thought, right away," Suzette said, "I thought, it'd be better if the ambulance got there… too late… it took me—" She hesitated. "—A while to call them…" She looked at Carolien imploringly.

"When the problem parent is removed from the child's life, I think it must be a relief in some ways, better than having your ex always hanging around, meddling in stuff," Carolien said.

"I am so happy you said that. It was a blessing, really, there's no question about it. It was the Lord's way of setting me free."

"I agree."

"I see it with my friends, always that tug of war with exes. The only thing I regret is that I got no child support, that's a bummer, it'd have come in handy. I didn't really want him in our lives anymore, but the money, well, you can never have enough, can you. It's not easy being a single mom."

"What happened to your second husband? The professor?"

"He ran off with some student, the bastard."

"Men."

"I think they just can't help themselves; you know. But sometimes they don't get away with it. I have this friend here at the university, also a PhD student, she's from Seattle, Sheryl, she had sex with some guy at a party, one time, got pregnant, he wanted her to abort, but she was already forty and who knew if she'd be able to have a kid again, so now he has to pay $650 per month for the next eighteen years."

"That was one expensive fuck."

Suzette laughed nervously. She was a bit taken aback by the word, coming from such a sophisticated woman like Carolien. Still, she had noticed that Europeans swore significantly more than Americans.

"You have to take responsibility for your actions," Suzette said.

"Absolutely. That will teach *him* a lesson."

"Exactly," said Suzette, feeling back on the same page with Carolien. Then she added, "So, now when anyone asks Toren about his dad, all he really says is, 'My dad was a very bad man.'"

"Everything worked out for the best."

"Yeah, I think so, too. Everything except for the money. So, now listen, tomorrow, I'll pick you up at ten a.m. I have a meeting before then, and I will take you to the crisis center, and now, Carolien, I don't want to hear any more about it, I know you love him, but we're going, OK? I am not taking 'no' for an answer."

"Do you really think—"

"Yes, I do. I'll see you at ten."

They hugged for some time. Tomorrow will be an important day. Carolien wiped her eyes and left.

THE ROAD TO HEAVEN (CONT.):

THEY drove wordlessly through the streets of Palm City. The car without license plates was unsteady from the fierce wind, and it was difficult to see with the pouring sheets of rain. Klara got a slight chill and pulled her jacket tighter. Up ahead, the street was better illuminated; on both sides of the road were beige strip malls, stores, and restaurants similar to any other city in America. Unlike Europe, looking out, not knowing where one was, it would have been impossible to determine which city one was in. Klara looked at the person driving the car. She had seen many people like her in her lifetime but now she didn't wish to think about those days anymore. She looked the person up and down and noticed between the jeans and shoe a gold ankle bracelet that she had not seen before.

    She had wondered, previously, what she would think about at a time like this. She had always assumed that it would be about childhood, or her parents, her brother and sister or perhaps about the time in the camps. But it wasn't and that surprised her. It was about Anton, and Anton's father, and how Anton was conceived and born. In some ways, she wasn't sure how much she had romanticized memories, or altered them. Most importantly, she knew that her son came back to her after the death of his father. Although it had not been an easy time for any of them, it had also provided the sort of happiness she had not felt since she had been a part of her family before the war; that only a family can provide, unless brutal and cruel. She now thought back to that time and realized she only had one regret; she couldn't entirely put her finger on it, or at least, not until the memory ran its course.

    She remembered Anton's birth, her third child. And how elated she had been when he was so fleetingly shown to her. He was, to her, the most beautiful child she'd ever seen, more beautiful even than her first, untainted by Nazi blood. True, it was dark in the dwelling, and of course, she was his mother and perhaps every mother thinks so about her baby, but still, it was how she saw him in the tepid light. His skin was light brown, soft, hair dark and curly. His features were gentle and, she thought, serene. She called him Anton, Joseph named him Kagiso. And now, she thought, she had never called him Kagiso, when he had been Kagiso for most of his life and how shortsighted it was and how selfish, and how kind of him to always let her call him Anton, and never requesting to be called Kagiso. She thought how she could at least text him, still, and tell him, or maybe even call him and then she remembered the cell phone lying at the bottom of the canal and she almost cried, but she didn't, she was brave, and she didn't want to give this person any satisfaction, or more than she'd already had. Klara thought that she would never hold him or kiss him again, or Annie or Lucie, and she thought suddenly about opening the car door or maybe putting down the window and calling for help. What was she doing, anyway, wasn't she going to her death, as had millions before her in the camps? Without a fight? When she swore she'd never walk to her death voluntarily? And yet, wasn't she doing the very same? The same that Arendt had accused her people of from the safe confines of a hotel room.

For a moment, Klara thought of attacking the person driving her, no different than a Nazi or a Kapo in her mind, but then she remembered Father Kolbe and the role she thought she had to play, and the man whose life Father Kolbe had saved, and that man reuniting with his wife and children after the war; so, she, too, was making a greater sacrifice.

How had Father Kolbe received the injection in the heart? She knew that he had prayed on his knees every day in the awful cell he was in, that he was the only one of the random ten to survive the starvation. She assumed he went with the guards and received the 'doctor's' injection with peace and tranquility, knowing he was giving life for a cause.

She suddenly felt much calmer and took her hand off the car door handle and even smiled to herself. How many people went to their deaths every day without any sense of destiny or purpose; whereas she knew precisely what sort of end awaited and why and although it was to be at the hands of an unkind person, the greater good overrode misgivings.

She returned to her ruminations about Anton-Kagiso. She regretted again how she had not asked Anton very much about the intervening years, his years as the son of a prominent member of the ANC, living in exile in London, and then his father's triumphant return to South Africa and he along with him; but perhaps it was because she found it difficult to hear about the times that were stolen, and if she had heard of any happiness he had experienced, it would have warmed and seared, perhaps unbearably.

There he was, the baby Anton Kagiso, born in a township in South Africa somewhere (or was it one of the homelands or even Swaziland? She had never been certain and now she realized she had never even asked). Born to a Slovak mother, and a Zulu father, Joseph, at a time when sexual relations between the races in South Africa were illegal. That act itself was brittle but defiant and Klara wouldn't have wanted it any other way. Whether conscious or not (she herself wasn't sure), it was perhaps the purest form of rebellion to the system at the time and place that she could have undertaken akin to a non-Jew having a child with a Jew under the Nazis.

Now, from a distance, her act made sense. After her experiences, she wasn't going to act like other people, was she? She was certainly not going to *think* like other people. Laws meant nothing. Conventions, nothing. They could all be taken away with a knock on the door in the middle of the night. All the things she had been brought up to believe and trust, in reality, meant little.

She remembered returning to Czechoslovakia after the war, her family dead, home seized by a Nazi sympathizer, now evicted to Germany; and she stayed a few years, not long, in a small town two hours from Prague; then, she went to the only country that would take her at the time, South Africa (she didn't want to go to Palestine, she had never felt sufficiently Jewish); she could have waited longer and perhaps reached Canada or Australia or the US, but she could no longer bear Europe without her family.

She had survived the camps as a young woman. It was an experience that profoundly affected her. Not outwardly, she thought. That was the tricky part. In the beginning, she had thought that, as a victim, all her pain and suffering were evident for all to see, as if forever surrounded by a puddle of blood or visibly branded by hot iron. But she realized that wasn't the case. That, to other people, especially those that had never lived through tragic circumstances, she appeared as a smiling, benevolent woman with shiny eyes. They saw none of the pain; were unaware of the perpetual grief and sorrow and pain. It was a miracle she had not become a *Musselman*.

Still, she hadn't lived fully, had she. She kept to herself, never had a family, spurned Joseph. And paid the price. She avoided friendships and relationships, until Anton came back into her life. So, perhaps she *had* become a *Musselman,* after all.

When Anton had been taken, she had searched for an entire year, hopelessly. At the time, she couldn't go to a police station and ask for help to find her black child. And of course, nobody would help. She was again alone. She had heard rumors of Joseph being in Zambia, in Mozambique, in Zimbabwe, in Swaziland, even in the UK, of being a member of the ANC, but she could never be sure and there was no way to find out.

One day, unable to remain in South Africa with its segregation, which reminded her of an earlier, terrible time, from neighborhoods to beaches to water fountains, she departed for the US (little realizing that she would end up in the American South, where every plantation had been a concentration camp of its own), walking away from her baby son. She did so involuntarily, she felt, but did so, nonetheless. He had disappeared no less than her children had in the camps. And it was easier to tell herself that he, too, was deceased.

It was all so long ago. She tried to remember now how she had met Joseph. Was she introduced to him by some enlightened white South Africans? She preferred another version — she had seen him standing at the back entrance of a butchery, marked 'servants and boys'. He, a man, was in this world a demeaning 'boy'. A male servant. She saw him, she liked to think, in line and she remembered it as love at first sight. Or was it something else? Did he remind her of Alfons, her husband? She thought he might have. The look in the eyes, the gentleness. The inquisitiveness without imposition. She couldn't be sure. One thing she did know, in that instant, was that this man would father her third and last child. And that her last act of fornication would not be entirely without eroticism but would be a symbolic act that she herself would not fully understand, either then or now. An act of defiance, perhaps. An act of love in a sweeping sense, but also anger, resistance, freedom, of no one imposing upon her an illogical will in the guise of *laws*. And ultimately of victory and survival. Maybe all that; and maybe none of that.

She remembered how she had gone to the line of black people waiting for white peoples' discarded cuts of meat — the fattiest, the most meatless, the necks, the feet. She remembered how the line retreated as she approached. How only Joseph stood still. He even managed a smile, she now liked to think. Out of surprise maybe, she thought. To the Africans' astonishment, if not Joseph's, Klara took him by the hand and led him from the line. A white lady exclaimed as the couple walked past. Joseph had no idea where she was leading him. But it could not be far as a few concerned white people looked on. She went down an alleyway, she reminisced; then, when she was sure no one could see her — or as sure as she could be — she climbed stairs in the back of a building that led to her one-bedroom flat. Inside, she led him to the middle of the room, let go of his hand, and stared at him wordlessly for a prolonged moment. She liked what she saw, a kind, handsome, open, honest face. Alfons. Joseph.

"You will be the father of my child," Klara had said, not realizing that she had just objectified him as the country had done, as she had once been and that perhaps he had different plans for how events would turn out. She led him again by the hand into the bedroom and they undressed each other. They made love three times (or maybe it was five) that afternoon and night for several hours, awkwardly at first and inexpertly, but improving each time and for a moment she remembered a rare, emaciated couple fornicating mournfully in the cold, dirty barracks of the camp. Her eyes watered, which he thought he understood and slowed and stroked her cheek and held her tenderly. The myriad of emotions coursing through her body she could no more explain than a philosopher the meaning of existence. Still, enwrapped within, she felt resistance and determination and a victory of sorts.

After the second round of lovemaking, as they lay sweaty staring at the high, pressed ceiling, the ever-present Johannesburg breeze flailing the curtains, hardly cooling the summer December day, she said, "You are going to give me a child and I am going to take him to America."

That was how she remembered it, and no one was going to tell her otherwise. She remembered Joseph being genuinely taken aback by the incongruous statement but purposefully trying to hide his surprise.

Klara at the time misunderstood that a father's love could be no less fierce than a mother's; she erroneously thought she'd give birth and depart. That Joseph would simply let her go and let her take their son, his son, with her, never to see him again (the irony of this would become apparent, of course, years later).

For nine months they had played an elaborate dance. He took her home to his sprawling village somewhere in Southern Africa to remain for the duration of the pregnancy, his hut far from the rest. She had to hide in the hut and only came out occasionally late at night. She remembered being treated like royalty by Joseph and his mother. Although the living quarters were meager, she felt spoiled. Joseph was the doting father-to-be, although he did disappear for weeks on 'official duty'. When present, she was amazed how loving he was, knowing he'd never see his son (she was as sure as he that it would be a son). Often, Joseph came and asked her to remain in Africa with him once their son was born. He said they could live freely in one of the other African countries until South Africa changed (which he believed was a matter of time). He had proposed marriage although he was saddened that his male elders could not take her male elders through the intricacies of an African courtship and marriage. Still, each time she had declined, both marriage and staying with him, he would leave, mournful. What seemed to dismay him further was that she never once asked if he'd accompany her to America, for he would have done so, unhesitatingly, he declared. He had fallen in love with her, he declared, so seriously and solemnly that she almost laughed.

But she remained distant and unmoved; she never told him it was because of the horrors she had experienced. It wasn't that she wasn't kind and gentle to him. It was simply that she had barriers in place that she could not remove, barriers that had protected her in the camps, but that now prevented her from accepting another husband — for fear of losing him as she had the first.

The next to last words she would hear Joseph utter while she was going into labor, as he had a hundred times since her arrival in the village, were, "Will you stay by my side and let me raise our son together?"

And she replied as she had always done, "You know I must travel to America with him, alone." She remembered his eyes watering as they did every time he asked her to stay, and she said no. And Klara remembered looking away uncomfortably. After she gave birth, utterly exhausted but serene and ecstatic, she gave the baby (unbeknownst to the child), the only gift she'd give him for the next thirty-four years — a Slavic name, Anton — although he'd not use it just as long and go by his Zulu name, Kagiso. That is how she remembered the birth and loss of Anton.

She looked at the person next to her, driving. A person with a steely determination and disposition, driven by one purpose and goal only. And she thought of Levi's recounting of eighteen Frenchmen, camp abandoned by the guards, eating in the dining room of the Waffen-SS, all killed by random SS men fleeing from the front who by chance came upon the camp, a mere five days before liberation. *Five* days. Knowing the war was lost, running for their lives from the Russians, they still killed these about-to-be-freed Frenchmen. Those Germans knew the war was lost. The person next to her still believed in 'final victory', a most illusory notion. Klara wasn't sure who was worse.

She looked out the passenger window at the palm trees bending in the wind and the town she had called home for some time and realized it had been more a home to her since Anton and his family arrived. And again, she suddenly wasn't sure she wanted any of that to end, although she knew it must. She involuntarily hugged herself, as Lucie always did, and Annie, too, and she just hoped that they would forever be happy and out of harm's way and that Lucie would develop, despite all this tragedy, into a young woman not too scarred. And she'd give anything to see that day, but knew it was not to be. She tried to breathe a bit deeper and a bit slower now. She looked straight ahead; the bridge was not far. There was no traffic here because the bridge had been closed off for construction and they weren't really allowed on it; besides, in this weather unless they could help it, people were at home, keeping dry and warm. The work crews had gone home by now, in any event, and wouldn't be back till Monday. That day would be one of commotion and questions, she thought, but Annie and Anton would know and at least Annie would understand and prepare for the next part of the journey. And now she could only think of (strange how the mind worked, she thought), *Himmelfahrtsstrasse*, the road from the railway tracks to the gas chambers at Sobibor — the Road to Heaven. All those before her had gone in their own way — most quietly, some cursing, some singing a national or Zionist anthem. Still, they all went as she was going now. Road to Heaven. Was there a heaven? If only she believed. But it was so terribly hard to believe after what she had witnessed. Terribly hard. Either God was good and just, in which case He allowing the atrocities to go unpunished, and therefore His existence, was illogical; or God was malevolent (in which case why believe in a malevolent deity?).

The person that drove — she could not even think her name let alone pronounce it lest it dignify her — the *blázen*. And suddenly she realized they had misnamed her. She wasn't the *blázen*. She recognized those eyes at last for what they were. They *were* indeed the eyes of a Kapo. The Kapo now stopped the car and got out. The Kapo walked ahead, unfazed by the rain. It was a dark night, the moon veiled. Still, the bridge, because of its whiteness, stood out and they could see enough to get through the gate in the fence and between the concrete obstacles placed to keep traffic out. The obstacles aptly reminded her of *Drachenazähne*, dragon's teeth, that she has seen on a beach in France.

The Kapo went ahead, through the 'dragon's teeth', and stopped in the middle of the bridge. Klara got out of the car with some difficulty (her hip hurt), preferring her right side, and followed, walking slowly after the Kapo. She walked through the gateway of the fence. On the other side, she tried to straighten her back as she walked. She stood near the edge, close to the Kapo. Down below to the right, poorly lit by scattered streetlights, was what remained of a tennis club, now overgrown, and she could see, barely in the heavy rain, an old abandoned wooden pier where Anton and Annie liked to fish, and beyond that was a place called European Town. It was a modern structure with shops at the bottom and apartments on the top levels and a tall brick chimney. It was built to resemble an old structure, with cracks and rust, but it looked more dilapidated than ancient. The only thing missing, she thought, was perpetual smoke bellowing ominously from the chimney.

"So obedient," the Kapo said.

It was true, the Kapos (and the SS) didn't like much fuss, they liked the prisoners to do as much of the dirty work on their fellow prisoners as possible — clothing removed, cajoled or forced into and closed inside and minutes later removed from gas chambers, corpses desperate and blue, probed for valuables, gold teeth removed, bodies dragged, inserted into furnaces and burned. Even the phenol injections were helped along by two Jewish assistants. Klara thought that if the prisoners, the *Häflinge*, could have done the entire operation without any assistance, that would have been ideal in the eyes of the SS. As it was, the *Häflinge* did by far the dirtiest work. Still, the SS had to do *some* of the work, someone had to throw in the Zyklon B blue-green crystals, for example, or inject the phenol.

"You know why you're here." That was how the Kapo punished Lucie. *You know what you've done. You have chosen the punishment yourself.*

And, like Lucie, Klara said, "I do."

"And yet you're here." *You know you are to be gassed and yet you walk into the gas chambers.*

"What do you expect of *Untermenschen*?" Klara said.

"Any final words?"

"Zuzana."

"What?"

"That was my baby's name. I *had* named her."

"You people are so sickeningly sentimental. That's why it was so easy to kill you. All of you."

The Kapo moved closer, but this was where the plan took a different turn. Before she had a chance to push Klara, Klara moved backwards. It was Klara's one final denial of passivity. The Kapo had to do none of the work herself. This was the concentration camp of the future — prisoners killing themselves. The heart stopped without the phenol injection. But the end was just as fast, and just as unequivocal. Still, it was not at the hands of another. That took some of the joy from the Kapo. And here was the final realization and regret. Klara had tried to deprive Joseph of a son, and, by doing so, had deprived Anton of a mother. But she had done it on a continent that took a different view of justice. And yet, once again, the child lost out.

"I love you, Kagiso," Klara whispered.

Then it was over at last. The Kapo looked over the edge, indifferent, at the *Stücke,* the *Untermensch,* on the ground below. There was one more person left now for 'special treatment'.

At that precise moment, Lucie awoke with a start. She knew instantly, felt instantly, that her grandmother had died.

She didn't know how, but she did; and she knew at whose hand. She cried into the night, uncontrollably, "*Gogo* is dead, *Gogo* is dead," over and over, tears streaming, clutching herself, and she cried like that for hours until falling asleep again towards the morning. Intermittently, she heard Chuck roaming the hallway and muttering and cursing at the noise she made, but mercifully leaving her alone. When she awoke in the morning, feeling as if she'd not slept at all, she had no respite, and wouldn't have any for a long time to come.

Carolien woke up, groggy. First, she smelled pipe tobacco. Then she tried to open her eyes. They felt stuck together. She had a headache. She tried to move her hands and feet but neither budged, tied together with rope, tight. She was tied to a chair. It took a moment to discern her surroundings; she had no idea where she was. As she looked about, she realized that she sat on a chair on a wooden deck leading to a small, dilapidated house on stilts, surrounded by thick foliage. The house didn't look in better shape than the walkway.

On a chair in front sat a black man smoking a pipe. On his neck was what looked like a tattoo of a heart and a 'four' next to it. He looked oblivious, smoking the pipe as if he were alone and paid no attention except the occasional sly glance.

"Who the fuck are you and why am I here."

"Hmm," the man said. "I ain't used to a woman swearin' like that first thing she wakes up."

"I don't give a fuck what you're used to. Untie me."

"No can do."

He didn't look particularly dangerous, Carolien thought, nor was he particularly helpful. He just continued to sit, smoking his pipe. Carolien wondered how she had ended up here; she looked at her mini skirt (torn on the side), the tight top (dirty), long red nails (two broken), high heels (one missing), and the gold ankle bracelet from Chuck.

Carolien looked up. The house was surrounded on all sides by the endless, quiet swamp. Attached to the side of the deck were two boats, one seemingly old, one new. These were, evidently, the only means to leave. She assumed that was also how she got here, by boat, but when and how and with whom, she had little recollection.

"Katrin — I believe your guest is awake."

"Thanks, Carl," a woman with a German accent said measuredly from inside the house. She walked outside and pulled up a chair, with its back towards Carolien, and straddled it. Suddenly things were becoming a little clearer. Carolien remembered the police officer who had come to the house and wouldn't arrest Anton. Palm City had forty thousand inhabitants; small enough that sometimes people looked familiar; large enough that most didn't. She also remembered the police officer calling her, and then coming to her house — well, not her house, Chuck's house — Chuck had been out at the country club — it had been dark, and when she opened the door, the officer took something out of her pocket and next thing Carolien remembered she was in terrible pain and after that she woke up here.

"How did I get here. Where am I. That police officer who came to the house... I remember—"

"Annie."

"Where is she? Who are you?"

"Annie couldn't be here today, sadly. I'm Katrin — and this is Carl."

"Ma'am, " said Carl in greeting.

"I don't understand. Why am I tied up? Where are we? Are you her friends?"

"You might say that. Carl has known Annie much longer than me."

"But... I don't understand. She called me, and said Anton broke up with her because he still loves me. That she wanted to get back at him, that's why I agreed to meet. She came to Chuck's house. Why am I here? Tied up? Who are you? This makes no sense. You're German."

"That's right. Don't tell me you want your bicycle back." Katrin turned to Carl. "That's what the Dutch sing at soccer games with us, give us back our bicycles. We smelted them during the war, apparently."

"I'm sorry to hear that," said Carl. "Not much use for a bicycle out here, I'm afraid."

"Yeah," said Katrin. *Ya.* "Never cared much for the Dutch, they really love themselves and think the whole world loves them. You should ask the Indonesians about that. They are really Germans in orange uniforms. Inventors of the world's two greatest evils, the Dutch, capitalism and reality TV."

"Ouch," Carl said.

"My grandfather fought with the Waffen-SS. He volunteered," Carolien said.

"That doesn't surprise me," Katrin said.

"I'm not the enemy. It's Anton. I can help you. No one knows Anton better than me. I know all his weaknesses. You know... Chuck?"

"No."

"I'm confused. Why are we... where am I? What is this place?" She softened her tone. "Can you please untie me?"

"Not just yet," Katrin said. "Sorry."

"Why?"

"Because first I'm going to tell you a story and then you're going to answer some questions."

"What are you talking about? What sort of bullshit is this? Untie me. Now! You can't do this."

"Yeah, I know. Just bear with me for a bit if you don't mind."

"I'm thirsty."

"You know what, let me start by asking you some questions first. Did you ever hit Anton?"

"What? Is that what he told you? *He* used to beat *me*. And Lucie. I had to report him to the crisis center. And at the school. You can ask them; they know all about it."

"Ask her if *she* ever hit Lucie," Carl said.

"Have *you* ever hit Lucie?"

"No! Of course not. I am her *mother*."

"You're the person who gave her birth. Not quite the same thing. Did you kill Klara?"

"No, I loved Klara, she was like a mother to me. She jumped off the bridge, I saw it on the news. It was awful. I was — I am — just devastated." Katrin stared at her. Carolien looked away. Who was this person and what did she know exactly? Carolien thought. There had been nobody on the bridge, nobody on the wooden pier. The weather had been atrocious. Hurricane weather, almost. It had been pouring down, windy. There was no way anybody had been there. She was bluffing. Still, she didn't like her eyes, steely, unmoving.

"How did I get here?"

"Annie tasered you. Then she drugged you. And then we brought you out here on the boat. Carl was great help, too."

"I am going to report her. All of you. This is kidnapping. You can't do this."

"Not sure that's going to be possible. She's on administrative leave anyway, I think, because she helped Carl steal some money."

"That is an unsubstantiated rumor," Carl said. "Fact is, she made me give it back to Johnny."

"What?" said Carolien.

"Long story."

"Did he… rape me."

"Girl, dream on. You should be so lucky. What do you take me for."

"Now, Carolien, I'm going to tell you a story and then I'm going to ask you questions and this time you'll tell me the truth and we'll see where it all leads, what do you say."

"I did tell you the truth."

"It's a true story, Carolien, I think you're really going to like it, I think it's just right down your alley."

"I'm thirsty."

"She's thirsty, Carl."

"Me, too, I think I'm going to get myself a beer, you want one, too, Katrin?"

"No, let me go on with the story."

"I'm getting bitten by mosquitos out here," Carolien said.

"Yeah, me too," said Carl. "I think I'm going to go inside and spray myself. Katrin — you?"

"No, thanks, Carl, I don't have delicate skin like you. Now can I please go on with my story?"

"Oh, yeah, I'm sorry about that." Carl went inside. They could hear an aerosol spray and then he came out with a beer. He twisted off the screw-top and took a drink. "Man, that's good."

"I'm happy for you. So, where was I. Oh, yes, now this is a true story, Carolien, my great-uncle was Odilo Globocnik. Ever hear of him?"

"No."

"My great-uncle turned killing into a modern factory. He was in charge of the extermination camps."

"I told you, we're on the same side. Our grandfathers may have known each other. My grandfather was an amazing man. I remember him well. He loved the Germans. After the war, he worked in Germany. We're both descendants of the SS, you and I."

"You say it like it's a good thing."

"My grandfather is a hero there. I went to the Ukraine a few years ago for a commemoration of the fallen Germans and Ukrainians. Everybody wanted to shake my hand."

"That might explain why Putin calls them a bunch of fascists."

"They said my grandfather was a good man. I'm proud of him."

"That's where we differ. I am ashamed of mine. I am ashamed of being German. My grandfather was responsible for the deaths of millions of people."

"*Untermenschen.*"

"Some believe that our crimes made *us Untermenschen*."

"You know better than that. Look at the riffraff coming into Europe. Besides, there's no proof the Holocaust ever happened. It's Jewish propaganda."

"Klara was proof—"

"Klara was a whore. She probably volunteered her services. You know what those people are like. They'll do anything for money."

Katrin's jaw clenched, but she remained calm. "Klara, the woman you just called a whore, was like a mother to me. She was the kindest woman I've ever known."

"Strange. She never spoke about you."

"But she did write me about *you*."

"All lies, I'm sure."

"Let's get back to why I'm here. Annie hadn't expected you to kill Klara—"

"Klara fell off a bridge."

"Not 'productive annihilation'? *Produktive Vernichtung*?"

"What?"

"Her death broke my heart, and Annie's heart and Anton's and Lucie's—"

"Children are resilient."

"That's what adults say to make themselves feel better," Katrin said. "You know, I thought I was going to get to you first, but you're fast. Besides, Klara made sure to send a postcard, something that would take time to arrive. When she could have emailed, called…"

"I didn't do anything."

"I have this thing from Annie to help you remember." Katrin pulled a large sturdy plastic bag from her pocket. Inside were what appeared to be remnants of ashes.

"What is that? You're sick. You can't get away with this."

"Maybe. Let's try this on for size, shall we?" Carolien tried to struggle; Katrin put the bag over her head. She closed it around her neck and watched as Carolien, terror stricken, inhaled the plastic in and out. She tried to thrash about. When her face started turning blue, Katrin pulled off the bag.

"If Klara could see us now, I think she'd really be enjoying this. Well, in a way she is here, isn't she. I am sorry, it's the best I could do—"

"You're c-c-crazy," Carolien said, gasping for air. "You can't do this. They will catch you."

"The thing is, I'm just a tourist, came for the beaches and warm weather. I don't know anyone in Florida."

"I'm going to tell—" Carolien started saying, then stopped.

"Ah, yes, that is the sad part, Carolien, I'm afraid you won't be able to say much to anyone. You see, I don't think that much will remain of you. Especially if you don't start talking."

"They will blame Anton."

"Smart one, this, eh, Carl."

"Very smart."

"Thing is, Anton is in Kentucky for a few days."

"What?"

"I guess you didn't know Anton as well as you thought you did. He's there for a horse race. Big fan, apparently. Oh, and I believe he's on a bourbon tour, too."

"Lucky man," said Carl.

"I don't believe you."

"I'm afraid so. Not everybody lies. It's just the three of us here, Carolien, and, well, nobody knows about this place except Carl and Annie and now me — which is really a shame."

"Don't forget Odilo," Carl said.

"Oh, yes, of course, Odilo, how could I forget. My grandfather's namesake. How appropriate."

"Who is Odilo."

"Hmm, you want to tell her, Carl, or should I?"

"Maybe we should just let her find out for herself?"

"Good idea."

Carolien started to pull at the ropes viciously, but they were too tight. She managed to fall to the ground with a loud bang, then remained stuck on her side and couldn't move.

"Now, I can either place the bag over your head again, or you can tell me the truth, which do you prefer."

"Fuck you."

Katrin placed the bag over Carolien's head again, leaving it for longer. When Carolien was about to pass out, she pulled it off. It took Carolien longer to regain her breath this time; she was no longer in a fighting spirit.

"Will you let me g-g-go if I tell you."

"There's a chance of that, right, Carl?"

"Right."

"What do you want to know."

"You had someone call Annie to warn her about Anton."

"So?"

"You used to watch them when they were fishing, at the intracoastal."

"No law against that."

"Do you hit Anton and Lucie?"

"No." Katrin moved closer with the bag. "OK, OK, wait. Yes, so?"

"Did you kill Klara."

"I wanted to, but at the last second, she jumped… by herself."

Katrin looked mournfully in the distance. "Why did you want to kill her?"

"Because I fucking hate her, that's why, I hate him, I hate everything about them."

"Why."

"Because they're weak. Like him. He always just took it, the way I treated him. And she just came with me. No fight. They are pathetic. I couldn't stand her."

"And Anton is next."

"So, what? What do you care?"

"And then? Chuck? Chuck's family? Lucie? Where does it stop?"

"No, I love Chuck."

"Right. Chuck's not *Untermensch*, like Anton?"

"No," Carolien said.

Katrin sat down onto the wooden walkway and looked at Carolien for some time. Carl handed her an opened bottle of beer. She took a drink; he sat beside her.

"Carl, I'm tired. Of everything. Of life. The way Klara used to be. I remember, as a child, looking at her. On hot days, days when it was at least twenty-seven degrees Celsius, she would always light a candle. I have always done it ever since. Do you know why she did that?"

"Why?" Carl said.

"That was the temperature at which the Zyklon B crystals turned to gas. It was one reason why they packed the gas chambers so full of people, not only to get rid of so many at once, but so that the body heat would rise quickly, and the crystals turn to gas." Katrin paused and wiped a tear. "My countrymen. My grandfather. My family."

"Sentimental drivel," Carolien said.

Carl ignored her. "World's a fucked-up place, all right, Katrin. It can grind you down."

"Do you live out here alone?"

"Except for Annie's visits. Lucky me, right?"

"What are you going to do with me?"

"Well, Carolien, I might have lied. But then, to you, lying is first nature, let alone second, so, it won't surprise you too much."

"What are you going to do?"

"Carl — can you help me?"

"Of course."

Carl got up and held Carolien from behind the chair tightly. Katrin came closer and put the plastic bag over Carolien's head, holding it tightly around her neck. The bag expanded and deflated with each breath. Carolien thrashed violently, but Carl was too strong. The breaths decreased until the bag moved no more.

Katrin stared at Carolien's open, terrified eyes through the plastic bag. Carl cut the limp body from the chair; it slumped to the deck. He picked the body up by the head and Katrin held her feet. They threw the body over the side into the swamp and within seconds heard the chomping of jaws and the crunching of bone and flesh.

"*Nacht und Nebel*," Katrin said.

"Meaning?" said Carl.

"Night and mist. One of my countrymen's favorites. Opponents of the regime were taken and killed, mostly at night. Their loved ones knew nothing of their whereabouts or fates. And now, Carolien is *vernebelt*. Turned into mist."

"Quite the poets, your country. I also like the other one you said, 'productive annihilation'."

"I've always thought I was different. Now—"

Suddenly Katrin felt an overwhelming fatigue and sadness. She put her head on Carl's shoulder and started to weep. He held onto her tightly, letting her cry as long as she needed. Finally, she put her head back up, wiped her tears with a sleeve and took a drink of his beer.

"Tell me we did the right thing, Carl. Somehow, I thought that it would correct wrongs, fix things, make a change, that it would make me feel... better. Set me free, at least a little. As if purging all the crimes we committed, my grandfather... But it doesn't..."

"We did the only thing we could."

"Tell me we're nothing like her."

"Let me tell you somethin', Katrin. You made sure she'll never hurt another human being again — not Lucie, not Anton, not Annie, not Chuck, not anyone. You made sure that Anton and Annie and Lucie had another chance at life, that they won't end up like me, living alone in the damn swamp. So, if you're not patting yourself on the back, I'm doing it for you. As we threw her over, I said, good riddance. It was bittersweet. I had visions of my ex-wife tossed over, too. It was therapeutic. Too late for me, for my kids, too late for others. But not too late for them. It felt like a tiny victory, that. I had absolutely no sympathy for that woman. She was poison. So, be kind to yerself. You just rid the world of a very nasty person. Evil as hell. My only regret is that we ain't done it sooner, then Klara would still be alive."

"Yeah." *Ya.*

Carl took a sip of his beer. "Katrin, when you're back in Germany, drinking good beer and eatin' sausage and kraut, feeling sorry for yerself, and having doubts, think of me, hiding away in the swamp, having lost everything. I will never see my kids; I will never have a life. I have no idea why I go on."

"You can't give up."

"What have I got to live for? I'm tired, too, Katrin. Damn tired."

"How would you feel if I stayed a while?"

"What? Why would you do that?"

"I have no one and nothing in Germany."

"This is no life, Katrin, believe me."

"It'd be temporary. Unless you are attached to the swamp."

"Right. Me and Odilo. Match made in heaven. He serenades me at night."

"You don't deserve to live like this. And, with Annie gone, how will you survive. I am thinking of smuggling you out of this godforsaken place and taking you to a civilized country."

"Germany?"

"Mexico. I'm never going back to Germany. A new beginning. Where no one knows either of us. I figure, with so many people smuggled into the US, we go against the tide. Can't be that difficult. Before this idiot builds his wall. Couldn't somebody have bought him a building set when he was a kid?"

"I don't…I was kind of resigned—"

"Not going to leave you out here on your own. How do you feel about basset hounds?"

"What?"

"Dogs."

"I love dogs."

"I can't have kids."

"I'm finished with that."

"That settles it then. But… I must warn you…" She grew still, serious, melancholic. "The blood of a monster runs through my veins."

"I'll take my chances. And sleep with one eye open."

"I will do my best to get you to Mexico. After that, I can't make any promises. Should we see how it goes?"

"That's fair."

"One more thing I must do. Have you a lighter?"

"Matches."

"Please."

He went into the house and came back with a book of matches. In the meantime, Katrin had taken from her pocket a photograph and a postcard.

He pointed at the photograph. "Who's that?"

"My grandfather, shortly after they hanged him. I carry it with me always, to make sure he really is dead." Carl stared at the figure of a man lying in a grey jacket, eyes closed. "And this is the postcard I received from Klara." She took the matches from Carl and lit both photo and postcard and smiled sadly at Carl as she watched both turn to ashes and with a light breeze blow into the swamp. Then she let Carl give her a long hug. She felt small in his arms, and safe. She wasn't sure why, but the feeling of safety was immense. They finished the beers, fished for a souvenir of sorts from the shallow water below and went inside.

An hour later, Katrin took the human souvenir, got on the boat, and returned to Palm City.

THE PRESENT AND AFTER

The Present

THE road to the southernmost tip of Africa now lay ahead, but it still had to be carefully executed. Nevertheless, Annie had planned diligently. She had been prepared to do what had to be done. Katrin's arrival surprised her. But she realized that for her and Anton, Katrin was a godsend, a final gift from Klara. And that Klara at last had been able to protect the ones she loved.

It had been a terrible tragedy, everyone agreed, when Carolien's severed leg was found at the water fountain and moat at the entrance to Palm City. She had already been declared missing by her boyfriend Chuck the night before. The DNA results confirmed that the body was indeed Carolien's, but Chuck had had no doubt anyway. He recognized the gold ankle bracelet that still remained. He also recognized the two high-heeled shoes nearby. As for the rest, nothing remained, but the coroner confirmed that the bites were those of a large alligator. For good measure, two alligators near the moat were cut open but no human remains were found; the culprit, it was decided, must have meanwhile gone into the not-too-distant swamp.

A further mystery was what she had been doing by the moat in the middle of the night in the first place, but then again, she was Dutch and there had been instances of tourists, Europeans especially, getting too close to the gators, especially when they had tried to take selfies. Strange time for a selfie, everyone agreed, but Europeans, the locals concurred, had peculiar habits. Two things there could be no doubt about, it was her leg, and it had been snapped in two by a gator.

The only potential suspects, her ex-husband, had in any case been away, in Kentucky, to a horse race and a bourbon tasting tour. That was easily verified with CCTV footage obtained by the Lexington police. And Chuck, her boyfriend, had been at the country club having dinner with golfing buddies. Finally, suicide was not likely. Improbable, the detective in charge had said, but not something that could be entirely ruled out. After all, her ex-mother-in-law had just jumped off the intracoastal bridge, and the Dutch woman's friend, Suzette, confirmed that Carolien had been absolutely devastated by the news. Additionally, she had gone through a terribly painful divorce several months earlier which she didn't want — again, as told by Suzette and confirmed by her ex-husband — well, suicide could not be discounted. Odd way to go, to be sure, they all agreed, but with people, you just never knew. In any event, foul play had been decisively ruled out.

Meanwhile Suzette made a stunning confession at the crisis center. It turned out that Carolien had entirely fabricated her accusations regarding Anton, to get custody and hefty child support. Suzette said that she had only found out from Carolien after their visit together to the center and right before she died and that she had counselled Carolien to set the record straight and now took it upon herself. What the crisis center didn't know was that Suzette had spent a weekend at an unknown destination in the middle of the swamp. It was a weekend that she didn't remember fondly, but she survived it, that was the main thing (she had been very worried about Toren at the time but, admittedly, not as worried as she had been about herself). True, many people remarked afterwards, not knowing about her harrowing weekend, that she had changed, she was not nearly as sociable afterwards, keeping very much to herself. Some said she had aged overnight. Many attributed that to losing in such tragic circumstances her friend Carolien, whom she had known only several months but to whom she had seemed to become inordinately close.

As for Annie, she had been put on administrative leave for the incident at the restaurant. The manager, Johnny, had reported it a few days later, and Annie had been under suspicion for some time in the department for being too soft on criminals. This was simply a straw too many, letting a robber run off with money. On her behalf pleaded an elderly woman who had eaten at the restaurant that very morning and who had volunteered to pay whatever the restaurant had lost. But it was explained that it was really a matter of principle, not money (though it was that, too), and that you couldn't have police officers letting criminals do whatever they wanted. Reluctantly, the woman had agreed and left.

Of course, it didn't help matters that the criminal was never apprehended. All sorts of witness descriptions came forward, many entirely contradictory, but most agreed that it had been a nondescript light-skinned black or Hispanic or Arabic man of medium height with or without a tattoo that read, or didn't read, 'four' and a heart, or it may have been a heart and a 'four', pudgy or not, nondescript, a little overweight maybe, with a thick Cajun/Hispanic/Arabic accent, depending on whom you asked, or possibly a speech impediment because he was extremely difficult to understand, except when he said 'floor', 'money' and 'kids' — they all agreed on that.

One young heavily tattooed man with a beard and a baseball cap even said that Annie had disarmed him so she could let the criminal go. He had run after him into the forest, but it had quickly turned into a swamp, and he couldn't go any farther. The man had completely disappeared, the young man said, hopefully eaten by gators. He fully agreed with the police officer's suspension and subsequent firing.

And of course, that Klara's death was also suicide hardly needed an explanation. She was a Holocaust survivor and suicides rates amongst them, the police department said, were not uncommon, especially in old age; her son's family had disintegrated in front of her eyes, her son had been accused of domestic abuse; and he and she had their daughter and granddaughter taken away (Florida family law having no visitation rights for grandparents). The son had only been exonerated after she had jumped off the bridge. The fact that her cell phone was never found wasn't troublesome. It had, in all likelihood, fallen out of her pocket and into the waters of the intracoastal.

With that, Annie had been fired and was at loose ends. She moved away from Palm City without great fanfare. She wasn't close to people, not her colleagues or others, as far as anyone knew. And frankly, with her track record, she knew that it was good riddance at the station. She had been soft on crime. No one would really know where she'd gone, but most, she supposed, would suspect that she went home to Kentucky.

Anton and Lucie were reunited. It was a very painful reunion, joyous and painful. Lucie was like all abused people, like all abused children. She still loved and missed her mother. She still believed, had she been a better child, she would not have been beaten by her mother; and her mother might still be alive. These were wounds that would take a long time to heal, and would perhaps, as with survivors of the camps, always remain under the surface and one day potentially passed on to her own children. Still, the love that she and her father shared was palpable, and many in the neighborhood and in the school, including the mothers who had been against him, now that he was exonerated, wished to welcome him into their fold. He was unmoved, however, by the delayed display of acceptance. Courteous, but distant, is how most would have described him. He put his mother's house up for sale (it was now his) and the house sold quickly, being on the canal and the price being more than reasonable. He was in a hurry to sell and depart and the price was less important than leaving Palm City and the US behind. It had been one big source of tragedy since his arrival.

AFTER

THE day arrived that none thought they'd ever see. It was just as they'd expected, wanted, anticipated. It was a magnificent day on a beach on the southernmost tip of Africa. And, yes, Annie had to concede, it was precisely as Anton — Kagiso — had described. He had exaggerated nothing. The light was brighter, the sky bluer — a blue she'd never seen. The food tasted like nothing she'd ever had. The people, of all colors and backgrounds, Indian, Malay, White — English, Afrikaans, Africans of several tribes, were some of the genuinely friendliest people she'd ever met. Everywhere they went, she felt amongst people who cared. Not that it was a place of perfection, but it was perfection to them.

On this day of joy, when the two tied the knot, she in white with her hand on a slightly protruding belly, and he in a blue suit, with Lucie smiling joyously next to them, and Maria there, too, having rejoined them, it was a most beautiful ceremony performed by an old family friend of Kagiso from Durban. The only persons missing, of course, at fleeting moments when joy subsided, was Klara, to whom their intermittent thoughts turned, Annie's and Klara's and Lucie's, and a couple represented by a recently arrived bottle of tequila; and after the ceremony, Annie took a small wooden urn with a candle and tiny drawer and opened the drawer and poured a small amount of ashes into the sea, as Klara had wished, and this way she was with them, looking down perhaps, and she would always be with them, in this place, on this continent, where they now could be free. But Annie was very careful to leave half of the ashes still inside, those were destined for the Vltava River. For, in the end, as she had wished, Klara ended up in three places — the first, a place where she found a sense of family for the first time in decades, albeit short-lived; the second, permanently near her son and daughter-in-law and granddaughter, all of whom she inordinately loved and over whom she could always watch; and the third, near her parents and brother and sister, and in a way, near the babies she'd lost, and near her aunt and namesake, Klara; near all the places she either found a semblance of the peace and serenity and love she always sought and ran towards; and near the people she had in her life loved the most. If she was watching, Annie hoped, she could exhale with relief. She'd probably look at her granddaughter and her son and her daughter-in-law, she, *Gogo* at long last and now forever, who'd seen the worst and best of humanity, would clasp her hands and probably say, *pane bože*, but this time, in a good way, with relief.

That evening, when together, the three of them (Maria retired early after the emotional day), Lucie said, "*Baba*, what sort of story was this?" And Anton looked at Annie, who was smiling, curling a strand of hair with her finger.

And he said, "It's our story. It's everyone's story — the oppressed, those that oppress, and those that refuse to be oppressed; it is the last who are of any real consequence, may there be many more."

And with that, Lucie tenderly fingered the gold necklace inlaid with garnet stones around her neck, once her great-grandmothers and later grandmother's, to her signifying so much and so many more. They lit the candle that had come with the small wooden urn and thought of Klara and went to sleep as peacefully as none of them had ever expected to sleep. They dreamt, smiling as they slept, of all the days to come on the southernmost tip of Africa, home at last. And on hot days, those over twenty-seven degrees Celsius, they'd always place a candle on a windowsill and light it and think of Klara and those she'd loved and lost and regained.